"Wonderfully witty, often very funny, even when it is most serious... it is recognizably feminine, but men will enjoy reading it nonetheless... Margaret Drabble is an immensely gifted writer, one of the best."

The Boston Globe

"A conspicuous pleasure to read... Margaret Drabble is the only writer we can think of who uses experience and social commentary almost interchangeably and always to astute advantage.... Her human data has always been superb and now, how readily she succeeds in informing the mind and engaging the heart."

The Kirkus Reviews

Also by Margaret Drabble:

A SUMMER BIRD-CAGE

THE GARRICK YEAR

THE MILLSTONE

JERUSALEM THE GOLDEN

THE WATERFALL

THE NEEDLE'S EYE

THE ICE AGE

THE MIDDLE GROUND*

THE RADIANT WAY*

Nonfiction

A WRITER'S BRITAIN

THE OXFORD COMPANION TO ENGLISH LITERATURE, 5th Ed.

ARNOLD BENNETT

*Published by Ivy Books

THE REALMS OF GOLD

Margaret Drabble

IVY BOOKS • NEW YORK

Ivy Books
Published by Ballantine Books
Copyright © 1975 by Margaret Drabble

Library of Congress Catalog Card Number: 75-8229

ISBN 0-8041-0363-1

This edition published by arrangement with Alfred A. Knopf, Inc.

Printed in Canada

First Ballantine Books Edition: January 1989
Third Printing: January 1991

Cover Photo by Suzzane Opton

For
FRANCIS HOPE

T

HE octopus lived in a square plastic box with holes for his arms. He had touched her with his gray wet hand, and had shrunk quickly from the contact. Back into his box he went, as she into this rather nice hotel room.

He had suckers all the way along his arms. She thought of them with affection and amusement. He was the best thing she had seen for some time, better even than the view of the bay. He had seemed quite friendly, even though he hadn't wanted to touch her, even though she didn't quite like the smell of formaldehyde that filled the research laboratory. The most intelligent of the invertebrates. Perhaps the octopus had no sense of smell.

Idly, she reached for her perfume bottle and dabbed a little on her neck. Silly, really, to travel with such a big bottle. Her case was so heavy. But it gave one something to do, packing, unpacking. There stood a few of her things, though she was only here for a couple of nights—a bottle or two, a hairbrush, a few books, photographs, talcum, a ballpoint pen, lecture notes, her glasses. She had made her mark on the room. She never understood people who said they felt submerged by hotel rooms, that they felt extinguished, annihilated, depersonalized. She had occasionally felt the reverse—that herself, suddenly put down in transit, was so powerful that it might burst through the frail partition walls and send all the things swirling. Towels, fittings, coathangers, things like that. On the whole, she was happy to be in hotel rooms. A little rest, one got there, from the strain of adjusting oneself constantly, putting oneself as it were under a shade, muting oneself, lowering one's eyes. In a hotel room one could look oneself at least in the eyes, throw oneself upon the bed, take a bath naked, and no harm done to anyone. In this hotel room, one could even have a drink without any effort. She was delighted with the little humming refrigerator full of miniature bottles and fruit juices and halves of champagne and chocolate cherries. It was a nice room. The bed was old and ornate, with an inlaid headboard, the curtains were heavy and shut out the light, the windows were double glazed and shut out the noise of the traffic, and there was a view of the bay. The appliances were modern. In the last hotel, the night before, everything had been a little old and dusty—they had apologized, and she had said she liked old hotels better, but really, she did like a nice modern bath and a little refrigerator humming away as well. This one was just about right. It was fine. She had a sip of the drink at her elbow, and then a larger gulp. It wasn't one of those miniature drinks, it was a good healthy tumbler full of duty-free brandy with some water in it.

There was a very attractive gilt-edged mirror, on the wall just over the desk. Sitting down, she couldn't see herself in it, but didn't much want to. The desk had little pigeonholes and inlay. What period was it? She didn't know, she wasn't very good on furniture. It looked good, though. So did those carved black people supporting the door. There was a description of the building somewhere downstairs, she'd seen it at Reception, and it mentioned those black people. Blackamoors, it called them, in its quaint English translation. Had there been slave trade here? It seemed likely. There were a lot of Arabs. It was a big port.

It was, in fact, indisputably the best bedroom in the hotel.

There was no doing anything about it. They had given the best room, in what seemed to be the best hotel.

Things were getting bad. No matter what she did about it, they were going from bad to worse. It wasn't as though she hadn't expected it, she told herself. She had, exactly, expected it. This was precisely the stage for it to happen. Eight days away from home, and it would happen, like clockwork.

However had she got herself here, into this good room? It was madness, really. Why hadn't Professor Andersson seen how mad it was, when he showed her up to the room? (A rather personal touch, that had been, but she was used to such personal touches, she even appreciated them, she liked his delicacy about it, he was a nice man, he had wanted to be sure that the hotel had done all it promised.) Professor Andersson had seemed to accept her—not quite to take her for granted, because nobody took her for granted, everyone was far too polite for that. Ah, what attentions she had purchased. But he hadn't said, "There's your room, and it's too good for you." At the thought of him saying that (which he might have said, instead of what he did say, which was, "Here's your room, I hope you find it comfortable, there will be a good view in the morning") she smiled to herself, but rather dourly, the kind of smile that old-world heroes made on their way to the gallows. To the gallows I go, she said to herself, and had another large drink.

It was bound to be bad, this evening. Did that make it better or worse, as a prospect? That was something she could debate at leisure. There was something rather dreary about the inevitability of it all. Let us postpone it, she said brightly, aloud, to herself. She was an eccentric woman, and often talked to herself, aloud, in hotel rooms.

Perhaps it wouldn't be dreary. Perhaps it would be gripping. She walked over to the window and pulled back the thick curtain. There, below the double glazing, were the yachts, the bay, the port, the cars, the restaurants. All very lit up, though it was out of season. It was better than the last town she had been to. That had been really dusty. But then,

it was farther south. At this time of the year, very early spring,
life lay in the north rather than in the south: the colder, the
gayer. The south had been truly shabby, faded and desperate.
The taps had been large and brass, the floor had been of
spotted marble, the staircases had been wide, the porter had
been thirteen years old, and the roof garden had been utterly
empty, deserted like a closed building site. She had stumbled
over spades and a heap of geranium roots. It was livelier,
here. An all-the-year-round city. The octopus industry flourished, as did her own. Further south, she had felt like a
prophet, a wanderer (which in a sense she was). Perhaps that
had made it better. She had felt a purpose there. Here, she
had none, she was one of many, there was no reason why
she should not be down there in one of those flashy cars, or
dining in one of those illuminated restaurants, rather than
sitting here alone, with an empty evening, an utterly empty
evening ahead of her. (It was only six o'clock.) She could
have accepted a dinner at one of those restaurants down there:
the Professor and his wife would have been glad to take her
out.

The octopus, intelligent creature that he was, could survive in a plastic box. Though why he bothered, who could
say. And the female of the species died, invariably, after
giving birth.

It's all a question of programming, she said to herself, as
she began to walk up and down the room. It wasn't presumably possible that an individual mother octopus could refuse
to die. They always made the same decision, even when
tempted from their deathbeds by choice morsels. Their role
accomplished, they preferred death. She often wondered what
she herself was programmed for. This curious mood, into
which she was now just about to fall, seemed to be part of
her plan. And as it was part of her, so she had made plans
for it. She was good at plans and programs—she had a program for her lecture tour, full of times, dates, names, addresses, hotels, she had left behind her a complicated
program for her children, with meals, Wednesday swimming

day, Thursday window cleaner, and such things written upon it. And she had by now a well-established program for the horrible thing that was about to get her. (Sometimes she dignified it with the name of Despair—had usually done so, in fact, as a child, but now she was less respectful to it, and saw it as some kind of illness. A family illness, but more of that later.) A tutor of hers (and indeed her first seducer) when she used to complain about Despair had said that she must learn to familiarize herself with it, and treat it as a part of a pattern, part of a cycle. She had thought him a foolish and cynical old bore (he had been twenty-nine) but time had in fact proved him right. You must learn to see life as a cycle, not as a meaningless succession of mutually exclusive absolute states, he had said.

She had tried to learn to do just that, but wasn't too pleased with some of the results. She did indeed know now, of her states of mind, that they would arrive, and pass, and that each time they'd seem to be there forever. It was largely a question of sticking it out. She also knew, more sinister knowledge, that she tended deliberately to choose every now and then a situation in which nothing else could possibly happen. Solitude, enforced, as now. As though she wanted it? This was something she by no means understood.

Programming. She thought about that again, it was a pleasant distraction, it occupied the brain, while whatever it was gathered behind her eyes, in her chest. It had been interesting, the experience of being programmed for maternity. She had been a fairly responsive case; yet not utterly responsive. Now that her younger child was seven, and some of her finer responses were no longer needed. She had felt, had noticed her heart hardening. She no longer softened at the sight of other people's babies: in fact she would avoid them and leave railway compartments when they entered. She no longer wept over newspaper stories about battered and abandoned infants. Advertisements for the NSPCC and the Salvation Army failed to draw automatic tears, as they had done. But she didn't seem to be developing other, compensatory areas of softness. Her heart didn't bleed for divorced wives or retired pensioners. She was just getting harder. These days, she blamed people for what happened to them, instead of excusing them. Perhaps, her children now so old, and no longer needing her care so much, there was nowhere else for her to go. What were women supposed to do, in their middle years, biologically speaking? Have more babies, she supposed. The idea appalled her. Unlike the octopus, she seemed resolved on a course of defying nature. Maybe that was why she felt so bad?

The male octopus hadn't known his limitations. He thought he could have a full, active, healthy life in that box, or surely he would have sat down and died?

It wasn't much good, really; speculations about the octopus were interesting, but not interesting enough. She looked at her watch. (A bad sign.) Ten past six, said her watch. Only ten past six.

She walked up and down the room a few more times, and looked again. Still only ten past. And here it came, this indescribable event, which as soon as it had passed would be gone and forgotten, leaving nothing in its wake, though in other ways one could have compared it to a change in the weather, to a feared approaching squall or hurricane, and it was true that the air did grow very dark at that moment, but it would pass (she told herself), and leave nothing, it broke nothing, it hurt nothing, she would be all right soon, inevitably she would be all right. She repeated these words, a careful formula. It grew darker, a kind of blue-gray watery darkness, and she began to moan (as she had always moaned as a child, tossing her head backward and forward on the pillow, finally beating her head against the wall or the rails of the bed). Indescribable, how bad it was, when it came. And yet, she told herself (a little, safe, monotonous voice speaking) it doesn't matter, it doesn't matter, it will pass, up and down, up and down, she walked and walked, and the tears rose, and she breathed with difficulty, and the hot tears spilled down her cheeks, and she thought that's better, it's nearly over, when the tears come, for though the tears had no healing power, they took off the edge of it, like cold water on a burn, which similarly has no healing power, and before she knew where she was she was weeping and gulping as she walked, and moaning at the same time, and for a moment it seemed to be happening, in time, and then whatever it was was over, and she was left feeling obscurely cheated, as though she had missed something of final importance by not concentrating hard enough. This was the worst thing of all, the sense of loss. As though one waited, constantly, for something that never happened, was never revealed. That, too, was familiar. And now it was all over, the tears that still fell were falling meaninglessly, unfelt; she pulled out her handkerchief and blew her nose. It wasn't so bad, really, after all. More of a nuisance, really.

She honestly couldn't tell whether it was the depths of her being that she fell toward, at such moments, or whether it was some squalid muddy intersecting gutter or canal, from which she would struggle wisely back to dry land. At times she would willingly have fallen farther. But never achieved it. Always, the struggling back, the drying of eyes, the reassembling of parts.

She still didn't feel exactly cheerful, though the worst was over. She walked up and down for half an hour or more, muttering to herself, trying to divert the energy of the experience to some more useful end, but she was exhausted. It was, after all, as though some bad weather had passed over her, leaving her a little flattened, like a field after heavy rain. It would take her some time to shake it off and slowly uncrackle and unfurl herself again. Meanwhile, she walked up and down, and had another drink. She was a large woman and could drink more than was good for her, and moreover had got into the habit of doing so. Sometimes she had thought she could drown her bad moments in drink, but had never managed to yet; they always lurked and waited for her, and got her later, when she had a hangover. (Her brother, of much the same temperament, had pursued drink more effectively, and seemed to have had good results, though accompanied by deplorable side effects.) At one patch in her life, the bad moments had been so frequent (this was just before she decided, finally, to leave her husband) that she had gone to her doctor like an adult woman and asked for tranquilizers, as all her friends did: she'd swallowed the things, mouthfuls of them, and waited for some Nirvana of happy irresponsibility to take over, but nothing at all had happened. Absolutely nothing. She'd been back to the doctor and complained, and he'd tried her with some others, and again, nothing at all had happened. (She'd found much the same resistance to amphetamines, at Oxford.) She still wept endlessly, and moaned and beat her head on the wall, in almost incessant stormy weather. After a while, she'd abandoned the whole idea of drugs, and had subsequently been relieved that they hadn't worked: it made her misery more, not less, respectable, she felt; she was glad it hadn't been so feeble as to respond to a few chemicals. As soon avert an avalanche with a wall, or quench a volcano with firehoses, as they had vainly and recently tried to do in Iceland.

(In fact, it was largely Frances Wingate's own fault that she did not respond to drugs: it is true that she had a happy constitution, a metabolism able to deal with large quantities of foreign substances, but it is also true that she never followed instructions on bottles, and failed to grasp the point that many pills are geared for cumulative or long-term effect, not for instant relief. Her doctor, unable to believe that Frances could be so stupid, never thought to question her more closely about her pill-taking habits, and remained puzzled by her resistance. But then, he had never been convinced that there was anything much wrong with her.)

When she left her husband, the thing stopped altogether, for a while. Aha, she had said to herself.

It started up again some time later, and had continued, though very intermittently, through the happiest years of her life. It was back again now, but not surprisingly. She poured herself another drink, and wandered over to the gilt-edged mirror and looked at herself, while thinking of the happiest years of her life, and wondered if they could really be over, as it now seemed. She looked at herself, red and blotchy, her skin with broken veins (drink, of course, as much as age), and thought that she certainly didn't look as though she had much future. The notion amused her, because she was after all only in her mid-thirties, and doing very well for herself in other ways. She blew her nose, and decided to feel better, if she possibly could.

It was partly her own fault that she was feeling so bad. She must, in some way, have wanted it. Otherwise, she wouldn't have come back to this very town, where she had parted from the only man she had ever loved, the only man in Europe. (She liked that phrase and said it to herself from time to time, and in a sense it was appropriate as well as melodramatic, for the man in question had been a Middle-European, born in Pilsen though reared in Palmers Green.) She deserved to feel bad, after all. One had to relive one's own worst moments. (Part of her said, if one must be miserable, one might as well have something to be miserable *about*.)

Though she was feeling, distinctly, better. Blowing her nose, powdering her nose, wiping her eyes. It's all your own fault, she said to herself, you shouldn't spend so much time alone. You should have gone to dinner with Andersson, as you were supposed to.

But I didn't *want* to, she answered herself. I'd seen enough people, I'd met too many people.

Oh, heavens, she said to herself, and looked at her watch. It was, amazingly, mercifully, ten to eight. One good thing about one's bad moments, they did speed up once they got going. It was only the approach that was so laboriously, so boringly, so painfully slow. It was rather like work. Settling down to work was agonizingly tedious, and yet once one got into it the time flew away. Ten to eight. If she went out now for dinner, and had a little walk on the way there, and a little walk on the way back, it would be time to go to bed when she got back to the hotel, and the whole evening would be over, polished off, finished forever. She looked at herself. Did she look ill, did she look drunk? She must not shame the Institute, whose honored guest she was. She didn't look too bad; surely, she would pass.

She put on the coat, picked up her bag, walked smartly down the stairs and handed in her key, with a familiar deceptive briskness, as though she were very busy and slightly late for an important assignation.

Over a plate of soup, a little later, she thought about the only man in Europe, that man from Palmers Green. (He lived in Fulham now.) She thought about him a great deal of the time. She wondered again why it was that she had left him, and why she was sitting here alone, and whether it had been her fault or his. Had he driven her away, or had she departed? The latter, surely. The issue had become confused, by her insistence that it wasn't in any way his fault that she was leaving, that it had been entirely her own, and that it was her wicked nature that was to blame. As she recalled, she had blamed her bad nature, and her work. He was ruining both, she had said. He was making her better natured, and he was preventing her from wanting to work. This had been true, but she doubted if it could really have been her reason for leaving him—more like a reason for staying, it sounded now, after the event. Why on earth had she left him? She added pepper to her soup. Pride? Fear?

She had been rather afraid of him. He had been something of a salvationist, he had wished to save her, with evangelical passion, and she was afraid of disappointing him, and simultaneously rather afraid of being saved. So she had told him firmly that she was mad and beyond redemption and that he'd better leave her alone or he'd be in for some nasty disappointments. Out she had gone into the wilderness, and now she stayed in expensive hotel bedrooms, in beds large enough at least for two. (Perhaps it was the third that had really driven her away, though she and he had never talked about it much, and she never thought about it if she could possibly prevent herself.)

She certainly wasn't going to start thinking about his wife now. It was neither the time nor the place. She stirred her soup vigorously. It was full of fish bones. Amazing, how keen one was to eat even when thoroughly depressed. Or was one simply keen to pass the time? The man at the other end of the restaurant was staring at her rather nastily, a large, mustached, huge-chested person. He was the only other customer in the place. It was a horrid little eating house, as cheap as she could find, tucked away down a dark back street strewn with cabbage stalks and fish heads, slapping with washing. One could say this for Frances Wingate, she really didn't care where she went or what she did or what she ate, she didn't care what risks she ran. (She was careful about foreign water these days, but with good cause.) And yet, of course, she didn't really run any risks, she had an excellent sense of judgment, she was well used to eating alone, and she had recognized at once, from the outside, that this place, though a dump, was in no way a sinister dump, and the man who was staring at her was doing it idly, and the fat proprietor and his fat wife and skinny daughter who were sitting in a sulky group around a table at the other end of her room would protect her interests, though with some contempt. Safe, safe as houses. She took out a little embossed hotel notepaper and started to write a long drunken unpostable letter to her long-lost lover (six months lost, he was in fact, but it seemed like an age). Darling, darling, beautiful darling, I love you forever, I miss you forever, she wrote idly. There wasn't really much to say in a love letter. He had been good at the genre, inventive and devious. He had also been good at telegrams. I love you, she wrote again, underlining the words for emphasis.

Then she wrote a real postcard to her children: that one she would post. And another to her parents, and one to her alcoholic brother Hugh and his wife Natasha. And another to her brother Hugh's son Stephen, who had (rather early in life) a new baby, which he took as seriously as a mother octopus would its many offspring. There were various other friends to whom she would have liked to send cards, but she did not know their addresses. Her family was hardly a close-knit one, but at least she knew where most of its immediate members lived. She made a note or two, for her lecture in the morning, thinking of ex-colleagues who would have been pleased and surprised to hear from her, if only she knew where they were. The past had been so full: overfull. What of the future? What on earth could it still hold for her? Her mind hovered over her soup plate, contemplating its skeletal omens. There must surely still be something in store. Hope springs eternal, she said to herself. Such clichés amused her. But it was not hope that seemed to be springing and flourishing in her spiritual breast, it was a malignant and meaningless growth of grief. She felt as though she had swallowed a stone, or a whole hardboiled egg. A dull sad ache. Perhaps the soup would cure it, but she doubted it.

The soup was really quite good, though bony. She had told the children about the octopus on the postcard—they would be pleased, they had watched the television program with her about the programmed octopus, indeed they had summoned her with cries from the kitchen to watch it, one of them with tears in her eyes about the poor mother dying in her nest, and it was because of them really, that she'd told Professor Andersson that she'd like to see the research laboratory. They'd be interested in that. Though she might well get home before the postcard, the post was dreadfully slow. Somebody told her there'd been a postal strike in this country, but that wasn't so bad, in fact, because they were delivering all the most recently posted things, it was the very old ones that had to wait, lingering in the boxes for months till all the backlog was cleared, and if it wasn't cleared before the next inevitable strike, well, too bad, there they would stay for another few months. Not that it mattered, she'd be home soon.

A piece of bone had lodged itself between her wisdom tooth and her back molar. Annoying. She prodded at it with her tongue, but failed to dislodge it. She had another glass of wine, swilling it around hopefully—weren't fish bones supposed to melt? And this wine was acid enough to melt anything, even Cleopatra's pearl. Wine of the house, in a smeared carafe. Sometimes she did wish she didn't drink so much. Though she'd only just finished that bottle of brandy, hadn't she? But then she'd been dined out every night. An eighth of a bottle a day, on top of what she'd been given and the experimental little bottles she'd taken out of the convenient little refrigerators. Modest, really, quite a reassuring calculation. Though not quite *so* reassuring, because there'd also been that open half bottle of scotch that she'd finished off on the first night with Peter Borg, and she'd noticed he'd hardly had any. Oh, dear. It would be too awful to become a real alcoholic, and to have to make these little self-deceiving calculations all the time—but I only had three doubles, and wine doesn't count, and I am sure John drank *some* of that bottle, and anyway I'm going to give it up tomorrow— all that kind of thing. The wine really was sour. She quite liked sour wine. She had another half glass, and then began to prod at the bone with a toothpick—funny how they were so lavish with toothpicks abroad, even in places like this. (She'd come here really because it would have been too embarrassing to meet Andersson or Galletti or any of her other contacts in any other restaurant when she'd promised them she was going to eat in the hotel and go to bed early. Which she might even have done, but eating in the hotel wouldn't have filled in enough of the evening. It was still only nine o'clock.) She was prodding at her teeth more energetically than she would have done if she had been entirely sober, as she thought these dull thoughts, and so she was not particularly surprised, though rather alarmed, when she dislodged not only the fish bone, but also a fair-sized piece of filling from her wisdom tooth. As the tooth consisted of little but filling (the dentist had wanted to pull it out last time, and she hadn't let him, because it seemed such a bad omen, to lose a wisdom tooth), she couldn't feel she had lost anything very important—he'd warned her that he was filling it for the last time. But the lump of silvery metal which she extracted, delicately, with her finger, and laid upon the side of her soup plate, did look rather large. Nervously, she explored what was left. There seemed to be very little left, but at least it didn't hurt. She washed a little more wine around it, and was grateful that she had ordered an omelette for her next course. Stringy foreign bifteck would have been the end.

She was beginning to feel quite cheerful. The man at the other table, right across the other side of the room, was staring at her. She stared back and he dropped his eyes. That done, she decided to have a little read of her book. She was reading a novel by Virginia Woolf—*The Years*. One had to be so careful what one read on journeys, because the book would forever bear the mark of the journey, so she always tried to read something not too important but not too trivial either. She remembered reading a volume of short stories by Wells—why, she couldn't remember—while waiting for Karel to arrive at some incredibly elaborate and doubtful assignation, and the book had been ruined forever: she had to turn its spine to the wall nowadays so she couldn't read its lettering. And while one of the children had been having his appendix out, she had read Iris Murdoch. On a train, when she had just left her husband forever, she had read *Mr. Norris Changes Trains*. Crying, turning the pages, gazing out of the window, crying again, reading a few more pages. Just like now, in fact. The soup plate and the filling were removed by the proprietor's sulky daughter, the omelette arrived.

She read a few pages of *The Years*, but she couldn't concentrate for long. Such gallant old people lived in those pages, but the writer had died young by her own hand. Shall I become a lonely gallant old lady? thought Frances Wingate. All in all, it seemed quite likely. She did seem to have amazing powers of survival and adaptation. And it wasn't surprising, at all, that she had felt bad, here in this strange city. It had been quite a significant place, in her life. A strange place, with its bleached salty buildings, its fortifications, its serious naval power, its fish bones and conferences, and a few luxury yachts moored amongst the fishing boats, well away from the tankers and the destroyers. She had been here quite often. The first time, many years ago, she had been eighteen years old, and she had sat on that bench on the sea front, and cried and cried—the disaster had been so petty that she had often laughed about it, when recalling or recounting it, but it had seemed the end of the world at the time. She'd been on her way home from a fortnight's hitchhiking in Calabria, and here, in this city, where she and her friend were to part, and her friend to catch her train home, she found that she had lost her passport. It must have been stolen from her bag, on their last lift, for nothing else was gone. Bravely she had waved her friend goodbye (she was off back to England, the lucky girl; Frances still had a week more abroad to endure), and then she had wandered down from the station, back down the long steps from the height of the town to its depth, down to the sea front, and there she had sat on the bench, and watched the oily sea. Hopeless, she felt, hopeless and stateless. She hadn't even got anywhere to spend the night, and two days to wait before her next companion reached her. She wept, tired and dirty. In the end, she pulled herself together and found herself a bed in a convent: it had been a frightening place, with rows of girls sleeping in uncurtained beds, and a curtained nun shuffling behind a screen in a corner, where a candle burned, as though it were a hospital, not a youth center.

The candle had upset her. Was it for religion, or for surveillance? she had wondered then, and wondered now. She had had a bad night. But in the morning, she had got up and gone off to the consulate and bought herself a new passport, it had been as simple as that, as easy as that to reinstate oneself, in those days. And now she did not sleep with rows of girls and a nun, but in the best room in the best hotel. Alone.

Her second visit had been three years later, with the man she was just about to marry. She had known at the time that it was a mistake to marry him, that on no account ought she to marry him, that she would be no use to him nor he to her. She also knew it was inevitable that the mistake would be made. It was partly that he was so insistent. He thought he loved her; he could not be dissuaded from this fixed and neurotic idea, and in the end she had decided that he could find out for himself that he didn't. But oh, how long and horrible the process of discovery had been. He hadn't been a man to give in easily. Anthony Wingate. She rarely thought of him now, though she bore his name. On that evening, when she was twenty, she had escaped from him for half an hour, and had sat watching the sea and thinking of what it would be like, married to Anthony.

Her third visit had been with Anthony and some of their children, on their way south, on holiday. (How many children? She could hardly remember. Two? Three? Or maybe even four?) How odd these family holidays had been, how painful, and yet at times how poignant, how lovely the moments salvaged. They had been bitter with one another most of the time, she and her husband: he was a cold man with a violent temper, and she was frightened of him, but she was not easily intimidated, she refused to submit. Obstinate to the last degree, she had pursued her career, her interests, her own self, in his despite. She had hardened herself on him. On holidays, she had tried to soften, for the children's sake, but it was impossible—they would quarrel in the car, fight bitter disputes over meal times, shout and throw things at one another at night, quarrel over trivia: where to stop, where to stay, what to eat, what to buy, how to treat the children. (The children, tough, resilient, good-natured, ignored their parents' folly, and amused themselves.) Holidays, from the adult point of view, had been largely an occasion for intensive, undistracted warfare. But even then, there had been strange lakes of time when a view of a mountain, a tree in flower, a courtyard, had seemed to retain its own self despite their destructive passions, when they would have, the two of them, even a moment of peace in the face of some more powerful natural phenomenon. They had been overcome, from time to time, in their littleness. It had not happened here: it was one of the most famous views in the world, but it had not done its famous trick, for they had spent their two hours here (they were passing through, they had stopped for lunch) arguing about where to have lunch. Anthony had wanted an expensive meal, she could tell, but hadn't been able to stand the thought of the children larking around in a good restaurant. Frances didn't give a damn what the children did, they never embarrassed her. They had compromised, and both had sulked, looking over the famous bay. But later that day, a little farther south, they had had a moment of remission: they had driven through a small forest, high over the sea, and the roots of the trees had been crazily exposed and twisted, and strange undergrowth flourished, and they had stopped the car, and looked at the improbable vegetation in some awe. Fungi, odd fleshy plants, brown leaves, spotted leaves, thin needle leaves, mold and heaped curving interweaving branches, like nothing in nature, showing what?— that there was hope, that there were more manifestations than man's miserable limited mind could dream of, that not even she, all-thoughtful, never-resting, never-rested, could either create or destroy by her own misery the variety of the earth's creation, for such a sight she had never dreamed of.

She thought of the octopus again, and smiled. Why did she love it so? She had loved its gray fleshy body, its lovely tinted iridescent gray muscles, its faint blushes and changes, its round suckers, its responsiveness, its sensibility, its grace. And, smiling, she thought of that last, that most significant visit to this city. She had been there with Karel. They had had two days here together, a lifetime. On one of the days they had gone out for a walk, and with their usual lack of success they had found the most terrible place in the world for walking—Karel, a city man, had no sense of maps or countryside, and would always deliver them, thus, in some impossible place. This time he had looked at the map, at the empty spaces on either side of the port—it must be good there, he said, pointing at a large flat patch without towns or villages, and they had set off, along the coast road, hoping for seclusion, and indeed seclusion they had found, for they ended up in a flat yellow swamp, crossed by long straight muddy tracks. They left the road and turned down a track through what seemed to be fields, though what they were growing who could have said, for the soil was both yellow and salty, an unpromising combination. There were ditches by either side of the track: the tracks intersected, regularly, at right angles. They aimed for the sea, but the terrain grew more and more difficult, the mud clinging to the tires of Karel's car, and the ditches turning in a sinister fashion into banks, until finally they were driving along a kind of yellow muddy tunnel, and then the car went into a deep rut, and stopped. They hadn't much cared: they had sat and kissed and talked for a while of other matters, and then they'd got out to investigate. The car was deeply embedded: they would clearly have to push it out and reverse out the way they had come. They stood there in the mud, holding hands, his shoes sinking, her sandals full of wet clay. It was one of the most unattractive spots one could have imagined. Frances, being a practical woman and used to excavations, hadn't worried much: she was more worried about losing Karel the next day than about standing there forever in a muddy estuary. She said this to him. I'll never leave you, he said, with his usual air of slight panic. You're leaving me tomorrow, she said, unable to keep a plaintive tremor from her voice. I'll see you next week, he said. And they stood there, in the immense wet flat silence, where nothing grew.

Only it wasn't silence. As they stood and listened, they became aware of a most peculiar noise—a kind of honking and squawking and bubbling, a comic and sinister sound.

"What on earth is that?" said Karel.

"I've no idea," she said.

It continued, rhythmically: it came from the end of the canal they were stuck in. They went to see what it was, curious, like children, and located its source: it was coming from a round, erect drainage pipe, about four feet across, standing at an arbitrary cross road. Shall we look down? said

Frances, standing at a safe distance, her feet squelching. I think we must, said Karel.

So they went up to the yellow pottery pipe, and stared down it. And there they saw a most amazing sight. Hundreds and hundreds of frogs were sitting down that pipe, and they were all honking, all of them, not in unison but constantly, their little throats going, their mouths open, their eyes staring up with curiosity at Karel and Frances and their large human shadows. Honk, honk, koax, koax, they cried. They were all different shapes and sizes—the same species, probably, all a yellowy gray in color, but madly, but crazily varied in size, as though some law of nature had gone wrong. Huge big ones, tiny little ones, fat ones, skinny ones, they all sat and honked. Down the pipe they sat, as happy as can be, croaking for joy. Karel and Frances stared, awestruck, amused: the sight was repulsive and at the same time profoundly comic, they loved the little frogs and the big ones. Oh, I love them, said Frances. They looked as though they had been bred from the clay, as in some medieval natural history. A natural product of the landscape, they were. And every time she thought of them, in later years, she felt such pleasure and amusement deep within her, a deep source of it, much deeper than that pipe.

It had taken them some time to get the car out, she remembered, as she finished up her omelette and chewed a lettuce leaf. In fact, they had given up the attempt for a while, and had made their way finally down to the sea—a strange sea, derelict and morbid, not at all the same sea that filled the bay a few miles down the coast. There had been no beach to speak of, but a clay shore where the tideless Mediterranean dully curled its idle dirty little waves. Long reeds and rushes grew. But it had at least been secluded, so they lay down on the mud and made love, which was, after all, the purpose of their expedition. Frances kept her filthy sandals on, because she knew that although they felt quite nice, almost part of her foot at the moment, she would never be able to face putting them back on again once they had caked and dried.

She could remember the sight of that dirty sandal, somewhere up behind Karel's shoulder. She thought of Karel's
shoulder, forever lost, renounced forever.

Then they had gone back to the car, and pushed it out.
She, expert in dislodging jeeps and Land-Rovers, had finally
taken off her dress, and used it to give the wheels some grip:
she'd arrived back at the hotel in a quite amazing condition.

The next day, when Karel drove back to his wife, it crossed
her mind that she would leave him. She was tired of being
treated so badly—abandoned in inconvenient places, pushed
into muddy ditches. She had had enough of it. Something in
her finally rebelled—pride, conscience, something like that—
and when she got back to England she found herself behaving, somewhat to her own surprise, quite oddly. She told
Karel that they should part, and stuck to it. He didn't believe
her at first: he refused to let her go, suggesting ludicrous
compromises (but not, she noted, marriage). She became
equally persistent. They were ruining one another's life, she
said, and off she went, firmly, after a fortnight of recrimi-
nation, to North Africa, on a perfectly legitimate piece of
work. He could not pursue her there: she had always had the
upper hand, as far as mobility went. She stayed there for a
month, half expecting each day to see him appear on a camel,
sunstruck, across the sands to rescue her, as he had threatened to do: but he didn't. And when she got back to England,
she didn't see him, didn't hear from him. She was rather
surprised. They had left it that if she ever changed her mind,
she had only to let him know, but she hadn't exactly changed
her mind. It was as though he had ceased to exist. She was
not likely to come across him by accident. They did not move
in the same circles. And now she had not seen him or heard
of him for months.

Going over this old ground, she poked through the pile of
papers she had brought with her to chaperone her during her
dinner. There was the card for the children, there were the
lecture notes, there was the note she had written to Karel.
She tore it up, and pushed the pieces into the folder. The

folder was full of such scraps. Then, wavering, she lit upon
another new postcard—well, it wasn't exactly new, she'd
picked it up a year or two ago on another lecture tour in
Florence, around the Uffizi she'd been, and there she must
have bought this rather attractive card. (Her folder was full
of such things also—a sediment of past journeys, tickets, old
cards, street plans, hotel bills, letters, addresses.) The card
was a detail from a painting by Hugo van der Goes, of the
adoration of the shepherds: it showed a bunch of straw, a
glass with some Canterbury bells, a painted pot with two red
lilies, two white irises, and one blue iris. It was extraordinarily beautiful. She looked at it and her eyes filled with
tears. Beautiful, beautiful. She turned it over, and she wrote

Karel Schmidt Esq.,
11 Huntingdon Rd,
SW6

She stared at that for some time, and then she filled in the
message space. First of all she put the date. Carefully then
she wrote: *I miss you.* Then, underneath that, she wrote, *I
love you.*

There didn't seem to be much point in signing it. She had
no intention of posting it, and anyway, he would know who
she was.

Silly, really, the things she had found herself doing since
she fell in love with Karel. Love was certainly a madness, as
the poets said, and it made even quite adult people behave
in a most peculiar way—hoarding, hoping, promising, sending messages. It was the last resort, the last deliverance, for
those who could not aspire to the holy love of God. She was
not well balanced enough for the holy love of God, she had
not the spiritual capacity for it, though she had spiritual concepts from time to time. No, passion had been the only hope
for her. It had worked in a way, but the circumstances had
been so inconvenient. For instance, Karel's wife hadn't liked
it at all. And she had so much to put up with from Karel

anyway that Frances had sympathized with her unpleasant-
ness.

I love you, I miss you. It was true, she did miss him, but
she'd missed him even while she was in theory with him,
because of all the times when in practice she wasn't. Incred-
ible subterfuges she had been driven to—you tell me what
program you'll be watching on the telly and I'll watch it too,
you give me a ring at nine exactly but I won't answer, I'll
know it's you, you think of me when you're at college and
I'll think of you in the library. When he got some new false
teeth (he had two on a bridge) she made him give her the old
set. She carried them around for ages, then put them in a
drawer by her bed with his letters. Later, when she had left
him, she got them out again, and when she returned from
Africa and started again upon social life, she had taken to
putting the teeth down the front of her brassière. She liked
the feel of them, Karel's teeth resting gently and delicately
and wirily against her soft evening breast, they kept her company. She had one low-cut dress that she was rather fond of,
a soft black one, soft black wool, and one night at a party
she caught a man in the act of staring down her cleavage and
meeting, entranced, and horrified the sight of Karel's glaring
teeth, the guardians of her virtue. She had taken a man back
home with her from that party, an old colleague and friend,
and as they got undressed for bed, she got out the teeth and
put them on the bedside table, and John had stared at them
in alarm, and she had told him what and whose they were,
and they had lain in each other's arms all night, quietly,
watched over by those almost luminous dentures, gleaming
pale like ivory, more vigilant than a nun's candle. John had
been good and solicitous to her after that, ringing her up
sometimes, asking her out to dinner once in a while. He must
have thought she was mad, and in need of care and attention.
A little of Karel's virtue had breathed its way through even
so poor a relic.

She and Karel had planned, once, to visit Pilsen, but they
hadn't made it. He had not been there since he was a small

child. Most of his family had perished in concentration camps. He alone of his generation had escaped. Teeth and bones. Profanely she cherished his fragments.

Suddenly she wanted the teeth very badly. She hadn't had them out for ages. She didn't even know where they were. It was just possible that she might have them with her, in one of the rarely opened zip pockets of her luggage: she had taken them to Turin, hadn't she, on that last trip? Or had she? She couldn't remember.

Perhaps he has forgotten me, she thought, as she waved to the girl, to bring her bill.

She woke up in the morning in a most frightful panic. She had been dreaming—she dreamed every night, all night, exhaustingly—that she was standing in a bathroom, with blue-tiled walls and chrome fittings, and that every detail was as clear to her as if she were really there, though she had never been there and knew it was a dream. This is impossible, she was saying to herself, as she stood there in her dream gazing at every tiny detail of the unexistent wall's surface, at every thread of the dark blue towel, at every little silver screw in the frame of the mirror. Impossible, impossible, I could never create so powerfully in such detail, she said to herself, quite consciously panic-stricken even in her dream. And then she woke up. It was pitch black, and her heart was pounding high up in her bosom—too much black coffee, as people on the continent always say. Also, her tooth was aching shockingly. Help, help, please God it is morning, she said to herself, and switched on her bedside light and looked at her watch.

It was. It was seven o'clock.

Thank God for that, she said, and got out of bed, and went over to the window, nervously exploring the hole in her tooth as she walked. The curtains were so thick they let in no light. She opened them, and there was the autumn sunshine, there was the harbor, there were the boats and their forest of masts, and there was all the dazzling bay, with the islands

far out, strung along the horizon. Her thudding heart lifted.
Lovely, said her waking heart.

While she was having breakfast, she had a good idea for her
lecture—nothing much, just an interesting new connection
about Phoenician trade which would interest, from what Galletti had said, this particular lay and local audience. She got
out her notes again, scribbled a few more, crossed out one
quotation and decided to use another. The breakfast was delicious—nice doughy rolls, thank God, instead of those hard
crusty things one sometimes got, and the coffee was hot. I
must get my tooth fixed, she thought (plugging up the cavity
with dough, swallowing down a couple of codeine) as soon
as I get back to England. I must get my tooth fixed, she
thought, and have a bath.

The water was hot, and there was a bath as well as a
shower. She didn't like showers. She liked to lie in a hot
bath. And like lying in a hot bath it was, two hours later, to
hear Professor Andersson introduce her to her audience. She
sat there, neatly, happily, listening to the long list of her
achievements: she let them flow over her, reassuring, relax-
ing, comforting, like water full of compliments. I did all that,
she thought to herself, as she heard the catalogue of her ac-
complishments: I, me, I stole all that from nature and got it
for myself. I am a vain, self-satisfied woman, she said to
herself, with satisfaction.

Professor Andersson was an amiable fellow: tall, stooping, urbane, Scandinavian, and chivalrous in a thoroughly
acceptable way, like most Scandinavians. (She didn't trust
Galletti: in her pre-Karel days, when she found it almost
impossible to stop herself sleeping with people whenever she
was away from home, she'd have been in trouble with Galletti.) But Andersson was delightful. He was even rather
handsome, thought Frances idly, watching his beaky profile
and his cold gray Nordic eye. She liked people with big
noses, having one herself. What about making a pass at Andersson? Would he respond? He was in a promising age group

for response. She looked down, modestly, to avoid her own improper speculations, and the image of a less tidy professor in her splendid hotel bed, and noticed that she should have cleaned her shoes, perhaps. But nobody would look at her shoes, they'd be behind the lectern. How filthy she had been, that day with Karel in the mud. She had got into the shower fully clothed, sandals and all, and it had run off her in great streaks and lumps, clogging up the drain: she'd had to pick lumps of mud out and mush them up with a hairpin before they would go down.

She shouldn't really think about Karel. It was unsuitable, memories of him threw her sometimes, they would flash across her mind in the middle of dinner parties and press conferences. His thinning yellow hair, his hollow creaky chest, his pedantic speaking, his mouth open in sleep, his long in-turning feet, his bony hands, his nose so sharp in the early morning, so handsome in the evening. His mouth against her, sucking strength into her. An interesting physical exchange. Was there a term for it in physics, maybe, a formal term, or in biology? The replacement of one energy by the removal of another? Sometimes she thought, thinking of Karel, that he had filled her and given to her and charged her for years, so that she could run on for years without him, but still full of him. Opaque with goodness he had been, though he looked as brittle as glass, as transparent as a classifiable neurotic. Like thick old glass he was, like the sky or the sea, opaque, indestructible. She had thought to see through him with her quickness and clever knowingness. I mustn't think about all this, thought Frances Wingate, I must stop it, there'll be more coming if I don't watch it. Oh, how awful it is to be able to think of several things at once, thought Frances Wingate insincerely, as she listened to her own praises and decided to fix her attention upon the decor.

A large and ancient room it was, a dignified spot, though unlike most English halls of the same distinction it was peeling a bit, and the dark red Attic borders on the high ceiling could do with a bit of touching up. Funny how careless they

are about some things abroad, and how fussy about others.
A much-traveled woman, she never ceased to marvel. False
marbling filled the false and unnecessary arches in the walls.
The chairs were gilt, and the floor was polished wood. On
the chairs sat a curiously mixed audience, of students, dig-
nitaries, Anglophiles, exiles, even one or two academics.
There sat, though she did not know it, her distant cousin
David Ollerenshaw, geologist. David Ollerenshaw did not
know that he was her cousin, nor did he know much about
her. He had come to her lecture largely through boredom,
having nothing better to do. Though he had always been
interested in archaeology, fossils, and that kind of thing. He
had come across several archaeologists on his travels, and
had been interested in their pursuits.

Professor Andersson was drawing his eloquent introduction to a close. He had recounted her early academic career,
dwelling lovingly on her thesis, *Carthage and the Saharan
Hinterland*, on her later seminal paper, *Carthage and the
Garamantes*, and moving on to her later travels in Chad,
Adra, and the Sudan. Finally, he described the well-known
story of her discovery of Tizouk, which had established her
theory of Punic-Meroitic contacts, as well as introducing
some interesting new speculations about trade routes from
the south. "Inspired," said Professor Andersson, "by a fine
mixture of faith and scholarly expectation, Dr. Wingate had
the perseverance to communicate to others the belief that she
had located and could usefully excavate her Saharan highland
emporium—a missing link in so many scholars' speculations. And, with an exceptional perseverance, she was able
to overcome all the practical and financial obstacles that lay
between her and the city of her imagination. . . ." (Yes,
thought Frances, Andersson would do. But he wouldn't be
very cheerful about it. Too serious. Galletti looked a more
cheerful prospect.) "As we all know," said the Professor,
"in 1968 she discovered . . ." And he proceeded, politely,
to recap what they all ought to have known but undoubtedly
didn't: Frances, who was realistic if not modest about her

own achievements and their notoriety, was always grateful
for such summaries. There was nothing more embarrassing
or embarrassed than an audience who did not know what it
was there for, or who its speaker was. Why such people went
to lectures remained a mystery, but as they did, it was sensible of people like Andersson to take them into account.

Professor Andersson concluded. "It is a great personal
pleasure," he said, "for me to be able to introduce to you
Dr. Frances Wingate, whose work I have followed with the
greatest enthusiasm, and who has proved to be as interesting
as a person as she is" (here he fumbled slightly for words)
"as she is as a . . . as . . ." (triumphantly but not wholly
happily) "as an archaeologist." And he sat down, leaving
her the floor. He won't do, thought Frances. Too unhappy,
too worn, too guilty. Too deep lines from the nose to the
mouth, too elaborate a manner. She warmed pointlessly to
his courtesy. She wished she'd had dinner with him and his
wife the night before.

Frances Wingate cleared her throat, rose neatly to her feet,
and lectured. She felt on form. Something in what Andersson
had said had lifted her—she wasn't quite sure what, but it
had been there. Perhaps it had been that phrase, the city of
her imagination. An ordinary phrase, but so precisely what
Tizouk had been. She gave more or less her usual lay lecture—a description of her early interest in the Carthaginians,
her studies in Tunis and the Sahara, her visit to Meroë, her
visit to Nigeria, filled out for this local audience by a few
polite references to the trade between this famous seaport
and ancient Carthage: then she moved onto Tizouk itself.
People often told her that she must get tired of talking about
Tizouk, which always annoyed her, because the truth was
that she never got tired of it, she always enjoyed it, it was
just that they got tired of hearing about it and assumed in
their incorrect sophisticated way that she must be as bored
as they. Not so, not so: she loved Tizouk. She could no more
get tired of it than she could tire of living. If she relinquished
Tizouk, she would relinquish all things. It never bored her.

But at times, it frightened her, and now, talking as evocatively as she could about her discovery and excavation of it, she remembered with awesome clarity the emotions of triumph and terror that had accompanied that discovery. Those, she could not relate.

The triumph had been natural. All alone she had worked it out, putting bits together from here and there—the tablets at Carthage, the strangely Meroitic lion in Kano, the curiously Nok-like face on the tablet in Kush. A phrase or two from Athenaeus, who said that the Carthaginians had crossed the Sahara eating barley. A sentence from Herodotus, a remark by Heinrich Barth, a visit with the children to the Ethnological Museum, a conversation about *négritude* with Joe Ayida, a vague memory of a heap of ruins, glimpsed like so many heaps from a passing Land-Rover, in mountainous country near the Chad-Libyan border, going north. And then, one night, sitting at Rome airport waiting for a delayed flight home (she'd promised to see the children by breakfast, those poor children, they'd been dragged to some strange sites in their time till they grew so old that they had to stay at home to be educated)—sitting there, worn out by a two-day dispute with her one-time professor, a man so fixed in his views of classical antiquity that nothing south of Leptis Magna could be taken seriously in his presence, sitting there, idly staring at a map of the Sahara, wondering if there was any possible reason for her sense of certainty about her own arbitrary interpretation of the evidence, wondering if she were not, as her one-time professor had suggested, suffering from womanly intuition: sitting there, gazing at the relief of the mountains, suddenly she knew exactly where to look. She knew with such conviction that it was like a revelation—the evidence was all there, it was simply that she alone had produced the correct interpretation of it, and being correct, of course it had fitted. It was as simple as that. But why, there at the airport, had she been allowed to know? This is what puzzled her slightly. If her flight had been on time, she might never have hit on it. Or she might have hit on it two days later in the bath. Who can tell? It was so arbitrary, it had frightened her terribly. She had known that the city was there, she had gone out to dig for it, and she had found it. But all because of one flash of knowledge. Where had it come from, and why had she been allowed to have it, that revelation on which so much else had depended?

Digging in the cold dawn, her city rising from its burial in the sand, a building in reverse. Walls, buildings. Stacked. Pots, beads, figurines. Gold bars even, though they had not been the greatest wealth. Each afternoon they had retired to their tents to lie and inspect their discoveries—matchboxes and cigarette packs, and little plastic bags full of relics, dried and preserved and hidden by the sand for millennia. They had waited for her, quiet and obedient. Silently they had waited, to provide her with this unique delight.

It had all been too much. She had suffered dreadfully, afterward, from anxiety—not from guilt, exactly, for after all she had taken nothing from anyone, she had not even pillaged the dead, on the contrary she had made them live again, and she had loved them, her traders, her merchants, her agents, she had loved and defended them, with their caravans and their date palms, their peaceful negotiations. Men of peace, not war, they had been exchanging useful commodities and works of art. But she suffered from anxiety at the narrowness of her triumph, and its seeming inevitability. I must be mad, she thought to herself. I imagine a city, and it exists. If I hadn't imagined it, it wouldn't have existed. All her life, things had been like that. She had imagined herself doing well at school, and had done well. Marrying, and had married. Bearing children, and had borne them. Being rich, and had become rich. Being free, and was free. Finding true love, and had found it. Losing it, and had lost it. What next should she imagine? What terrifying enormity should she next conjure forth? Should she dig again in the desert and uncover gold? Should she plant down her foot and let water spring from the dry land? Should she wave her arm and let the rocks blossom? She had been as arid as a rock, but she had learned to flow. Or should she conceive of desolation? Defoliate forests? Slaughter innocent children and bury them in little jars with Punic inscriptions? Their small bones had made her weep, but her own children had stared coldly with no sense of kinship.

Sometimes she thought that it was all an elaborate mistake, and that she would wake up one morning and discover that the city was not there, and had never been there. Just as she imagined that she would wake up and find that Karel had deceived her, that he had never loved her. Faith and certainty, bricks and mortar. Once she had rung up the Archaeological Institute and asked to speak to her professor. (This was just after her return from Tizouk: she was expecting his sincere if jealous approbation. Instead she was told he did not exist. Instead of thinking, I have the wrong number, she thought, oh, God, I have gone mad, I have been suffering from a lengthy delusion and I never went to Tizouk, never studied under Bryers, never went to Oxford, never had the things I have had. In fact, she had a wrong number.)

It was difficult to know what to imagine next, when one had had so much. And with such alarming powers, it was so important to imagine the right things. As she talked, about the pots in Tizouk, and subsequent confirmatory discoveries near Kano, she felt some vague stirring of aspiration. She had been quiet for too long, living in the past on her laurels for too long. Time for some new excursion. She would be home soon, there might be something new waiting in the post. No wonder she got morbid and depressed late at night; it was years since she had really got moving. It was there, something was waiting, something must be waiting. But she must imagine it well. She must get it right. She had too much force to be able to afford even minor errors.

She concluded her lecture on a note of expectation, fed back from her own thinking. Scholarly expectation, it is true—who can tell, she said, what rich finds await us, all we need is the finance. She said a few words about preserving what we have (Carthage, for example) and a few more about finding what we haven't found. Then she sat down.

The applause was gratifying, the questions confused. As so often these days, she found herself warming more to the lay questions than to the professional ones: perhaps that was her alleged lust for domination manifesting itself, along with her alleged fear of serious competition, or perhaps it was simply that she and all the professionals there knew perfectly well that nothing very precise or interesting could be asked or answered in a lecture. She often wondered why the lecture was still so popular as a form. Why did all these people still come to them, when they could read her views far more comfortably at home, or watch her on the box, or cut her photograph out of the *National Geographic*, if that was what they wanted? Still, she rather liked the elderly lady who asked about the heat. Yes, she agreed, it was indeed hot in the Sahara, and digging there was at times not much fun.

She told an anecdote or two about others who had suffered in the heat: they liked the story of poor Father Julian, who had gone off to convert the Nubians in the sixth century and had found the climate so appalling that he had to sit from nine until four every day in caves full of water, undressed save for a damp linen garment. "Presumably," said Frances, "he accomplished his conversion before nine in the morning, when we used to dig. But he was better off than us in one respect—he could go on converting in the evening, nobody can dig in the dark."

(As she spoke, a vision of herself, Derek Palmer, Bruce Wyatt, and John Sinclair-Davies flashed across her mind, lying prostrate in their tent, in their underpants, drinking tepid Coke and irritably playing poker. It had indeed been hot. Bruce had won fifteen pounds off them and Derek hadn't been amused.)

She also liked a man who asked about mining in the desert: he obviously knew what he was talking about, a geologist or engineer she thought, for he'd seen the Tassili rock paintings, and had visited the tin mines in Nigeria where some of

the Nok terra cottas had been found. Did she think, he asked,
that the intensive geological surveys of the Sahara that were
now being undertaken (he must have been on one himself,
she thought) would unearth new archaeological treasures? Or
make it, at least, easier for the archaeologists to unearth
them? Or might there be a conflict between the two interests?
It was a question too interesting to suggest an immediate
answer: the desert's a large place, she said, as I'm sure you
know, and I don't suppose anyone's very likely to sink an oil
well through my next Saharan emporium, she said, playing
for time, but you're right, she said, as communications im-
prove, for commercial reasons, as roads and vehicles im-
prove, perhaps it would become easier for the archaeologist
to explore possibilities that would previously have been too
expensive to touch. Too expensive, and too hot, she said,
smiling at the old lady who had inquired about the heat. The
old lady nodded and smiled, glad that the relevance of her
question had been so fully appreciated.

One last question, said Professor Andersson, but flatter-
ingly, there were two. One was a question from a professional, about the quality of her Arab diggers, and her relations
with them, as a woman employer, which enabled her to give
her usual chivalrous praise for the chivalry and courtesy of
the Arabs who inhabited her particular area—well known,
they were, for the emancipation if not the domination of their
women, and they had taken Frances, unveiled and bare-
legged, as a natural commander. In that area, the men it was
that wore the veils. She was also able to praise, in a comic
vignette, the brave and tireless Amos, of the tribe of the well-
diggers, most of whom were now employed in oilfields, who
had been so loyal, so interested, so foolhardy, so inexhaust-
ible. She often thought of Amos, who had tramped off one
day, when the dig was nearing its end, with a nonchalant and
gallant smile, and a few photographs of the site in his pocket.
The Arabs had despised him, and treated him like a dog,
which was a fact she never mentioned in lectures: he had
accepted his role, and was puzzled to find himself as well

paid as the others. She wondered what had become of him. She liked to pay her tribute at least.

The final question was one that she could have done without, in a sense, for it was a question to which she always overreacted. She was asked if she agreed with the conventional historical and archaeological estimate of the Phoenicians: was it true that they were "a reactionary, mercenary, cruel, inartistic, and unsympathetic people, whose disappearance from history was a boon to mankind," as at least one eminent historian had stated? Frances always found this question alarming, because of the confusion of her own response. It was a fact that she had first been drawn to the Phoenicians because of their bad reputation: no race could be as bad as *that*, she had decided while still at Oxford, and had set off from Carthage in her early twenties to prove it. But alas, she had found it difficult to do so. They had been, notoriously, destroyed: all their graces and little domestic ways had gone, leaving only pots of sacrifice and Roman legends. It was with relief that she had moved farther south, to peaceful trading outposts. So what could she do now, but say that we do not know enough about the Phoenicians to condemn them wholesale, as the Romans slaughtered them wholesale? She defended them by attacking the Romans, what else could one do? And they had left some good things. A dove, a lamp, a mask. The pink baths on the rocky point at Kerkouane. She had bathed naked there from the rocks. We must remember that there were Phoenicians and Phoenicians, she said. Some perhaps slaughtered their children, others perhaps refused. As some denounced their families in the last war, and some refused. As some collaborated, and some refused. (An inspired point, that, in this city.) And then she moved to her last defense, of her own men, the men of Tizouk, the men who passed through Tizouk. "What is wrong with trade?" she inquired rhetorically. "Why should men not be merchants? Which is more civilized, a Roman legion, or a caravan of merchandise?"

She sat down quickly, before anyone spoke of slaves. There

were still slaves in the Sahara. One couldn't really pretend
her men had traded only in salt and pots and ironware. But
she tried to, just the same.

She looked at her watch. Just after twelve. Drinks time.
She could do with a drink. Her tooth had begun to throb
again, slightly, now that the false excitement of lecturing had
passed away. She remembered, suddenly, that horrible dream
bathroom. Better not have any more visions of that nature,
she told herself.

The drinks were in the room behind the lecture hall, and
people came up and shook her hand, and she downed a gin
and tonic or two. She had hoped that the geologist would
come and speak to her, as she would have liked to make
some comparison between the excitement of finding ruins,
and the excitement of finding oil, and to ask him if there also
was an element of the accidental. Did one sometimes, with
all that expensive equipment, blow up the wrong bit of desert? And how, anyway, did one know what was underneath?
She would have liked to talk about these things to him, but
he wasn't there, clearly he hadn't been invited for drinks,
and she had to make do with a librarian, a representative of
the British Council, a diplomat or two, and Galletti, who
didn't leave her elbow, and who in fact was making himself
quite useful at her elbow, replenishing her glass, whenever
it seemed to be empty. She was feeling quite euphoric. Now
she would get a good lunch, then she could have a rest in the
hotel after it, and then she could catch the six o'clock over-
night train to Paris. Only two more lectures, and she'd be
home. It was all perfectly satisfactory and she did rather like
the way everyone kept telling her how marvelous she was.

She was feeling slightly lightheaded by the time they set
off for lunch, and did not at all object to the suggestion that
they should repair to the restaurant on foot. It's very near,
Galletti assured her, firmly grabbing her arm and her brief-
case. She let him have both. Why not? It was a pleasant walk,
though steep, with winding circular streets sharply ascend-
ing, glimpses of churches and washing lines, and finally a

narrow yellow stone staircase, with shallow steps, and vines drooping from the walls. It was a shortcut but nevertheless, by the time they reached the top of it, the others seemed already to have arrived: there they were, Andersson and his wife, a couple of archaeologists, the director of the Institute, and two or three others whom she didn't recognize, and whose names, as they sat down at the long table overlooking the bay, flowed over her without leaving any mark. Either the invitations had been highly selective, or the average age of archaeologists in this country was very much lower than it was in her own, she thought, looking around the table: she was usually one of the youngest in any professional gathering, and here this was not noticeably so.

She sat between Galletti and a British archaeologist called Hunter Wisbech, who knew a lot of people she knew; opposite sat Andersson, and behind him was the window and the sea. They were high up, she now realized: it was always the case in these steep naval cities, a short steep walk and one was on the top. There were the boats again, and the white light, one of the most famous views in Europe. She thought of leafy Putney and the Thames. The tablecloth was white, and there was a large quantity of glasses and cutlery, and some olives and radishes and things in little dishes. She began to nibble them. She was ravenously hungry. She liked all this kind of thing. Some people pretended not to; perhaps some people were so good that they really didn't (Karel, for instance, would hardly eat at all, and would certainly never be got into a place like this). Galletti poured her a glass of wine and asked what she thought of the view, which wasn't what he meant. I like it, she said, happily. What a pity you have to leave this evening, why don't you fly up tomorrow, he said. I quite *like* trains, she protested, and they talked about trains and journeys, and the terrible heat in Luxor. His subject was Egypt. They talked about Egypt, but not very seriously. He was an easygoing man, he wasn't going to take her seriously or talk to her about work because he couldn't believe in her because she was a woman. He thought she was a freak and would prefer a few silly jokes. He was right. He was an amusing fellow with a face like an aging elf and pointed ears sticking through his short crinkly hair. He told her about an amusing quarrel with a driver in Cairo.

Hunter, on the other side, turned out to be an old friend of Derek Palmer, and had talked about her much with Derek in her absence. He seemed to know quite a lot about her, rather accurately, and in other circumstances she might have felt rather uneasy at the knowledge that Derek had clearly recounted in some detail the night he and she had spent with the BBC man in Tunis, and the day when she had been so violently and embarrassingly ill in the back of the Land-Rover. But at the moment, with the wine flowing, and with delightful little morsels of shellfish and salad and mayonnaise and so forth following one another quickly upon her plate—it seemed to be her favorite kind of meal, a meal of endless hors d'oeuvres, or would she suddenly be called upon to tackle a huge steak or whole chicken?—at the moment she didn't much care, and even launched upon her own description of that famous illness. It was a real breakthrough in human relations for me, she said, for after all, after that, what worse could life hold, in what worse a light could one possibly appear? If people can take that, they can take anything. Derek was *wonderful*, she said warmly, absolutely *wonderful*, he held my hand right through and never once looked disgusted, and I kept explaining that we couldn't stop because we were behind schedule and had to get there before the sun came up, but oh, Lord, I thought I was dying.

But it was a good trip, after that, said Hunter.

Yes, it had been a good trip. She'd recovered the next day—it hadn't been typhoid at all, that time. I'm incredibly resilient, she said; yes, so Derek said, said Hunter. They had started work on good terms, her momentary illness had reinforced her authority, and they had become close, the four of them, sharing everything, sleeping in the same tent, hiding nothing. It had been companionable. Karel would have hated it, for he was a modest man; she sometimes wondered how he could ever have liked an immodest person like herself. She had become more and more immodest over the years; perhaps it was something to do with tent life and the curious kind of nonsexual group feeling that always evolved in a shared enterprise of that nature. She'd often argued with Karel (who inclined to be jealous, even of the past) that there was no sex at all in her feelings for Derek and John and Bruce, though there was evidently something that was physical—it's friendship, or comradeliness, she would say lamely, but she'd never been able to make it sound very convincing, there weren't any good words for what she was trying to describe—companionship, comradeship, fellowship, the very words made one wince, as did the stupid word "dig," which she avoided whenever possible. It wasn't always possible. A friend of hers who had read classics with her at university, and who was possessed of an even greater semantic squeamishness, had abandoned a career in archaeology because of this problem, and had stuck to book-bound ancient history instead. Frances herself was not such an extremist. Unlike pedantic Karel, she recognized the existence of things that lacked good words to describe them. And she was not easily deterred.

Hunter was very interested in her, no doubt about it. Or perhaps he was more interested in secondhand stories about Derek. She really must be very careful what she said, as it would clearly get around in no time, and she had lived to regret many an indiscretion: on the other hand, she couldn't resist telling him about Derek and the camel and the syphilis. (She could see Andersson looking at her more in sorrow than in anger. Galletti, on the other hand, was much entertained, though distracted slightly by the attentions he was having to pay to some unexplained and indeed inexplicable young lady on his other side. Who the hell could she be? She was far too young to be anyone's wife, and too well dressed to be a student. Someone's daughter, maybe? Anyway, she was old enough to hear echoes of the camel story.) Hunter enjoyed the story, she could see, though it was impossible to evoke

all it had meant to them, huddled together in their small
oasis, playing poker, playing Scrabble, drinking, recounting
the whole of their past histories to one another night after
night, laughing hysterically whenever the camel was mentioned, childishly referring to it, making Derek expose, night
after night, the infinitesimally small bump which he had mistaken for serious affliction, and which in the end admitted
had probably been there all his life. Even the words of the
Scrabble board had veered remarkably toward the camel, and
when one night they had been reduced to playing Consequences, they had produced some highly entertaining varia-
tions on the theme. None of those good jokes would stand
the chill of retelling, but they had been good at the time,
mingled as they had been with the extraordinary sensations
of relief and triumph, with the knowledge that there, just out
there in the sandhills, lay their own city, rising slowly from
the ground: a reputation made, it meant, for Frances Wingate, and a good step in the right direction, careerwise, for
Derek and Bruce, both of them acting as her assistants, both
of them on handsome grants from their respective universities, grants which would now be seen to have been amply
justified. No wonder they had laughed weakly with euphoria,
lying there in the cool evening, thinking of the long caravans
from Meroë, the bazaar, the palms, the chickens and dogs,
the bargaining, the donkeys and camels, probably not so different then from now, for the whole place had been miracu-
lously preserved by the fine dry sand, and it looked, as it
emerged habitable, homely, like any other small Saharan village today, not crushed out of recognition, like so many sites,
by earth and rain and trampling feet. It had been busy then,
but they had all gone away (she had had to think of reasons
for their departure, but that came later). Negroes, Arabs,
Phoenicians. John Sinclair-Davies, who had accompanied
them at his own expense, was the artist of the expedition; he
was there to draw pots and stones, but would also dash off
beautiful reconstructions—life in Tizouk and Meroë in 500
B.C., with giraffes and monkeys and ivory, with palm trees

and lions, interspersed with sketches of Frances in her bikini, Frances in the pose of Alexandrine Tinné, the first European woman to venture into the Sahara (she was hacked to death for her trouble), Frances in the full regalia of a Meroitic queen, Palmer grotesquely raddled in the last stages of tertiary syphilis, Bruce Wyatt as a sheik playing poker with Frances dressed as the ancient queen of the Tuareg. They had all been very silly, no doubt. They had played Scrabble, in the evenings, when the poker palled, allowing themselves to use the place names of the Sahara, which were full of *z* and *k* and *x*, and other useful consonants—after all, said Frances one night, regally adjudicating, bending the rules, allowing Tizouk to Derek, it is *our* place name, and we can allow ourselves to use it, can we not?

The Sahara had once been very different: fertile, grass-covered, and in places the hippopotamus had wallowed where there is now no water for hundreds of miles. Her people had left Tizouk when the water dried up: they had wandered off, from their little trading post, leaving it to the wind and the sand and Frances Wingate.

When she had finished her camel story, she and Hunter and Galletti discussed camels and their habits in general, contrasting their bad character with the nobility and fidelity of the horse and the dog, and then, suddenly out of the blue, Hunter said, "I met an old friend of yours a month ago. Karel Schmidt, his name was."

"Really?" said Frances, a little stunned, unable to change gear very quickly. She couldn't think of anything to say, her mind still ran on camels, but she longed to know more.

"Where did you meet him?" she said, after a pause, playing for time, afraid the topic would be changed, wondering desperately how much Hunter could know about her and Karel, what Karel had said about her and whether she dared ask, whether Karel still saw Derek Palmer ever, wishing she hadn't drunk so much.

"I met him at his polytechnic," said Hunter. "I went to give a talk there. He said that's where you first met him."

"Yes, I did," said Frances. "A good few years ago, now."

"A nice fellow," said Hunter, idly, probingly. She panicked, unsure what to do. Should she tell all and get the real news of Karel? Should she keep calm and disown him? Should she suggest ownership? Hunter, she thought, would like her to tell all, so that he could sympathize, but perhaps he would sympathize too much. If she disowned him, she wouldn't get the news. The only thing to do was to suggest a vague association, implying all and telling nothing: that would keep Hunter quiet and get her what she wanted. If only I still *had* Karel, she said to herself, I wouldn't get into these confusions, drinking too much at lunchtime and all this kind of thing.

Her tooth was beginning to ache: she had hit it, in her panic, on her pudding spoon.

"He's a *very* nice fellow," she said, warmly. "*Very* nice. In fact, quite one of my closest friends." She'd said that in a special enough way, she hoped, without too much of a leer. "And how *was* he?"

"Oh, he seemed very well," said Hunter. "Working hard. He does two evenings a week adult education as well, he says. We had quite a chat about it, because I was thinking of doing a class myself next year, if I can afford it. The pay's appalling. I don't know what he does it for."

"Two a week is too much," said Frances, faintly, emptying her glass quickly as Galletti reached for the replenishing decanter, and replenished. Waves of loneliness poured through her. Two a week. Last time she had spoken to him, he'd only been doing one. He had taken on a whole new class and she hadn't known. She felt insulted and bereft.

"One would be all right, though, I thought it might be fun," said Hunter. "Does he do it for fun?"

"I don't really know," said Frances, cautiously. "I think he enjoyed it, yes. He's a very good teacher," she said, primly and loyally.

"And he's got a large family," said Hunter. "Perhaps with all those children, even a fiver helps. . . ."

"It's not as large a family as *mine*," said Frances.

"Ah yes," said Hunter, with a touch of malice, "but then we all know you're the golden girl, don't we?"

"Tell me some more about Karel," said Frances, rather pleased by the malice: flattery was all very well, but it wasn't as good as real acknowledgment. "What else did you talk about?"

Hunter stared at her calmly. He had a peculiar baby face, soft and freckled and pale, and long wavy hair, straggling a little around his neck, as though it had passed the point where he usually cut it. He was very relaxed. He was years younger than she was.

"We talked about you, of course," said Hunter.

"But you don't know me," she said.

"I knew you through Derek. And I knew your work."

"Yes, I suppose so."

"Aren't you going to ask me what he said about you?"

"I don't know if I dare," said Frances, as the air turned very still: her heart was beating rather loudly, and her tooth seemed to be beating in time with it, with an incessant throb, like a generating machine. Suddenly Hunter's self, which she had taken so lightly, assumed a terrible significance: there he was, this bland young man, smiling at her, a fatal messenger. How much would he dare to say? If the news were bad, would he utter it, and would she blame him for delivering it? Or was he the kind of polite person who would never tell an unwelcome truth? It was important to know, but too late to discover. He smiled at her, knowingly. He was a quiet troublemaker, maybe. It was too late to escape. If Karel had disowned her, she would die.

"Oh, I think you dare ask," said Hunter.

"All right, then," said Frances. "Tell me. What did he say about me?"

"He said he loved you," said Hunter, with satisfaction, expecting applause.

She thought she was going to faint, for a moment, at the sound of this lovely news.

"How nice of him," she said, unable to stop herself from smiling. And then she handed over her reward. "And I love him, of course," she said, primly.

"He didn't say much about that," said Hunter.

"No. Well, he wouldn't," said Frances. She was so moved by Karel's loyalty, and by this boy's completely self-interested nerve, that she wanted to embrace Hunter as a substitute, but could see that that would not do. On the other hand, she could see that there was no point in pursuing the Karel theme: to pursue it would have ruined it, for she would have had to admit her failures, and at the moment it stood between them perfect, undiminished, neatly summarized, as though in a poem or a play. She decided that it would be better, after all, to devote her attention to Hunter himself.

"How kind of you to tell me," she said. "*Why* did you tell me, may I ask?"

"I thought you might like to know," said Hunter.

"It was rather a risk," she said. "You clearly don't mind taking a risk or two."

And in no time at all, she had Hunter discussing himself, with her knowledge of Karel filling her heart with such delight and joy that she could hardly breathe. She would rush straight back to him, she would ring him as soon as she reached England, no perhaps not ring because of his wife, she would write to him, they would meet again, how mad to have wasted all this time, she drunkenly reflected, as she listened to Hunter and the story of his divorce (he *can't* be divorced, she said to herself, he's only about twenty-eight, he can hardly be *married* yet, she thought, though she herself had married a rich man at the age of twenty).

Hunter walked her back to her hotel. She had a train to catch at six: it was now half-past three, and she hadn't packed. Hunter could help her pack. She had got him completely under her thumb. He had nothing better to do, anyway, and would enjoy telling the story of how he helped Frances Wingate to pack her bags. She hadn't behaved badly to him, after all. She'd listened to his stories about his wife with sympathy and had given him some excellent advice. She felt slightly bad about Galletti, but then one can't please everyone, and there hadn't after all been a contract between them, and even if there had been Galletti wouldn't have liked its terms. Whereas Hunter liked exactly what he was getting, she could tell. She was too old for him, but he liked watching.

He was impressed by her bedroom. He sat on the bed and accepted gracefully when she opened the refrigerator and offered him a little bottle of champagne. She herself swallowed a couple more codeine, and told him about her bad tooth, and started to pack her things.

"You don't exactly travel light, do you?" said Hunter, staring at her hairbrushes and photographs and books and scent bottles.

"No need, in Europe," she said.

"I'd pictured you keeping all your possessions in a carrier bag," he said.

"Oh, I get quite enough of that," she said, checking in her bag for the fiftieth time to make sure she'd got her passport, her money, and her escape ticket. "I quite like a little luxury, every now and then."

There in her bag was the postcard to Karel. She looked at it and read it, and then, very quickly, before she had time to think, she put a stamp on it. She would post it at the station, and it would all be fixed. He would be waiting for her, not exactly when she got back, because the card would take a day or two to get there, but almost as soon as she got back. She had perfect faith in him. He had always promised that, if asked, he would return, and she had believed him. In a way, that had made it easy to be good. He had persuaded her that he would never abandon her. An impressive achievement. She admired him for it.

Hunter was lying back, now, on her bed.

"Aren't you feeling tired," he said, "after all that lecturing?"

"Not particularly," said Frances, who was, in fact, but

who didn't want to get onto the bed with Hunter: so she busied herself by washing her feet and cleaning her shoes. When she looked around, Hunter's eyes were shut. He was breathing heavily. He was asleep. How very nice he looked, she thought maternally, with his wavy hair and his round white neck. His wife had gone off with their doctor and nearly got him struck off the medical register: a *wicked* woman, Hunter had called her, but had had to admit that it was all his own fault because he was never at home if he could help it and was not very good about the house.

Quietly, Frances edged herself onto the other side of the bed, kicked off her shoes, and fell asleep.

They both woke at five: she had a perfect timing mechanism, and could wake at will at any predecided moment. A life of babies and travel had taught her this excellent skill. She felt quite well, apart from her tooth, but Hunter looked worn out.

"Sorry," he said, pulling himself together.

"That's *quite* all right," said Frances.

"I'll drive you to the station," he said.

"I didn't know you'd got a car," she said.

"I have one, *somewhere*, but I've forgotten where." He looked vaguely puzzled.

"Oh well, we'll ring for a taxi."

So they did, and departed. There wasn't even a hotel bill to pay: the Institute had paid it. Learning this, Frances wished she had taken more advantage, drunk more and eaten more, but realized that that would have been impossible. Once, in an Eastern European country, she had been taken around by a fat little student interpreter, who had eaten colossally and drunk immensely on Frances's expense account, and had, at the end of the week, without the slightest note of embarrassment or apology, declared that it was necessary to eat as much as one could these days because it was the only thing They couldn't take off you. Frances had never thought to hear such a peasant declaration from a teenage student of lan-

guages in the late twentieth century. It had pleased her very
much.

At the station, she posted her card to Karel in a highly
official-looking and carefully chosen box. It fell into the welcome depths. Her fate was sealed, or rather unsealed. She
felt extraordinarily happy, standing there, in all the rightness
of her decision. She would make no more cities, she would
make love. The departure announcements clicked and
whizzed. She liked train journeys, she slept well on trains.

"Is there anything you need for the journey?" said Hunter.
"What about a drink?"

"That wouldn't be a bad idea," she said, thinking she
should make use of him for his own sake, so he went off and
bought her half a bottle of brandy.

"I'll see you onto the train," he said, and he carried her
bags to her sleeping car. They had twenty minutes in hand.

"Have a drink," said Frances, reaching for her tooth glass.

He accepted a drop of brandy with some mineral water.

"You must come and see me in England," she said, in a
friendly manner. "When did you say you finished here?"

"At the end of the year," he said.

He was washing the brandy around the glass in a quiet,
reflective way. He was about to say something else. She decided to let him.

"I admire you immensely," he said, looking at her with
what was almost insolence. Appraising her, he was.

"Do you?" she said. "What for?"

She expected the question to throw him slightly: she didn't
care for so much cool in one so young. But he continued to
stare at her, with his rather shortsighted brown eyes. He reflected.

"I enjoyed your lecture," he said.

She laughed, but despite herself she couldn't help feeling
pleased, even by so absurd a response.

"Well," she said, "I'm glad somebody appreciated it."

"Oh, everybody enjoyed it," he said, with that curiously
insincere tone of his. She wondered why he employed it.

Was it simply to prevent himself from sounding foolish? Or
was it meant to intrigue? Or had he a lot to hide? She couldn't
imagine why he had said he enjoyed her lecture if he hadn't,
and had to admit that on one not very important level she
needed reassurance so much that even reassurance of this
dubious nature was welcome. There was nothing she disliked
more than the blunt openhearted frankness of those who
sought to ingratiate themselves with her by telling her that
they didn't know anything about her subject, hadn't read any
of her work or seen any of her programs, and didn't intend
to. It was extraordinary how often people seemed to think
that such an approach would delight her. Perhaps Hunter's
line was simply a more sophisticated version of the same
thing. If so, she preferred it to the other.

"Do you like lecturing?" she said.

"Not much," he said, limply. "I don't do it if I can avoid
it. And I usually can. You," he said, this time with a positive
note of accusation, "you actually seem to *like* doing it."

"I don't mind it," she said. "Why shouldn't I like it?"

"No reason at all," he said, implying reasons. "I envy
you, that's all. I envy your energy. I admire you. I've just
said so. I'm the laziest person I've ever met. I admire you
for doing so much. I just wonder why you do it, that's all.
You needn't bother, need you?"

"Well, I have a family to support," she said, but as she
said it she knew that he knew quite well that that wasn't the
whole or real reason. What did he suspect her of? Histrion-
ics? Showmanship? Unprofessionalism? A slight panic began to flutter in her chest.

"I do it because I've got to keep moving," she said. "I
get so depressed if I don't."

The truth, baldly stated, sounded and was ridiculous. But
he looked at her with curiosity and concern.

"Depressed?" he said, gently, delicately, as though unwilling to probe. Her tooth had become very noticeable
again.

"Well, yes, depressed," she said. "But I find it quite easy

to cure depression by work. One just has to keep moving, that's all. Otherwise one sinks. I'm just an unnaturally energetic person, that's all. I even think sometimes that I'm not really depressive at all, it's just that for years I was underemployed. But I doubt if that's quite true, because my family are all depressives too."

"And what do your family do about it?"

"Oh, various things."

"What things?"

She thought. "Oh, the usual things. Suicide, drugs, drink, the madhouse."

"You make it sound quite serious."

"Oh, I don't know. Most families are like that, aren't they?"

He thought. He smiled.

"Yes," he said. "I suppose they are. Certainly I can think of examples of all those lines of attack in my fairly immediate family. I just never worry about them though. In fact, I hardly ever think about them."

"You have a lucky nature," she said.

"So have you."

"One could say that."

Her whole jaw was aching by now. She clutched at it.

"My tooth is killing me," she said. "I should have stayed and had it out."

The look of spurious concern returned to his face.

"Can I get you anything for it?"

"No, not really. I've got drink and pills, there's nothing else one can do about it, is there?"

"Not really," he said.

And they sat there for a few more minutes, until the brown-suited attendant came around, and said the train would be leaving shortly, and that dinner would be at seven. To her surprise, at the sound of dinner, she felt quite hungry. Eating would take her mind off her tooth, maybe.

Hunter left, politely saying goodbye, wishing her a pleasant journey. She shook his hand, and then inclined her cheek,

so that he could kiss it. He kissed the bone over her aching
tooth. She felt very friendly toward him, for he had after all
been the means of renewing her life with Karel. He had seen
Karel, in the flesh, quite recently. She almost wanted to tell
him of the role he had played, but having decided on discre-
tion, thought she would stick to it. Anyway, he probably
sensed it, as he was no fool. Cleopatra had hauled her mes-
sengers up and down by the hair when they brought bad
tidings. Antony had been reduced to sending his schoolmas-
ter to sue for peace. She looked at Hunter as he stood there
on the platform below the open window, expecting wings or
a halo, almost, or some other archaic sign of distinction to
sprout from him or encircle him. He was a nice boy, a worthy
messenger, a pleasant and probably talented (if lazy) archaeologist.

"Don't wait for the train to go," she said.

"I want to," he said, standing there below her on the
platform.

"Give my regards to Karel," he said, "when you see
him."

"I will," she said, "I will."

He looked like a piece of plot, standing there. An extra
character, about to return to his mislaid car and his own life.

"I hope your tooth isn't too bad," he said. "You must get
it seen to, in Paris."

The train lurched forward. She put her hand through the
window and he squeezed it. They were so high, continental
trains. He was still staring at her intently as the train drew
out. He admired her.

She returned to her compartment and sat on the bed and
poured herself a drink. She was pleased with the Hunter
episode. She thought she had handled it well. She looked out
of the window, and watched the station and the city. It was
dusk, and beautiful. She thought of Karel, and the day she
had met him here: the train had pulled into the station in the
early morning, through an amazing pink and lilac dawn, and
her heart had been so full of love and anxiety, and she had

taken a taxi to the hotel where they had arranged to meet,
and there he was in bed asleep. It would be like that again,
she would have all that again. What a fool she had been to
lose him.

Husband, I come, she thought to herself, thinking again
of Cleopatra and grand passion. *Now to that name my courage prove my title.*

David Ollerenshaw, by this time, was back in his own institute. It stood next door to the octopus research laboratory,
on the sea front beneath the date palms. He too, like Frances,
had paid a courtesy visit to see the octopus, and several to
the public aquarium, where he had stared at the fish and the
coral, and pondered on the possibilities of marine geology.
He was bored. He was held up, waiting for some rocks in a
bag, and some information about the rocks, which he was
hoping to feed into a new kind of computer. The rocks should
have arrived three days earlier. He had spent the three days
idly, strolling along the front, gazing at ships, going to films
in foreign languages, reading periodicals in the institute library, drifting into zoo and aquarium and museums and
churches, and wondering whether he needed a new pair of
glasses. There was something wrong with his eyes, but he
was damned if he was going to have them tested abroad.

He was quite used to being abroad, and quite used to being
alone. He didn't mind either. He was just a little bored, by
the lack of action. And he was rather keen to have a closer
look at his rocks.

Meanwhile, he leafed aimlessly through an old copy of the
Guardian, and thought about the Tassili rock paintings. They
had been impressive, and he liked the thought that the Sahara
had been thoroughly inhabited so long ago. Though he was
himself, in the course of work, constantly setting off for uninhabited places, he was no conservationist: his aim was after
all the exploitation and not the preservation of the world's
resources. The stuff was there to be got, and man was merely

another agent of change, like wind or water, or earthquakes. Ridiculous, to look at it any other way.

Here, in the *Guardian*, as usual, was another crappy conservationist article about the way of life in the Shetlands, and its threat from North Sea oil. There was a quaint ill-printed picture of an old lady clutching a shawl around her head, and a lot of nonsense by a female journalist about dying customs and mainland mentality. The female journalist had of course traveled up from London and no doubt had sampled the local customs for all of three or four days. It amazed him, the way in which people these days seemed to admire the primitive. If they admired it so much, why didn't they go off like himself and try it? There were still plenty of extraordinarily uncomfortable places left in the world, and he had been to many of them. He was a useful geologist: the company he worked for made good use of his liking for unpleasant places.

He read on, of the possibility of striking oil near Rockall, near the Hebrides: it was by no means as unlikely a discovery as it would once have seemed. Gold in the Sahara, oil at Rockall. David Ollerenshaw, perhaps understandably, held the minority view, that the earth's resources are more or less illimitable, and also self-renewing: as yet, man, in the shape of men very much like himself, had simply wandered around picking up lumps as they lay scattered on, or very near, the earth's crust, lumps of coal, lumps of iron, of tin, of copper, gathered as unscientifically as Elgin (he was thinking of Frances Wingate) had gathered the marble of Athens. It was only recently that the intellect had been engaged at all in such searches.

And yet. He stared at the photograph of the old lady. Perhaps, after all, he would be rather put out if the North West Highlands were to be transformed by oil rigs and property speculators. He remembered the first time that he had been there, alone, as a young man, for a holiday, in a summer so splendid that it had become legendary. He had taken his motorbike, had slept in bed-and-breakfast places, eating too much bacon and eggs, chipping bits of rock and measuring angles of strike, discovering outcrops, tracing faults, examining crystals, awestruck by the predominance of water, by the sudden lowering loaves of Torridonian sandstone, by the pink sands of Mull and the white sands of Sutherland; and, finally, ending up late one night in the dark middle of nowhere, he had taken a winding path down to the sea between lochs and mountains, hoping to find a small village or a hamlet with a bed to let (the Ordnance Survey map marked a cluster of cottages), and had nearly turned back, but in the end reached the sea, in a deep sudden inlet, and there at the land's end stood four cottages, and one of them had a sign out: BED AND BREAKFAST. In the morning, when he looked out of the bedroom window, there was the sea, right beneath him: he could see into the depths of clear and rocky water, he could see each limpet, each barnacle, each anemone, pink stone, blue stone, gray stone, and silvery crystalline crevasses. And looking up, there was the sea, an enormously high horizon, welling up above him.

Hurried, he struggled into his clothes, and out through the garden where his motorbike stood amongst chickens and lobster pots: he struggled through a profusion of flowers, purple, yellow, blue, green, growing in a dense and lush long-stemmed abundance, monkey flowers with yellow throats deep-spotted with red, forget-me-nots straggling in the hedge bottom, their pale blue faces small and perfect, so much perfection in so small a space, as lovely and as oft-repeated as crystals, as sure, as infallible, yet as different as snowflakes. He walked through the flowers as though it were the first morning, and through a little gate and up a hill, where the ground changed suddenly from the gulf-stream haven to a shorter turf starred with saxifrage and thyme and milkweed and speedwell, and there, most beautiful flower of all, grew the Grass of Parnassus, so aptly named, its white carved petals streaked with its own faint green blood. But he climbed on, upward, to see the sea, as yet obscured by the brow of the hill: he climbed, breathing heavily, for the hill was steep though small, and there at the top lay a view more splendid, more wild, more various than anything he could have imagined in the darkness of the night, for there before him lay a sea full of small islands, rising like gray seals, raising their backs like dolphins from the water, heaving and burgeoning, as far as the eye could see, an expanse of rocky islands lying in a blue-green sea. The landscape seemed alive, as though seething in the act of its own creation, for around every island the waves broke white and fell and glittered, in a perpetual swell and heave. The Isles of the Blest, he said to himself. Uninhabited, ancient. Out they stretched forever, to the north and west, to the ultimate reaches of man's desiring, where man was lost and nothing, at the edges of the world. For what did man desire, but those edges? David Ollerenshaw stood there and gazed, his heart beating strangely. Those islands were granite: Lewisian gneiss, the most ancient rock in Britain.

He had known they were ancient, he said to himself, as he scrambled back down the hill to his hard-scrambled eggs. He had a Geiger counter in his blood, a mechanism that responded to rock, as swallows to the magnetism of the earth. He did not really need a computer: all that the computer would do would be to confirm his own innate response. This was what was called a feeling for the subject, he supposed.

And now they were going to dig it all up. He had to admit that he would himself rather dig up the Sahara. The Grass of Parnassus did not blossom there, nor the pale-blue water lobelia and the marsh orchid. If the company sent him off to the Hebrides, should he on grounds of conscience refuse? Not that they were likely to: he was a hard rock man, not an oil man. He wished that his hard rocks would arrive from Africa: he knew what they were made of, but equally knew that the company would prefer confirmation from this convenient new computer. He gazed out of the institute window, at the famous view. The blue lobelia had pallid flowers, blue-white, and it broke the still mirror surface of the lochs, of the all-covering water, of the cold brown peaty water. It was more water than land, that part of Scotland. That, too, could not be said of the Sahara.

If the rocks turned out to be what he expected (and they would) then he would have been as lucky, in his way, as Frances Wingate. Though he would never get the credit. She, he thought (though without ill-will), seemed to have had more than her fair share of credit. Her performance had amused him.

He rubbed his glasses on his handkerchief. Remember him, for it will be some months before he and Frances Wingate meet again.

By the time Frances got to the dinner on the train, she was in intense pain. The whole of the side of her head was aching and drumming, not quite in time with the train's rhythm. She thought she probably had an abscess. From time to time she hit at it with her knuckles, horribly aware of bone and mortality, thinking of the poor Pharaohs with their tooth rot, and the insufferable dental decay of the ancient world. She had two more codeine, and got the waiter to open a whole bottle of wine. The meal was quite pleasant, and she had a table to herself: it was a quiet time of year. She read *The Years*, and ate her eggs in aspic, and her veal, and forgot about her tooth for a second or two while doing it, being an exceptionally greedy person, and then returned seriously, over the fruit and cheese, to the subject of pain.

It was too much. She wanted to cry. The codeine had no effect at all. She took another. It was as bad as typhoid and slightly worse than childbirth, up till then her high-water marks of pain. She tried to remember how awful it had been in the back of the Land-Rover, with the vomiting and the diarrhea and the appalling cramping and clutching in her guts, and above all the sickening anxiety about actual death. Nobody ever died of a toothache, though somebody—was it Dr. Johnson?—had said that if toothache were mortal, it would be the most dreaded of all illnesses. That was a reassuring thought, and she quoted it to herself several times while waiting for her bill, then went through a speech from Shakespeare and a sonnet or two from Keats and Milton, an ode from Horace, and a piece of Virgil.

The train was thumping unnaturally. She wanted to lie down and cry. When the waiter brought her the bill, she went back to her compartment and lay down on the bed and cried, but it didn't do much good. Desperately, she rang for the attendant and told him she had a toothache. He clucked and shook his head and said he was desolated and offered her an aspirin. She declined it. It had been good to speak to somebody, however.

After another half hour, she took a couple of sleeping pills and got into bed and had another drink. She had ceased to care whether or not she made herself ill, and wished only to knock herself out. She repeated "On His Blindness" and "Westminster Bridge" several times to herself; they had always been a good charm against pain, and she had gone through them many a time while trying to comply with her husband's desire for sexual intercourse, for instance, and had shouted them aloud very wildly in childbirth, till the nurses told her to shut up.

Her head felt like a skull. There was no flesh feeling about it at all, the flesh seemed such irrelevance, a silly perishable covering of the serious matter, which was diseased bone. One might as well *be* dead, she found herself thinking. She had seen a statue once which had weathered so badly that the head had looked like a skull. The rest of it had been all right, it was only the head that had gone. She felt a bit like that herself. She pinched her leg. It was all right, it was still there, it didn't hurt. She would try and concentrate on how well her legs felt.

She must have dozed off at some point, because she was woken up by the feeling of the train grinding to a halt. She opened her blind, and found that they were on the middle of high, dark mountains, at a tiny station. The pain of returning consciousness was so bad that she felt like leaping off and demanding extraction from a local dentist. She couldn't see

a place name: perhaps it was some kind of frontier. A lot of
people were getting down from the train and heading for the
buffet, which curiously enough (it was one o'clock in the
morning) seemed to be open and doing good business. Just
as she was wondering whether or not to join them, the attendant knocked on her door and told her the train had stopped
for three-quarters of an hour, and how was she, and would
she like to get out and have a drink with him in the bar. Why
not, she thought to herself, and pulled her coat on over her
nightdress, and pushed her feet into her shoes, and staggered
out onto the icy platform.

Her coat was fur lined. It felt rather good momentarily on
her bare arms. The whole of the rest of her body felt numb
and weightless: she couldn't feel her legs move. She followed
the attendant to the buffet, where he bought her a brandy.
The buffet was full of people, positively humming with some
curious mountain life of its own: not all of the customers
were passengers, some were clearly locals, playing cards,
drinking beer, eating omelettes. She stood there in her nightdress drinking. Was it France, Austria, Germany, Switzer-
land, Italy? She had no idea. Her head wasn't exactly turning,
it wasn't there. She was disembodied. The attendant, a
smooth-faced young man of about forty, was trying to chat
her up in French, but she couldn't hear a word he was saying.
She held on to the rail of the bar. Everything had dissolved
away, except, amazingly enough, her toothache. That was
still at its job, plunging and beating and knocking at her
persistently, demanding attention but not getting it: it felt
removed, her resistance to it had gone but so had her anxiety,
and it raged and throbbed furiously, getting no reply.

The woman behind the bar was sallow and stringy, her
hair tied up in a black bun. She wore a black dress and a
small white apron. There were men wearing braces. The
menu was multilingual. The attendant went on talking. She
bought him a drink, not listening. Then she wandered back
onto the platform.

The sky was full of stars, the air bitterly cold. There was

a smell of pine, and snow on the hillside. They must be high up: the air felt clear and thin. She ground her knuckles into her cheekbone. My life is amazing, she thought to herself dimly. Did anyone ever die to escape the toothache? The rails gleamed. Suicide ran in the family: her younger sister had killed herself, while at the university. It had been called an accident. By accident I was spared. To whom should I feel gratitude?

She had elected Karel. She stood there in the steep and cruel mountains, hitting herself, moaning slightly. The jagged edges soared above her. She looked up and felt faint. Sometimes she had thought she would like to live her life under an anesthetic. She wasn't up to it; she would fail, yet again. The mountains were, in fact, too high, the desert was, in fact, too hot, the stones were, in fact, too dry. Too much of the world was inhospitable, intractable. Why prove that it had ever once been green? And yet, here, on these steep slopes, people lived, played cards, drank beer in the small hours, perched on a gradient too perilous to contemplate, in the path of avalanches. The octopus lived on in its plastic box. The effort of comprehension was beyond her, she felt like despairing; love and understanding were beyond her. In the middle of nowhere, high up, a solitary lunatic, in her dry crater. The world was drying out, and everything she touched would die. Manic. Down on her gleamed the ancient and romantic moon, through the clear sky. It lit the snow. Frantically she hit the other cheekbone, to distribute the pain. Inside the buffet, people ate sausages and talked in an unknown tongue. She did not even know which species was her own.

When she reached Paris, she was too ill to lecture. She was whisked off to a dental hospital, and had her tooth extracted. There was no abscess, but the tooth was fanged and green. She kept it as a souvenir.

The next morning, she was put on the airplane home. Her gum where the tooth had been was soft and bloody, and she probed it constantly, anxiously, with a surprised relief. Her jaw ached, but pleasantly.

When she got home, she gave the children their presents, and listened to their stories, and kissed them, and was pulled around by them: they were an excitable, assertive, healthy, resolute, daring bunch, her children, constantly milling and seething with an excess of energy, conditioned by herself, perhaps into an irregular way of life, all stops and starts, departures and homecomings, presents and dramas and disasters. It was not a peaceful home, and after half an hour of Daisy, Josh, Spike, and Pru she felt quite shattered and whole again at the same time, and had to shut them up (they got very loud, with any encouragement at all) by showing them her extracted tooth. They admired it as it lay wicked in its gauze wrapping, and then her daughter Daisy embalmed it for her, in her Plasticraft Kit. It was a kit for making plastic jewelry— one could embed in it small shells, seaweed, beads, pebbles. Frances's tooth gleamed from a clear white bed, against a blue ground, preserved forever, a smooth oval. Frances put it in the drawer of her bedside table, along with the false ones Karel had given her. Then she began to wait for Karel.

The postcard she had sent the children arrived a couple of days after her: the post was slow, but not so slow. She calculated when Karel would receive his. She waited for him to write or ring.

He neither wrote nor rang. There was silence from Karel. For a fortnight or two, she hoped. Then she began to abandon hope. After a month, she despaired, and fell ill.

First of all she caught flu. Though she was never ill, had never had flu in her life. Then she had to have another tooth out. Then, just after Whitsun, she developed a lump on her breast, and had to go into hospital to have it off: she had to sign a paper saying they could take the breast off if they wanted. They didn't: the lump had proved benign. But she was depressed: unreasonably depressed.

Writing Karel off as missing was a process she had never thought to undergo. It was slower and more painful than she

had thought possible. Lying feverish in bed at home, lying
awake in hospital listening to the heavy breathing of women
in pain, she tried to reconcile herself to his loss. She could
not really believe that he would not return. He was a kind
man: he had shown perplexing kindness to people much less
pleasant than herself. His desertion obliged her to reconsider
the whole affair.

He had always sworn loyalty, and she had believed him.
Only now, nearly a year later, could she measure by the depth
of her shock how much she had trusted and believed him.
She had thought that at the slightest hint from her, he would
return. She had always been so lucky, and now her luck had
run out.

Of course, she'd never quite trusted her luck. She'd rarely
put it to the test, in case it failed. She'd taken no chances;
her guesses had been certainties. She applied for jobs she
could not fail to get, she avoided too keen competition, she
gave herself a wide margin, she covered her bets. She left
Karel before he had a chance of leaving her. And yet, even
so, he had managed, posthumously as it were, to reject her.
And she had trusted him. He hadn't seemed a gamble; he
had seemed, for various reasons, a certainty.

She had known Karel Schmidt for years, and had had good
cause to trust him. She had trusted him surely as much as
any wife who is not an entire fool can trust any husband—
possibly even more so, for not being married, their relationship had had a whole extra scaffold of uncertainty and
inconvenience and shortage of time to prevent the usual
cracks of boredom and familiarity from creeping into the
structure. Their relationship, she had thought, had been perfect. He had been perfect.

It was, in reality (she had to count the years) only seven
years that she had known him. It seemed much longer. She
often looked back on their first meeting. It had taken place
at a propitious time in her life, just as she was on the verge
of her major excavations on the Chad-Libyan border. She'd
already done her preliminary survey, and had got enough

grants and backing for a larger expedition. She was full of certainty: she knew the stuff was there, all she had to do was to go and find it. And, almost on the eve of her departure, she'd gone to give a lecture to Karel's students at the South Western Polytechnic. She was going to talk about her discoveries on the last trip, her hopes of the next. She was pleased with herself, cheerful, expectant.

Karel met her at the station, took her to the Poly, gave her a cup of tea, and told her about the students. The students everywhere were in their angriest phase, for it was a troubled time in the universities and polytechnics: but they were quite eager to listen to Frances, because after all one of her themes was the fashionable one that black culture had been consistently neglected and underestimated by scholars, who preferred the Greeks and the Romans, and who couldn't believe that any good thing could come out of Africa. Do they expect me to sing a hymn of *négritude*, she had asked Karel, over that first (of many thousands) cup of tea, and he had sighed heavily, and said that after all the students weren't really very well informed, and it didn't matter much what she said. A few antirationalist, anti-Western culture remarks would no doubt go down well, he said. If *that's* the way they look at it, I won't make any, she said primly, and Karel smiled at her, a peculiar exhausted intimate smile, as of one who acknowledged her reluctance.

She thought, looking at him in these first minutes: a familiar type. She had been met by so many strange men on strange stations, she had drunk so many cups of tea with so many heads of departments, headmasters, students. Karel she classified as an aging beauty: he had long fair stringy ringlet thinning hair, a long stringy mustache, a huge beak of a nose, a tired and oddly foreign look, the look of one much battered by overwork and a refusal to admit the advance of the years. She guessed he had domestic problems, or amorous problems: all men of his age in his kind of job had that kind of problem. She guessed, rightly, that he was in his mid-thirties, if not already in his late thirties. He must once have been good-looking, she thought to herself; as so many of them had once been. A certain gallantry still lingered, in the prow of the nose, the shabbiness of the clothes. After a certain age, men get tidier or shabbier: Karel had chosen the latter course. Again, like so many. (She herself on this occasion was wearing a rather strange purple dress, which she had put on that morning by mistake, having found a large hole in the seam of the skirt she had meant to wear: she'd intended to change all day, but hadn't got around to it. What will it matter what I look like, in the South Western Poly? she had thought. Who cares?)

The lecture went as well as could be expected: she talked about trade routes and showed them some slides of Carthage, declaimed some Herodotus in Greek, and handed around a piece of mid-first-millennium poetry. I'm going to find more of that stuff, and better, she told them. She kept off politics, and when asked by a rather astute grinning student with corkscrew ringlets about the attitudes of the Nigerian and Libyan governments, she managed to restrain herself from telling her favorite horror story about the episode on the Libyan frontier, and told them instead about delightful, rationalist, responsible, scholarly, Quaker, black Mr. Manowe, who had been in charge of the first dig she had visited in Africa: an expert on Nok terra cottas, he had been deeply comforting. Manowe believed in her trade routes, he believed in the history of Africa, he was a friend of Leakey, his views were impeccable: she recited them, and the students didn't seem to notice that they had been diverted, if not exactly deceived. Except, perhaps, for the corkscrew ringlets, who continued to grin. (He had modeled his hair style on what Karel's might once have been, she decided.)

Afterward, Karel said she had done it very nicely, and thanked her, and took her up to his room for a drink. He was a historian; he said apologetically that he didn't know much about her period, but he had enjoyed her talk and admired her tact. She asked him about student revolt, and he sighed again, and said it was tiring.

She liked him, more than most of his kind. He was without vanity, she thought, and he looked tired, and did not conceal the fact that he was tired. Gently he rolled himself a cigarette, with yellow fingers. His hair was thinning, his nose was sharp, and his eyes were a hard blue, an unnaturally deep blue. He did not look at her directly. His shirt was dirty, his room was untidy, deep in papers and books and periodicals and old cups of tea. It was a poky little room, with a window that looked onto a brick wall. While she was there, the phone went five times, and two students knocked on the door; he dealt with all these interruptions at excessive length, keeping her sitting there, drinking gin and water. (There had been no tonic in the cupboard, not much to his surprise.) A weak man, she said to herself. Nice, but weak.

After a while, she said that she had to be going, and he said he'd drive her to the station. Outside the station, he said where was she going ultimately, and she said home, to Putney.

I'll take you, he said, I'm going that way myself.

It was half-past nine. He drove her across South London, and told her that he lived in Fulham, so it wasn't really out of his way. She could see that it wasn't much, but nevertheless thought he was the nice harmless kind of person who would quite like to do another person a kindness even if it inconvenienced himself. As they got within a mile or two of home, she began to worry about whether or not she ought to ask him in, when they got there: what a bore it would be, she was thinking to herself, if I asked him in and he stayed for hours and hours, being dull and boring. She was quite tired and wanted an early night. She was trying to think of ways of handling him, which made her rather silent, and inattentive, as they neared her house. As they turned the corner of her street, he said, "I'll have to get straight off, I'm afraid," as though to forestall any polite invitation, when they both at once saw the ambulance standing outside her front door.

"Oh, my God," said Frances, and scrambled for the door,

and jumped out before he had had much time to park. He must have dumped the car and run after her, because he was there when she reached the open door of her house. There were two men standing in the drive, and her housekeeper Polly.

Reassurance began to pour from them as soon as they saw her. "It's nothing," said Polly, nearly in tears. And it was nothing: the baby had shoved a bead down its ear, Polly had panicked, been unable to get a taxi, had dialed an ambulance, couldn't leave the other children, and was being told off by the ambulance men for being an alarmist and a waster of public funds. The bead had been extracted, but the baby was wailing in its not very big sister's arms.

Frances felt her knees shaking, as the ambulance men explained what had happened: when they saw how frightened she looked, they stopped being angry and became quite civil. Karel was hanging about, nervously and aimlessly, clearly not sure how or whether to participate. The ambulance went away, and Frances went in with the baby, and tried to pacify the other three bigger children, who were all standing about in their pajamas and nightdresses, waiting for more action. Polly's baby was howling too, from its cot upstairs, so Frances sent Polly off to deal with it, and when she had gathered herself together, Karel was still there, standing in the wide hallway, leaning on a bookcase, and she looked at him in the shadowy hall, and caught on his face such an expression of concern, such profoundly harassed embarrassed anxious protective participation, that she fell in love with him at once.

"I'm sorry," he said, meeting her eyes. "I haven't been very useful. I didn't know what to do."

She stared at him. As an aging beauty, she had classed him. She must have been mad. She had never seen anyone so beautiful. As a type, she had typed him, whereas the truth was that she had never seen anything like him in her life before.

"Come and have a drink," she said. "Please, I need a drink." She was far more terrified now that he would refuse, than she had earlier been anxious that he might accept such an offer. "Please," she said, as he hesitated, "I know it's late and you look tired. But please."

He followed her into her large sitting room, full of plants and archaeological objects in and out of glass cases and maps and cats and parrots and children, and he poured her a drink because she was still holding the baby, and they sat down, and drank, and after a few minutes she chased the other children off to bed having listened to seven different versions of where Baby had got the bead from, why Polly had panicked (no more unmarried-mother housekeepers, said Frances to herself), what the ambulance man had said, what the doctor in the Outpatients had said. Her eldest, Daisy, had accompanied Baby to hospital, and was proud of her initiative. "He said Baby might have been *deafened* if we hadn't taken her in at once," said this child with satisfaction. "And he gave me some Smarties too," she added, with equal satisfaction.

When they had gone, Frances looked at Karel again. He still looked the same: astonishing, that she had missed it for so long.

"Cheer up," she said, "it's all right now, it's all over."

"It gave me such a fright," he said. "One's worst nightmare, the ambulance at the door."

"You must have children of your own," she said, dumping the baby in the corner of the settee, refilling her glass. "How many have you got?"

"Three," he said.

And they talked of the children, and the time he had got home to find one covered with burns from a birthday cake candle, the time another of his had fallen from a first-floor window, the time she had lost one on a hovercraft and had been convinced it was overboard, and had made them stop the boat, only to find the child in question (a girl) locked in the First Class Gents.

She drank a lot, from nervousness and relief. He drank a lot too, she noticed, for reasons as yet unknown to her. After a while the baby fell asleep, but she hadn't the strength to move it. Lectures and ambulances take it out of one, she said.

He wandered around and looked at her objects. She was proud of her room; she hoped he liked it. He was tall and bony and slightly stooping. Whatever was she to do about him? It wouldn't be fair to do anything about him. If she seduced him, he would be tortured, and he looked tortured enough already. One couldn't seduce, in cold blood, a man who was so fond of his children.

He hadn't mentioned his wife. A signal, of some sort? Frances found herself thinking that his wife must be a feckless woman, to let her children fall out of windows so often. (Thereby finding an attitude of censure from the outset which was to make life a great deal simpler than it might otherwise have been.)

They looked at some of her photographs of the excavations at Carthage, and talked about child sacrifice, and whether perhaps the children had been already dead when sacrificed. They talked about primitive beliefs, about fertility and magic and barbarism and cruelty and progress and angry students. Trendy though he looked, in some ways, his views were of a deep-hued universal pessimism: a hopeless rationalist, he called himself. She was desperate not to let him go: she wanted to go on watching him. But just after midnight, he said he'd better be getting home. She managed to keep him for another half hour, doing her best to retain him (though already she could see that it would be better not to let him drink too much, she didn't want him to kill himself, perhaps sensing already that Karel's survival was essential for her own). She wondered whether to embark on the subject of marriage, her own lack of marriage, but thought better of it: it was too powerful a card to play. She was a woman used to getting her own way, but she did not want to cheat, particularly at the outset. They talked, instead, of the origins of agriculture.

In the end, he left. She had to let him go; he was deter-

mined to go. She did not say that she would like to see him
again: pride, honor, a desire not to cheat, restrained her.
Instead, they shook hands, at the door, and parted. She went
to bed, with the baby. She had been asleep for half an hour
when he rang. They talked, for another hour. They agreed
to meet, for lunch the next day.

They met the next day, and the next, and the next. They
met every day, in the three weeks before she went off to
Africa, though she was busy with preparations for her journey, and he was working full time. But they made time.
While she was in Africa, they corresponded, in so far as the
postal service and the remoteness of her position admitted.
In his letters, he said that he loved her. She replied, saying
that she loved him, and suggesting that he should fly out to
see her to check up on it. He said he was too busy and
couldn't afford it. I'll wait till you come back, he said. It will
keep till then.

And it kept. When she got back to England, he met her at
the airport, and drove her and her vast amounts of luggage
home to Putney. Shortly after their reunion, they started to
sleep together. For Frances, it was one of the most amazing
patches of her altogether amazing life. She couldn't believe
it. She'd been sleeping with people for years, on principle
almost, but nothing much had ever happened to her. Some
affairs had been more interesting than others, but none had
been serious. With Karel, it was serious. The first time she
slept with him (and the first time wasn't even very satisfactory, from some points of view) she knew that it was serious,
that she had entered a new world of events. She heard herself
cry out with astonishment, again and again.

She couldn't explain what it was in him that affected her
so profoundly. He was beautiful, but even she could still see
hovering behind his real self the ghost of the seedy aging
harassed family man who had met her on a Southern Region
station. Anyway, she decided, it couldn't be just the look of
him. She liked the way he talked, the things he said. But it
couldn't be just that, either. She liked the things he did to

her, she liked them very much indeed. Altogether, perhaps
all these things added up to love. Though perhaps love had
nothing to do with any of them.

In short, she loved him. She didn't know why, but she did.
She could tell that she did because she had never loved anyone before, though she had sometimes fancied that she had.
She could tell, because this was so different. Otherwise, it
was a bit of a mystery, to them both. It wasn't even as though
she were blind to his irritating qualities—there were many
things about him that annoyed her; his friends, his wife, his
indecisiveness, his unpunctuality, the way in which he let his
colleagues and his students exploit him; his meaningless con-
scientious time-wasting inefficiency. He was one of those
people who are hopelessly inefficient through an excess of
goodwill—he never liked to say no, was always promising to
do things that conflicted with other things that he had already
promised to do, could never leave a conversation or a room
for fear of hurting other people's feelings, and thus was frequently late and frequently causing offense. When he had
caused offense, he would, on randomly selected occasions,
lose his temper. Frances, an efficient woman, found such
conduct exasperating, and longed to intervene when she
overheard him make totally impossible assignations—I'll see
you in half an hour, he would say from Putney, arranging to
meet someone twenty miles away on the other side of London in the rush hour. But it was impossible to intervene. His
conduct had its own logic. She learned to adapt herself to it.

They got on well: they learned to get on better. They talked
to each other a great deal about their work, a pleasure neither
had ever before experienced, finding that with a little inge-
nuity their subjects could be made to have a considerable
overlap. (After all, it was in a professional context that they
had first met: it was Karel who had selected Frances's name
from a list of possible external lecturers.) They talked of
students and colleagues, of history and progress; also of their
children, and what was in the newspapers. They argued about
Northern Ireland and overpopulation. It was a good time, for

Frances. With Tizouk behind her and Karel before her, she felt herself a made woman, in every sense. Flattered and courted, she flourished and blossomed. She enjoyed the attentions of the public: she enjoyed even more her ability to live, at last, in private.

It was so good that at times she would tell herself: I must remember, I must record for myself, how good it is, in case things go wrong again. But she knew in her heart that it was as impossible to recall the good times during the bad, as it was to recall the bad during the good. One moved from one state to another helplessly, in forgetfulness, with merely a dry shadowy knowledge of the other, as unlike the real thing as a dried hard seed pod, a hard dry brittle box full of small black seeds of forgetfulness, is unlike the living flower. At times, during the flowering, one could hear the dry seeds rattle, ominously: moods, depressions, meaningless distortions of consciousness. This was why she persevered, and tried to make a conscious effort to control the process, to remember moments, to store them and preserve them, as though she could in some way carry them with her through the dark winter when it closed in; like a talisman, a seed, a pledge of the unimaginable spring. For how had the first sowers ever learned to trust the wheat to survive the winter? On such acts of faith has human life been built. And if the spring were never to come again, she told herself, I must at least know that it has been. I owe it to fate, to chance, to Karel.

Moments. The children in the garden on swing and seesaw (struck into silence by the harmony of the double glazing), herself watching from an upstairs room. A meal in the Poly canteen. A game of poker with Karel and the children. Bed, of course. One of the days that she remembered most often, in her effort to trick time (as she was later to remember the frogs in the pipe) was a day when she and Karel had been together in Surrey. It had been very early spring, her favorite season, the safest season. (A long time, till winter.) Karel had been to give a lecture in Farnham, she to visit a colleague to consult him about her Tizouk figurines. Karel had picked

her up from her friend's house, after his lecture, and they
had chatted a while, all three, watching through the window
the sunlight on the brown earth and the pale garden green of
January, on a pink primula, a Christmas rose, and a little
white honeysuckle, timorously blossoming. She liked the
early plants of the year: her own garden had aconites, now.
She and Jeremy Harding and Karel spoke of aconites a little
while (she was proud of Karel, she liked to be with him in
company), and then they declined a cup of tea, and set off
home.

In the car, they agreed that they would have liked a cup of
tea, really. They discussed why they had declined. To be
together, they agreed, alone together.

It was early afternoon; the light was bright but fading.
They drove through the suburban countryside, through the
pine woods and the bracken, as the color deepened. It was
pink and silver, russet and coral, the silver birches pink in
the faint premonition of a sunset, the bark of the pine trees
darkening to a wilder Scots redness, a few leaves of last year
pink and copper, but above all the bracken, the dead bracken,
with its lovely special eccentric cold burnished leafy metallic
dead but promising beauty. A countryside tamed but burning. She kept her hand on his knee. A lovely afternoon it
was, a lovely evening it would be. Karel's lecture had gone
well: her friend had been helpful. She should wash Spike's
hair when they got back, then they would have spaghetti car-
bonara for supper, and some salad, and go to bed early.
Thinking of the spaghetti, she realized how hungry she was,
and as though reading her mind, he said, "Let's stop, shall
we, for a cup of tea?"

They stopped at a cafe by the roadside: standing at the
counter, Karel ordered two teas, one with and one without,
and she saw him looking hungrily at the sandwiches, and
hunger overcame her too, for the sandwiches (unlike the
doughnuts and the fruit pies) looked so delicious, and she
and Karel looked at one another, by the Formica-topped

counter, and both hesitated, and he said, "Shall we have one, then?" and she said, "Yes, *please*."

All the sandwiches looked so good that they could not decide which to get. Cheese and chutney, cheese and tomato, ham? She watched him, as he examined the sandwiches in their several-storied glass steel-rimmed box.

"I love you, Karel," she said. "I really love you."

"Do you, my darling?" he said. "Shall we have cheese and tomato?"

She had never enjoyed a sandwich so much in her life. Sitting together at the small table amongst the ketchup bottles.

"There's nothing like a sandwich, is there," said Karel, after a pause, "when it's what one really wants?"

They looked down at the two halves on the plate, each with large bites taken out of the soft white bread, lying together. Both had taken identical-sized bites.

"I enjoyed deciding to buy this sandwich," said Karel. "And now I'm going to enjoy eating it."

And hearing him speak, she shivered slightly, as though a moment of intense joy had come to its proper completion, and it occurred to her that she had never been as happy in her life as she was there, sitting at that shabby table gazing through a white net curtain at the road, with two half-eaten sandwiches in front of her, signifying union. To have it was one thing: to know one was having it was something else, more than one could have hoped for.

On such things did life consist. She enjoyed it all. At times she said to herself, it's so good it can't last; but not very often. There was no reason why one should not enjoy sandwiches and love forever. Unlike some pleasures, they seemed to have no inbuilt destructive elements.

There were, however, other elements in the affair that were destructive, of course. They became more obtrusive with time, though at first she hardly noticed them. The chief of these elements was Karel's wife. Frances had little idea what his relations with her were, and did not intend to upset herself by inquiring more closely: she resolutely ignored the guilt she at times suffered. But she was compelled, after a year or two, to notice that the wife existed, and that Karel did not seem to intend to leave her. Frances had never expected him to. She was used to admiring men who didn't want to leave their wives. Unlike most of them, Karel did leave his wife from time to time, and came to live with Frances, but then he would go back home again. He seemed eager to keep everybody happy. As he was successfully keeping her happy, Frances accepted his arrivals and disappearances without question. She wasn't even sure if she wanted him to come and live with her permanently. She was all right on her own. And he was, in his own way, thoroughly reliable: even if he went away, at least he always came back again, which is more than one could say of most people. And she had to go away herself, quite often, for professional reasons, so why should she complain? The strange tempo of their life suited her quite well.

She was obliged to admit, after a couple of years, however, that the situation wasn't quite as simple as she assumed. It was Karel's wife who forced this awareness rather violently upon her. She called around late one night, and started throwing things through the window. In order not to have all her windows broken, Frances got out of bed and went down and let her in. She had not met her before and did not need an introduction. Karel's wife had come around to look for Karel: he wasn't there, a fact which seemed to surprise her, but which did not deter her from throwing more objects around the sitting room, some of them quite valuable, though luckily she didn't seem to have grasped the principle that the duller the object in appearance, the greater its archaeological value: she went for the showy items, the nineteenth-century African masks, and spared the boring, priceless, irreplacable bits of Saharan sherd. While she wrecked the place, she screamed loudly and hysterically that Frances was a wicked wealthy promiscuous whore who was simply amusing herself

at Karel's expense, that if she saw the *hovel* where she and
Karel lived in squalor she would know what Karel was after
her for, that Frances grossly neglected her children, that
Frances's mother was a murderer, that Frances's entire family was part of the vicious power structure of the land, and
deserved to have bombs thrown at its country houses.

Such a welter of emotional misapprehensions, albeit mingled with a little truth, had left Frances speechless: she had
stood and watched in amazement, smiling in what she later
realized must have been an infuriating manner, though at the
time she had meant it to be soothing and encouraging. After
a while Karel's wife (her name was Joy) seemed to run out
of insults, and sank down on a corner of the settee. Frances
half expected her to burst into tears, but she was made of
sterner stuff. She sat there, grimly, and after a while she said,
"I'm sitting here till he turns up."

"You might have to wait a long time," said Frances, "because I'm not really expecting him."

"I'll wait," said Joy.

"Do you mind if I go back to bed?" said Frances: an ill-
judged remark, for Joy leaped to her feet, seized another
glass, chucked it at Frances's head, hit her, then followed it
up by a personal assault, which resulted in her pulling out a
lump or two of Frances's hair. Frances, who was a much
bigger woman, retaliated by kicking her smartly in the shins.

Joy sat down again. Frances poured herself a drink, but
didn't feel that the laws of hospitality demanded that she
should pour one for Joy, who had clearly had a drop too much
already. Quietly, she started to pick up some of the broken
objects from the floor, in as unobtrusive a way as possible,
watching Joy out of the corner of her eye, and recalling the
descriptions of similar incidents recounted to her by friends
and neighbors. It was her first experience of such a scene,
though these days they seemed to be a commonplace: marriage in the middle classes had become a violent affair. She
and her husband, Anthony, had thrown things at each other,
but that had been an internal matter. She'd never yet come

up against a third party, and was not sure of the rules of the game. She had heard of strange alliances between wives and mistresses. Of one thing she was certain: she did not wish to ally herself with Joy at all.

Joy, she noticed, had a black eye. Her face was thin and angry, and the lines from her nose to her mouth signified a permanent rage. Frances found herself worried for Karel, on more than one score. What had he done, to make another woman look like that? While she herself was sitting amidst her finery, brown and blooming? It was so long since she herself had been through the misery of marital violence that she had forgotten what it was like. This was one of the things that seemed to annoy Joy most: you get rid of your husband, she had yelled, then you sit here at his expense and just take what you fancy of mine. This, again, had been an inaccuracy, for it had been many years since Frances had needed any subsidy from her admittedly rather wealthy husband, but it did not seem worth correcting, in the mood of the moment. Frances felt more like asking why Joy considered her mother to be a murderer, but didn't dare to do that either: she tended to agree with her, and would have been prepared to discuss the subject in an amicable and joint manner, but it took her some time to learn (from Karel) that Joy, before he married her, had had an abortion, and considered Mrs. Ollerenshaw (who happened to be a gynecologist much in favor of abortion) as part of a conspiracy to sterilize the lower classes.

Meanwhile, they sat there and waited. After a while, Joy said, with intense bitterness, "Don't you think you have anything like a profound relationship with Karel, will you? He doesn't tell you a thing."

"Doesn't he?" said Frances.

She wondered if it was true, in the ensuing silence. Maybe he didn't; it hadn't seemed to matter much.

"For instance," said Joy, "he didn't tell you about me, did he?"

"What about you?"

"Anything about me," said Joy.

"He certainly didn't tell me how awful you were, if that's what you mean," said Frances, mildly stung, then adding. "Did he tell you about me?"

"Of course," said Joy, with a nasty snap of the lips. "I don't suppose you've even noticed," said Joy, "how ill he's been looking of late?"

"He's been looking tired," said Frances.

"He didn't tell you about Bob?" said Joy.

"What about Bob?" said Frances, suddenly losing her nerve. Bob was the name of Karel's eldest child.

"He's terribly ill. Seriously ill," said Joy, with a malicious satisfaction so intense that Frances felt her head swim. "He didn't tell you that, did he? I bet he didn't tell you that. He wouldn't tell *you* a thing."

Frances sat back and shut her eyes, feeling sick. Perhaps the woman was lying. She looked mad, acted mad; she might well lie. But it was true, Karel had been horribly ill and tired of late. He had said it was work and the mortgage.

"I don't believe you," said Frances after a while. "If it were true, you couldn't conceivably sound so bloody pleased about it."

"I'm past caring," said Joy.

Frances reflected. "I'm going to ring Karel," she said. "Perhaps he's at your place by now."

This remark precipitated another flood of abuse, mostly about mysterious telephone calls, implausible wrong numbers, and the size of the Schmidt phone bill.

"You're quite wrong," said Frances, "I'd never ring your place. I was always too unwilling to speak to you. Now I see how wise I was." And she got up and went over to the telephone, only to find herself once more assaulted on the way, Joy screaming this time that she wasn't going to have a woman like Frances disturbing her children.

"You don't seem to mind disturbing mine," said Frances, between blows: blood was running down the side of her face from where the glass had hit it, and now Joy was beating her over the head with a copy of the *Oxford Book of Twentieth*

Century Verse which had been conveniently lying around. After a short skirmish, she managed to push Joy back into her corner of the settee, where she sat, breathing heavily, and looking crosser than ever.

It was upon this scene that Karel entered. He had a key and let himself in, but seemed to be expecting this sight before him, because he already looked harassed to death. He was greeted by another flying book, and half a bottle of wine, which went all over the place.

"Oh, Christ," said Karel.

Frances felt like bursting into tears, but instead sat there. Karel stood in the doorway, dripping wine, and trying vaguely to wipe it off the paintwork with his hand.

"Have a drink," said Frances. "If there's anything left."

"Darling," said Karel, in rather an uncertain and undirected way.

"Darling *who*?" said Joy, pulling herself together again.

"Please have a drink," said Frances, and got up and poured him one.

"Always the perfect hostess," said Joy, with childish savagery.

Karel crossed over and took the drink. He held her hand. "I'm sorry," he said. "What a mess, what a mess."

"I don't mind," said Frances, hopelessly. She was beginning to mind, rather badly, now that Karel was there, and couldn't see how he could possibly cope with the situation. It crossed her mind that the best thing to do would be, quietly, to leave the room and let them get on with it, whatever it was: she started to detach her fingers from Karel's, but he held on.

"I'd better go," she said.

"Why should you go?" said Karel. "It's your house."

This remark, perhaps understandably, aroused Joy again from her corner of the settee: she went for them both this time, flailing but effective, inflicting rather a lot of damage. After a while Karel hit her very hard, and she sat down on the floor, and shut her eyes, as though that was what she had been waiting for. She sat there, propped up against a table leg, and appeared to pass out.

Frances, weeping at last, took a disconsolate gulp of scotch and sat down on the settee. She didn't dare to look at Karel. The violence of his blow had silenced her too.

"What on earth was all this about?" said Karel, after a minute or two, coming to sit down by her.

Frances explained that she didn't know, that Joy had just turned up and gone for her, that she had no idea what it was all about. Talking about it, she began to feel better. Karel, on the other hand, seemed to get worse and worse, sunk into a more and more profound gloom. Frances ended up stroking his hair and his face. "You didn't tell me Bob was ill," she said, after a while, whispering, as though Joy were asleep, which maybe she was. And he told her about Bob: he'd been very ill, he'd had some mysterious and permanent high fever, he'd been for a month in hospital waiting for the worst, they'd expected the worst, and then, in the end, somebody had diagnosed it as a curable but extremely obscure virus, and now he was all right and home again.

"You didn't tell me a word," said Frances, struck to the heart. "Not one word."

"I didn't want to worry you," said Karel.

"Why not?" said Frances. "I love you. I'm here to be worried. I *want* to be worried. I fell in love with you because you worried so much about me, why do you deny me the same privilege?"

And they went over it all: love, fear, commitment, fear of commitment, lack of mutual living. Joy slept through it all, worn out by emotion. I'll never leave you, Karel told Frances. She said that she believed him. As a pale green watery dawn broke, and the birds began to sing in the trees in her large garden, Karel and Frances started to pick up the pieces, throwing broken glass into one corner, assembling precious ancient fragments, trying to prop up the mangled ferns and pot plants. There was earth all over the carpet, as well as wine and blood and glass. Karel got the Hoover, and began to vacuum, but it was clearly a major task, and Frances persuaded him to abandon it.

Joy lay inert. "She *is* irresponsible," said Karel, dishcloth in hand. "She's left those children alone all night. I wish she wouldn't do that kind of thing."

"And where were *you*? So late at night?"

"Me?" said Karel. He looked slightly shifty and embarrassed. "Oh, I got stuck at college. Then I had to go home with Mrs. Mayfield."

"Darling," said Frances, with reproach. Mrs. Mayfield was a tedious old lady, an ex-student, who had wasted many years of Karel's life.

"I'm sorry," said Karel, nervously.

"You should have been either here or at home," said Frances, "and then all this wouldn't have happened. You haven't any time to waste on Mrs. Mayfield."

"Nor has anybody else any time to waste on Mrs. Mayfield," said Karel. "So I must."

"I love you," said Frances, with conviction.

"I make such a mess," said Karel, irresolutely, "through trying to give people what they want. She" (pointing to Joy) "wants to be knocked about. I hate doing it, I really do."

She had rarely heard him speak of himself in this way.

And you, he went on to her, all you seem to want is exactly what I want to give. How couldn't I like it better with you?

They stood there in the wrecked room, holding hands, contemplating the debris of their own confusions. They were both strong and healthy people, able to take a lot more of the same kind of thing. One blow, one row, was nothing. They would tidy up and begin again.

After a while Joy began to stir and mumble, and Karel picked her up and took her home, and Frances went to bed for what was left of the night.

The incident did not part them, as perhaps Joy had intended. If Joy had thought Frances a kind person or a nervous person, who would be disturbed by the sight of another's grief and rage, she had miscalculated. At times Frances wished she was a little nicer and kinder, but she wasn't, and that was that. Indeed, in a sense Joy had demonstrated how right Karel had been to seek an alternative, and Frances felt marginally less guilty than before. For his part, Karel seemed determined to take Frances more into his confidence: though naturally a secretive person, he made an effort to tell her about himself, his family, he introduced her to his past, his children. He even offered to show her where he lived, when Joy was out, and seemed surprised when she said she didn't want to see the flat off the Fulham Road. In other respects, their affair became like a second marriage. Frances's friends and children accepted Karel as her man: they went out together sometimes, though not often, for their chief problem was lack of time. Frances was an energetic and successful woman, with a life full of domestic, social, and professional engagements, and Karel was also busy. He took on far too much, he spread himself far too thin. His life was full of past obligations, old Jewish refugees, impoverished college friends, old school friends, wealthy and boring fools, silly students, mad entrepreneurs, con men, thieves, and liars of every kind. Frances accused him once of not knowing a single sane or interesting person, and he had agreed with her, but had defended his case: it was wicked, he said, to discriminate amongst people on the grounds of whether or not they were interesting. One should love all. (Frances privately believed that he had married Joy because she was so awful: she hated to think that Karel had made her awful, and very little research had reassured her that she had been to pieces before Karel got to her—paranoid, miserable, mad. He might have liked her for her bad qualities, he might even have connived at and encouraged them, but at least he wasn't their sole origin.)

And so you love me, said Frances, awful though I am?

You're different, of course, he would say. You're my one indulgence in life. You're the one person I choose, who also chooses me. That's why you can't leave me. I can't survive without you.

She listened, anxious to believe.

And as he seemed to her to be incapable of organizing himself, she organized herself, over the years. She cut down on unnecessary work, she stopped traveling so much, she tried to stop going out to see people. She no longer needed other people: she got plenty of attention from Karel. It was all right, really. Sometimes she thought she had constructed a perfect situation for herself. And yet, she herself had destroyed it. After that holiday, their one holiday abroad, she had had enough. Something rebelled in her, something began to make trouble: she found herself saying to herself things like, ''It simply isn't in me to spend the rest of my life ruining my career for a man who will never marry me.'' Though that wasn't it, at all: for one thing, she wasn't ruining her career, and for another thing, she didn't much want to marry Karel. She was quite happy on her own. The words seemed to come into her head from nowhere, but once they started to come, that had been the end of it: she couldn't resist them. Karel wasn't as unresisting: he shouted at her, pleaded with her, wept at her, not minding that she should see how much he suffered. She was awestruck. If *he* had left *her*, how she would have dissimulated, how she would have pretended that she did not care, that it did not matter, that it had never mattered. How she would have pretended never to have loved him. His difference of approach stunned her. It had a grandeur, a generosity, a simplicity, of which she felt herself utterly incapable. He was far, far beyond her, in some different land. She would never be able to join him. She would return to her trivial round of excavations and lectures and television series and parties, suffering in the upper mountain reaches of her being, while his nature lay deep and opaque, leveled to base level, without the jagged cataracts of the self, deep, persistent, continuous, deep like the river meeting the sea.

And so it was something of a shock to her, to find that water dry. She'd sent him an unambiguous postcard, telling him she loved him and missed him, and he hadn't rushed in love or pity to her side. He would have taken pity on a dog, a cat, a hamster, but he'd lost pity for her. Whatever could have happened to him, what had she done? She had been so certain that he would take her back. At times she said to herself, he would have taken pity on a dog, but the fact that he takes no pity on me can only mean he loves me still, thus he distinguishes me. But she didn't think much of this explanation. She knew it was nonsense. She knew he would have to come to her. (The true explanation never crossed her mind.)

In the end, she began to wonder whether he *had* loved her. She was obliged to. Perhaps he had another woman by now? He was an attractive man, he had had plenty of offers. His students solicited him constantly.

She began to doubt his nature. In astonishment, she said to herself, he *deceived* me. This is how it must be, she said, for a woman when her husband suddenly tells her, out of the blue, that he's got another woman. And she can't believe it, because she had always trusted him, had never had any suspicions.

It was the one experience she had tried to avoid. Rejection. Betrayal. Surprise.

Doubting him, she grew ill, as I have said. As she lay in bed in the hospital, she looked at the worst things in herself, and did not like them much. She had behaved badly. She had left him frivolously, she saw that now. She had left because she was a woman used to having the initiative, and she must have been afraid of losing it. Had she been offended, over the years, by the fact that he had not even spoken of leaving Joy for her? Her pride, her self-esteem, the most trivial parts of herself, had been wounded, and in revenge for them, she had lost all. She had lost him because she had believed that if she relented, he would come back.

She did not like herself much for this.

But even more, she disliked the way that Karel now, finally, had accepted her departure. Oh yes, he'd made a fuss at the time, she'd been taken in by his wails of anguish at her desertion. She'd been vain enough, even at that point, to be taken in. But Karel hadn't even meant it. It hadn't been love or generosity in him, to make that kind of fuss, it was simply the way he expressed himself. Middle-European. It didn't mean anything. It had simply been a conventional row from a man who had chosen to cast himself in a certain role. All right, she had behaved badly, pettily. But he should have seen through her pettiness and redeemed her. That was what he was there for. But instead, he had clearly vowed to take upon her the revenge that she had taken upon him. He would ignore her appeals, as she had his. And this was the man she had thought so good.

It wasn't his fault, maybe, that he was no better than herself. It was the situation's. But if he couldn't rise above it, she wasn't interested. She determined, halfheartedly, not to be interested. She would cast him off. A future without him stretched like the desert, dry and hot. She had always hated the heat, and wished often that she had specialized in some more Nordic branch of her field.

She would think of him no more, she told herself. Or if she thought of him, she would try to think the worst. (She did not succeed. She had too strong a sense of reality.)

In her illness she found herself turning rather weakly to her family. There was nowhere else to turn. She had no real friends, only colleagues and acquaintances, and she'd lost a lot of these during her years with Karel. Karel had been bad for her, she told herself. He had cut her off from her kind, had made her into a recluse. When she got better, she would have to apply herself seriously to the business of living in the world again. She hadn't really faced that problem yet, she'd always been expecting to get Karel back, since their parting she had lived in a kind of nothingness, a kind of limbo. She would have to come to terms with the future. She would have to make new connections.

Her family were quite kind to her. They visited her in hospital, sent her flowers, entertained her children in her absence, asked her to stay in their houses while she recuper-

ated. Joy had been wrong about the country houses which
she believed the Ollerenshaws to possess in such abundance.
Frances's brother Hugh had a cottage in the country, but that
wasn't quite the same thing. And her parents lived on a campus, which could hardly have been described as the country:
her father was vice-chancellor of a fairly new university, and
one of the perks or penalties of this post was that one had to
live in the building designed for the job. Frances, who went
to stay with them for the weekend after she emerged from
hospital, thought that she wouldn't have liked it at all, but
they didn't seem to mind. The campus was composed of
plate glass and grassy lawns and duck ponds and covered
alleyways, quite a change from the Oxford where she had
been brought up. She suspected that they both liked its an-
onymity, and the fact that they need take no personal responsibility for its shortcomings. Neither of them cared much
for style: her father, brought up in the flat East Midlands,
the only child of a nursery gardener, was quite exceptionally
unaware of his surroundings, while her mother, who came
from a notable family of Oxford intellectuals (mostly scientific ones) had always believed in functional living conditions. She had certainly got them now, thought Frances,
slumped into a corner of the modern very comfortable undyed tweed settee, gazing out of the huge picture window at
the vast artificially hummocky garden, trying to avoid her
mother's eye, trying not to be drawn into discussion about
the lump now removed from her breast. Her mother was a
gynecologist, and had the most extraordinary views on sex.
One really had to keep off the subject, but it was more or
less impossible, for Lady Ollerenshaw was an enthusiast,
ardently caught up in population control and abortion law
reform—she wanted more abortion, not less. She spent much
of her time now telling others from the lecture platform that
they ought not to have more than two children per family.
This was reasonable enough, Frances supposed, but her tone
when delivering her views was peculiarly unfortunate—
upper-class, patronizing, shrill, and dogmatic. Perhaps Joy

had had the misfortune to hear her speak. At least, thought
Frances, if nothing else, I'm a better speaker than my mother.

Frances had always suspected that her mother didn't care
much for sex. (That would be one explanation for the domestic moodiness of her father: in public life, he was pleasant, amiable, a good chap, a reliable administrator, efficient
and calm but at home he tended toward the morose and ab-
stracted. In fact, it was reported to Frances that he was forgetting to be pleasant in public, these days, as though he were
brooding all the time over some important problem as he
grew older.) Her mother had never disparaged sex: on the
contrary, she had talked about it too much, too sensibly, too
medically. How could anyone who talked like that ever have
enjoyed the least sensible, the messiest, and most amazing
of mysteries? On the other hand, she was an attractive
woman—she was still an attractive woman—and enjoyed the
company of men. Although in theory a feminist, speaking
frequently of the need to emancipate woman from the chores
of domesticity and child-rearing, she seemed not to like other
women, and had few friends. She liked sexual attention, and
demanded it from the men around her (in university circles,
there were always plenty of men) in a way that was both coy
and calculating: she manipulated the most unwilling and reluctant old dons and young undergraduates into attitudes of
gallantry that Frances certainly found embarrassing, even if
they didn't. There was no resisting her: she would not be
ignored in a gathering, she had to be noticed, as a woman.
And yet she hadn't got quite the style to manipulate gracefully: perhaps she lacked confidence, somewhere along the
line, for her conquests always eyed her with a faint air of
uneasiness, as though they knew something was demanded
of them, knew they had to give, and were unsure whether
they had given enough. She had the power to demand, without the charm to make tributes easy. She made people uncomfortable, she made them feel guilty, as though they were
somehow at fault.

She had been very difficult to deal with, during Frances's

adolescence and years at university. Frances had since discovered that it is more commonly a daughter's father who
makes problems over his daughter's friends, but Frank Ollerenshaw had ignored her social life completely, never even
bothering to inquire where she was going, with whom she
had just been to stay. Her mother, on the other hand, took
an excessive, a proprietorial interest. Young men, brought
home for tea or dinner, would be interrogated, charmed,
bullied, provoked. Many was the time that Frances found
herself sulking silently and ungraciously in a corner of the
sitting room, or weeping upstairs on her bed, while her
mother talked to her boyfriend on the settee. Some of them
succumbed easily: she was after all an intelligent, highly
educated woman, from a family of famous names, with some
interesting anecdotes to tell, and a good deal of social power
in the university. Others resisted, hoping to please Frances.
Frances found herself disliking both those who gave in and
those who didn't. She couldn't bear her mother to get away
with it, but she couldn't bear to know she was being criticized either. Thus, successfully, were many of her early attempts at friendship brought to an end. It was only fairly
recently that she'd begun to wonder whether her mother might
not have done it deliberately, through jealousy. But she didn't
think that was it. It was more likely that her mother simply
needed attention, whatever the source.

In the end, she had learned to keep her real friends away
from her mother. She would feed to her mother harmless
friends, meaningless people, as one might feed dead rabbits
to a snake, twitching them a little every now and then by a
string so that they simulated signs of life. She was careful
not to introduce complete duds—her mother was no fool,
after all, she would not be taken in by anything too mangy,
too bedraggled. But there was always an intermediate cate-
gory of friends, would-be suitors most of them (for Frances
was not a particularly kind person herself), who would do
for her mother—to this day, Lady Ollerenshaw would still
inquire in a possessive and self-congratulatory way about

Miles who became a doctor, Stephen who became an art historian, Malcolm who went off to Iowa, and that very nice boy Rickie who always brought her flowers. Miles, Stephen, Malcolm, and Rickie had played their parts well, and graced the dinner table many times. Rickie had been truly charmed. Frances, perversely, had been grateful to him for that.

But her real friends, her formidable friends, she kept to herself. Until Anthony, her husband. And as she had to marry him, so she had to introduce him to her mother. Cold-blooded and dominating himself, Anthony had set out to charm her mother as she set out to charm him, and they had eyed one another with a mutually hypnotic stare, both of them conniving at what seemed to be a rather sordid agreement. Anthony allowed himself to be bullied into flattery: her mother allowed him to marry Frances, as long as he continued to flatter and pay court. The relationship seemed to give them both satisfaction, for which she, again perversely, gave them both black marks.

A friend of hers told her in bed late one night that he sometimes slept with his wife's mother, and didn't mind which he had, mother or daughter. Frances had been temporarily shocked by this near-incest, but had since decided that if Anthony had been capable of sleeping with her mother, or her mother capable of sleeping with Anthony, they would both of them have been happier and nicer people. Frigidity and gynecology seemed to her a deadly combination, and possibly a common one.

Common or not, they had overshadowed her adolescence, and in an effort to escape them she had pursued sex with determination rather than pleasure, resolving that whatever she turned out like, at least she wouldn't be like her mother. Before Anthony, she slept with anyone she fancied, while taking home the men with whom she did not sleep. It had done her no good, she had ended up with Anthony, who could never forgive her for his inability to control her. One cannot escape one's destiny. And one day, in a moment of comic horror, it had occurred to her that in seeking to avoid her mother's ghost, she had in fact behaved exactly like her mother—she too had turned into a promiscuous and dominating flirt, the only difference being a technical one, in that she slept with the men instead of satisfying herself with verbal homage. But for Karel, she would have ended up like her mother.

She'd never been able to understand her father's attitude to her mother. As a child, she had taken his side, blaming her mother for his moodiness, imagining that she herself knew what went on in his head during the long domestic silences. He obviously didn't like the spectacle of her social behavior any more than Frances did, and had been on occasions remarkably rude about her public crusades. Whatever their differences, they had stayed together, as couples of their generation tended so submissively to do. He sat now, silent, doing *The Times* crossword, in a corner of the large room. Impossible to know what he was thinking. Perhaps he had had a bad effect on her, as perhaps Karel had had on Joy. Perhaps she would have been all right, with another man.

Lady Ollerenshaw, sipping her sherry, had now moved from the subject of the lump in Frances's breast to the subject of the extreme productivity of her own children, which had naturally shocked her greatly. Frances's elder brother Hugh had produced three, Frances herself had produced four, partly at least, she supposed, through the same defiant impulse that had driven her into so many strange beds, partly through a deep dislike of the birth control of which she had heard so much too much, partly out of a need to compensate for her lack of affection for her husband, partly to prove she could, partly because she liked being pregnant, and partly (no not partly, all, of course all) because she loved children, and would have wanted more and more, loving each one as it arrived. So much for the population problem. Still, four was excessive, yes, she knew it, it was extravagant and disgraceful, as her behavior had always been. (Her mother had had three: listening to her now, Frances felt like remarking that her younger sister Alice, now dead and beyond reproduction, had doubtless killed herself to reduce the family average. She might have made the remark had she not feared that her mother would not mind it. She is a woman without real affections, said Frances to herself.)

To make matters worse, Hugh's eldest son Stephen had got himself married while still at university, and had produced a baby, which made Lady Ollerenshaw, the pioneer of planning, a great-grandmother at the modest age of sixty-two. She did not like it at all.

"It makes me look *ridiculous*," she said, leaning back in her chair, brushing her blue-white hair from her unwrinkled brow.

"I don't suppose it was you they were thinking of when they did it," said Frances, knowing that even so obvious a truth could not fail to disturb her mother's picture of how things ought to be. Luckily, she was not listening. "It's too disgraceful," she continued, moaning slightly, for the fiftieth time, and for the fiftieth time a large duck flew into the plate glass window and dropped, stunned and ornamental, upon the Basil Spence greensward.

"I wish to God they wouldn't do that," said her father, and looked down again at the crossword. They were waiting for dinner, they were to dine in Hall. They had asked Frances if she would mind, and she had said she wouldn't mind, she felt (reproachfully) quite well enough, of course. Oh, you poor thing, how awful, I'd quite *forgotten* you were ill, you look so *well*, cried her mother—I don't mind at all, insisted Frances—oh well, if you really don't *mind*, Dr. Billing would so like to meet you. Ha, ha, thought Frances nastily, forced to admit I'm worth showing off, even with a severed breast, she thought, but the truth was she quite liked dining in Hall, it was a change after all, she didn't do that kind of thing often these days.

"I mean to say," pursued her mother, relentlessly, "do I *look* like a great-grandmother?"

Frances regarded her with amusement and affection. She certainly didn't, one had to admit. She looked younger than her years, despite the fact that she tended to dress in a rather old-world manner, preferring well-cut suits and cashmere twinsets to the more casual shirts and skirts and long dresses that most of the other women on the campus now wore, and despite the fact that her luxurious white hair was rinsed blue, and carefully waved, and despite the fact that she wore very large diamond and sapphire earrings in her ears, and red lipstick on her lips. Frances had never understood her mother's attitude to clothes. Well-off, well-brought up, she had always groomed herself with a slightly excessive care, rather like a member of the royal family, while other stylish dons and dons' wives, equally well-born, tended to despise make-up as vulgar, and earrings as a waste of time. Some interesting social distinctions lurked in the upper middle classes. Frances had never come to terms with them. Herself, she was of mixed blood. But it was certainly true that Lady Ollerenshaw looked as though she could not possibly be a great-grandmother. Her face was unlined, her back straight, her skin clear, her hands with their large emerald fine and white and smooth and dimpled, mysteriously more youthful, in fact, than Frances's own large veined freckled buckled hands. She had almost an unused look, as though there was something in her that was still waiting. Her legs were like a girl's, straight-shinned, neat-ankled, well-shod. What was she waiting for, at the age of sixty-three? So clean, so well-groomed, so neat, so womanly? How dare she sit there, so unsatisfied? Perhaps she had been waiting in a trance for all the forty-one years of her marriage. Would it ever come to her, now? Watching her, Frances struggled with onslaughts of fear, of pity, and of love. Her mother disappointed in eternity, forever protected from knowing she would be so by the quicker wits of others. Frances sought for the only tone in which she could speak to her—a tone positive, jocular, teasing, bracing. (A patronizing tone?) She was frightened by her mother, but more frightened for her. She was too vulnerable. One shouldn't be like that, at her age, thought Frances.

"No," she said, "you don't look at all like a great-grandmother. But then, do you think I look like a great-aunt? Think what a shock it was for me, suddenly finding myself a great-aunt. At my age."

"In my day," said her father, suddenly, exceptionally conversational, "great-aunts were about ninety. Weren't they, Stella? Do you remember Great-Aunt Dorrie?"

"Something has happened to the nation," said Frances. "People get married so young these days. It must be your fault, mother. You set the trend."

"Don't be silly," said her mother. "Seriously, Frances, I am surprised by Hugh. Letting that boy get married. He's only nineteen."

"The girl was pregnant," said Frances.

"Yes, I know, that's what I'm *complaining* about. Haven't they ever heard of contraception? Haven't they ever heard of abortion?"

"It wasn't Hugh's fault," said Frances. "I don't suppose he much likes being a grandfather, either."

"Of course it was his fault. The man's an alcoholic."

"That's another matter," said Frances, thinking of her brother, who had escaped his mother and his heritage at some cost to his liver. It doubtless caused Stella pain, to find her golden boy a drunken grandfather. Hugh had been so literally a golden boy, more golden than even Frances had ever been, flaxen-curled, beautiful, smiling, ingratiating. And then, as occasionally happens with blond children, the sun had gone in and darkness had overtaken him: his hair had turned not brown, but pitch black, his skin had darkened to gypsy changeling darkness, and as a youth he had grown thick hair like a bear curling all over his brown chest. He had to shave twice a day if he wanted to look respectable. It was a freak transformation, inexplicable in terms of immediate heredity. One night, after a heavy drinking session, Frances and Hugh and Hugh's wife Natasha had constructed the theory that Hugh had produced this transformation by sheer will, in order to escape the seductive powers of his mother,

who had certainly been slightly unnerved by her son's in-
creasingly masculine and swarthy appearance. Having constructed the theory in a moment of idle fancy, all of them
had been struck with its solemn truth, and had been unable
to forget it.

Lady Ollerenshaw decided to drop the subject of her son's
condition.

"Anyway, darling," she went on, "you should know what
happened, if anyone does. You're on good terms with Stephen, aren't you? I thought you were the person he talks to?
Have you seen him, lately?"

"He came to see me in hospital," said Frances, not quite
wanting to deliver him up: he was so delicate, Stephen, so
insubstantial, she would have to talk about him in a deceitful
jolly family tone, if she talked about him at all, in order not
to hurt him. She would protect him from their curiosity, for
it was true that he confided in her. He had attached himself
to her, while he was still a schoolboy, and she had taken him
in, at first as a duty (remembering Karel's amazing patience
with tedious young and old dependents, modeling herself as
so often on Karel's virtues), and then through affection. He
wasn't much trouble to her, once she had got over the surprise of finding him a young man rather than a child. He was
good practice, she told him, she could learn through him to
adjust to the eventual aging of her own children. He would
arrive unannounced on her doorstep in Putney, with his thin
white face and his clouds of frizzy dark hair, he would sit at
her kitchen table while she chopped vegetables, he would tell
her his anxieties, some of which seemed to her (her hands
reeking with onions, her chopping block ornamented with
slices of liver) curiously metaphysical. She would smile and
soothe and listen. She went to hear him sing, once, in his
school choir—he had a fine voice, a tenor, they were singing
the *St. Matthew Passion*, and tears of nostalgia had flowed
down her cheeks as she heard the tall long-haired boys singing the familiar tragic music, and Stephen there in the back
row in his vague dark halo, remote and useless, beautiful

and gone. Give. Oh, give me back my lord. He loved music, but he wouldn't work, he was lazy, sometimes she would reproach him for this, as perhaps he wanted her to do. He lived in a cloud of grass, the full dry wrinkled sheaves of his hair symbolizing too aptly the clouds in which he drifted, with the white star of his anxious face like an indestructible center of human knowledge, undrifting, unchanging, fixed, intent, unappeased—and he would return for more reproaches. He admired her, he said so. "Aunt Frances," he would say, earnestly, mockingly, with devotion, "where do you get it all from?"

"All what?" she would say.

"The energy, the movement," he would say, as she briskly sliced a tomato or two.

"It's a phenomenon of our generation. Your father's got it too."

"My father's an alcoholic. It's all artificial," said Stephen.

"Nonsense," Frances would say, proving how dynamic she was by the manner in which she mixed the salad dressing.

"How can you possibly imagine," he would say, again, returning to the same theme, "that the things you do are worth doing?"

"I don't know," she would say, helplessly, attacked, not knowing. "I like them, that's all."

"You mean you enjoy them?"

"Yes, yes, I enjoy them."

And he would gaze at her in wonder, as though she belonged to another species, as though she were an angel floating in the upper reaches of meaningless heavenly activity, as though she were a bird or a fish.

"Aren't you bored?" he would say.

"No," she would say, truthfully. "Though I *was* bored, often, at your age."

"Why, why, tell me why?" he would ask, and she would speculate, trying to tell him and he would listen, genuinely eager. He was never impertinent, he was the soul of tact. He was a delightful child, she had great hopes of him. She could understand why he distrusted Hugh, why he confided in her rather than in his remarkable mother. (His mother was fully occupied trying to amuse Hugh, an impossible task at which she seemed to have been, over the years, remarkably successful.) So she had been anxious, conventionally anxious, she had to admit, like a mother or a grandmother, when he arrived on her doorstep in Putney one day with his prospective bride, and had asked her to intercede with his father to allow them to get married.

The bride was a shabby, neurotic little creature, as skinny as a rabbit, with bitten nails and stringy hair, hair the very opposite of Stephen's fine abundance. (Though Stephen, too, was skinny. One could see that they had a similarity.) She hardly spoke. She was called Beata, though Frances doubted the name's authenticity, and her voice, when one was lucky enough to hear it, had a horrible nasal whine. She wore limp old clothes, in the fashion of the day, and painted her nails green. Frances, like a jealous mother, found herself deeply resenting the fact that such a miserable creature had found the life-force to buy nail varnish, and had wasted it on nail varnish. The human race, looking at her, appeared threatened with extinction.

Then Stephen had told her that Beata was pregnant.

"Do you *want* the baby?" said Frances, to both of them, wondering if she were being employed as devil's advocate, and resenting the role, indeed thinking that she would not forgive Stephen if such was his conception of her quasi-maternal relationship. But they had insisted that they both wanted the baby, that it had to be born. They talked about it as though it already existed, which she found disquieting— but no more logically disquieting, she had to remind herself, than her mother's less imaginative attitude.

So she had encouraged them, and had talked to Hugh at length on the telephone, and Stephen and Beata had married. She did not go to the wedding. The baby was born at the end of Stephen's second year at university. It was a girl. She was only faintly surprised, if at all, to learn that Beata was the daughter of an oil millionaire, that she expected to inherit a fortune, and that she was suffering from anorexia nervosa. She managed to eat enough to survive during pregnancy, spoon fed by Stephen (this she did see, in her own home, before her own eyes: she saw Stephen, talking of the baby's survival, spoon leek soup down her retching bony throat): but after the baby was born, she relapsed, and was taken into hospital, where she lay inert for weeks. For all Frances knew she was still there. And Stephen had refused to allow his daughter to be taken from him. He had turned quite savage and rejected all suggestions that she should be removed though he would soon be in his final year, and was working hard. He had, independently, devised a rota of girlfriends and tutors' wives' au pair girls to cope when he was absolutely obliged to be elsewhere, and the rest of the time he carried the baby on his hip in a canvas bag. Hugh thought he had gone mad; Beata lay uncaring; Lady Ollerenshaw did not seem to think that it might be partly the fault of her own policies. Frances thought he was mad, but was also moved. He had shown perseverance, at last. He had simply been waiting for some occasion worthy of his effort. He was even working better, now. There wasn't so much to worry about.

Though he had upset her slightly, when he had called to see her in hospital. He had brought the baby, of course: she sat on his hip and smiled, and waved her squashy fingers. But he had talked oddly, sadly. He had said that the conditions of survival were so dreadful that it was undignified to survive. This is what Beata feels, he had said: that living is a crime. What do you mean, Frances said, look at your lovely baby, she is innocent, she smiles, innocent of any crimes. Yes, he had said, but keeping a baby alive is such a labor, such a labor, can God have intended survival? Not knowing whether he seriously believed in God or not, she did not know how to answer, though she knew she was on thin ground. Perhaps, her rational self had said to herself, he is simply worn out, with trying to deal with the baby and the work and the ill wife, and she had offered to look after the

baby for a few days when well enough herself: he declined
the offer, as she had expected he would. But anyway, she
knew that there was more at stake than simple fatigue. He
had asked her about her own illness in a strange, probing,
intent way: he had looked at the other women in the ward
with an air of assessment. He talked at some length about
the Jews (his mother was Jewish) and why they had submitted
to their own fate, and what he felt about Israel and its struggling for survival, and its racism, and its militarism. "I used
to despise the Jews," he said at one point, "for their cow-
ardice. Whoever, looking at the Jews, could call Christianity
a slave religion? But now I like them even less."

"You're a child of your time," said Frances, recognizing
familiar arguments. "We, we're too old to renounce Israel."

"You're too addicted to living," said Stephen, with what
seemed to her an uncharacteristic unkindness: for there she
lay, as he well knew, awaiting the final results of her biopsy.
And then he had looked at his child, wriggling there against
him, and he had looked with such desperate unconcealed
yearning, and had begun to talk strangely about his fears of
having her immunized and vaccinated, for he had read in the
paper that even such routine measures could kill, could cause
irreversible brain damage, "and if a hair of her head," he
said, with a miserable ferocity, "were harmed, I would—I
would—I don't know what I wouldn't do."

The baby, almost hairless, smiled happily.

"You mustn't worry so much," said Frances, gently,
reaching for his hand, squeezing it in an avuncular fashion.
"Babies aren't so fragile, you know. They survive an awful
lot. Don't worry yourself, Stephen. I know it's hell, worrying
about them, you just have to accept that that's how it is and
that it doesn't matter, and that they'll survive. You read too
many papers. You shouldn't read the papers, you should read
Dr. Spock, you know."

"Dr. Spock is so hideously *reassuring*," Stephen had said,
"and so obviously a *liar*. . . ."

And they had both laughed, and Stephen had gone on to

ask her, in a different tone, what Karel thought of Israel: for him this was a conversational matter, he was perhaps curious about where Karel had gone to, why he had disappeared from the scene; she sometimes thought he was too young and self-absorbed ever to have noticed what Karel had meant to her, and so she was not prepared to speak of Karel's views on Israel, of his anxiety, his loyalty, his distress. Why should she deliver these things up to a teenager who believed blindly in the Third World?

She kept the memory of Karel to herself, and fobbed Stephen off with some of her own views on the Arabs. She knew a lot about the Arabs, he could not answer her back.

While Frances Wingate sat in her parents' sitting room gazing over the darkening wastes, fobbing off her parents with some account of their grandson and great-granddaughter which quite denied her true anxiety (why should they be given her true feelings?) Karel Schmidt sat in his room at the Polytechnic, staring at a pile of essays, and thought of Frances Wingate. He hadn't really yet got around to believing she had left him. Surely she would summon him back. They had loved each other, it had all been so simple, it had been so silly to part.

Love was such a rare commodity, too rare to waste. He didn't love anyone else much, except his children, and they were growing up in a most tiresome way and no longer required his devotion. Joy required devotion, but she would honorably admit from time to time that she hardly expected to get it, and that only a saint would love her after the things she had said and done to him: and you, she would point out, are no saint. He didn't love Joy: neither did he love Mrs. Mayfield, or Dick Wilkie, or Slater, or Ken Stuart, or Gloria Hussein, or Eli Kulunka, or all the other people who counted themselves his intimate friends. He ought to be a saint, and love Joy and Mrs. Mayfield, but he wasn't, though he had tried hard. From time to time, through the years, through a lifetime of endeavor, he had felt welling up in him a kind of compelled and induced love, and had felt as though he were on the brink of a discovery so wonderful that all the doubts and hours of boredom and inadequate responses would be justified: Mrs. Mayfield or Dick Wilkie would suddenly bask in his unforced, real, shining love, and would at last be made whole. Nobody else could do it, they were too unlovable: he alone, with his years of practice, could achieve the transformation. But the vision would fade, and he would be forced to see himself in the light of common day: weak, over-identifying with the unlovely, unable to say no, with a peculiar capacity for enduring hours and hours of unremitting boredom. At least he put the capacity to good use. Every now and then one of his more energetic friends (and he still had a few left, by some miracle) would try to encourage him to see himself in more worldly terms: you ought to try to enjoy yourself, you ought to get out, you ought to get rid of all these dreary people, they would say. In other words, they would say, you ought to come with us.

Karel wondered why they bothered with him, and was too modest to see clearly that his conversion would have been a considerable triumph. He did suspect that there was some hypnotic quality in his own drab but passionate life: it drew people, and the only reason why it didn't draw more of the exciting ones was that they got tired of finding his flat full of the interminable others. Karel is all right, they would say, but I can't stand another evening of Eli/Ken/Gloria. And yet they would return to Karel, for Karel was a man of weird and crazy principle, and in part they wanted to destroy it, in part to have it. Karel, never knowing how others saw him, would mildly respond to all claims, from the most trivial to the most demanding: he would sit up all night talking and drinking and smoking, he would lend his money, he would drive people to railway stations, he would fix them up with psychiatrists or degree courses in the Open University or drug contacts, each according to his need. It was one of his favorite principles (again closely resembling inertia) that one should never question what the other person wanted, or try to impose a view of one's own upon another: he believed, against all the evidence, that people knew what they were doing and ought to be allowed to do it. Occasionally, behind their backs, being human, he would explode into a terrible rage, and condemn and disapprove as violently as anyone: but always, when he had got over his rage, he would again accept even the most hardened, most disagreeable cases. Joy, who had been driven into excessive intolerance by his excessive tolerance, amused herself by inventing all kinds of degrading explanations for his social habits—that he felt himself to be so unacceptable that even the acceptance of a Mrs. Mayfield was welcome, that he was himself so boring that the concept of boredom had never darkened his mind, that he wanted to play at being Jesus Christ. This last explanation often managed to enrage him, and as he was not particularly Christ-like in his domestic life, he would usually beat her up whenever she expanded upon it: a result which gave her a peculiar satisfaction, and which left him feeling worse than ever, and even less able to discriminate morally between his acquaintances. There were evenings when Karel did not dare move out of his office, for dread of the inevitable encounter with Ken: he would sit on for hours longer than he needed, and then Ken would get him, late, and keep him even later. Ken was one of the few students who never knocked on the door: he always lurked around waiting, and his timing of his confrontations was brilliant. He was mad, Ken, and like many madmen he was a brilliant manipulator. He was one of the most exhausting people even Karel had ever met: a session with Ken would leave him limp and drained, bloodless and sweating, depressed and savage, hopeless and bitter, as though Ken had managed to transfer all his own psychic and chemical content into Karel's own body. Karel tried not to think of Ken: he thought of Frances instead.

He had reduced Frances, for such times, into a series of images. First of all, he would think of the color of her. She was brown and yellow. Her skin was golden, and it was an interesting mixture of coarseness and sensitivity: it had been weathered, as she was fond of pointing out, by sun and sand, like an ancient monument. She was covered in blemishes: scars, rough patches, corns, permanently damaged nails, moles, and a large brown birthmark on her bottom. He would think of these details, one after the other. Then he would think of making love to her, and how much she seemed to like it. Ow, help, lovely, ow, Karel, she would yell. She certainly hadn't weathered right through: inside, there was plenty going on. He had known there would be, from the beginning. All that had astonished him had been her assertion (love, or truth?) that nobody had got there before.

After he had thought about this kind of thing (and it was getting hard to remember details, all the separate years of occasions had begun to blur into a single archetypal event), he would go on to remember other kinds of incidents with her: conversations, meals, journeys, the odd social outing. Sometimes, he would nostalgically start again at the beginning, remembering the first time they had met, the rather dauntingly bland lecture she had given, the odd purple dress she'd been wearing, the pleasant way in which she hadn't seemed to mind the lack of tonic in the gin. He would think of the drive home, and the slight uneasiness that had overcome both of them toward the end of the journey: over her, because she wanted to get rid of him, over him, because he was aware of this, and concurred with her, for he too was tired and wanted to get to bed. Then he would remember the shock of seeing, as in one's worst nightmare, an ambulance at one's own front door (he was an overanxious person himself, a constant foreseer of disaster, and was not at this point to know that she herself was much less given to nightmare speculations); and then he would recall what was for him the decisive moment, which was the moment when he saw, under the streetlamp, all the color drain out of her face. It was an astonishing, a beautiful effect. That brown-yellow, freckled face of hers had turned gray: the blood had poured away, leaving the brown freckles standing there on her skin, strained, pallid, deadly, in the yellow-gray waste of her cheek, on the prow of her large nose. Even her lips had turned gray, parted dry with shock. How lovely, how responsive, how beautifully knit, how in the body she had been. The texture and the color remained with him forever. Later, as tragedy turned to farce, as the blood came back into her face, he hung around and watched her, to see what would happen next: and her swoop of recovery, her instant relief, her instant command, had been irresistible. He forgot that he was tired, that he ought to get home early. Love had got hold of him, yet again.

As he got to know her better, Karel found that there were many things about Frances that he did not exactly approve. He didn't like the way she kept leaving her children to go off to foreign parts. He slightly disapproved of her excessive interest in her work. He didn't like the way she threw her money and her husband's money around. He didn't like what he took to be her predatory instincts about people—her liking to be liked, her need to collect admirers, her need for flattery. He slightly distrusted the imbalance of her nature, and the way it would swing from meaningless but infectious gloom to meaningless but infectious euphoria. And yet for all that, he loved her, he admired her. What did it matter whether he approved or disapproved? There she was—or there, at least, she had been. He couldn't really believe that she shouldn't come back to him again. Surely she would write to him, one of these days.

(Her postcard, months old, lay in the bottom of an enormous heap of mail in a strike-bound letterbox in a railway station somewhere in Europe.)

He couldn't think why her loss hadn't finished him off. Because he hadn't believed it, maybe? He gave one more thought to her body, and, groaning slightly in his spirit, turned his attention to Ken, whose peaky schizoid face would be lying in wait for him in the shadowy gauntlet of the foyer. He was no use to anyone, why go through with it? But there wasn't really any choice.

* * *

Frances Wingate, sitting at High Table in Leofric College, talked about heredity and environment to a psychologist who worked with rats and hamsters. The depressing session over poor Stephen had stimulated her, and she was drinking more than the doctor had said she should, and propounding to this rather opinionated young man her view that there were factors in the environment—the human environment—that had never yet been taken into consideration when assessing the human personality. She could tell that he did not know how to take her: he did not know whether she was trying to be serious or amusing, and she was not sure herself. "The point is," she was saying, "that the Romantics took all this seriously, even if we don't. They understood the effects of landscape on the soul. What about all that stuff about frost at midnight, and moon shine sweetly, and the formative influences of the Lake District? Hartley, and all that? I've never yet met a psychiatrist or a psychologist who went into all that kind of thing when trying to diagnose an illness, have you? They never ask one if one was brought up in the mountains or the suburbs. And yet *anyone* could tell you it must have *some* effect. It's obvious that it does. Look at America, you must have been to America. Well, it's on too large a scale. It drives people mad. Everything there is too big, the rivers are too wide, the mountains are too high, the canyons are too deep, the geology is too dramatic, the deserts are too large, it just isn't possible to live in spaces like that. They've taken centuries trying to adapt to it and they can't. It's driving them insane. In Europe one gets proper-scale landscapes, but there it's just all out of proportion. The whole nation is suffering from collective agoraphobia."

"And what about us? What do we suffer from?"

"Oh, it depends what part of the country one comes from. There are small distinctions, you know. I only really know about the parts I come from. Oxford and the East Midlands. A fine mixture. And of course, like your rats, we are all products of mixed environmental heredity."

"Do you mean that one can inherit a landscape?"

"Yes, I think so. Though it's not quite as simple as that. After all, one does still have family links, kinship links, with the landscapes one's parents and grandparents were born in. One goes back to visit relatives. One hears about them from one's parents. One might even take sentimental journeys to see them."

"What do you still see of the East Midlands? You weren't even born there, were you?"

"No, I was born in Oxford. But I used to go and stay with my grandmother. My father's mother. She's dead now, of course. But I used to know it quite well. There are still members of the family there, I think, though we don't see them. I haven't been back for years." She paused, prodding at the tablecloth with her knife, thoughtfully. "You know," she said, slowly, "I've often thought that there must be something in the *soil* there, in the very earth and water, that sours the nature. I often think that in our family—we've got some hereditary deficiency. Or excess. I wouldn't know which. Like fluoride. And that, combined with the flatness of the landscape, was what did it."

"Did what?"

"Oh, I don't know. Created the family temperament, I suppose I mean. If there is such a thing. Though, quite obviously, there is. Don't you agree?"

"In general, do you mean, or in your family? I couldn't say about your family. I've only met you and your father. Oh, and once, I think, your brother. In general, I think I agree. Of course certain families have very pronounced characteristics—take your mother's for example, or the Huxleys, or the Darwins, or the Mitchisons . . ."

"I wasn't so much meaning families like that," said Frances, flatly. "I meant just ordinary families. Rat families. Without genius or too much inbreeding. I'm certain," she said, rousing herself slightly, "that there must be something positively *poisoning* the whole of South Yorkshire and the Midlands, or they wouldn't all be so bloody miserable up there, and live in such *appalling* conditions. One day they'll work out what it is, and give everyone a pill to counteract it. Meanwhile, we've all got to accommodate ourselves to it as best we can.''

"To the Midlands sickness?" He laughed, politely.

"That's it. One could call it that." She too laughed, to prove that she wasn't serious. "I manage to accommodate myself quite well. I'm never there. I'm always abroad."

"But you carry it with you in your bones."

"Oh yes. Even in the middle of the Sahara, it flattens me out if I'm not careful."

"You're lucky to be able to move."

"Oh yes, I believe in keeping on the move. I get quite upset when I think about all the people that can't."

"They probably like it there."

"Do you think so? How could they?"

"Lucky for you that your father got out, anyway."

"Yes, I suppose so." She looked down the table at her father, who was staring blankly into the far distance. "But he's a bad case," she confided, conspiratorially. "A bad case of the Midlands." And, disloyally, they both laughed.

She thought about this conversation in bed, at length. She had been joking, or so she thought: the psychologist's description of his rats and his discoveries about social and anti-social behavior had both depressed and excited her, as did all suggestions of mechanism in behavior, and she had tried to change the subject. But she had not succeeded. The more she thought about it, the more she feared that Stephen was suffering from some incurable and ratlike family disease, yet another manifestation of the same illness that had killed her sister, driven Hugh manic to the bottle, and drive her father into a world of silent brooding. She herself suffered from the same thing: it would come over her, periodically, meaninglessly. She had learned to deal with it by ignoring it, by denying its significance: she had refused to take it too seriously, but had let it sweat itself out like a dose of malaria. She had clung to activity and movement as an escape, and

on the whole her remedy had worked: she had been able to
evade the effects of the sickness, if not the sickness itself. At
times she thought Hugh in his own way had been as successful: though often in a hopeless condition, he could still
operate, he still by some freak which she failed to understand
managed to do well in the city, and when drunk he was
sometimes quite amusing. Not always, but sometimes. But
was this all she was doing, feverishly seeking health by trying
to avoid illness? And what of her convictions, when in the
illness, that the illness had some deep spiritual significance?
She suspected that her father thought it had: any talk of chemical imbalance or hereditary disorder upset him wildly. He
thought God was after him alone. Frances could not give
herself such dignity, but, lying awake at night, feeling the
stitches in her once perfect breast, she felt that she would
like to know where she began and the family ended. God
was certainly not hounding her down the nights and down
the days, but on the other hand it was possible that she had
set up her individual will too firmly against him, had tried
too much to cheat him, had ignored his portents too coldly.
Where would it take her? She had often thought it would take
her to a spectacular collapse in her forties, at the approach
of the change of life, maybe. That was now not too far ahead.
Would there be some stunning reckoning, would she crawl
around the walls and stick forever in one of those black
phases, eating her own excrement?

The family history was in fact far from cheerful. Without
exaggeration (and often she and Hugh exaggerated, care-
lessly, for effect, to dispel the gloom), the record was not too
good. It was not on her mother's brilliant side that things
were black: there, eccentricity and talent had mingled and
expressed themselves happily, collecting Nobel Prizes on the
way, and condemning only an odd maiden aunt or two to a
quiet retreat. It was her father's family, that so-called ordinary family, that gave rise for alarm.

Thinking of them, she thought with a sudden panic of her
own children. As an adolescent, she had sworn that she would

have no children: she seriously feared that she and they would go mad. And then, through some quirk of nature, she had quite forgotten her doubts, she had married, had given birth cheerfully, and produced as it seemed cheerful children. Maybe she shouldn't have done it? Maybe she had had a brief period of light between two darknesses, long enough to condemn four others to perpetual gloom, before returning there herself? Why hadn't she listened to her fifteen-year-old self? Those violent forebodings hadn't been adolescent extravagances, they had been true warnings, as she had known at the time.

Nonsense, nonsense, she said to herself, turning in some discomfort. This is post-operative depression I am suffering from, and worry about poor Stephen.

She resolved to ring Stephen in the morning.

But still she couldn't get to sleep. Thoughts of her childhood, of the flat Midlands, obtruded. She thought of her visits to her grandmother, visits both dreaded and desired. She remembered stories of the great-uncle who had hanged the cat and then himself, of the distant cousin who had thrown himself under a train, of aunts in lunatic asylums and another ancient cousin who had tramped the country preaching the word until he was found dead in a ditch. Some said murdered, though it was never known. With such stories her grandmother would lighten the dark evenings, though she would never tell all: she always implied there was worse to tell, if she only could, if Hugh and Frances and Alice were only old enough to hear it. It had been such a fascinating mixture of morbidity and coziness, her grandmother's house. She wondered whether it was still standing.

After she had rung Stephen, she would leave her parents, and spend a few days in Tockley. Her children were all with their father for the week, while she convalesced. She would take herself off to the fens, and stay in a hotel, and visit all the old places, and find out what it was that was worrying her. Maybe it was nothing. Maybe the old blackbird would flap off on its dirty old wings if she went to catch it.

Morbid, morbid, said Frances to herself, as she curled up
more comfortably, her hand tucked between her legs, ceasing
to finger the irritating stitches. She felt better already. The
prospect of action always cheered her up.

As Frances Wingate sat in a first-class carriage (her car was
in service) on the way to Tockley, her second cousin Janet
Bird (née Ollerenshaw) pushed her baby and her pram along
Tockley High Street.

They had never met, and were not yet to meet.

Frances Wingate had not been to Tockley for many years—
she could not remember how many. Her grandfather had died
when she was fourteen, and her grandmother ten years later,
but she had been out of the country at the time and had not
been to the funeral. In fact, after her grandfather's death she
had hardly visited Tockley at all, she now remembered guiltily: the place had begun to weigh on her adolescent spirits,
she could no longer stand the slow pace, the solitude, the
emptiness, the very things which had charmed her as a small
child, and her grandmother had turned odd and crabby, even
more short-tempered than she had been when younger, even
more given to disconcerting attacks and long silences.

She thought of it, then as now, as "going to Tockley," but
the house wasn't really in Tockley: it was about six miles
out, a distance that had then seemed enormous, as it had to
be negotiated by a bus. The town was a medium-sized ordinary provincial town, with much light industry: it was
easy enough to get to, but it was the kind of place one
goes through, rather than stops at. Frances had booked herself into the King's Head, a British Rail hotel, because it
was next to the station, and because her guidebook said it was
well run and that the food was acceptable. She looked out of
the window and wondered what she remembered of the town.
Little, she thought. It hadn't meant much to her grandparents: they went there once a fortnight, to shop, depending
otherwise on the shop in the nearest village, and on their own
produce. There was a famous church, rising out of the flat

plain, a landmark for miles: her guidebook gave it a star and a glowing description, but she didn't remember that she had ever been in it. She remembered, vaguely, the wool shop, the shoe shop, Woolworth's. It had probably all changed by now.

The cottage, too, had probably changed. She remembered it with a peculiar intensity. It had been the one fixed point in her childhood, for her parents had been itinerant, constantly moving as they climbed the academic ladder of promotion— five years here, three years there, had been the pattern. Granny Ollerenshaw, in the cottage, had been immovable, unchanged and unchanging. They called it Eel Cottage: over the doorway there was a square which announced EEL, 1779. For years Frances had thought that the eel was the eel of the fens and ditches: only later, looking more closely, did she consider that the mysterious and evocative word must have represented the builder or owner's initials. The cottage was a basic cottage, the kind that children draw: low, a door in the middle, two windows with small panes downstairs, two windows with small panes upstairs. It was in red brick, the brick of the district, with a red-tiled fluted roof. There were no rose bushes on either side of the door; though there were plenty in the fields behind, for it was a good district for roses, as for other things. On either side was a long low red-roofed barn: behind and around stretched fields and greenhouses. It stood a little back from the road, in the middle of nowhere in particular, alone, with a strange look of basic survival as well as basic shape about it. It looked old, part of the land- scape, and yet in some way uncertain and pathetic, as though the landscape would never really accept it. In the front garden was a large notice, which said NURSERY GARDEN *Please call at house for,* and then would follow a list of seasonal treats: stick beans, peas, cut flowers (tulips, gladioli, daffodils), apples, pears, lettuce, marrows. It was a paradise for chil- dren.

Perhaps the uneasiness of the landscape sprang from the fact that it was all reclaimed land. Its very fertility was un- natural. The country needed drainage, and it was crossed and crossed again by dikes and ditches, sometimes many feet deeper than the land surface, sometimes, frighteningly, banked higher than the fields. If man did not cherish it, the earth would sink beneath the sea, as the Romans had sunk beneath the Midlands marshes: bits of Roman pot sunk into the marsh were forever being unearthed by local ploughmen. Not for nothing was a neighboring district called after Holland. Frances remembered being enthralled and terrified, as a child, by stories of Dutch courage: the boy with his finger in the hole in the dike, Hans Brinker and the silver skates, and just beyond the raging water. A small tilt of the earth's surface and everything would be swamped and disappear forever. She and Alice had been frightened, on the car journey from Oxford, or Leeds, or Bristol: the car (a small Austin) had seemed so low, the country so flat, the ditches so deep, the banks so high, the cabbages so huge. And then, at Eel Cottage, one reached safety: one went into the small low rooms where the paraffin lamps glowed and the small panes shut out the darkness, one went into a small-scale human world, with pot plants instead of shrub-sized cauliflowers, with knick-knacks and sewing boxes and souvenirs and proximity. It was a tiny cottage: her father, not a tall man, banged his head on the door frames, and her mother would fill the living room with her presence when she sat on the immensely decayed, patched, and cat-filled couch. She never sat there for long: she would never stay the night. There wasn't room for her.

The children would stay there alone. For Frances, at first, it was like paradise, like the original garden. She was fascinated by the garden itself, and would hang around helping while her grandfather, a fat round man with check trousers and boots and muddy fingernails and a mustache, would dig, or hoe, or sow, or mutter to himself. She sprayed insects, dug up weeds, picked tomatoes. It was a little business, just enough to live on nicely. It supplied various local greengrocers and florists, and did a little passing trade at the door. Frances adored the passing trade, and would wait passionately for the moment when her grandfather would be out in the field, and her gran in the orchard hanging out the washing, so that she could rush importantly to answer the bell, to weigh out a pound of tomatoes or sell a bunch of tulips. She would often be given a sixpence for her trouble, which she pocketed with pleasure, though there was nothing in the neighborhood to spend it on except more tomatoes or more dahlias. Hugh, for some reason which she could never discover, didn't like answering the bell: he would hide in the shed if anyone called. He spent most of his time there, in fact, reading books: Dickens, Walter Scott, Shakespeare, the *Reader's Digest*, whatever the cottage had to offer. Alice didn't like serving either: she would slink off, then slink back enviously as Frances collected her sixpence. Sometimes she crept back just in time to get a penny herself, which always annoyed Frances: a sign of weakness of character, she thought, to want to get something for nothing.

Alice was dead now, and Hugh a grandfather.

There had been other pleasures. The very ditches, which seemed so unnatural and threatening elsewhere, were a source of delight when close enough to the safety of the cottage. There was one at the end of the potato field (new potatoes clinging like little white marbles to their delicate network of hairy roots, even Gran, normally lazy and cross, would sometimes take the trouble to wash them and scrape them, boil them and butter them and exclaim on their flavor)—it was a deep one, steep-sided, and utterly private. Frances remembered the sides of it as being ten feet tall, a dangerous descent, but she had herself been small at the time. She would slip off there alone, when bored with helping, or when Gran shouted at her once too often: Clear off, bugger off, Gran would yell every now and then at her gently nutured grandchildren, an instruction which both shocked and thrilled them. And Hugh would disappear with a book, Alice would wheedle around till she was in favor, and Frances would make for the ditch.

It was full of creatures. Its flora varied from section to

section: some bits were chocked with duckweed, bright green and thick and scummy, others were clear, with forget-me-nots, and pale yellow comfrey, and even bits of watercress. Canadian pondweed grew in the water: purple spikes and poppies and ragwort and teasels grew on the banks. In the spring there were celandines and cowslips. It was untouched, undisturbed, and the water, over the yellow mud, was clear and cold. Frances often drank from it, and found it delicious. The animals that lived in the ditch were as varied as the flora, though more evenly distributed: there were water boatmen, large beetles, tadpoles, frogs, minnows, stickleback, grubs, caddis larvae, water rats, newts, a whole unnecessary and teeming world of creation. Frances, a speculative child, would lie there on her stomach with her face against the frontier of the water and peer for hours and hours, wondering what God had bothered to make it all for, and pondering on the origin of species; coming near at times to an apprehension of a real answer: God had done it all for fun, for joy, for excitement in creation, for variety, for delight. Why seek to justify? There it all was. One year there was a plague of frogs, there were millions of them everywhere, something had gone wrong with nature's regulations, they got into the fields and all over the back yard and into the house, and Gran nearly went mad beating them to death with the broom, poor little hopping tadpoles, Gran hated nature, and no wonder, she had to keep it at bay, or it would be in under the doors and through the cracks in the bricks, oozing like flood water, irresistible, spoiling her little dry haven.

Frances liked the newts best. They were elusive, and therefore something of a sign of favor. One day she had gone down there, in tears over some trivial row with Hugh, and had found several of the small ancient special creatures, floating on the surface, their little arms outstretched, taking the sun. Breathless, quiet, she sat there and watched them. They were surely a sign to her, a blessing. They floated there, green-gray, pink-bellied, frill-backed, survivors from a world of prehistory, born before the Romans arrived, before the bits of bronze-age pot sank in the swamp, remembering in their tiny bones the great bones of the stegosaurus, a symbol of God's undying contract with the earth. They floated with an intense pleasure: she felt it herself, in the warm sun. And then, suddenly, silently, with one accord, they sank, swimming downward with their small graceful limbs, leaving bubbles to rise behind them from the depths. She had been left on the bank. But did not forget them.

She had always wanted to see an eel. There were eels, she knew, but she never saw one. It was her one failure.

In the end, things had changed: inevitably, she supposed. It wasn't exactly an angel with a flaming sword that had expelled her: nor was it, as she had at one Freudian stage assumed, simply the sins of sex, though she had in fact reached puberty at Eel Cottage one hot summer, to her terror and alarm, miles from sanitary belts and sanitary towels, nearly a year earlier than most of her contemporaries, and unable to confide in crosspatch Gran, who, she was sure, had never heard of such a thing. In the end, weeping bitterly, appalled by the rust-colored guilty stain, she had told Hugh, and he, noble boy that he was, had borrowed Grandad's bike and cycled into Tockley for her and bought the things. She had always loved Hugh for that, and had also been forced to recognize that she couldn't have been all that neurotic about sex if she had managed to confide in him about such a matter. He had often thanked her for the opportunity to prove himself a hero: always rather dashing in his own sexual exploits, he had been delighted by this early chance to show his courage. (He had been fifteen at the time: she, twelve.) In fact, one of the amusing aspects of life at the Eel had been the fact that she and Hugh had been allowed, indeed compelled, to share a bedroom, and there late at night they would discuss such subjects as atom bombs, homosexuality, procreation, contraception, masturbation, and love, while Alice slept or pretended to sleep: Hugh would quote to Frances Shakespeare's sonnets (there really was rather a dearth of reading matter at the cottage, and by the age of fifteen Hugh had been through it all several times, though he always refused to import much, for to him the Eel reading matter was as special as, for Frances, were the Eel newts)—and they would discuss Shakespeare, and whether he was or wasn't a homosexual. Hugh took the line that he was clearly bisexual: Frances tended, even at that early age, to defend her sex by claiming that the sonnets to the young man (W.H., or H.W., or whoever he was) were clearly not written from the heart, whereas those to the dark lady were hot with unwilling passion. She could get quite cross about it at times.

So it can't have been wholly the fact of sexual development that spoiled her stays at the cottage. Perhaps it was somehow connected with growing large, for the rooms began to seem cramped and pokey, instead of deep and comfortable: she too, a tall girl, would occasionally hit her head going through a door. Or maybe her grandmother's temper really had deteriorated. Her grandfather fell ill, two years before he died, and became slower and slower and quieter and quieter, delegating most of his work to two lads from the next village who came in to help him: one of them was simple, and would stand for hours leaning on a spade gazing vacantly and dribbling, and the other could not really manage on his own, though he tried. The garden went to seed: first one patch was left, then another. Nobody bothered to dig up the new potatoes or to plant carrots. Even the fruit trees seemed to be growing old, for each year they produced fewer plums, fewer pears, fewer apples, and what they did produce was left to the wasps and the birds. Grandfather kept the flowers going, and the tomatoes; because they were his favorites, and they were nearer to the house, but bit by bit the garden frayed around its outer edges: the ditches grew over, the fields were overgrown, the spinach leaped into trees then withered into yellow decay. Nobody talked about what would happen when Grandfather died: at home, once, Frances heard her father say that they were all right, his parents, they'd got quite a bit put away, but it seemed depressing to her, just the same. The one good thing about those last years was that, toward the end, Gran let her husband have a dog. She had always hated dogs, and swore she would never have one in the house: she was a cat lover herself, and sometimes filled the house with as many as eight cats. Then, suddenly, eighteen months before the end, she got rid of the cats. Just like that. Her favorite cat, the matriarch, died, and she sent the boy off with the others to shoot them or drown them. Frances never dared to ask which he had done, for she had liked the cats, and was horrified by this brutal act of treachery. And then she let her husband have a dog.

It was a little yellow puppy: Frances saw it when it was very small. Her grandfather would hobble along, immensely fat by now, leaning on his stick, and the silly little dog would trail after him: every now and then he would gently garner it with his stick, when it strayed away. He talked to it with pride. In the evenings, it sat on his knee, and it would lap hot tea out of his saucer. Gran watched all this sourly, and said nothing. Frances, of an age now to be sentimental, was deeply moved by the thought that this man had all his life wanted a dog—when she was little, he had told her about the dogs of his childhood—and had had to wait like this, till the end. The big man and the little pup made her want to cry, but no tears came. She had wept over the dead cats.

When her grandfather died, visits to the cottage became a duty rather than a pleasure. Her grandmother refused to move, and lived on there alone. Frances, deep in school life, emotional entanglements, the classics, adolescence, nearly died of boredom while she was there. Her grandmother had developed so great a grudge against life that there was nothing left to discuss with her. The world was made up of villains and liars, the shopkeepers were out to ruin her, the income tax plagued her, the post office persecuted her, her own son neglected her, the radio and the television annoyed her. She lived out of tins, and on sliced bread from the traveling baker: she never ate a vegetable or a leaf of salad. Sometimes Frances would slip out furtively into the fields and dig, but all she found were huge old potatoes full of

worms and eyes, or carrots like wood. Gran refused to do
anything about the place: refused to sell up, refused to have
it taken over. Here I live and here I die, she would say mo-
rosely, when propositioned. She kept the tomatoes going,
after a fashion, though panes of glass would fall in and lie
unreplaced for months. To her horror, Frances now found
herself hating to serve passing customers: she felt it was
beneath her dignity to sell tomatoes, she blushed deeply when
inoffensive passers-by asked if she was the little girl they'd
seen years ago, when they asked where her grandad was,
when they looked with surprise around the derelict gardens.
She had grown used, at home, to seeing herself as a customer, not as a supplier: the charm of playing shop had faded,
to be replaced by a deadly threat. One of the most humiliating memories of this period was a day when a car drew up:
a middle-aged couple got out, with their two teenage children, all smiles and friendliness, he in shorts, she in a flowery dress, the children shy and hanging back. They were on
their way home from holiday on the coast, could they have
some tomatoes and some vegetables, and what was there in
the way of fruit? Embarrassed, Frances weighed out tomatoes, and explained that there was nothing else. The pleasant
red-faced man looked round (Dutch, he looked, like many
people in this region) and said, oh, dear, what a pity, what
had happened? Where's your grandad? he said, I knew him
well, I always stop for a chat.

He's dead, said Frances, knowing she should have put it
more politely.

Oh, dear, oh, dear, oh, dear, said the man. "And what
about your gran, then? She still here?"

"Yes," said Frances.

"You've come to look after her then?" he said, and Frances nodded, and then, realizing that he might mean permanently, forever, shook her head violently, thinking with
longing of Horace and Ovid, of Sappho and Sophocles, of
lipstick and cinemas, of pavements and Marks and Spencers.

"Is your gran there?" said the man. "I'd better have a word."

Frances didn't know how to say that he'd better not have a word, and she stood there immobile, unable to prevent him from striding over to the door and banging on it and swinging it open.

"You there, Mrs. Ollerenshaw?" he yelled, making the cottage and all its bits and pieces jangle.

Gran emerged, sullenly, from the back regions, wiping her hands on her apron. "What's that, then?" she said. "What's all this noise, then?"

"It's me, Mrs. Ollerenshaw. You'll remember me, I used to call by every year, we missed last year. . . ."

"Don't remember yer," she said, and turned away.

He called after her, offering sympathy, but she had gone into the kitchen: stood there muttering and cursing, for all the world, thought Frances, like an old witch.

The man had been as upset as Frances.

"She's taken it bad," he said, and to her horror he pressed into her hand a ten-bob note. She tried desperately to thrust it back, but failed. "You buy yourself something pretty, cheer yourself up," he said. And off he went, red from shame and from the East Coast sun, ashamed of his kindness.

Frances nearly tore the note up, but in the end she kept it and bought herself some nylon stockings.

In those later days, the poor yellow dog led a dog's life. Gran kept it and hated it. It wasn't pretty any more, it was just an ordinary dog. It didn't go out into the fields to escape, as it could have done: it hung around the kitchen, tripping Gran up and waiting to be kicked. When Frances visited, she would try to take it for walks, but it was hard to shift. It preferred to stick around at home, in the memory of its glorious infancy. She didn't suppose it could really remember. She hoped it couldn't. She hoped it liked being kicked. It seemed to, after all.

* * *

The cottage, of course, might have been pulled down, thought Frances, as the train drew into Tockley station. I might have come all this way for nothing. She couldn't even remember who had bought it: it and the land had been sold up separately, she thought.

There was the gas works, the river, the church spire, the factory chimneys. Her heart beat rather noisily, and her stomach churned.

The hotel was just across the yard from the station entrance; square, yellow-brick, three-star, Victorian, reassuring. She carried her bag and her typewriter over, registered herself, went up to her twin-bedded room, sat on the bed. It was lunchtime. She would have some lunch, then in the afternoon she would brace herself to go for a walk.

Lunch was something called Eggs Joinville, which turned out to be half a hardboiled egg in pink sauce with three shrimps on it, then salmon mayonnaise (quite nice, fresh salmon at least) and then a piece of Stilton so old and green and salty and crystalline that it was quite a pleasure in itself, though hardly a Stilton-type pleasure. It was dark green and brown, a rich bruised ripe dead color. They were quite near Stilton, here, they could surely have found her a better piece. The dining room was hushed like a church, and only one other couple was lunching: an elderly couple who did not speak. Frances read her notes on her own footnotes to her own book on trans-Saharan trade, edition two: she was supposed to be bringing them up to date. After lunch, feeling rather tired, she went back to her bedroom and took her shoes off and fell asleep. When she woke up, it was half-past three. She sat up quickly, put her shoes back on, and set off.

She half wished she had the car, but knew that her purpose, obscure as it was, could not have been accomplished with one, so she set off on foot, through the town center, thinking that if she got tired she could catch a bus. The doctors had told her to take it easy, but not even they could object to her plodding along at an even pace along these exceedingly even streets.

The town had changed. Some of the old shops were still there, but those that remained looked shabby and full of old useless bits: only Elfrida Maple, a little dress shop that sold autumnal suits and felt hats, was unchanged. Even her suits and her hats were unchanged. But nearly everything else had gone. There were two new enormous supermarkets, filling a street each: Woolworth's had rebuilt itself into a characteristic tall blank-back-walled factory building, all the banks except the dignified Midland had new plate-glass modern frontages. Instead of tea shops there were Wimpy Bars, dirty coffee shops and sandwich bars, a Chinese restaurant. A cake shop, showing faintly regional cakes, remained, and a butcher or two had hung on, with windows full of pork pies and home-made brawn and faggots and plastic parsley. A whole street full of shops was empty and derelict, awaiting demolition: notices on the doors said that new branches would be opening shortly in the Holland Shopping Centre. But what struck her most of all was the number of estate agents, building societies, investment societies, banks, central heating firms, and lighting firms that filled the best positions in the main streets. Had they always been there, and had she as a child never thought to register their names—the Norwich, the Leeds, the Loughborough, the Peterborough, the Leicester, the Lincoln, the Tockley, the Bradford and Bingley? What were they all doing, what was it all about, what was all this building and money, why had she never noticed it before? And it was a time, too, when building societies were desperately short of cash: the interest rate and the bank rate had never been higher. How had they managed to fill the whole of Tockley High Street with their gleaming panes?

She felt slightly ill, as she walked along, and decided she would have to visit the ladies' lavatory in the coach station. Her stomach felt upset; it was heaving ominously. She wondered whether it was nerves: nervousness often went straight to her guts. It was too soon for it to have been the Station Hotel shrimps, but it could have been the peculiar veal from the night before. It had been a very odd meal, the meal at

High Table; the college, being a new one, appeared to have a policy of fine living, which manifested itself in extremely expensive modern china and silver and glass, and pretentious cooking the like of which she had never sampled. Elaborate dish had followed elaborate dish, but the curious thing about the courses was that there was something wrong with each of them. The fish soup, for instance, though excellent, was tepid, the rolls were dry, the piece of smoked trout was served with wilted lettuce, and the veal, with its accompaniment of strangely carved tomatoes, tinned asparagus, ice-cream-shaped potatoes and cheese, had been tough. It had been rather depressing to see so much effort put to so little effect. She had felt sorry for her parents, but they assured her later that they didn't eat in Hall often.

It might well have been the veal. Or possibly the fish soup. She reached the lavatory in time, feeling shocking: her bowels had turned to water. At least, she thought with relief, I know it's not cholera, and very unlikely to be typhoid: salmonella at the worst. Or maybe simply fear.

The lavatory was unmodernized. It stank. Pools of water lay on the concrete floor, there was no toilet paper, the door was covered with graffiti, boys' names, drawings of cocks and balls, sad declarations. *Here am I,* declared one of them, *Sally Prince, I'll do it any time.* Boredom stank in the dark stall. The walls were of a peculiarly nasty dark-red granite and concrete chip mix: in other circumstances she could imagine herself admiring the texture in porphyry or marble. As there was no toilet paper, she had to choose between using her last Kleenex and an unused airmail letter: she used the airmail letter. She felt much better as she emerged: her guts, though responsive, were also efficient, and she hoped that that would be that.

The coach station was much the same. So were the coaches. Single-decker, green and red, Eastern Counties. She toyed with the idea of walking the six miles, decided it would be silly when she wasn't feeling too good, and went to the bus stop, resolving to get off a few stops before the cottage, so she could approach it on foot. In fact, she would get off at the village before. She felt embarrassed about the nature of her expedition, afraid she would be caught out, almost afraid that somebody might recognize her.

She had remembered the route well, but it was utterly, utterly changed. Nothing was left as it had been. Landmarks had disappeared, new ones in the form of garages and discount stores had risen. And, to her mounting dismay, she realized that there was no country left. The whole road was built up, lined with houses. In the old days, it had taken five minutes to get out of the town, right out, into a dull but rural country. Now, it seemed, there was no country. After a quarter of an hour they were still driving through semidetached houses, bungalows, and estates: where country roads had once led off the main road there were sign posts saying EASTERN INDUSTRY, INDUSTRIAL ESTATE, PRIESTMAN'S PLANT. By the time they had reached the village of Hesley, they had not passed a single field. And there was only a mile to go to Eel Cottage.

Frances got out and sat down in the bus shelter. She should have known it was going to be like this: things always were like this. She had known. This was what she had feared. What had she expected, some untouched corner of Britain, a rustic paradise, unreached by road and supermarket and overpopulation? The town was thriving, anyone could see, it was expanding. One ought, almost, to be pleased: the fields of cabbage and spinach and onion had been depressing too, in their own way. Let the people choose. Agricultural wages were at subsistence level, no life was grimmer than tilling the soil.

She thought of the tomatoes and the new potatoes and the waist-high grasses by the ditch. She stood up, to walk on. She almost hoped the cottage had been pulled down, to make way for developers.

But in the last mile, things improved, slightly. The bungalows thinned out making way for undeveloped building plots covered with brown dock and thistle and bramble and groundsel: flights of small birds rose from the dry stalks as she passed. Eventually, she reached a field. It was full of onions. The smell, pungent, cressy, green, violent, rose all around. The air was full of triumphant onion. After all, one cannot do without the onion, she said to herself. A few houses later there was another field, containing black bean stalks, then another, with stubble. The houses had come to an end, and still she had not reached the cottage. Her heart rose, it was reprieved.

The road was so flat that one could not see far ahead: there were no perspectives in this district. She came upon it almost unexpectedly: it had always been unexpected, like that, slightly hidden by a large tree on the wayside. It was still there. She stood, at a safe distance, and looked at it, wondering if she would have the courage to go and knock on the door: whoever had it would surely remember the Ollerenshaws, and let her in. If that was what she wanted. She wasn't sure what she wanted, or why she had come, but her heart was quick, the shape of the roof and the windows and the big tree, so long unseen, so often imagined in her inward eye was calling up some corresponding pattern in her mind, its lines were the lines of memory, a shorthand carving, like the graph of her heart or brain, like the points of its movements. There, that shape, imperfectly remembered, and yet perfectly there: an electrocardiogram of her childhood, a map of her past. The angle of roof and window, the shapes of the sheds, the colors of the tiles. Sick with excitement, faint with emotion, she went on: but there was no need to knock, for on the nursery garden notice—the same one, unchanged after ten years, a good solid wooden notice—there was another notice, saying *Gone on Holiday, back end of July.*

So even the garden was still there. There were still tomatoes. She paused, on the roadway, and looked around: there might be somebody here, they would have had to leave somebody looking after the produce, one can't just leave a garden, as her grandfather had said many a time, with happy submission. (He didn't like moving: once he went to London and came back on the next train, because he thought he'd forgotten to water the new seedlings. He hadn't forgotten to water them, of course.) But there seemed to be nobody there. She went up the garden path, past the notice, and tapped on the door, just in case. Nobody answered. She peered through the small windows. There were still pots of plants on the windowsills, as there always had been: ferns, cacti, flowering plants. She couldn't see into the rooms, it was too dark. The front lawn was as tidy as it had been in her grandfather's day, far tidier than in her grandmother's, and the barn walls had been newly painted. She could have wept with relief: there were tears in her eyes.

Growing more confident, she went around the side of the house to the back. The greenhouses were in good repair. Beyond them, she could see a field of roses, a field of cabbage. There were changes—there was a new garage (the Ollerenshaws had never had a car), and the old pump had gone. There was a plastic gyrating clothesdryer in the orchard, and a sandpit in a corner of the yard, and a new swing. So they had children. For some reason she was surprised, she had thought of the cottage's inhabitants as inevitably old. She peered through the kitchen window, into that room which with its blackened range and white deal table and cats had been a source of so much misery and ancestral joy, and she saw that it was changed. The range had gone, and a new red Aga stood in its place. The floor, which had been stone in her day, covered with ants and peg rugs, was now done in Marley tiles. There was a new dresser, replacing the shelves of her gran, and on the dresser plates and cups and—she peered harder—yes, books. She could not say why she was surprised to see books.

The white deal table was still there. Somebody had liked it, and kept it.

There was nothing else to be seen through the windows: she wondered if she dared set off through the fields and look at the ditch. There was nobody to stop her, she was harming nobody.

The walk to the ditch was less reassuring. Some of the land had clearly been sold off when the house was sold: she could tell that the farmer who owned the property on the right, a man whom her grandfather had always disliked for no known reason (perhaps merely because he was a neighbor) had got hold of the two fields he had always wanted, for they were now ploughed into his own, and a new ditch had been dug to cut them off. (It was a land without hedges.) And on the left, things were even worse. Her favorite ditch, which had run parallel to the road behind the whole property, turned finally toward the village behind: and as she approached the ditch, she could see that the village had spread to meet the main road. Like Tockley itself, it had overflowed. She couldn't believe it—a hamlet like Hussey, to overflow? There had been nothing there in her day except a few cottages, the big house, an empty church, a duckpond, and a hairdresser. Whoever would want to live in Hussey? Why on earth should Hussey flow along Back Lane to Eel Cottage?

Anxious for her ditch, she made her way through the cabbages, tripping in the deep dry ruts. It was a dry summer. The cabbages were gray and silver, and clouds of white butterflies rose from them at her approach. Perhaps the new Eel people were organic farmers and didn't believe in killing caterpillars. She recalled her happy days with the spray gun in the greenhouse, the lovely afternoon when they had smoked the ants out of the kitchen with a rag soaked in gasoline.

The ditch was still there, but she could tell before she was close enough to peer into it that its prime days were over. There was a building site just on the other side of it, with concrete mixers and signs and heaps of bricks, where once there had been another pure and endless field of cabbages. Knowing the worst already, but unable to see, owing to the lie of the land, until the last moment, she climbed over the small ridge before the descent into the ditch, and saw what she had feared. A thick oily scum covered the water: bits of paper, fag ends, Coca-Cola bottles, an old tire, a chunk of polystyrene, and a car seat floated in it. Bubbles, not from fish or newts, but from some invisible putrescence rose to the surface. There was still, surprisingly, a little greenery: a patch of slimy duckweed, a slippery moss. And that was that. Ah well, never mind, she said to herself, one could hope for no better. And she climbed out of the ditch, and went on to Hussey, to see what was going on in the new metropolis.

Nothing much was going on there, it appeared. There were some new houses, some new shops, a garage. Back Lane had been widened into a road. There were babies in prams in gardens, old men taking dogs for walks. It was much the same as it had been in her own day, but bigger: the people had the same faces, the same voices. It wasn't even Hussey translated into a commuter's suburb. It was simply Hussey up to date. Frances began to feel ashamed of her conserva- tionist notions, as she watched two young mothers, babies on their hips, talking over their hedge on their brand-new lawns in front of their brand-new picture-windowed houses (one could see right through the houses, into the flat fields behind), by their brand-new goldfish ponds. In her day, only Colonel Blake at Hinkley had had a goldfish pond, and it had been a wonder of the district.

Still, it was a pity about the scum on the ditch.

She walked through the village, thinking of her grandpar- ents and of their circumscribed lives. Had her grandmother wanted more, was that why she had been so sour? And what had they made of her father's success? They never spoke of it much, and had dealt with her mother's superiority by ig- noring it, in a manner that Frances at the time had found natural, and now found wholly admirable. Unruffled, they had fed her on strong tea and kippers: they had turned a deaf ear to her requests for coffee. They had listened blankly at her mannered praise of fresh vegetables and duck eggs (they had had a duck-keeping phase) and plied her with biscuits and cake. Thinking back, Frances remembered how she had loved the diet, and how incredibly greedy she had been all her life, a most undignified failing in a woman. What a fool she had made of herself over meals, at times. She wondered what the Station Hotel would provide for dinner. The salmon had really been very nice. What a miracle that she wasn't monstrously fat. Though of course she could survive on nothing, as she had proved, and had a capacity like a camel for doing without drink, except in the most appalling heat.

She recognized somebody in Hussey, but was not recognized in turn. It was the village postmistress, now no doubt long retired: a little bent woman of infinite gentility, with a voice so faint that one had had to stand on tiptoe to catch it. She was wearing the same long black suit that she had always worn in Frances's childhood, but she had a new hat. Her black buttoned shoes looked the same, and not unlike the pair that Frances herself was wearing. The wheel comes full circle. A little further on, on the far outskirts of now monstrously inflated Hussey (grown from forty souls to four hundred) she saw another familiar face: it was Mr. Bazeley, who had worked at the big seed merchants' in Tockley, and who had called at her grandparents' for tea regularly, every Sunday afternoon. She remembered those teas. They had said little, the three of them: they had sat in companionable silence, the two men smoking, Gran sewing, drinking cups of strong tea and eating pieces of home-made custard tart and rock cakes and fairy cakes and fruitcake. (After, Gran had taken to buying everything from the traveling baker.) When she was small, Frances had thought this silence quite acceptable. Why should they talk, and what about? Later, she had thought it horrible, and had writhed with misery during the event, sweating with fear lest one of the odd remarks should be addressed to her. (Literally sweating, for she had sweated much during adolescence, to add to its other inconveniences.) Yet later, on her last visit before Gran's death, when she had found loyal aging fifty-year-old bachelor Mr. Bazeley, still loyal, still there, still sitting it out with his cups of poisonous tea, she had taken another line. She had studied her anthropology by then, she knew about primitive societies, kinship, social networks, nonverbal communication.

And therefore, now, she greeted him with a smile. "Hello," she said, extending her hand, "you won't remember me, I'm Frances Ollerenshaw, you used to come to tea with my grandparents."

And his weathered red-veined face lit with certain recollection, and they stood there painfully for a few moments, exchanging platitudes. Yes, she said, she was married now: yes, she had four children. And how was he? Retired now? Was he enjoying it? Not much to do? But surely he had always had plenty to do, in the district. What was she doing here? Just looking around a little. Yes, that's right, for old times' sake. Yes, it was changed. A lot of new buildings. Nice for the young people.

"I miss your gran," said Mr. Bazeley, digging his stick into the turf: but he said it flatly, dully. How could she know whether he spoke with passion, with loss, with respect, with duty? He spoke a foreign language, the signs of which she could read less well than the signs of a Punic inscription or a Latin text.

"She reached a good age, though," said Frances.

"Yes," he said, brightening slightly. "Eighty-two. A fair age."

"And the new people at Eel Cottage," she dared to ask. "How long have they been there? Do you know them?"

His face darkened. A rum couple, was all that he would say. She had known it, somehow. Triumphant at her own reading of signs and portents (here thwarted with Mr. Bazeley) she knew that she had known it.

He asked after her parents, she was able to tell him that she had seen them alive and well the night before, which made her feel ultrarespectable, as though in fact there might have been something not quite respectable involved in wandering around alone in a Lincolnshire lane, like a tramp, as though she needed the stamp of respectability: and so they parted, cordially. She was glad she had spoken.

She had to move on, though she had been intending to turn back, because she was afraid of overtaking him. He was aging and walked slowly, with his stick. She had to walk on briskly, as though that was what she had intended, though she was feeling tired and the road led to nowhere. Past the last two buildings she went—a chapel, closed forever, and a school once closed but now, apparently, with the new growth of population, reopened. Beyond lay nothing but fields. How far would she have to walk, before she dared return without fear of encountering once more Mr. Bazeley? She thought of the Station Hotel and its solid comforts. She would have a bath, when she got back, and write up those notes, or some of them at least.

She was about to turn back, judging that she had let enough time pass, when she saw ahead of her a sight that drew her forward. It was a field full of people, and the vision of it flashed across her unprepared eye, shaking her in a way that she could not comprehend. A field full of people, only women and children, in a bare ploughed field. Stooping and bending under the large sky. They had baskets, they were filling the baskets. What were they doing, in that bare field? There were no crops, there was nothing. Small children stooped, women in head scarves stooped, like an ancestral memory. She shivered as she drew nearer, and her first impression dispelled itself—for of course, they were ordinary women and children gathering stones, and when she leaned on the gate and asked the nearest what they were doing, they said they were clearing the new school playing field, and she could see that that was what they were doing, and that they were enjoying it—it was a voluntary effort, a communal effort, and the children were nicely dressed and the women were exchanging jokes as they worked. Why then had she seen something quite different? For what she had seen had been an image of forced labor, of barrenness, of futility, of toil, of women and children stooping for survival, harvesting nothing but stones. The big field stretched aimlessly, the people at the far reaches looked small and aimless. Shivering, she went back and caught the bus to Tockley.

On the way back to the hotel, she called in at the museum.

Forlornly it represented culture amidst the Building Society windows: she needed it, after the stones and the potatoes. It had been done up since her day. There was still the same collection of Roman coins and pots, the same old bones, but they had been put in new cases with new charts, and re-labeled. And there was a whole new section, a sign of the cultural times, devoted to agricultural implements and ar-chaeology, with photographs and reconstructions and exhib-its. The most interesting exhibit, to Frances, was a thing called an eel stang. It was a black pronged fork, and staring at it, she felt the same shiver as she had felt watching the bare field. Something is the matter with me, she thought, her teeth chattering. Flu again, or salmonella. The label attached to the eel stang said, or so she thought, that it was an imple-ment used for turning eels in ditches. At the description, she shivered again, and looked again, and saw that it said not turning, but trapping: it was a useful implement, for trapping eels. She felt an unaccountable relief. She had a vision, she had to admit it to herself, of old men pointlessly turning over eels in ditches in meaningless labor, just as those women and children in the field had appeared to her at first sight as an allegory of pointless rural toil. We dig, we plant, we reap, we dig again, and barely we survive. The thought made her feel ill. A man with an eel stang, like Wordsworth's leech gatherer, stood around portentously in her mind, aimlessly searching the ditches for eels to turn. He meant something to her, she had not conjured him from nothing, she had not misread that notice for nothing. What did he personify, that ancient laborer? She looked in horror at his black pronged fork, and turned away. She turned back to modernity and her bedroom's efficient plumbing.

She had a bath, and washed her jersey, and washed her hair, and then sat in front of her typewriter drying off. She squeezed the water out of her jersey very tightly, and piled it in a neat little heap on top of the bulb of the reading lamp, where it steamed gently, like a little household god. Then she looked at her notes and thought about primitive societies

and why she had become an archaeologist and what on earth
it was that she was trying to prove about the past. She felt as
though she had been visited by ghosts. Karel's special subject
was the history of agriculture in the eighteenth century, and
she had often talked about the matter with him—the whole
story of enclosures, of laborers' wages, of rural poverty, of
Captain Swing and peasants' revolts, she knew only through
him. She had often teased him about his interest in these
things, for he was the most urban of men, and could not tell
a turnip from a swede, or wheat from barley, and it had
seemed strange to find him so attached to the history of the
countryside. I am reclaiming the lost land of the Jew, he
would say. You should go to Israel, she would say, but he
would shake his head and say that he belonged to the cabbage
plots and mustard fields of Europe, for all that his father had
been a Jewish doctor and his mother a Polish journalist.

The primitive life appalled her. Why had she chosen to
struggle with it? Why had she chosen to divert her attention
from the Greeks and the Romans? Classical archaeology, the
praise of Western thought, would have been quite good
enough for her. She could have spent her time digging the
ditches of Norfolk and Lincolnshire for relics of Roman oc-
cupation, instead of confronting the problems of the Sahara.

The incense steamed upward from her jersey. She had to
turn it from time to time so it would not scorch, as the man
in her mind turned his eels. John Clare, she remembered,
had lived not too far from here. Karel had much admired the
poetry of John Clare. John Clare had gone mad, another case
of the Midlands sickness, but before his madness he had
deplored the loss of the commons and the death of moles, in
his great tenderness for the creation.

The pursuit of archaeology, she said to herself, like the
pursuit of history, is for such as myself and Karel a fruitless
attempt to prove the possibility of the future through the past.
We seek a utopia in the past, a possible if not an ideal society.
We seek golden worlds from which we are banished, they
recede infinitely, for there never was a golden world, there

was never anything but toil and subsistence, cruelty and dullness.

Ah, if I believed that, she said to herself. But we unearth horrors, and justify them. Child sacrifice we label benevolent birth control, a dull and endless struggle against nature we label communion with the earth. We see an Eskimo child drag a dead sea gull along a bleak beach by a piece of seal gut, and we praise its diverse customary joys.

A friend of hers, another archaeologist, had recently discovered unmistakable evidence that the civilization he had been investigating had, contrary to all previous suggestions, practiced cannibalism. He was still close enough to the discovery to admit that it had shocked him: the practices of a people centuries dead had shocked him, because he had invested them with his own values, he had learned to like them. In time, he said, I know I shall justify them. I will see why they did it, and why I am wrong to judge them. It is simply a question of investing five more years of thought.

What for, what for, said Frances to herself. What is it for, the past, one's own or the world's. To what end question it so closely.

Generations of her ancestors had gathered stones in those fields. Her grandfather had grown tomatoes and potatoes. Her father had studied newts and become a professor of zoology. And for herself, as a result of their labors, the world lay open. That was why she sat here, so comfortably, with a tumbler of brandy at her elbow, a portable typewriter in front of her, a choice of two single beds (odd, how they never seemed to have single rooms with baths in hotels these days), and a handy nylon jersey smoking by her side. Even her lumps were benign. Her spirits soared with the steam. The choice of two beds, both with clean sheets, was after all quite something.

Janet Bird née Ollerenshaw was pushing her pram along Tockley High Street. The fact that she was doing this, as she was some 23 pages ago, does not indicate that no time has passed since that last brief encounter. Nor does it indicate a desire on the part of the narrator to impose an arbitrary order or significance upon events. It is simply a fact that Janet Bird spent a great deal of time pushing her pram up and down Tockley High Street. She had not much choice. She had little else to do. One could, arguably, have picked her up at one or another of the various monotonous and repetitive tasks that filled her day, but she might as well be allowed some exercise. For she gets little.

It was now autumn. Nothing much had changed in Tockley in the last three months since Frances Wingate paid her pilgrimage. The coats and hats in Elfrida Maple's window were still autumnal in tint, the butchers still flourished plastic parsley, the Holland Shopping Precinct was not yet finished. The notices for evening classes, which had been up already when Frances Wingate née Ollerenshaw walked the same street in July, were still exactly where they had been, with the difference that they now applied to current, not future events. It was at one of these notices, in the Sportshop window, that Janet Bird was now staring. Her baby, three months older than on his last appearance, was sitting in his pram with two red fingers stuck in his mouth, rubbing his gum. He was teething, and from time to time seemed to be in great pain. Two white isolated pointed icebergs of teeth rose from the raw red bottom gum, and he sucked his fingers perpetually, making them wet and red and consequently, in the cold wind, chapped. She had tried to make him wear gloves, but gloves made him scream. He sucked miserably, while Janet read the notice for the twentieth time.

She was wondering whether to join a class on classical music, or a class on upholstery, or a class on bird-watching. It was strange that Tockley offered these things, but it offered them with some persistence. She did not really want to join an evening class at all. She was feeling too low to profit from an evening class, but she felt that if she did not join, her husband would be angry with her, and she was so tired of him being angry with her that she would do quite a lot to avoid it. But maybe not upholstery. Cookery she could have faced, but he would have thought that was stupid. And so it would have been, but she had almost ceased to mind how stupid she appeared.

The main reason why she did not want to go to an evening class was that she did not want either her husband or her mother to gain the moral advantage of baby-sitting for her. If she were to let either of them make any inroads on her misery, they would destroy her. Her only hope lay in total resistance. They must not be allowed to pity her or help her. She had dedicated her life to resistance, but her resistance must be both total and secret. On the other hand, it was possible to deceive them both, as she had already discovered—she could allow one or the other of them to baby-sit, while she went off to a course on sociology or the Russian novel, as long as she didn't actually enjoy herself while she was out. Perhaps, after all, that would be the best line. It would give Mark less opportunity to complain that she was turning into a cabbage, or whatever it was that he was complaining she was doing. As long as she didn't find herself actually enjoying herself, or taking an interest, she would be safe enough. And there was, after all, little likelihood of that.

She took the brake off the pram, and jerked it forward. The baby's fingers jerked out of his mouth, and he let out a despairing wail, then crammed them back in again, glaring at her reproachfully, with incommunicable distress. She stared back, not knowing what to do. Her regret was immense, but what was there to do about it? She could not even smile at him in his angry captive state. "There, there," she said, weakly. Her voice sounded very odd. Often she didn't speak to anyone all day except the baby and the people in the shops. I'll forget how to talk one of these days, she said to herself, as she set off home. She would give the baby a bit of biscuit when she got back, perhaps he would feel better with something to chew on. She didn't want him to be miserable. But what on earth could she do about his teeth?

On the way home, she wondered why she had ever got

married. She spent a good deal of each day wondering about this question, and as yet had come up with very little in the way of an answer. The answers that did from time to time float toward her, before floating off again, were too trivial as well as too unpleasant to grasp. Could she possibly have done it because her younger sister had just done it before her, and she was jealous? Such things did happen, she knew. Was it because her mother had put a bit of pressure on her? Was it because she couldn't think of any other way of getting away from her mother? Was it because she couldn't think of anything else in the world to do? She would scan the back pages of women's magazines for hints about her own behavior, but found little: there was some conspiracy afoot, to make people believe that marriage was necessary and desirable, and nobody seemed at all concerned to justify it, as though it needed no justification. Occasionally one of the more expensive and avant-garde of the women's magazines would suggest that there were other ways of doing things, but she could tell at once that the other ways would not have suited her, and that the kind of women who did the other things did not live in Tockley.

She never wasted time on wondering whether or not she had married Mark because she loved him. That would at least have simplified the issue. One could feel sorry for people who married in love and then fell out of love. It must happen quite frequently. Janet had seen it happen to her own acquaintances. No, her own case had been very different. She had certainly not loved Mark when she had agreed to marry him. She had been quite interested in him at one point, she admitted that much to herself—otherwise she wouldn't have gone out with him, would she? But as for love—she had always known that she hadn't loved him. Why on earth had she agreed to marry him?

Walking past Mason's, seeing the new displays of crockery and household goods in the windows, she had a twinge of shame, as she remembered how hard she had worked on making herself take an interest in wedding presents. What a crazy binge of objects a wedding produces. Insane. Tea sets, coffee sets, Pyrex dishes with different designs, fish knives, ironing boards, toasters, electric kettles, what kind of refrigerator, what color bedroom curtains. They had been quite distracting, the objects, they had taken her mind off Mark for days on end. (Frances Wingate, her oh so much cleverer cousin, had been a little taken up with the whole thing herself too, though she would never in a million years have admitted it. She had been particularly taken, when young, twenty-one and foolish, by a writing desk that her mother-in-law to be— now her ex-mother-in-law—had given her. She hadn't minded the Gallé vase, either. There is some tribal insanity that comes over women, as they approach marriage: society offers Pyrex dishes and silver teaspoons as bribes, as bargains, as anesthesia against self-sacrifice. Stuck about with silver forks and new carving knives, as in a form of acupuncture, the woman lays herself upon the altar, upon the couch, half numb. Even sensible women, like Frances Wingate: sensible women, who later struggle, as their senses return, and throw their Gallé vases and fish knives violently around their dwellings, as a protest.)

Mason's window was like an altar, a shrine to matrimony. So thought Janet Bird, as she walked past it, and thought of all the poor fools who would make their offerings, their purchases, who would receive coffee percolators and ice buckets and hot plates and pressure cookers, and then live forever disconsolate amidst their useless indestructible relics. Janet's closets (and she was a tidy woman, who had been married only four years) were already filled with unrepairable toasters and handleless nonstick frying pans.

Why did one let it all happen? She would have liked some kind of an explanation. But there was very little in the way of an explanation, in the streets of Tockley. Aided by a psychoanalyst, or even by a reading of Freud in his new Pelican edition, she might have been able to construct some kind of answer. But there were no psychoanalysts in Tockley. There was not even a bookshop that stocked Pelicans. And she wouldn't have understood the Freud, had she got hold of it. She was on her own, in a solitude that was so bleak that it was a thing on its own, almost a possession, almost company. She and the baby were in it together: at first she'd been afraid that he would have been on his own too, somewhere out there, but they shared the same envelope of darkness. It was a relief, to find that they constituted a unit, instead of two separate solitudes. She was not a natural mother: mothering did not come easily to her, for she was overanxious, overfastidious, she sterilized bottles too carefully, she read the baby book too often, she had no instinct for easy margins or leeways. The sight of the baby crawling on a less than spotless floor, or raising an unsterilized object to his mouth, would fill her with panic. But despite her apprehensions, she cared for him: he was her small powerless ally, and it was not him that she resented, from him there was no need to close herself away. He was an innocent victim of larger forces. And at the moment, the poor mite was miserable. His teeth hurt him, and she could not do nothing to help. He would wail all evening, while she tried to entertain Mark's colleagues, and felt inadequate, in all directions. She foresaw it all.

Perhaps she would buy some jelly for the baby's gums. It did no good, but it did no harm either. Even the book said it did no harm. She paused, in front of the drugstore, and then pushed on, to a larger, more anonymous self-service store further down the road, which had a drug department. She didn't like small shops, where one recognized the staff, and were recognized by them. She preferred larger places, like this one, with long counters and cash desks and cut prices, with its rapid turnover of assistants. Queueing at the cash desk, she watched peaky, undernourished little girls, in high platform shoes and ludicrously short skirts pushing trolleys around, restocking shelves: girls of sixteen, with tough, scrappy, vacant faces and pink and blue plastic shoes. And boys of sixteen, in overalls with long drooping hair, and thin lips. She ached, with either sympathy or envy for them: she was not sure which.

(Frances Wingate, watching these same girls and boys three months earlier, had reflected on the extraordinary style of the provinces: so avant-garde in some respects, so out of date in others. The short skirts had long vanished from the London scene, but the platform shoes had reached heights of exaggeration, in color and form, that none but the boldest would yet have dared to wear.)

Outside the church, Janet paused, and stared at the notice board, waiting idly for the church bells to strike. It was almost midday. There had been moments, when things had been bad, when she had thought of turning to the church for help. She could have joined a mother's group, now that she had a baby. She could speak to the vicar. The vicar must be used to problems such as hers. But what could he do about them? Nothing. He could not change Mark's nature, or her own nature, or Tockley, or their life in it, and without some change on that kind of scale she didn't see much hope. It was better, really, not to give in: to keep one's self to one's self. A vicar would wheedle one's misery away, minimize it, stroke it and soothe it, and leave her nothing in its stead, leave her ashamed and betrayed. Vicars and doctors were all the same, they told one it was natural to suffer from headaches and misery at puberty, to dread marriage, to feel ill and get cystitis when newly married, to dread pregnancy and feel ill and cry a lot when pregnant, to cry a lot with postnatal depression. It was all so natural.

She was tired of hearing that kind of thing. It hadn't done her much good. It had brought her here, to this full stop.

She read the church notice boards, as she had read the evening class notice boards. One leaflet invited her to a jumble sale, another to an evening with slides about a mission in India. A larger, more garish poster, with black print on a yellow ground, declared, "I will lift up mine eyes unto the hills: from whence cometh my help." There were of course no hills around here, and therefore no help: though she remembered being told in a modern Bible class at school that the lines didn't mean that help came from the hills at all, they should have been punctuated differently, thus: "I will lift up mine eyes unto the hills: from whence cometh my help?" As though it were the enemies that were to descend from the hills, and the Lord to save one from them. Either way, there was no Lord, and there were no hills. It was all of an even flatness. She would quite have liked to see the warriors descending from the mountains, rattling their sabers, aiming for her heart.

The church bells tolled. She looked up at the tall spire. It was an exceptionally beautiful church, or so she had been informed since she was a small child, by local schoolteachers and local papers. Once she had climbed to the top of it. From the top of the spire one could see many flat miles, and the flat wide river, and the town's outskirts, and the chemical factory where her husband was to work. (She hadn't met him then.) And she had clung to the old worn stone, alarmed by her vertigo, alarmed by the almost over-powering impulse to jump off and crash into the churchyard below. That again was something that puzzled her. A lot of people suffered from vertigo, she knew, it was considered quite natural, and the top of the tower was often crowded with giggling, gasping, squeaking schoolchildren, or with parents blenching with fear as their children tried to stand on tiptoe to see over the parapet. But why, why was it natural? And if it was natural, why did people continue to build and climb towers? Why didn't they stay safely on the ground? They did not climb merely for the view.

The church had been no help. She was too young for the women's institute. The baby clinic was, she supposed, intended to be some kind of support, and it had been reassuring to discover that Hugh was gaining, not losing weight. But that was about it. Against her one-time friends she had hardened her heart, for fear lest they should discover her secret, and anyway the nicest of them had left the district. As who would not?

The church bells fell silent. She would walk through the churchyard home, she decided. There were yellow leaves on the graves, and the berries of the holly were already red. She found herself thinking, despite herself, of the mushroom soup and the chicken that she was going to cook for the evening. She was not a confident cook, as she was not a confident mother, and always deeply dreaded that she would do something wrong. Every meal that she prepared seemed to contain in it the charred or bleeding ghosts of her first disasters: they could never be properly concealed or exorcised. However unexceptionable the meal, she felt that her guests could discern in it her past mistakes. It was in vain that she told herself that it didn't matter, that she didn't even like the guests, that she didn't care whether they liked their dinner or not, that anyway Cynthia's roast lamb hadn't been much to boast about, New Zealand it must have been, and not properly unfrozen at that—it was in vain to repeat these arguments to herself, for she knew that she cared deeply though she despised herself for caring. Sliced peaches and sliced mushrooms floated in her head: she must be careful with the sauce, the last sauce she had made had been a little lumpy, and Mark had made an elaborate pantomime of dissecting one of the lumps.

(For Frances Wingate tolled the Christian bells of the church. Happily neglectful, confident mother, no agonizer she over bits of bread salvaged from the carpet, over mud and diseases: haphazard, confident, efficient cook. To them that have, it shall be given. There was no need for Frances Wingate to bury her talents. Stony ground, stony ground, tolled the bells, for Janet Bird.)

Janet was nearly home. She wondered if anything nice could possibly have happened there while she was out. What could she imagine that might cheer her up? This was a game she had played since adolescence—on the way back from school, she would try to imagine something, anything, that would make life seem better, and at times would admit to herself that she would have welcomed a cataclysm, a vol-

cano, a fire, an outbreak of war, anything to break the unremitting nothingness of her existence. What would she feel
like now, if she got back and found that the whole new estate
they lived in had been burned to the ground? She had to admit
that she would have felt nothing but delight to see the black
ruins and the smoldering ash. It was even possible. A gas
main might have leaked and blown up, that old bore Mr.
Blaney next door might at last have fallen asleep over his
pipe and newspaper and set the place on fire. If such a thing
happened, at least something would have happened, and she
and Hugh would have been safely out of it, and free—but
free for what? She could not imagine. But perhaps for something. If the shell were burned, she dimly sensed, she might
work her way into a new life. Alone, she was not strong
enough to do it. It would take a cataclysm to release her, and
a cataclysm, even via the gas main, was not likely to come
her way.

She had been of late more and more drawn toward disasters. She hadn't quite taken stock of this yet, hadn't quite
even noticed it, but the fact was that her heart quickened
with excitement when she read of factories going up in
flames, of explosions in Northern Ireland and central London, of floods in Italy and car crashes on motorways. She
longed to see an airplane drop burning from the sky. She had
even started to read books about holocausts. She had always
been an idle reader, picking things up in the library, able to
involve herself easily in the adventures of Nurse Brown or
the life of Anne Boleyn or the voyage of the Kon-Tiki. But
recently, since the child was born, she had found herself
reading of horrors. She did not know why. She started mildly,
with *A Town Like Alice*, and other such war stories, then
moved on to heavier stuff—the literature of the concentration
camps, war memoirs, even Solzhenitsyn. She could not have
said what drew her to it. Was it fear or pleasure? She did not
know. As she walked home, picturing Aragon Court in ruins,
she thought of the book she was reading at the moment—a
heart-rending account, it was, a fictional account, of a

mother in Poland, a Jewish woman, who had been taken off to the concentration camps on a train, and who had thrown her baby out of the train window as the train moved through a flat field. She had thrown the baby into the arms of a Polish peasant woman, who was hoeing the turnip field, and as the train moved on inexorably to extinction, the Polish woman and the Jewish woman had exchanged looks of profound significance, and the Polish woman had picked up the baby and had embraced and kissed it with a promise of devotion as the train moved out of sight. That was as far as Janet had got with the story: there were at least five-sixths of the book still to come, including no doubt a description of the mother's death, in the labor camp or gas chambers.

What was it that attracted her to these subjects? The death and the destruction? Or the baby salvaged and harvested like a turnip from the field?

Janet Bird, who was after all a post-war baby, knew quite well that the Poles were not distinguished for their love of the Jews, and that she was reading a romantic fiction. She took it seriously, nevertheless.

(Karel Schmidt, who had been born in Pilsen, took such fantasies seriously too, for other reasons.)

She looked at her small baby, who was dribbling miserably onto the stained front of his tiny anorak. She would never have to throw him for his salvation from a train window as she went on to her death, or at least she imagined that she would not have to. But perhaps, with her, a doom as dreadful he was inheriting. Not the gas chamber, not the labor camp, but some lengthy disaster. Perhaps it was for this reason that her soul yearned for the holocaust. Perhaps, now, she should fling him from her, for his own sake. I won't do, as a mother, she thought sadly. The sight of his wet jacket filled her with despair. She could not endure it, she could not endure it. But she had to endure it. There was no way of getting off this train.

(Stephen Ollerenshaw, on this theme, was to have other views, alas.)

The estate, of course had not been burned down. It was not even smoking slightly. It looked perfectly normal, established forever, in the late October air. There it stood, so conveniently near the center of town, only a twenty-minute pram-push away. It was supposed to be a good address, a cut above the council and factory housing that lay farther out on the long ribbon roads that wandered in their desultory manner through the surrounding countryside. Its inhabitants were nice people, as Janet's mother was fond of pointing out: even Janet was not above reflecting that her neighbors were at least, most of them, "nice." There was a schoolteacher or two, a journalist on the local paper, a retired military man, and a few executives from local firms, as well as a wealthy bookie and a greengrocer. Nevertheless, Janet thought to herself frequently, if this is a good address, what can a bad one be like? Her parents' home (they had lived on top of their little shop, in an outlying village, in increasing comfort as the village and trade expanded) had been a hundred times more pleasant, more homely.

The estate had been built in the late fifties, and had the characteristics of the period. The little houses—maisonettes, they were described as, but Mark and his friends thought the word silly, and laughed when her mother used it—were two-story, with an entrance hall, a kitchen, and a large lounge with windows back and front downstairs, and three small bedrooms and a bathroom upstairs. They were semidetached, though the detachment was extremely narrow, and consisted of a small alleyway along which one could wheel a bicycle, so one's neighbors were rather close.

Janet hated her home. She hated more or less everything about it—the color of the brick, the color of the linoleum tiles, the color of the bathroom fittings, the shape of the banisters. She hated her own efforts to make it look pleasanter, to give it individuality (as she had put it to herself) and she approached it now with a sinking in her spirits as she saw yet again the gleaming windowpane, framed by its orange curtains, and within the glow of the red sofa, and the red painted piano. Once, Janet had cared about such things. She had even been quite good at them: she had had "taste," as her mother called it. She had opinions about shapes and colors, and as a child she had been good at making things: she hadn't received much encouragement at school, where the art mistress, a tearful woman, never got past the stage of teaching them perspective, but she had watched the handicrafts programs on television, and had worked with glue and paper and paint, carefully, fastidiously. Everyone recognized that Janet had quite a flair for that kind of thing. It wasn't a gift that ran in the family at all. As she grew older, unaided, she began to make collages of felt and paper and pebbles and leaves. Her own designs.

While she was working at the town hall in Leicester, she'd summoned up the courage to go to an evening class. The instructor didn't seem to like her. He told her that her work was tight and neat and persnickety, and that she'd never get anywhere that way; she must learn to be free and express herself. He had yelled this at her several times, staring contemptuously at her small tidy creations, and she had tried, for a few weeks, to do as he advised: she had got her hands and her overalls dirty, she had got paint under her nails. But she had made nothing, and the process had sickened her: she couldn't stand the smell of oils, and the texture of clay disturbed her. Thinking it was her own fault, she withdrew from the class. The instructor was sorry: she had been the most promising of an unpromising year. But she was uptight and repressed, he said to himself. He never thought to reproach himself for her absence.

She had more or less given up trying, these days. Anyway, there wasn't much time, with Hugh. There sat Hugh, in his plastic chair, staring at her, and fretting while she warmed up his soup. He was sad and hungry. She gave him a rusk to chew on while he waited. His blue anorak, dirtily streaked with spittle, she hung up in the airing closet by the boiler to dry, and noted with something approaching anguish that the front of her jersey was matted and damp as well. The texture of the wool, sodden with dribbling, horrified her. She knew what it would be like when it dried out—it would be stiff and prickly and woolly, all the stitches somehow sogged into one another. He waved his octopus hands, his anemone hands. His gums were raw, his eyes were wide with passion. He looked at her and moaned. She could do nothing, nothing. It's no use looking at *me*, she said, desperately, aloud. I will look up unto the hill. From whence cometh my help? From whence but from me, poor poor thing, thought poor Janet, and kissed the baby passionately on its red and angry cheek, its taut and cracked and red and flaming cheek.

(A goodenoughmother.)

The baby had bone broth for its meal. She had some Weetabix, a bit of cheese, some leftover salad from the night before, a rotting banana, and one raw mushroom, stolen from the evening's mushroom soup. It must be admitted that despite the prevailing melancholy, she enjoyed this meal, and felt a little cheered by it (the human mind can bear plenty of reality but not too much unintermittent gloom) and even when she realized that her son Hugh had no intention of having his afternoon sleep, unless she slept with him, she managed to face the prospect of a communal nap. On the other hand, she did rather want to read the paper, which she hadn't had time to look at earlier in the day, and wasn't quite sure if she'd be able to persuade him to sleep through the crackling of the pages.

She managed it, in the end; she laid him by her side on the double bed, crooked in her arm, and joggled him, having previously spread the paper ready on the other side. When he turned up the whites of his eyes to the white ceiling and dozed, she turned over to the newspaper, quietly and breathlessly, and read the front page. It was concerned with incipient strikes and a royal wedding. It took some courage to turn the page and look within, as Hugh could be very cross if aroused prematurely—in fact he was one of those tiresome babies who always sink into sleep with a deep reluctance, forcibly lulled, and wake with howls of cheated rage, and

Janet herself could not but sympathize with his attitude—he was surely right to suspect that oblivion was a danger, and that enemies would knife him in the back if he ever lost his guard? She recognized all too well his awakening wails—they expressed resentment against the tricks of nature and convention, which would cheat one out of existence, if they could. Poisoned while sleeping, like Hamlet's father. Oh yes. Sleep, marriage, adultery: all, all knives in the back. Stay awake, baby. The inner pages of the paper contained news about Northern Ireland (which she skipped) about the dangers of the pill (which she read with interest) and about a baby that had been battered to death by its father, because it cried while Match of the Day was on. If she had been reading a paper with more news in it, she might have read in a very small, dull item that her cousin David Ollerenshaw, and her second cousin Frances Wingate were among the members about to attend an international conference in Adra. She would not have known where Adra was—somewhere in Africa, she would have rightly guessed—nor would she have known who Frances Wingate was, although they had passed one another on Tockley High Street that summer: but the name of David Ollerenshaw would certainly have caught her attention, for he was not some infinitely remote relative, but her own first cousin, the son of her father's brother, and she had actually met him quite often in her childhood, and heard a lot about him until her father and his father had quarreled about Great-Aunt Dorrie's furniture. She had looked up to him: he had been the clever one, as had his father before him.

But she didn't read all this, because her husband didn't take *The Times*. So we can skip her supposed reflections on David's success and her own failure in life: we can skip her childhood memories of family parties, of the eventual family feud, and of her mother's oft-voiced suspicions that David's parents had pushed him too hard, he would break down if they weren't careful.

Instead, Janet, dozing, breathing heavily and chestily

through the thin bones of her pigeon chest, through the small covering of her dry breasts, thought of the battered baby and fell asleep, rolling up the whites of her eyes to the ceiling like her son: a family trick.

Frances Wingate, reading of the same battering in the same paper at more or less the same hour, as she sat over a cup of coffee at home in Putney, was rather surprised to feel tears rising in her eyes. She'd thought she was past that kind of thing. Not that it seemed very meaningful. She moved on to the article about the pill. At least she didn't have to worry about thrombosis now. There was something to be said for celibacy.

David Ollerenshaw, while his cousins were indulging in the female pastimes of cups of coffee and afternoon naps, was making preparations for his visit to Adra. His preparations were of necessity elaborate, as he had decided to drive there, through Europe, and across the Sahara. He was looking forward to the journey: he liked driving, and he particularly liked driving alone across difficult terrain.

At the moment, he was sitting in his rarely occupied rooms, filling in an insurance form which he had to send off to the secretary of the conference. The secretary had not approved of David's plans: he thought David would arrive late for the conference, and would much have preferred him to arrive on an airplane like everybody else. But David had persisted. In the old French colonial days, one hadn't been allowed to drive alone across the Sahara: one had to go in convoy, which quite spoiled the whole point of the enterprise. Nowadays, one could get lost as one pleased. A great improvement. David had just been reading a review of a book by a man who had tried to cross the desert on a camel, and who had had a quite horrible time: he had been seeking Loneliness and Suffering, for personal domestic reasons, the reviewer suggested. David had no personal domestic reasons: nobody lived in his rooms but himself. Nor did he

intend to suffer as spectacularly as Geoffrey Moorhouse. A
little mild suffering was all he wanted—that moment of intense expectation, when the map has clearly been mislead-
ing, when the wheels stick in the sand, when the engine fails,
when the water is low. But even more than the disasters, he
liked the complete isolation. Don't you get bored, or lonely?
people would ask him, as he set out on similar expeditions,
and he could truly answer: No. To be completely free of all
human contact was in itself a pleasure. People were all right:
intermittently he enjoyed company. But solitude had its own
quality.

The insurance form wanted to know who was his next of
kin. He had no wife, no brothers, no sisters, no children,
and he did not wish to enter the names of his aging parents,
with whom his contact was almost nonexistent: he did not
like the thought of a police officer calling on them to tell
them that his desiccated corpse had been found in the Hoggar
Mountains. (He was looking forward particularly to the Hoggar.) So he put down the name of his friend and ex-colleague
Banks, with whom he was to have dinner that night. Lying,
he declared that Banks was his cousin. He had got some real
cousins, up in Tockley, but he didn't want to embarrass them
with his corpse either. Banks, a hardened earthquake inspec-
tor, wouldn't care either way about David Ollerenshaw's
corpse. That was one of the reasons why David kept in fitful
touch with him.

Janet, half an hour later, woke to the angry wails of Hugh.
Furious at being tricked into unawareness, tricked out of the
masochistic satisfaction of the toothache, he yelled and
bawled so loudly that she bundled him up in his dried-out
anorak and shoved him in his pram in the back garden with
a load of broken toys. He could sit out there, she said firmly,
while she made the soup and peeled the vegetables. Then he
could come in again. Her violent handling of him seemed to
silence him: he sat there, pink-cheeked and a little awestruck, plucking at his yellow harness and watching the leaves

fall off the trees. What a boring life, being a baby, she thought to herself, as she went in to her neat and tidy kitchen and put on her apron and waved to him through the window. He waved back, rather grudgingly.

She started to peel the mushrooms, heaping up a little pile of thin papery silky skin, and slicing them neatly with her sharp knife. The shape of them, the white moonlike crescent and its stalk, with its darker pink brown fringe, satisfied her. If one sliced neatly and thinly, one could make a perfect section of each, like a specimen for a slide in biology. Mushrooms around here were still sometimes proper, perfect mushrooms—not those huge black-gilled fraying things that one could sometimes get cheap, nor the other extreme, those so white and overcultured underground that they were deformed, embryonic, with no proper distinction between stalk and cap. These were really lovely ones. She arranged them on the chopping board, and went to melt the butter in the pan. One could not go wrong with mushroom soup, Di Hutchins had told her, if one put enough sherry and cream in it. That was the kind of advice people were always giving her, and it was all very well, but sherry and cream were expensive, and Mark had been so difficult about money lately, and it was indeed true that the mortgage was crippling and going up as it seemed every day, and the baby had proved more expensive than she had dreamed possible. She would thicken the soup with a tin of Heinz, and perhaps put a spot of cream in later, leaving the rest for the coffee and the sweet. She must remember never to give mushroom soup to the Hutchins. And come to think of it, what had she given Cynthia and Ted for their main course last time? And Bill and Anthea? She honestly couldn't remember. Too bad if it had been chicken. Too bad if any of them had yet tried on each other the chicken recipe in last month's *Femina*. It looked all right, and not too complicated and expensive. After all, how the hell was one expected to know what other people in Tockley were eating every night? One couldn't go and snoop through their windows of an evening, could one, spying on their supper, one couldn't trail them to the butcher and the greengrocer. And anyway, that wouldn't do much good these days, as everyone but herself seemed to have a deep freeze. She didn't know how they afforded all the things they had. Cynthia Street, she thought firmly, should have taken her lamb out of her deep freeze much much earlier. It had been tough and bloody.

She got the mushroom soup simmering, looked out the window and saw that Hugh had been joined by the cat and seemed quite happy for the moment, and started to joint the chickens, a job which always drove her into a frenzy. It was so messy, the meat was so translucent and slimy and slippery, the joints were never quite where they ought to be, but she had to do it, the recipe said so, and anyway the last time she had left a chicken whole Mark had made such a hash of carving it that he had sulked for the rest of the evening. How cruel he was to her. What pleasure did it give him, to be so unkind? She sawed at the knobbly thighbone of the fowl, severing a tattered drumstick, and hoped that he would not provoke her so much that she would be obliged to stick a knife in him one day. It was unlikely; she was a very feeble timid person. He counted on that, she was sure. But people did stick knives into one another. When younger she had never been able to understand why, she had always thought of knife-stickers as another species, a breed apart. Now she knew that she was one of them in her spirit. Now she knew why people did it. It was a wonder to her that people did not do it more often. The self-restraint around in the world filled her with awestruck admiration. How wonderful people were, herself included, to control themselves so well. And how nasty, bloodless, and underground chickens are: yellow skin, purple and white flesh. Reared in a battery. Not as good quality as the mushrooms, but doubtless nobody would notice, when she had sufficiently covered them with tinned peach sauce. She hacked away. Odd, how the flesh seemed to disappear as one hacked. There was never much left on a jointed chicken.

The cat sat on the baby's pram. She was glad that she liked
it there, and that Hugh accepted it so nicely. She had been
so fond of her little cat, before Hugh's arrival, but everybody
had tried to stop her from feeling fond—repressed maternal
instincts, the clever ones had said. You're a spinster at heart,
Mark would say in company, and in private he would push
the cat around, not quite cruelly, but as though he resented
its very existence. He would shut the door too sharply on the
cat's tail, he would tip it too abruptly off chairs, he would
push it away from its own dish with his foot if he wanted to
go out by the back door, though he could perfectly well have
walked around it. And when the baby was born, people tried
to make her get rid of the poor creature, implying that it
would be sure to suffocate the baby if she didn't, that it was
unhygienic, that she wouldn't miss it if she had a baby instead. She had been really upset by these arguments, as she
was terrified of germs, and had never thought of her little cat
as being dirty before. She was even more upset by the vigor
and venom with which her neighbors and relations pursued
these arguments—it was almost as though they *wanted* to kill
her cat, as though they enjoyed the idea of killing her cat. It
was their zeal that finally persuaded her to keep it—she burst
into tears one day, heavily pregnant, when a neighbor had
called in one evening for a cup of coffee and started to tell
her yet more horror stories of suffocated babies, and said,
"You can kill her yourself, now, if you like, but if you don't
do it right now, here and now, in this room, I'm keeping
her." And the neighbor had looked with shocked and narrow
eyes at the little black and white cat, sitting there so inno-
cently and peacefully, and had changed the subject, and
backed away without the cat's blood on her hands. Poor Janet,
she said later, vaguely, to both Janet and Mark, she's upset,
she's overwrought, we all know how upset people get when
the time gets near—and Janet, the palm of one hand flat
in the swell of her lower ribs, had felt like saying who's she,
the cat's mother, but her moment of rebellion was past, and
she had to accept sympathy, excuses made on her behalf for

her own bad behavior, and meekly bow her head, as though she admitted her folly, her pregnancy-induced folly. Extraordinary, the way people had of explaining away in quite false but oddly plausible terms one's own most violent emotions.

She accepted reproof, but the cat lived. She had equipped herself with cat nets and DDT (but hadn't dared to use the DDT because it said not to put it near babies), she had washed blankets and brushed cushions, she had sterilized teething rings and dummies ten times more frequently than she needed, and she had let the cat live. Somewhere, deep inside herself, she knew that the cat wasn't going to kill the baby. She didn't know where this knowledge came from, for she had no such instinctive feeling about slightly old soup, or unboiled water, or extremes of temperature. The baby had responded perfectly. He liked the cat. He never hurt her or pulled her about or dropped things on her. And there she sat, on the end of his pram, while he chewed on a plastic beaker and mumbled (she couldn't hear him, but she could see he was mumbling) and let spittle drip once more onto his anorak.

She had nearly finished the chicken when she heard the doorbell. Her heart sank, for it could not conceivably be anyone she wanted to see. Still, she had to answer it. Once she had hidden under the front-room windowsill, so horrified had she been by the approach of a neighbor down the front path, but people always got one in the end. They just came back later. Wiping her hands, hoping it would be a salesman she could send away, she went to the front door. But it wasn't a salesman, it was her mother.

"Getting dark early, isn't it?" said her mother, by way of greeting, as she stepped in. "Yes, it is," said Janet, though it wasn't, it was only three o'clock, and not yet dark or even very cloudy.

"I thought I'd better just pop in," said her mother, with no explanation.

"Yes," said Janet.

"You're busy, I see," said her mother, following her into the kitchen.

"Yes," said Janet.

"People coming for the evening?"

"Yes."

"That's nice for you then."

"Yes, it is."

"A lot of work, though," said her mother, wandering around, peering at the simmering soup, and almost-jointed chicken, the bowl of peaches, the peeled carrots, the green beans, the salad. "Messy, too."

"Would you like a cup of tea, mummy?" said Janet. "Would you mind putting the kettle on? My hands are all chickeny."

"Don't let me hold you up," said her mother, going to fill the kettle, noting, as Janet had known she would, the persistent stain in the sink, and the cat on the baby's pram in the garden.

"You're having a lot of people then?" asked her mother, and Janet sighed and said, "No, not really."

Her mother waited expectantly.

"We're having the Streets, and Anthea and Bill David," said Janet patiently.

"Ah," said her mother, paused, and then said, "I don't think I know the Davids, do I?"

"I don't know, mummy. Bill works at Patterson's. I'm sure you must have seen Anthea around in town. Very smart, she is."

"Oh? Smart? Would I have met her here, then?"

"I'm not sure. I don't know her very well really."

"I like the Streets very much," said her mother, in a speculative tone, as though she meant the opposite, and was waiting for her daughter to contradict her. "I'll never forget how kind they were that day when I'd been waiting so long at the bus stop at the end of your road and they gave me a lift. I thought that was very nice of them."

"Well, it was no trouble to them," said Janet, neutrally.

It was difficult, this game of nonadmission, because even neutrality could be interpreted.

Her mother made the tea, while Janet finished the chicken, and started on the sauce. She found it difficult to do things with her mother watching: the deliberately careful silence, the tactful lack of comment unnerved her, and she sliced her thumb on the last assault. She did not even like to look for a bandage. The carcasses stood there, hollow and ribby. Her own chest felt like that sometimes. Her mother would take her blood to be chicken blood.

"You'll make soup, I suppose, with the bones," said her mother, drinking her tea.

"Yes, I suppose so," said Janet, who had thought of bundling the nasty objects into a newspaper and bunging them in the bin.

"Is that a *peach* sauce you're making? For the chicken? How unusual."

"Yes, it is, rather."

"Did one of your friends give it to you?"

"I got it out of *Femina.*"

"Oh? Really? I've never heard of peaches and chicken. That's very unusual."

"Yes, it is, isn't it," said Janet, almost prepared to admit that the combination was not only unusual but potentially disgusting, but as that was the kind of thing her friends cooked, that was the kind of thing they were going to get back in return.

"And what will you serve it with?"

"Rice," said Janet, with a new note of finality. She could, occasionally, put her foot down, and she had had this rice-potato debate too often to be able to face it again. Her mother still seemed to believe that potatoes were an essential accompaniment to every meal, and that rice was a foreign, unsatisfying, and unwelcome substitute. Janet had actually, on previous occasions, been obliged to support her own use of rice by detailed descriptions of the menus and habits of her acquaintances, and she had found the process, tainted as it was with defensiveness, and laying her open as it did to further prying (as long as her mother didn't *know* what she was doing, it was safe)—she had found the process painful, and had no wish ever to repeat it. So now she said "Rice," with authority, and her mother repeated "Oh, rice," with submission, and changed her tack.

"Hugh's being very good," she said, after a while. "He doesn't seem to mind that cat at all."

"He likes the cat," said Janet.

"I do admire your confidence," said her mother. "I'd never have dared. But you mothers these days are so sure of yourselves."

"Would you like a piece of cake?" asked Janet. "I think I've got a cake somewhere."

"I wouldn't say no," said her mother. Janet could have sworn that her mother was positively hoping that there would be no cake, so that she could make a show of not minding not having any—but if that were so, why on earth had she offered her a piece? The minutest attention to Mrs. Ollerenshaw's behavior could not have discerned a suppressed desire for cake, nor a desire to catch Janet out at not having any: it was perfectly respectable to have a cup of tea at half-past three without cake, and as Mrs. Ollerenshaw was always going on about getting fat and dieting she ought not to want cake anyway. The fact remained that Janet had, unwilled, compelled, drawn by fatal threads, offered cake, and was not sure if there was a presentable piece in the cake tin. She didn't eat much cake herself. Still, the cake had at least provided a distraction from Hugh, the cat, and motherhood, and when she looked in the blue enamel tin she found to her relief a few Garibaldi cookies in the end of a cellophane wrapper, the end of a ginger cake, and a few digestive biscuits. If only her mother hadn't been sitting so close, she would have been able to make them look quite proper and attractive, on a cake plate, but as it was she could see that she was going to have to thrust the tin at her, crumbs and all, tatty bits of cellophane

and all, brand names and all. Not that one could ever have
pretended that such a cake was home-made.

Mrs. Ollerenshaw accepted a digestive biscuit, and commented that when the shop had still been going, they'd always
done better with the other well-known brand of ginger cake.
"I don't know why, really," she said. "There's not much to
choose between them, is there?" There followed a discussion on food prices, and whether small grocers were going
well or losing out on the increases: the Ollerenshaws could
take an Olympian view, for they had retired a year ago and
sold the business, and were now living in a new bungalow
in the small village, a village which had been almost swallowed up into the growing stretches of Tockley. Janet had
thought she would be sorry to see the shop go, though it was
obvious her parents couldn't live there forever—for one thing,
her father couldn't manage the stairs any more, since his
illness—but when the moment of departure came, she found
herself surprisingly unmoved, for the truth was that the shop
had changed beyond all recognition since the days when she
had loved it, those early days of infancy and grace, those
childish days when the apple trees had borne fruit, and the
counter in the shop had been a scrubbed wooden slab, and
bacon had been kept in a muslin cloth, and cheese in a cold
cheese safe, when tea had been measured out of large oval
enameled tins, and crackers kept in large boxes and sold by
the ounce, when an indescribable smell of coffee and ham
and beans and sugar had hung over all. It was all gone now.
The changes she could remember clearly—the first large refrigerator, which had seemed such a miracle, followed a few
years later by a deep freeze and a decision to stock the new
frozen foods. She had peered awestruck into the icy depths,
humming away, and admired the piles of peas and crinkle-
cut chips lying in the arctic jeweled white and blue, but at
the same time she had grieved for the old larder and its solid
smell of damp, she had felt a kind of pity for the stone and
marble slabs. In the end even the shop itself had been pulled
down and rebuilt—not the whole building, but the shopping

space itself. The small square windowpanes had been replaced by a huge plate-glass frontage, goods had been dis-
played on a central shelf unit, and Frank Ollerenshaw had
introduced wire baskets and called himself a self-service
store, though he still sat there in person, weighing out cheese
and bacon just as he had done in the old days, for there were
still old customers who were not content to buy everything
in plastic wrappers from New Zealand and Denmark, and
who would ask for a quarter of red cheese and a quarter of
yellow, expecting to be understood.

But he had had a slight stroke, and had sold the business
and retired. Janet knew she must ask after him, but did not
like to, for she knew her mother would complain. Nevertheless, as Mrs. Ollerenshaw nibbled her cracker—was she trying to imply by the movement of her lips that it had gone
soft?—Janet asked, "And how's dad keeping?"

"Oh, he's not so bad," said her mother. "He complains
a lot, though. He's very down, really. And he won't stick to
his diet, you know. I can't make him stick to his diet."

Launched on the subject of diet, she talked for a quarter
of an hour, about doctors and cholesterol and fat and flour
and butter and margarine and cooking oil and cakes and
chocolates, and the great lengths she had gone to in order to
provide appetizing meals that Frank would eat, and how he
was always sneaking off to the larder to help himself to for-
bidden things, and how tired she was of listening to his complaints, and how she wished Janet and Mark would come out
and see him more often but she supposed Mark must be very
busy. Janet listened dully: she knew that nothing in earth
would persuade either her father or her mother to change their
eating habits, and that talking about diet was substitute for
following it. In reality, deceiving themselves profoundly, they
would sit and eat mounds of bread, butter, and jam, they
would eat fried eggs and chips and bacon, they would eat
buttered kippers, and roast lamb with roast potatoes on Sun-
days, and that was that. The fact that her father was over-
weight and ill would make no difference to their behavior at

all: like a smoker who believes he will never die, he would go on eating. She had seen them eat half a pound of chocolates in an evening, after a large meal, and yet they still said they never ate sweets, or only on special occasions.

When her mother had finished talking about food, they noticed that Hugh in the garden was getting restless, and Janet went to get him in, and then her mother looked at her watch and said that she must be going.

"Give dad my love," said Janet, accompanying her to the front door. The baby, tactlessly, was too cross to be very agreeable to his grandmother, and struggled and wriggled when she tried to hold him. "He's teething," said Janet, apologetically.

"I'll bring you some spirits of salts next time I come," said her mother, poised on the threshold. "For that stain in the sink. I've been meaning to, but I keep forgetting, I'm so busy these days."

"I don't believe in having that stuff in the house," said Janet, feeling rather powerful as soon as she had got her mother over the step and out onto the path. "It's terribly poisonous. What if the baby got hold of it?"

"You could surely find somewhere where he *wouldn't* get hold of it," said her mother, almost sharply, and then nodded and marched off. Janet turned back into her house, and shut the frosted-glass-paned door with its stainless steel knob, and thought that after all her own house was her own house, and while she was alone in it there was something to be said for *that*. She felt almost cheerful as she went back to tidy up the kitchen.

Mrs. Ollerenshaw, standing at the bus stop, thought about her daughter. There was something wrong there, but if Janet couldn't tell her, what could she do? Janet was unhappy. Was she tired, with the baby? Small babies were tiring, and Hugh was a bad sleeper, she could tell. She'd offer to have him for the night more often, but Janet didn't seem to like it, and she didn't want to interfere. Was there something wrong between her and Mark? She'd never much cared for Mark, a snobby little fellow he was, too full of himself, always putting people's backs up with his superior jokes—she'd tried to say something to Janet about him, but she hadn't been able to, Janet was so prickly and difficult, but anybody could see how unhappy she was during the engagement, and how peaked she looked when she got back from the honeymoon. And now it was too late. Never interfere between husband and wife. But she couldn't stop herself calling around, to see how Janet was. She was worried about her. She wished she could speak to her, but somehow whenever she got there, the words wouldn't come right, and she'd find herself talking about cholesterol and recipes and spirits of salts. Janet was quite right not to want spirits of salts in the house. It was nasty evil corrosive dangerous stuff, fizzing away like the devil given half a chance, and smelling strong enough to knock you over. She didn't know why she'd ever suggested it. She couldn't help herself, that was the solemn truth.

She shivered, a fat woman in a big coat, as she waited for the bus. There was a cold wind blowing, and it was, now, growing dark. Marriage, what a business it was. Why didn't one drag one's daughters back from the altar, instead of pushing them up the aisle? She wouldn't like to live with Mark Bird, she could tell that, and have to keep everything just so. She'd be glad to get back to Frank and have a bit of tea and toast. And yet Frank hadn't been up to much in many ways. They were a funny family, the Ollerenshaws, a temperamental lot, for all that they looked so quiet. It was a cold bed that Janet lay on. What could one ever do for one's daughter? Nothing, nothing. Everything she tried to do came out wrong. Perhaps it did some good, just to be around. But perhaps it didn't do any good at all. It's hard, that's what it is, thought Mrs. Ollerenshaw, as she waited for the East Midlands County Bus in the gathering gloom, helpless and concerned.

Janet, safely back in her own house, shut the door on the falling leaves, put the baby on the polished wood living-room floor, and went into the kitchen to clear up. The meal was all organized, except for the things that had to be done at the last minute. She washed the tea cups, stared at the stain in the sink, and was just about to go out of the back door to empty the tea pot down the grate when she noticed her neighbor in the next door garden getting in some washing off the line, and decided not to: the last thing she wanted to do was to have to have a word with her neighbor, and the low hedge between the two back gardens made an interchange impossible to avoid. Her neighbor was a constant threat to her, and she would avoid encounters if she possibly could. It was not that there was anything overtly threatening about her—on the contrary, it was her very meekness that constituted the menace. She was an awful warning, poor Jean Cooper, of what Janet herself so nearly was—timid, nervous, gauche, sad, unfinished. She lived in the downstairs flat of the house next door, with her silent husband, and she was going mad, Janet thought, from boredom, so mad that she would even overcome her shyness to talk, endlessly, nervously, over the garden hedge. Once she started one could not get away. She had been already there, four years earlier, when Janet moved in, and Janet had at first thought she was much younger than herself, for her face had that curious washed blank unlined unregistering look which from a distance looks like youth, and she had worn her hair in childish styles, tied back with a ribbon or even, occasionally, in bunches: and she had worn childish clothes, school-type skirts and jerseys and blouses. But after a while Janet had noticed she was at least her own age, if not a couple of years older, and that she continued to look young because nothing ever happened to her.

She had been married for two years before Janet met her, in a union even more inexplicable than her own with Mark. Indeed, the element of parody and exaggeration was what most upset her about the Coopers. Not that Derek Cooper resembled Mark: on the contrary. He was silent, unaggressive, unambitious: he seemed quite content to sit in his downstairs flat in Aragon Court and read books about sailing and the Boer War and smoke his pipe. If Jean looked young for her age, he looked old. They were both, now, in their late twenties. It was hard to imagine why they had married, or how they had ever managed to say enough to each other to get themselves engaged, and Janet found herself wondering curiously from time to time whether the whole thing had been a complete misunderstanding, arising from some improperly heard remark.

Janet had pieced together a little of it, from remarks that Jean had dropped over the garden fence. Jean had at first tried to take a superior line, the experienced wife speaking to the raw bride: she had whispered shyly yet insistently that it was better to hang one's washing line at this end rather than that end of the garden, because of the trees, and that she wouldn't advise Janet to order eggs from the milkman, they were cheaper and fresher at the shop down the road. Janet, feeling sorry for this evidently timid person, had allowed herself to be advised, but she had done her best to keep Jean out of the house, because she did not want her to see that she had no idea how to boil potatoes, and that when she tried to make cheese sauce it always went lumpy. After some time, she began to realize that Jean was incompetent as well as shy: she might make wise remarks about where to hang the washing, but she was always leaving it out too late (as on this very evening) or hanging it up when it was about to start raining. And when, after a year's acquaintance, she had confided that she didn't dare to give Derek a lamb chop for supper, he always said there was nothing on a lamb chop, Janet felt that the balance had swung, and that no matter how badly she herself coped with daily affairs, she was never going to be as bad as Jean Cooper. Oddly enough, this knowledge did not cheer her: but for the grace of God, she might say to herself daily, but the smell of burning reached her nostrils nevertheless, and she knew that there was no true escape, that she was herself, at some point, if not now, equally condemned to those same flames.

Jean Cooper said over the garden hedge, a pair of shears

in her hands, one fine spring morning while Janet was expecting Hugh, that she would have liked to have a baby, but that it didn't seem to happen. Janet, embarrassed, extremely doubtful about her own feelings about her own rather late pregnancy (she had after all been married for well over two years before it happened, and then it had happened by accident) had not known what to say, and had not wanted to hear any more, but she had not been able to avoid it. "I've always wanted a baby," said Jean, "but the truth is, Derek isn't very masterful." Like the confession about the lamb chop, this remark turned Janet's blood to ice, and made the hair stand up with fear on her head: for what could the woman mean? She could not endure sexual revelations over the hedge, but it did seem as though the Coopers were in need of a marriage guidance counselor at the least, if not of a doctor. Again, her own sexual experiences had been far from happy, for Mark, though masterful enough out of bed, had been much in need of assistance in it; they had between them worked out some kind of compromise, and Mark was by now quite pleased with himself, though she suspected it was at her own expense. But if they had been one degree less able, they would have been like the Coopers.

For these reasons Janet Bird looked out of her kitchen window at the dusky shadow of Jean Cooper, in her white Arran sweater and gray-flannel skirt, as she took in her tea towels, and felt moved by an enormous fear and pity. Pity so intense was not endurable, that white shadow flitting grayly in the autumn evening, longing for a word—"Was that your mother I saw?" "How's little Hugh today?"—was like a soul in torment, and she herself, Janet Bird, could do nothing, she had no saving words, she was herself if not in torment at least in limbo, and if Jean were to speak to her she would sink into the lower depths. Like a sad white bird, like the stranded sea gulls that sometimes swooped and mewed, far from the sea, in the elms, Jean Cooper fluttered and swooped in her suburban garden, watched by Janet Bird, who was waiting for a private moment to empty her tea pot.

On the other side lived a retired civil servant and his wife. The wife never went into the garden, but he was there constantly, digging and hoping for a word. Janet tried to avoid him too, because he was a bore and also nosy, asking difficult and intimate questions, but at least she could take satisfaction in disliking him. At least he did not fill her with dread.

The back yard, at last, seemed unobserved, and Janet opened her back door and emptied the brown leaves down the disinfected grate. As she straightened herself up, she caught sight of the huge sky, which was an amazing color, dark blue, with a foreground of dark pink and purple clouds, light but regular clouds, a whole heaven of them, spread like flowing hair or weed over the growing darkness. It arrested her. She stood there, and stared upward. It was beautiful, beyond anything. The two colors were charged and heavy, and against them stood the black boughs of the tree at the end of the small garden, where black leaves, left desolate, struggled to fall in their death throes. The day before she had watched from the bedroom window a single leaf on that tree, twisting and turning and tugging at its stalk, in a frenzy of death, rattling dry with death, pulling for its final release. So must the soul leave the body, when its time comes. The amazing splendor of the shapes and colors held her there, the tea pot in her hand. I will lift up mine eyes, she thought to herself. I should lift them up more often.

When she went in again, she found Hugh eating a magazine, and smiled at him in quite a friendly fashion as she took it from him and put it back in the magazine rack. It was after all time for Hugh's tea. She wiped up his spittle off the floor (how nice the wood was looking, it was quite a pleasure to wipe something off it) and took him into the kitchen and popped him into the high chair and boiled him an egg. How she liked eggs, particularly boiled eggs—so solid and hygienic and tidy and neat and organic and healthy they were, so much nicer than a baby tin, so much neater than a squashed banana or a sieved tomato. They were getting expensive these days, but even so they were good value, and at least one knew what was in them. She sliced some bread and butter, thinly, into strips, and let him squash them into his mouth himself, though she would much have preferred to chop them into tiny morsels and pop them tidily in, and she fed him the egg on a small stainless steel egg spoon, efficiently, smartly, catching the dribble, scraping his chin with the spoon when it got buttery, keeping him as neat as she could, and smiling at him when she heard the spoon clank on his two small teeth. "You'll have some more soon," she said to him, and he smiled back at her and kicked his legs and blew some bubbles.

When she had wiped him up, she took him into the other room and sat him in front of the television, which he liked, though he was far too young to know what was happening on it, she supposed. She would set the table, then give him his bath and his bottle and put him to bed, then she would just have time to change before Mark and the others arrived. Mark was going straight from work with Bill to pick up Anthea in the car, because they hadn't got a car at the moment— they were in a conservationist phase and thought it was smart to do without one, which meant that their friends had to drive them around all the time in a most inconvenient fashion.

She enjoyed setting the table. Hugh gazed at the end of a cartoon and the beginning of the news (more strikes, a fuel crisis, threatened power cuts, an Irish bomb in distant London). He sucked his thumb happily. She gave a final wipe to the white Formica dining table top, and began to get out the placemats from the drawers. She would use brown and gold ones. They were some of the nicest, they went with the season, and Anthea would think they were smart—she herself rather liked the Redoute roses, but she wasn't quite sure if Anthea would. She remembered with dismay the time when she had put out the Stately Homes placemats, and Mark's friend Christopher had made such horrible jokes about them, when she'd honestly thought that they'd be just the kind of thing that he (rather a country type, Mark had proudly described him) would like.

Mark and Janet had been given four different sets of place-mats as wedding presents. They had been given two more as subsequent anniversary and Christmas presents. And the Formica table was in fact heatproof, and that was why they had bought it.

Six brown and gold mats on the white circular top looked very good. She added six cut-glass Waterford goblets, and paused. Would Anthea prefer those chunky Italian glasses with thick bottoms? Maybe. But the cut-glass ones looked so lovely, winking and glittering and jeweled in the orange light. (She pulled the lamp over the table down, on its extending cord, so it gave a more discreet, intimate glow.) She would leave the Waterford. They couldn't possibly be the wrong thing, they were so stunningly expensive.

There was no problem with the cutlery, as they had only the one set, a stainless steel set specially designed to go in the dishwasher they couldn't yet afford. (Janet pretended she didn't want a dishwasher, and really didn't want one either. She wondered how the two attitudes to dishwashers could be combined in one person, sometimes.) But choice arose again when it came to the question of plates. They had two dinner services, the best and the everyday. The everyday was quite attractive and she had always rather liked it (she'd chosen it herself, after all, as her present from Auntie Barbara from Lincoln) until one day she saw a rather similar though not identical set in Woolworth's, and ever after she'd wondered if it hadn't after all looked rather cheap. In fact, she wouldn't even have thought of using it, had it not been for the fact that the best set had two pieces missing. The best set was Royal Worcester, white, with a thin gold band around the edges, but the last time she'd used it, somebody (had it been Jackie Price?) had made a remark about how plates got broken in the happiest of homes, and how she'd thrown one herself at her husband's head only a week before, and Janet had been deeply upset, because she would at that stage simply never have been able to throw a plate at Mark's head, and did not believe that other people did either; she thought that throwing plates was just a convention of marriage, a film convention, a romantic notion, like happy union, or eternal love. She was beginning to wonder about this now—she had doubted her certainties, ever since she had first felt like sticking a knife in her husband—but nevertheless, indeed all the more, she did not want any more jokes about broken plates.

However, her social doubts about the ordinary set were by now so profound that she used the Royal Worcester after all, giving herself the odd side plate, and covering them all with brown napkins. Then she stood back, and surveyed her arrangement. She was pleased with it. If only there weren't any guests involved, she would be quite happy, setting tables.

(Her second cousin Frances Wingate had always taken the opposite view. In the old days, when she had given dinner parties, she hadn't minded the guests; it was the bore of feeding them and setting tables for them to which she had objected. She never had anything that went with anything: all her sets were broken, and elderly professors or middle-aged stockbrokers were obliged to eat off children's plates decorated with pictures of Babar, and drink out of glasses from the Greenshield stamp shop. Being however indirectly related to the heritage of Janet Bird née Ollerenshaw, she hadn't felt quite as indifferent to these deficiencies as she might have done, and had always been slightly anxious each time she was forced to survey the confusion of her dining table: but she had usually forgotten her anxiety in what she took to be the brilliance of her own conversation. She had the great advantage of being a confident cook: greedy people usually are.

She consoled herself not only with the wit of her conversation for her deficiencies as a hostess: she also argued with herself that if she *really* cared about appearances, as she seemed to care for a few moments when people came to dinner, then she would go out and buy some new sets of crockery and cutlery—being, unlike Janet Bird, well supplied with money. And as she didn't, then she couldn't care, could she? Such arguments were commonplace in her circle. She would sometimes, even, expound them over the cheese.

The last dinner party that Frances Wingate had given, as a wife and hostess, had been eight years earlier, and at the end of it she had thrown all her coffee cups, one after the other, at her husband's head, and advised him to get out of the house forever. He had done as advised.)

The table set, Janet carried the baby off for his bath: she was always slightly nervous about bathing him, he was such a slippery creature, and particularly since she'd read a book about a woman who'd drowned her baby in the bath after having a drink too many. But he seemed quite peaceful tonight: perhaps the new tooth would be through the next day. However could one let oneself get low enough to batter one's baby? She couldn't imagine it. She was glad she couldn't imagine it.

He went to bed like a lamb. He didn't even yell when she put him in his cot, and went off to get changed. She'd already decided to wear her long brown skirt, but wasn't sure what to wear on top: Anthea, of course, always overdressed, she went in for caftans and high boots and that kind of thing, so perhaps she'd better wear her low-cut sleeveless top. It looked all right, except for her collar bones, but there was nothing she could do about her collar bones.

(Frances Wingate, pouring herself a glass of gin, was worrying about getting fat. I can't give up both drinking *and* eating, she was saying to herself, and isn't it odd how the one kind of leads to the other?)

Downstairs, Janet fiddled around in the kitchen, and got out some sherry glasses. It was nearly seven, they would arrive soon. She drew the orange curtains, to shut out the night, and poured herself a tiny glass of sherry: she'd read an article about alcoholism amongst housewives only the week before, one had to be careful, she could see how people got that way. She sat down, and started to look through the pages of the magazine that Hugh had been chewing, and thought about evening classes, and the art instructor at Leicester, with his florid beard and messy jersey and dirty nails. He had attacked the very heart of her, out of malice. She wasn't going to expose herself to that kind of thing again. She sipped her sherry. The meal was all right, the soup couldn't go wrong, the chicken at least looked all right, the orange dessert was dull but foolproof, Hugh was asleep. Maybe it would all be all right. She looked at the table, she looked at herself, and she told herself not to worry: and then she heard the car draw up in the road outside, and she felt herself stiffen, and the cat jumped up in fear and off her, and all the certainty drained out of her like water from a cracked cup, and she felt her breath coming faster with agitation, and her heart beating, and she rose to her feet nervously, hearing steps on the path and voices, and all the fine pretense was over, and she was nothing again, anxious, waiting for pain, waiting for things to go wrong, as they surely would. And perfectly on cue, as though attached to her by a living cord, before the door was even opened, the baby began to cry.

So Mark Bird, coming through his own front door into his hall, with its telephone table, bookcase, linoleum tiles, and vase full of beech leaves, was greeted with the sound of wailing, and found his wife standing in the lounge door, tense, thin, pale and indecisive, smiling hard.

(Frances, that evening, at this moment, was chopping up leeks for her children's supper of soup: they eat early in the provinces, and children go to bed late in London. Is one meant to admire the one or the other style? One has to ask oneself, at least. She was already slightly drunk, for her peak drinking time, as has already been witnessed in a hotel room in some deliberately nameless city, was from six until seven: on the other hand, she tended to sober up thereafter, and was sometimes known to work quite late at night. She had long given up worrying about the alcoholism of housewives—or rather, being what she was, she worried about it as fleetingly and ineffectively as she worried about her cutlery.

What she was worrying about was her approaching visit to Adra. Should she have accepted the offer? Why had she accepted the offer? Would she be killed in the airplane? Had she prepared her paper well enough? Was she right in thinking that it might lead to some new archaeological venture of possible magnitude? Would she have time to pack properly when she got back from Hugh and Natasha's, where she meant to spend the next weekend? And should she take her black dress, or her brown dress, or both?

While she was thinking these things over, and slicing the concentric rings of strong-smelling leek, with much the same satisfaction as Janet had sliced her mushrooms, two of her children burst in, disrupting all thought, and yelled that one had stolen the other's pistol, that the other had pinched the one's pellets, and that Daisy, poor responsible eldest, was weeping over her physics homework, and would Frances like to sort all these things out? Frances, smiling dreamily, removed from and amused by these transitory and soluble disputes, tipped the sliced leeks into a pan of melting butter, and went off to see what she could do about Daisy, the most serious of these problems, having clipped the two youngest smartly over the ears, and thrown their pistol—or whoever's pistol, she was not sure—into the back garden, through the cat door. A lucky woman, you may say.)

Janet's baby wailed on, and Anthea and Cynthia proved full of good advice. Bring him down, said Anthea. Leave him, said Cynthia. Then they turned back to talk to the men. They were both rather talkative women, and had no intention of letting Ted, Bill, and Mark discuss the gravel pit unaided.

The subject of the gravel pit did not interest Janet greatly, and she did not really understand why it aroused such strong feeling in the others. She sipped her sherry (her second glass) and listened anxiously to Hugh's muffled cries, and dutifully to animated chat about local politics, and Councilor Biggs-Anderson (a local Tory villain) and the gravel pit, and the principle of the thing, and conservation. She could never quite tell who was on whose side in politics—national politics were bad enough, but Tockley affairs were worse. For instance, she did not quite see why Mark and Ted, who worked at a plastics factory trying to invent new kinds of indestructible matter, would be so interested in conservation, unless perhaps it was for guilt reasons. Maybe it was easier to understand Bill David's attitude—he was a lecturer at the local college of education, and had a strange habit of getting very worked up about things that had absolutely nothing to do with him at all, as far as Janet could see, like the railways, or nuclear power stations, or corruption in local government. He would talk about these things with such passion that Janet always felt he must be meaning to talk about something else really. Again, she couldn't understand why Mark and the Davids and the Streets all voted Labour—she'd nothing against voting Labour, but she'd been brought up to think that nice people voted Conservative, and they were all, at least by her mother's definition, "nice." She couldn't think what they were playing at. They were all ambitious, they all had mortgages, they all complained about income tax, they all made jokes about working-class ignorance, so what were they doing voting Labour? She could have understood it if they really hadn't liked people like Councilor Biggs-Anderson, but the truth was that they were all delighted when the Tory council invited them to functions, and the highlight of Anthea and Bill's life had been when Mrs. Reed-Wisbech had asked them to her New Year's party.

Another thing that she failed to understand was their interest in local amenities. None of them ever used them, if they could possibly avoid it—they never went to the local swimming pools or the local cinema or the local amateur dramatic group, they never went to watch the football team or took their children to the park. But they fought tooth and nail to protect them from others. The gravel pit was a case in point. It had been used by children for generations as an unofficial playground, and now somebody was trying to buy it and keep the children out. Janet couldn't understand why

Mark and Cynthia and Bill and Anthea and Ted were so committed to the issue. She was the only one of all of them who had been brought up in the district, who had played as a child in the gravel pit, and she certainly wouldn't have been prepared to go to great lengths to defend it. As far as she could remember, it was rather a nasty place, full of shit and litter even in her childhood, and doubtless much worse now: it was also dangerous, and several children had drowned there in her own memory. It was perhaps a pity that the children weren't going to be allowed to play there, but she could think of plenty of much nicer places, and it really wasn't as far as she could see anything to do with these five, discussing the matter now with such vigor, with so many scornful implications about the self-interest of certain parties, with such violent condemnation of local personalities who were more or less unknown to her, and she suspected not very intimately known to them. What did they know of Sir Harry Lonsdale? Nothing at all. It wasn't that she had much to say for him herself, she'd only ever once set eyes on him, and the Ollerenshaws had been no loyal supporters of the landed gentry, but she couldn't help but feel uneasy about the way he was being condemned out of hand. It wasn't as though Mark and the Davids and the Streets had any feeling at all for the local children. In fact, they hated them, and when they weren't talking about the gravel pit they would as likely as not be talking about what a dump Tockley was, and how backward, and how stupid its inhabitants, and how they wished they were in London.

Anthea was wearing a caftan, a green and blue one with a large paisley print. She had some large blue transparent plastic jewelry on, the expensive sort of plastic, and she waved her arms around to show off the rings and bracelets. She did look rather handsome, one couldn't deny, and the way Cynthia's husband was gazing at her would have boded ill, had they all been five years older and five years more dissatisfied. Cynthia was wearing a long black skirt with a gold lamé top. What a funny business it was, dressing up in one's best clothes to go out to one another's house to stare at one another's husband. Mark wasn't behaving too badly, Janet was glad to note. His most annoying specialty was to become extremely pedantic about demolishing other people's arguments, and as they were all on the same side about the gravel pit, they hadn't yet given him an opportunity. But he would doubtless find one. Just as he could always find an opportunity for upsetting her, as he now did, when she tried to move them toward the table: rising to his feet, he looked at her and smiled in that ominous way, and said, "Are you going upstairs to throttle that baby, or shall I?"

"He's a bit quieter now," said Janet. "I think he'll go to sleep." But she was raging inside, with a black fury. How could he use words like throttle, about her own baby?

"*How* you expect us to conduct a civilized conversation, with so much competition from the uninvited guest, I cannot imagine," he said, in that way which was meant to be a joke, but which made nobody smile. It was in that tone, in her childless years, that he had referred to her in company constantly as "my barren wife." What did he want, what did he want, she screamed inside to herself, and went out into the kitchen to pass the soup through the hatch.

When she got back again, they were talking about the power crisis, and the appalling way the Tory government was handling the matter. It never seemed to occur to them that a Labour government might have found some problems too. Surely she could remember power crises when Wilson had been in charge? She kept quiet. It was quite the vogue, these days, for women to do most of the talking: Women's Lib, they called it, and the men, who were keen to be fashionable, didn't like to put a stop to it. There was something rather comic in the spectacle of the poor men being obliged to connive at their own destruction, out of loyalty to an idea. It served them right, thought Janet, as she listened to Cynthia airing some very outspoken opinions about Phase Three: she could somehow tell, although she had no idea of the facts herself, that Cynthia had got her facts wrong, and that the others suspected it, but hadn't got the facts right enough themselves to contradict her. She could tell it partly, perhaps, from the uneasy look on Ted's face, and the way he caught her eye almost apologetically, and the way he said with a diffident smile when Cynthia paused for breath, "It's awfully nice soup, Janet, delicious." She found herself smiling back, gratefully, and thinking automatically, as though a button had been pushed—really, he's quite nice, Ted Street: and then thinking again, looking at him almost for the first time, at his neat straight brown hair and pleasant, capable face— thinking again, with genuine feeling, not pushbutton feeling, he *is* nice, after all. And she smiled at him again, and tried to think of something to say to him—no reason why they should *all* talk about the fuel crisis—and saw that he was trying to think of something to say to her, and he got there first, because he came out with, "And have you found your-self any new interests, then?" and then blushed slightly, as though it were an impertinent question, and followed it up with, "Cynthia tells me you're thinking of going to an eve-ning class, but you won't go to silk-screen printing with her, she says."

"I haven't quite decided yet," said Janet, scraping the last drop of soup, gray-beige, from her white bone-china plate. "I've left it too late to enroll for the popular things, anyway."

"What are the popular things?"

"Oh, yoga's always full at the beginning of term, and the cordon-bleu cookery class, and the local history class too."

"You don't *need* a cookery class," said Ted Street.

"Thank you," she said, and smiled quite warmly, in what she felt was quite an adult fashion.

He asked her why the local history class was so popular, and she explained that it was because a local hero was giving it, a handsome man in his sixties, the curator of the museum, a white-haired gallant, admired by ladies old and young. "But not by you?" suggested Ted Street.

"Oh no, I do admire him," said Janet. "I used to like it when he came to speak to us at school."

"So why don't you go to his class? Do you like to be different?"

"Oh no, not really. Not at all, in fact."

"And you won't go to the silk-screen printing, with Cynthia?"

"I don't think so. I've gone off that kind of thing."

"So what will you do?"

Ted Street stared at her, in his unusually amiable new mood. She wished she could think of something interesting to say, something unexpected. "I must get the next course," she said, and began to reach for the soup plates.

The others talked of radioactivity and nuclear reactors.

"Perhaps you really don't want to go to an evening class at all," said Ted.

"No," she said, considering the point seriously. "No, perhaps you're right."

And she left the room with the soup plates, and came back with the chicken and rice and peaches, and found that they had stopped talking heavily about fuel and had begun to talk about it lightly instead, joking about previous power cuts, saying that they were grateful that at least Janet had managed to get their delicious dinner cooked (they were all warming up a little with the wine), and that if all the lights went off now it wouldn't be too bad. Mark told quite a funny story about what somebody had said to him at the factory today about what would happen to the specimens if the electricity got switched off, and they discussed why it was that the telephone went on working when the electricity wasn't on, and Mark asked Janet where the candles were just in case (he asked this in quite a friendly fashion, but Janet could see he was going to punish her at some point for having enjoyed talking to his friend Ted), and they ate their chicken, and their salad, and their orange dessert, and just as Janet was going out to put the kettle on for coffee all the lights went out.

They all laughed, of course, and lit matches, and expressed thanks that dinner was over, and said that they could

do without coffee. The house was all-electric. It will get cold
soon, said Janet anxiously. Oh, then we'll all have to snuggle
up to one another, said Bill David, and laughed in an unpleasant manner that made her stiffen and shiver in the dark.
She would rather they talked about the gravel pit, than that
they got like *that*. But it was going to be hard to stop them,
now the lights were out. And Mark would hate it and resent
it as much as she would. Well, it was all his fault, he shouldn't
have such friends. She borrowed a cigarette lighter from
Cynthia, and went off into the kitchen to look for candles.
With any luck she'd at least be able to illuminate the place
brightly enough to stop any goings-on.

She found a whole packet of thick white candles in a cupboard, bought in the last emergency: she also had colored
ones, from the Christmas before. She put them in the pottery
holder that Cynthia and Ted had given her, and told them
what a useful gift it had been. They glowed, red and green
and orange. They left the table and sat in the easy chairs at
the other end of the room, in the soft light. Janet had always
liked candlelight: in the old days, in Leicester, that year she'd
lived on her own when she met Mark, she used to make her
own, and Mark had teased her about them, and made all
kinds of knowing remarks about nuns and candles, and wasn't
it time she got married, and she hadn't had the faintest
idea, but not the faintest idea, of what he'd been talking
about, and when she'd found out she'd been so upset, so
mortified, but by then it was too late, by then she had been
officially engaged, and anyway part of her still hoped that if
Mark were able to make such knowing remarks about nuns
and candles, then he would know some other useful facts of
life—but of course he hadn't known, all he had known had
been empty secondhand sterile vulgar jokes, and her knowledge, her instincts, when it came to it, had been better than
his, and God knows she had been hopeless enough. Looking
at the flickering candles, she had to repress these thoughts,
or they would have disturbed her too much. How dared Mark
come and take her from her safe solitude, and give her so

little in exchange for it? Whatever had he done it for? But, on the other hand, whatever had he got out of it? Nothing, nothing. He must have been mistaken as she had been, to have come to this pass. She bowed her head upon her knees, as she sat upon the floor (there were chairs for five people only), hoping to escape notice in the semi-darkness, but he had spotted her, he had heard her thoughts, he was on to her.

"Can't you go next *door* and make us some *coffee*," he said, in that curious whine that would come over him late at night or after a drink or two. "Haven't they got *gas* next *door*?"

"I don't think so," said Janet. "The whole estate's electric."

"Oh, *electric. Dynamic. Humming* with vitality. Never have you known"—he turned to his other guests—"such a vital, exciting, thrilling modern milieu. And is there nowhere we could get a cup of coffee? Surely your friend Mrs. Cooper next door, surely she'd have a primus stove or something like that? Or a *hay box*? Could one make coffee in a *hay box*? The mind boggles. I'm sure your friend Mrs. Cooper next door must have been a girl guide at some point in her dazzling career. Indeed, she may still be a girl guide now, she certainly dresses as though just about to present herself to *Brown Owl*, wouldn't you say, Janet? Wouldn't you say, my enchanting wife?"

"I don't know whether Jean's got a primus stove or not," said Janet, "but I can hardly go round and ask to borrow it without inviting her round for coffee. And in view of your views about her, you wouldn't be very likely to like that, would you?"

"*In view of your views—likely to like*—oh, she's getting quite witty and articulate in her old age, isn't she?" said Mark.

He is unbelievable, said Janet to herself. What could I have done to him to deserve what I get?

"We can manage without coffee," said Anthea, thinking things had gone far enough. "It's so pretty here, in the candlelight. Let's just sit here quietly until we freeze to death. They'll find us in the morning, dressed in our best. We could be put in a museum as a diorama, they could call it 'Dinner Party in the Provinces in the Nineteen Seventies.' They could transport your entire lounge to Tockley Museum and set it down as the next one on from all those Roman relics and bits of agricultural machinery, Janet. And I bet you people would look at it in a hundred years or two, and say, oh, look, isn't that nice, oh, I do wish I'd lived *then*."

"Isn't it funny, they'd say, that they still hadn't invented electricity?" suggested Ted. "And that the women were still wearing long skirts, they'd say," said Cynthia: and they went on for a while like that, imagining how others would see them, what mistakes they made in seeing other ages. Janet listened, thinking that perhaps she was inarticulate and a fool, as Mark proclaimed, because after all the others were quite entertaining at times: Anthea was being exceptionally pleasant, softened by the lights, and started to tell them about a visit she had made to Norwich Museum that summer with a nephew of hers (and Janet was surprised she had taken such trouble with a nephew, which proved how little she knew her), and how much he had liked the dioramas, and how gruesome life must have been in a really primitive society, in the stone or the bronze age, because there they were in all these reconstructed bits of history, poor buggers (it *must* be late, thought Janet, or Women's Lib was further advanced than she suspected), digging and hoeing and shivering and never resting. And Bill said that he'd seen an article recently proving that stone age Britons were cannibals, or something like that, and that wasn't very nice, was it, and they discussed morality and survival, and luxury and subsistence, and agreed that one of the causes of the present power crisis was that people had come to expect far too high a standard of living, far too much comfort, both at home and at work, but that it didn't do any good to know that, because there was no way of stopping the process.

As they talked, so cleverly, Janet remembered that after

all she had got a little cooking stove somewhere, she and
Mark had used it on their first holiday together in Wales, and
it might well have enough gas in it still for a cup of coffee
each. She went off to look for it, and there it was, in the
bottom of the broom closet. While she was fiddling with it
in the kitchen, trying to get it to light, Mark called to ask
what she was doing, and she told him, and Anthea said (how
nice Anthea was being, and why?) that she should bring it
into the lounge, and not stay out there in the dark, the even
darker kitchen—so she came through, and crouched on the
carpet, and finally managed, in the flickering shadows, to
ignite a pale blue flame. It flickered up, blue and spiritual,
sad and cold in color, although warming the small copper
pan. They all watched, spellbound, for the water to bubble,
as though watching the process of boiling for the first time.
Each small bubble seemed to swell from some deep spring.
It was not the coffee they wanted, it was the magic of the
process, it was not the triumph of the process but the magic
of it, not the will and the domination but the secret invocation, and as they watched Anthea told them how she had
taken her nephew to a reconstruction of an Iceni village in
Norfolk, one of the most beautiful historical reconstructions
she had ever seen (he was a history-struck little boy, her
nephew), and that she had read there that the process of
making iron had seemed to the iron age men so accidental,
so arbitrary, that they had been obliged to invoke success
from the deities, rather than from science. Let us now invoke
the God of boiling water, said Ted, as reluctant small bubbles
gathered around the pan's rim. They didn't know *how* it happened, it was so hit-and-miss, cried Anthea, but when it did,
that was a good day, a fine creation. They *made iron*! Imagine! But magic, it was to them. They didn't know how it
happened. Imagine!

The water bubbled, and Janet made tiny cups of coffee,
more an offering than a drink. They drank them solemnly,
facetiously invoking various gods. It was growing colder in
the room, but nobody knew what action to take, it seemed

better not to admit that it was cold at all. Gradually the conversation cooled, as well as the temperature, and Ted suggested that it would be as well to go home. It won't be any warmer at home, said Cynthia, and then came the moment that Janet had been dreading—oh yes it will, one can get into *bed* and warm oneself up at home, cried Anthea, and there followed inevitably a discussion of how the birth rate rose in power cuts, and how contraceptives would never do as much for world population in the East as the introduction of electric light in the evening, and how the Eskimos, although they had little to do but copulate, could never expand and overtake the world because their environment was *too* hostile, though at the same time, as Bill remarked, one had to wonder what kind of birth control they did use to keep the family size down. Abstinence, infanticide, the contraceptive pill?

Janet hated this kind of conversation. It kept the others warm for a while, and she watched them trying to be clever, giggling, making predictable jokes: all the temporary gleam had gone out of them, and they looked like they had looked at the beginning to her, mean, derivative, jaundiced, not golden but jaundiced in the mellow candlelight. It was amazing how none of them had a good word, ever, to say about anyone. They enjoyed sniping, about people they knew, people they didn't know, about whole cultures and countries they had never seen. They were a real opposition group, united in their suspicion of the outside world. Even Ted, whom she had been beginning to think that she might like, was being as silly as the others, in his speculation about the effect of central heating on sexual practices. She hated talk about sex. She didn't know what to make of the attitude of the others— perhaps they could talk about it in this way because they really enjoyed it and got on with it at home, perhaps Ted and Cynthia and Bill and Anthea had perfectly satisfactory private lives. If so, she admitted, they were free to make these jokes and to speculate. But in her heart she couldn't really believe that they were happy, she couldn't really believe that they enjoyed themselves in bed. It was just a convention,

THE REALMS OF GOLD 175

they were talking conventionally about something that did not exist. The emperor's new clothes. She had support for this view in the fact that Mark talked as well as anyone about sex, made the same jokes, seemed knowing and worldly—and yet she knew that he knew very little about it at all, when it came down to it. She remembered with a kind of disgust the way he used to go on about mini-skirts, in the days of the mini-skirt, about proportion, and the beauty of women's legs—he had a whole set speech about Art, the Human Body, Michelangelo (or was it Leonardo) and the Mini-Skirt, with which he used to entertain guests for months, till they too obviously tired of it. And yet he had no feeling for legs at all. He had never noticed any beauty in her own legs, he had never addressed them with any tenderness. All in the head, was his appreciation. She was glad that now she could cover her legs up in long skirts and keep them to herself, she had hated it when Mark would point at them in demonstration.

So they sat, and talked about sex—not rudely, not crudely, not tenderly. It was just talk. Perhaps, had they been five years older, there would have been a bit of action, a little more suggestiveness. As it was, there was nothing much. Janet sat and waited for them to go away, and hoped that the lights would not come back on again.

They did not. Somebody vaguely suggested that they should get coats, or rugs, and sit a little longer, but the conversation did not seem brilliant enough to warrant it, the little flare of intimacy had died down, they were all possessed with a kind of uneasiness. The time had come to go home, to confront one's own ghost privately, one's own skeleton. Anthea made rather a handsome skeleton, a well-covered one, rising dramatically to her feet, stretching, her bangles shaking and glinting, her huge heavy plastic beads catching the candlelight. Thank you, thank you for a *lovely* evening, she said, and kissed Janet on the cheek. She was a southerner and had imported southern manners, she kept herself going by frightening other women with her embraces; she rather enjoyed the way poor timid Janet stiffly shrank away. Cyn-

thia, a Sheffield girl, did not kiss, of course. Nor did the
men. They shuffled, and muttered thanks, not very good at
such things. Ted said several times over how much he had
enjoyed himself, and they must come to them soon. They
moved toward the door. The Streets, of course, had to give
the Davids a lift home. As soon as they were actually out on
the path, a new lease of life seemed to fill them: they stopped
muttering, spoke up, laughed loudly, commented on the size
of the moon and the large stars, told the Birds that they would
have to bring their gas stove with them next time they called
for dinner, waved cheerily, laughed some more, pledged
themselves to defend the gravel pit at a meeting on Thursday
night—all as though they had to prove to the neighbors that
they had had a good evening, thought Janet. The neighbors,
the Blaneys and the Coopers, sat silently in their dark houses,
and who could tell if they were watching or not?

The house was quite silent when Janet and Mark went back
into it, uncannily silent, without even the hum of electricity.
The baby had worn himself out with crying and was fast
asleep. Janet felt guilty about him: she should have gone up
to him, but had not dared, for fear the meal would be ruined
or Mark annoyed or Cynthia (who believed in letting them
yell) critical of her maternal behavior. She had sacrificed the
poor baby on the altar of their opinions, and now he slept,
exhausted. She felt bad. She also felt worried that she could
not clear up properly: it seemed silly to clear up in the dark,
one could do it so much more efficiently in the daylight, and
yet she really didn't like the thought of all those plates and
dishes and chicken bones and dirty glasses and ashtrays lying
around all evening. Of course it didn't matter, but it mattered
to her. She wondered what Mark would say if she started to
tidy up. Would he shout at her and tell her she was a fool?
She would start on it anyway.

Furtively, almost guiltily, she began to stack the dessert
plates that had been abandoned on the white table.

"Why don't you leave that till morning?" said Mark,

watching her from somewhere over in the shadows, standing
by the functionless, never-used fireplace.

"I'd rather get a bit of it done now," said Janet.

"Why? It'll wait till tomorrow. You've nothing else to do
tomorrow, have you? Nothing *pressing*, nothing particularly
urgent?"

"Of course not," said Janet. "It's just that I don't like the
thought of all this mess lying around all night. I'll just put a
few of the things away now. I'll just stack the dishes. It won't
take me a minute."

"You *are* neurotic. Everyone says you're neurotic, you
know. You know what it means, don't you, not being able to
leave the plates on the table all night?"

"No, I don't," she said, wearily, wondering what he was
going to come out with now—some dreary bit of half-baked
psychology out of a paperback, some pseudo-intellectual joke
from one of those silly games he and his friends sometimes
played. She often wondered how he and his friends dared to
play these games and say such things to one another, when
it was quite obvious that there must be something very wrong
with all of them. Skating on thin ice, they were. What if one
day one of them broke the convention and came up with some
real, some shocking truth: what if she were to say to Mark,
now, that the reason she wanted to stack the plates was that
she didn't want to go to bed with him, and that she'd do
anything to put off the evil moment of getting into bed with
her own husband. It was all very well making jokes about
barrenness, and frigidity, and neurosis. How dare he? Why
didn't she speak up? But she couldn't. She couldn't attack
him. She was terrified of destroying him. And Mark destroyed was worse than Mark potting shots at her as though
she were a duck at a fair.

Mark was still trying to think of something clever to say
about not putting the plates away, and failing: she got in
quickly, suddenly, with an obvious point. "Anyway," she said,
"I must at least put the chicken bones in the bin, or the cat'll
get them, and they can choke on chicken bones, cats can."

"I'm going to bed," said Mark. He was annoyed with himself for not being able to think of a joke about plates. Perhaps he'd have worked one out for her by the time she got upstairs.

"All right," said Janet. "I won't be long."

And she heard Mark go up, and clean his teeth in the dark, while she continued to pile up plates, and empty ashtrays, and put the bones, wrapped in newspaper, in the bin. She thought about doing the washing up, but of course there wasn't any hot water, it was tepid, and anyway she really couldn't see well enough to do it properly. It would be annoying to have to do it all again in the morning.

(Frances Wingate, a hundred and one miles away in Putney, was stacking her dishwasher, and thinking, not particularly coincidentally, about the museum in Tockley, and the eel stang, and her father watching before her the newts in the ditch, and becoming a professor of zoology. Had he ever been disappointed that she hadn't pursued her childish interest in nature? He'd never said anything about it, one way or the other. Daisy was getting on rather well with the physics, better than Frances had ever done: her tears had been caused by a fairly high level of frustration. Were there any women physicists?

She scraped a few neglected baked beans off a plate into the bin, and ate a cold piece of bacon rind. Though greedy, she was not fussy.

She shut the dishwasher door, and switched it on. She was wondering what her life would have been like, if her father hadn't become a zoologist. How would she have got on, if she'd had to live in Tockley? Though of course in those circumstances she could hardly have been born, because if her father hadn't gone to Oxford on a scholarship and met her mother, she wouldn't have existed, would she?

She looked at her watch. It was nearly bedtime. Perhaps she would go to bed and finish the novel that an old college friend of hers had written. It wasn't very good, but it was quite amusing, recognizing the characters, from so long ago.

The children were to go to her husband Anthony, while she was in Adra. How useful it was, to be divorced, she reflected, as she mounted the stairs with her pile of little distractions—the novel, a couple of learned journals, the *New Statesman*, a small whiskey, and some nail scissors that she'd used earlier, *faute de mieux*, to trim Spike's hair—how useful to be divorced, and how pleasant, if one cannot sleep with the man one loves, to sleep alone.)

When she had emptied the coffee pot, Janet Bird went back into the lounge, and sat down for a moment on the white sheepskin rug in front of the empty grate. It hadn't been too bad an evening, after all. Mark hadn't been too difficult, and Ted and Anthea had been rather nicer than usual. She sat back on her heels, and listened, to hear if Mark was making a noise. He couldn't be reading, he'd only got one candle. She heard a closet door shut, and wondered how much he'd had to drink. Not very much, she thought. Two glasses of sherry, and they'd only had three bottles of wine between them, and Bill always drank a lot more than his share. She wished that Mark had had some more. If he had had some more, he would be more likely to fall asleep. As it was, she knew that he was lying in wait.

Oh, God, oh, God, give me patience, give me strength, she said to herself, not to God particularly. Every night of her life, the same problem. What was she to do, what could she ever do, to escape this torment? There lay Mark waiting to grab her. She hated it, she hated him. She had thought of so many ways out—feeling ill, headaches, period pains, backaches. The baby had been a good excuse and had kept him off her for three months at a time. Perhaps she should have another baby, that would give her a bit of peace, but at what a price to herself, and it didn't seem quite fair to the baby either, one shouldn't use the poor little creatures as a kind of antisex device, it seemed all wrong somehow, but she bet it was quite common, however wrong. The queen had

babies they said to get out of having to appear in public all
the time, and so it perhaps wasn't all that rare to use babies
as a way of avoiding making love, she knew plenty of women
used them as an excuse, one could see that from the back
pages of the women's magazines, and the advice always was,
*don't worry, be patient, and your husband must be patient
too, and you will find that in good time all your natural
feelings will come back to you and you will enjoy your married life as much as you did before, it is quite natural to find
yourself less interested in sexual relations for a little while
after baby is born*—ah yes, but what if one had never been
interested, what if one had no natural feelings, what then,
Witch Doctor, what then? Oh, she knew all the tricks of
avoidance—pretending to be asleep, messing around downstairs for so long when Mark was tired that he fell asleep
first, little aches and pains all exploited to the full—it makes
one into a hypochondriac as well as inflicting other real
wounds, does marriage—pretending to be terribly worried
about altruistic things like her father's stroke or the mortgage
going up, or the reason why Mark hadn't got promotion yet,
so that Mark would feel a brute if he touched her, an insensitive brute. Oh yes, she had been through all that, and would
go through it still, as far as she could see, for every night of
her life, forever and ever, in sickness and in health. No wonder she wished for a volcano or an earthquake, neither of
them very likely in this flat terrain. A flood would be more
likely; what if the great river Don were to overflow and wash
them all away out to the cold North Sea? Sometimes she
wished that she could really catch some disabling disease—
not a fatal disease, for after all if it were truly death she
desired, she had the means to hand. No, what she wanted
was some universal disaster that would involve her in its fate,
or else some personal release, through paralysis, or a stroke,
or the threat of heart attacks.

She rocked backward and forward on the white rug in the
candlelight, and thought about all this.

Sometimes she had even woken the baby on purpose, as a

shield, as a protector. One can't make love (if that is what one could call it) in front of a baby, or not in Tockley, anyway. One may in the isles of the Pacific, or in Italy, or in the East End, or in Hampstead or Kensington, but not in Tockley.

Something had gone very wrong, somewhere. She recognized that. She did tend to think of herself as a norm and to see the world in her own image, finding enough evidence in Tockley at least to support her view, but she could tell that the rest of the world wasn't really like herself. The whole thing had been designed for some different end. Sex and babies had certainly not been intended by nature to be conflicting trials of interest, had they? Wasn't one meant to enjoy sex rather than grit one's teeth and bear it? She didn't even really like thinking about these things, but she had to; one of the most painful things about her present way of life (as a married woman) was that she had to think about it constantly, indeed she could never forget it, except on those rare and blessed occasions when Mark was away on business. Some people certainly enjoyed sex: literature and films and television and such like were full of their enjoyment. And if there *was* something real, why was she forever shut out from it, and forced to live in this horrible horrible mockery? What had she done wrong? What had been her mistake?

Somewhere in the back of her mind she had an image of what things ought to be like. It wasn't a very sexy image— sex she genuinely couldn't imagine as being anything other than humiliating—but it involved a mother, a father and a baby, all in some way happy together and united, though they didn't bear much inspection, this happy trio, because the more she tried to visualize them the stronger a resemblance they took on a Christmas crib with proud parents and babe in the manger, which wasn't the point at all, because Jesus had been produced by a virgin birth; it was yet another proof that she couldn't either want or imagine sex. Perhaps it was simply the Christmas candles that had suggested the image. She tried to remember an article she had read in *Nova*, by a man describing his emotion as he watched his baby daughter being born. It had made her cry. It had moved her so much that she had torn it out and thrown it away because she didn't want Mark to read it.

Things could be better, but not for her. It was a hard truth she held, hard like a nut. It would crack her teeth sooner than reveal its soft kernel for her.

It was time to go upstairs. She couldn't really pretend to be doing anything much for much longer down here. There was one more ashtray she could empty, over there by the corner of the settee. It was the one Ted had been using. She wondered why Ted had been so pleasant to her—was he just feeling sorry for her because she was so stupid and so unable to talk about gravel pits? She wondered how his marriage with Cynthia was. She could never make Cynthia out—she was brisk, busy, self-assured, outspoken, rather aggressive, she had two children already at school, one at nursery, one at primary, she worked part-time in the local hospital in the physiotherapy department and was very good at getting to know important people, she was into everything, she managed and manipulated and gossiped, she made Janet feel feeble and wilting, and she was getting fat. She wasn't, Janet had thought, the kind of person one could ever get to know really well: the nearest they had ever got to an intimate conversation (Janet was good at avoiding these too) had been when Cynthia had told her not to bother with natural childbirth classes, they were a waste of time, and had given her some gruesome hospital statistics about easy births by unnatural mothers and hard births by those who'd been breathing and doing exercises from the first week on. Don't you bother with all that, my girl, Cynthia had said, and Janet, relieved to be spared the embarrassment of doing exercises with a lot of other pregnant women, had followed her advice without noticeable ill effect; Cynthia came to see her in hospital and had actually been rather cheery and helpful, knowing all the doctors as she did, laughing loudly and making jokes about the nurses, admiring the baby. She was a no-

nonsense person, and had been good for morale, in those circumstances.

But to be married to, well, that was another matter. Ted must know her intimately, if anyone did. It was hard to imagine what they talked about. Ted was rather a quiet person, and Cynthia so noisy.

(Frances, brushing her teeth, was thinking of Karel and Joy. She hoped Joy didn't think she had given Karel up for Joy's sake. She didn't like to be underestimated.

Karel Schmidt, for his part, was thinking about Frances. So she was off to Adra, was she? Unlike Janet, he had read his morning papers thoroughly. Unlike Frances and Janet, he was nowhere near bed. He kept late hours. At the moment, while thinking of Frances, he was ostensibly listening to the drunken ramblings of a colleague whose wife had left him for the third time, and who was threatening suicide if he ever made her go back. They would go on for some time.

David Ollerenshaw was nowhere near bed either. Like Karel, he found himself in the listening role. His friend Banks, rather surprisingly, claimed to have fallen in love with a red-haired seismologist from Canada, who, like Banks, was already married. David listened with interest, over a rapidly emptying bottle of Glenfiddich, to Banks's story: it had had to wait till Mrs. Banks went to bed, so the whole of dinnertime had been devoted to earthquakes. How extraordinarily unexpected people are, thought David. He had always assumed that the heart of Banks was made of stone. How glad he was that he himself was not involved either with Mrs. Banks or with the red-haired seismologist. He opened the second pack of cigarettes, and listened on.)

Janet picked up the ashtray, and stared at the cigarette ends. White crushed cellulose, gray insubstantial ash. She picked up the large green scented Swedish candle at her elbow, idly, to look at it more closely, and some molten wax tipped into the pottery ashtray with its pottery sign of the zodiac. The combination of liquid wax and fag ends and burnt matches was singularly disgusting, but she tipped some more, trying to swamp the fag ends completely, leaving a burning hollow green crater in the wide candle. A friend of Mark's had spent years working for a tobacco company to invent the perfect synthetic cigarette. It seemed a strange way to spend one's life, but a useful one, it could be argued. Mark and Ted rarely spoke of the utility of their projects, they spoke instead of salaries and colleagues and the canteen food. They could not speak to her about such matters, she did not understand plastics, she tried to but she couldn't, and anyway part of her didn't want to. She melted more wax and tipped it into her molten green lake.

The translucent deep core of the candle glowed more brightly. Mark, upstairs, slammed a drawer in a threatening manner. Thus did he summon her. There would be no point tonight in trying to read in bed about the Jewish orphan in Poland. She must go up to her appointed, her chosen fate. Why could not Mark be more pleasant to her, if he wanted her to sleep with him?

She would go up when she had completely swamped Ted's cigarette ends and little heap of matches. She melted more wax, she tipped, she melted. She thought about what Anthea had said about the iron age. If anyone were to see her now, what would they think she was doing? Would they think she was a witch, would they think her mad, would they think the twentieth century mad? Here she sat, pouring wax onto an ancient symbol, pointlessly. If disinterred as from the ruins of Pompeii, what little rite would it be assumed she had been enacting, what gods would she have been seen to propitiate?

Her cat appeared from nowhere, as she melted the last drops. She sat by her side, fresh from the dry leaves outside, and watched the small flame with narrowed eyes and wide streaked golden irises. All the matches were sunk by now in the slowly hardening dead sea of wax, sunk like spars from some small shipwreck. Janet stared at her work with some satisfaction. And then she heard her husband call ''Janet'' from upstairs, and she shut the little cat into the kitchen, and blew out the green candle, and carried an ordinary white candle from the grocer's with her up to bed.

And that is enough, for the moment, of Janet Bird. More than enough, you might reasonably think, for her life is slow, even slower than its description, and her dinner party seemed to go on too long to her, as it did to you. Frances Wingate's life moves much faster. (Though it began rather slowly, in these pages—a tactical error, perhaps, and the idea of starting her off in a more manic moment has frequently suggested itself, but the reasons against such an opening are stronger, finally, than the reasons for it.) Because Frances Wingate's life moves faster, it is therefore more entertaining. We will return to it shortly, and will dwell no longer on its depressing aspects. It is depressing to read about depression. Frances Wingate, as you will have noticed, rarely feels depressed for long, anyway, and her opportunities for distraction are varied. Whereas Janet Bird's best hope of distraction is an evening class.

We will return to Frances with relief: her diseases are meaningless and mild, her prognosis is good, she is a cheering spectacle and should be given a fair chance. (Whether or not Janet Bird will be allowed a fair chance is another matter, as yet unresolved, and in the resolution, truth, likelihood, and a natural benevolence are at war.) But meanwhile, we must look briefly at David Ollerenshaw, the third of the Ollerenshaws, and I fear much the most impenetrable. I must confess I had at this point intended to introduce him in greater depth: indeed, I had a fine leap, from Janet staring at the small crater in her melted wax candle to David staring into the crater of a small volcano. It would have been an arbitrary link, but I liked it, and am sorry that I have messed it up by this perhaps unnecessary fit of explanation. The truth is that David was intended to play a much larger role in this narrative, but the more I looked at him, the more incomprehensible he became, and I simply have not the nerve to present what I saw in him in the detail I had intended. On the other hand, he continues to exist, he has a significance that might one day become clear, and meanwhile he will have to speak, as it were, for himself.

So: here is David Ollerenshaw, staring into the depths of a small and rather dull volcano. Banks had told him to have a look at it, but Banks must have been biased in its favor. It is a week after the long dull dinner party of Mark and Janet Bird, and David is well on his way to Adra, unlike Frances Wingate, who is still messing about in Putney wondering whether to take her black dress or her brown dress. You will remember (or, in other words, I fear you may have forgotten) that he has seen Frances Wingate once, at her lecture in the opening pages of this book, and is looking forward to meeting her again.

He has already crossed Europe: the next morning, he is to embark for Africa, with his new green Peugeot, which waits for him at the bottom of the volcano, with a docile and hopeful air, like a well-trained but spirited horse. So far he is enjoying himself, though the best is yet to come: the best, in terms of the solitude of the desert, and after that the highly transitory and therefore acceptable life of the conference. Once in a while he enjoys meeting his colleagues and members of allied professions.

Let us, without more ado, move him into a different focus, and into the past tense.

Banks had told him the volcano was of interest, but perhaps he had been too absentminded to concentrate on what he was saying, seduced inwardly by thoughts of the red-haired seismologist. It rumbled, heaved and spat, then sank back again like an old man into its ashen bed. Disappointing. David remembered the one in Iceland, which had truly merited a visit. It had been spectacular.

David liked the idea that nature could and would do worse than man, if it wanted, and that it was just biding its time: he liked to think of the earth as a living beast, blazing internally, waiting to revenge itself on insults, but it seemed to be getting old and docile, pitifully easy to tease. One stuck tubes into its guts and siphoned off oil: one blasted out quarries and mined and burrowed: one could even provoke artificial earthquakes, these days. And the old creature didn't seem to mind. It just twitched, occasionally, and a few hundred people died, but then it fell back into its senile torpor. David Ollerenshaw would have liked a large cataclysm, rather than this gritty bubbling at his feet.

He had always been fond of the more dramatic, dynamic, and dangerous manifestations of nature, a fondness that had led him to related activities such as pot-holing, rock-climbing, mountain-climbing. He wasn't quite sure what he was after—death, his more prudent colleagues had sometimes suggested—but he pursued it with some perseverance. His pursuit had taken him to some strange landscapes, and some strange extremes of heat and cold—the Falkland Islands, the Solomon Islands, Alaska, Australia, Adra. The last of these, his present destination, had proved rather dull in some ways: mostly flat, hot, dry, underpopulated. But in other ways, it had for him, as for Frances Wingate, been a scene of discovery, for up in the north, in the uninhabited part, on a government survey last year, he and his team had discovered a valley of tin. (We have already seen him, waiting to confirm the details of his discovery on a computer.)

The Adran government had been delighted: the company for which he worked had been delighted. For a country extremely low in mineral resources, David's valley represented wealth, and his company would have a large stake in the difficult job of extracting it. David too was delighted, for through the valley he had satisfied one of his childhood ambitions: he had contributed to changing the world charts of mineral distribution. This had always been his secret desire, though he had toyed at times with the thought of an academic career in volcanoes or earthquakes, a lucrative career in oil. Minerals had been his first love: minerals had made him a geologist. His favorite bedtime book, as a boy, had been an old blue Penguin about minerals in industry, in which he would read nightly, with inexplicable interest, of phosphates and bauxite and platinum, of the properties of molybdenum, nickel, and the solitary monazite, which appeared on the beach sands of Travancore, in occasional large crystals weighing up to thirty pounds. Most of all he liked the charts. Why should there be so much tungsten in China, so much tin in Malaya, so much mercury in Spain, so much platinum in Russia, such enormous quantities of cobalt in the Belgian Congo, when other countries seemed to have no minerals at all?

He had always suspected that the charts must be wrong, even as a boy: and so they had been proved. As a boy, he had dreamed of unlikely discoveries—opals in Sweden, asbestos in the Sudan, zirconium in the Cameroons: and now they had found oil under the North Sea, and valleys of tin in Adra. When you've tried all the obvious places, start to look in the silly ones: on this principle had the Adran government worked, with surprising success. David had in his car his papers on the likely distribution of tin, all written up neatly for the UNESCO Conference on Saharan Resources that he was about to attend.

He stared down abstractly into the reddish lava, thinking of the world chart in the limp blue Penguin, and as he stared, the volcano rumbled, made a noise like a gravel pit emptying, and spat up, suddenly, a few fair-sized bombs. One of them landed at David's feet, and he stepped back sharply. Perhaps the thing wasn't so quiescent after all. It would be a very second-rate fate, to be knocked out by an almost-spent volcano, and it would serve him right for wanting to see a bit of action. He stooped and picked up one of the bombs. It was hot and light and bubbled, newly congealed. He thought, not for the first time, that it would be his idea of heaven to sit on an observation platform somewhere and watch the earth change—watch mountains heave and fold, seas shrink, rivers wear down their valleys, continents drift and collide, forests dry into deserts and deserts burgeon into forests. The processes, the constant flux, enthralled him. Man's life span was too short to be interesting: he wanted to see all the slow great events, right to the final cinder, the black hole.

Weighing the light lump of lava in his hand, he stood there, and thought about order, and process. He thought a great deal about order, and about whether it went down to the very middle of things. In another age, these speculations might have been called religious. They were certainly concerned with the nature of the infinite. In many ways, David was a typical post-Darwinian scientist, who had adapted himself without effort to the faith of scientific determinism: he saw order in the universe, he traced it along faults and folds, knowing that it was only ignorance that concealed the pattern, that the next outcrop existed surely, if only one could find it, and he had abandoned happily, indeed had never had (being born too late) the slightest sense of man as a necessary part of creation, as in any way a significant part. Man's life, as the Bible says, is grass, a mere breath: so was the whole history of mankind. This did not perturb him at all: on the contrary, he found the idea reassuring, for what he knew of man did not justify his taking of any very dignified part in the scale of creation.

He was, however, perturbed by nuclear physics. Like a Victorian agonizing over the death of God and the inaccuracy of the Bible, David found himself worrying about the place of man in the universe, and fearing that, through the splitting of the atom, man had gained a power quite inappropriate, quite unsanctioned, a god-head which he disliked in every way. It was all very well to maintain (as he frequently did, to justify his own activities) that man was merely another agent of natural weathering and change, like wind and water, and that his mining and quarrying were at best superficial insults, insignificant contributions to a much more mightily organized whole: the fact was that it now seemed possible that man would take into his own hands the destruction of matter itself. And if that were possible, one would have to rethink the question of man's proper place, and of the order that had seemed to pre-exist. Nuclear fission had created a spiritual imbalance in the world which he did not like at all. It had elevated spirit against matter, the organic agent against the inorganic, and he found this as alarming as his ancestors had found the correct dating of fossils, and the evolutionary chain. (If questioned, he would also have agreed that he deplored the destruction of innocent human beings, at Nagasaki, at Hiroshima, and that he did not care for the thought of future destruction on such a scale, but he did not think of such things while alone. As a geologist, he took a long view of time: even longer than Francis Wingate, archaeologist, and very much longer than Karel Schmidt, historian.)

He tossed the lump of lava back into the volcano's gullet, and lit himself a cigarette. He thought of the voyage across the well-charted Mediterranean. The ancients, so Banks had told him, had held a variety of interesting superstitious beliefs about volcanoes and earthquakes; well, of course they had. Man has to find an explanation or two. Perhaps nuclear fission was not such a disaster after all: for even if man blew up the whole surface of the globe, the whole human race, and everything else with it, and filled the entire atmosphere to its known limits with fallout (as he was now filling it with fallout from aerosols), there would still follow natural cooling processes. Man could, it was true, upset the lovely weathering processes, but he could surely never ruin the world to the very center? And if he could, what of the other worlds? Man was, after all, surely, thank God, in all his wickedness, insignificant and weak, even now.

David Ollerenshaw threw his cigarette end into the crater. The volcano received it, spewing gently from its blackened lungs, like a tired old prophet. It would not overwhelm him with its wrath.

Imagine him, David Ollerenshaw, standing there, the only unbearded geologist in the business, fair-haired, long-necked, short-sighted, indefinably English, indefinably odd, with the oddness of one who spends much time alone, thinking about inhuman things. Watch him, as he begins to stumble, a small figure against a small volcano, down the mounds of pyroclastic rubble, back to his new car. Tomorrow, he sets sail for Africa.

And we can leave him there, on the eve of departure, and return home to Frances Wingate; she is a more familiar figure, a more manageable figure, in every way.

Frances Wingate spent the weekend before her departure for Adra with her brother's family, in the country. Her brother had a large cottage in the Cotswolds: once he had filled it at weekends with his own children, but now they were dispersed at boarding schools, and Frances had brought her own four. Hugh's children were dispersed only in theory the night before, the Friday night, his eldest son Stephen and his grandchild had arrived from Sussex, unexpectedly (though Frances privately fancied that they had come to see her). She was still worried about Stephen: something was up, she felt sure. So they were a large gathering, a family party, and there they sat, on the Saturday night, by an open fire, drinking, talking, remembering old times. Her own three younger ones had gone upstairs, though not to bed: they were expected to sleep in sleeping bags on mattresses on the floor (all the beds had had to be divided), and therefore they were fighting and jumping about and quarreling and reading damp spidery piles of their cousins' old comics. Frances's long-legged daughter Daisy was sitting below, with her niece on her knee, and keeping very quiet in case somebody noticed her and sent her to bed. Stephen, Frances, and Hugh were talking about Freud: Hugh's wife, Natasha, was leafing through a picture book of Ife and Nok sculptures that Frances had brought her. (It was an expensive book, but Frances had been sent a review copy, and anyway she doubted its thesis.) The fire crackled and popped: it smelt of wood and resin. There were yew boughs on it, lopped from the overhanging tree at the end of the church garden. It had seemed unlucky to lop them yet unlucky to leave them, so there they burned, with their pale poisonous gummy roasting berries. A pleasant scene, a rural scene, a family scene.

It was a pretty cottage, they were widely thought to have been lucky to find it. It was in a lovely part of the country—fertile, picturesque, with steep hills and valleys, verdant, unspoiled, expensive. Natasha, whose domestic touch Frances at times had time to envy, had made it exceptionally pretty. It was a large gray stone building—three cottages, in fact, knocked into one, with a large study, and upstairs a sequence of intercommunicating bedrooms. The garden outside sloped down to the churchyard: a gate led from the side onto a steep sloping field, with walks and sheep, and a small wood. The village contained a few shops, two pubs, a country crafts center. An idyllic position, everyone agreed. Natasha loved the country, she gardened with enthusiasm, she cooked and baked and painted, she chopped wood and tried to rear carp in the small pond. Frances admired her. She had just admired a large dinner cooked by her—farmhouse pâté, a casserole, salad, and home-made bread. The bread was brown and shining, with a woven plait on top of it, its crust a perfect brittle glaze, yellow-brown like a harvest offering. Everything that Natasha did was real and perfect. She took no shortcuts, she chopped with a hand chopper, she ground with a hand grinder, she made real stock, real bread, real marmalade, she preserved fruit. Her stone larder was full of jars of fruit, gleaming like jewels in bright rows.

Now she sat there, tired and comfortable, in a deep armchair, with her feet curled up under her, looking at the pictures. She wore a long wool skirt, and expensive shoes. She was tall, slight, and bony, her face was lined and hard and sweet. She had the gallant air of a woman fighting a losing battle, but nobody could guess the terms of her defeat, for she was discreet and silent about herself. She had a well-shaped mouth, curiously curved, with thin and conscious delicate lips, a careful and precise and gentle way of speech. Her hair was dyed. It had turned, in the course of nature, from brown to a miserable mustardy yellowy fuzzy gray, and so she dyed it, back to its original brown. It was her one weak gesture, and it was a realistic one, for she did, as she

had said to Frances one day some years ago, look like the
Witch of Endor with it undyed. And who wants to look like
that? she had said. It isn't fair to other people, she had said.
Who could tell what vanity lay concealed in her? Certainly
she always wore extremely expensive shoes. Now they were
tucked under her, out of sight. She sat there and looked at
photographs of wide-browed terra-cotta women, and read of
additive and subtractive techniques of sculpture, in terra
cotta and in wood.

Her husband was drunk, as he was every night of his life.
He drank at least half a bottle of scotch regularly, and if there
was anything to celebrate he drank more. He was arguing
with his son about Freud. He had not read Freud; Stephen
had. Frances was appealed to from time to time by either
side. She had read more than the former and less than the
latter—or perhaps more less recently than the latter. They
were discussing the uses of Freudian analysis, Hugh perhaps
predictably taking the view that it was useless, Stephen more
surprisingly claiming that it could be beneficial in certain
cases. It emerged that his wife (how strange to think such a
child has a wife, thought Frances) was thinking of struggling
out of the clutches of a drug-mad psychiatrist in hospital into
the embrace of a Freudian analyst at home—though what
home, whose home, where, was not at all clear. She's quite
right, Stephen was saying, it's no use her just lying there
swallowing pills and then being bullied into eating jam sandwiches. There must be a cause, it's the cause that needs
curing. He said this earnestly, and seemed to mean it.

Hugh, emphatic, vehement, as he always was later in the
evening, after a few drinks, took the line that if the pills made
her eat the sandwiches, then what was wrong with the pills?
Anyway, you lot, he said, you live on drugs anyway, why
object just because a doctor gives them to you in hospital?
What's the difference? And anyway, he went on, getting carried away, as arguments crowded into his head, I thought
young people disapproved of Freud, I thought he was sup-

posed to have a mechanical unspiritual view of human nature, and you're all spiritual aren't you?

"*I'm* not particularly spiritual," said Stephen, shaking his head gently, looking spiritual and aggrieved. "And I do wish you wouldn't talk about young people, Hugh. I'm not young people. I'm a young person. Be reasonable."

"Well, you share a good many characteristics of your generation."

"Of course I do. That doesn't mean I share them all. You do get so *animated* by the very *word* 'young,' dad."

"Well, do you blame me?" cried Hugh, feverishly pouring himself another drink, histrionically clutching his thick black curly hair, "do you blame me? Here I am, a grandfather at the age of forty. It's a joke, what kind of effect do you think it's likely to have on me? No wonder the adrenaline starts to flow the minute I *see* anyone under the age of thirty."

Watching them, Frances thought how true it was that Hugh got animated. She had rarely seen anyone with so much physical restlessness. He lived a sedentary life, an office life (how he managed to work so well she never knew), and in the evenings a violence of speech and gesture and emotion would take him over, like a spirit. His views were extreme, his language appalling, his behavior erratic. Stephen, on the other hand, sat still and careful like his mother, expressing himself in small movements of face and speech. As though, it suddenly occurred to Frances, as though afraid to move?

They moved on to a discussion of whether or not analysis was designed to make one fit into society, and if so, whether or not it destroyed rather than mended the individual psyche. Hugh argued that it destroyed, and that therefore people like Stephen, who were supposed to disapprove of society, ought also to disapprove of analysis. "Who ever said I disapproved of *society*?" said Stephen, in answer to this. "I've got nothing against it. Why should I disapprove of it?"

"Because of capitalism and all that crap. And policemen and drugs. And the Third World."

"I don't give a fuck about the Third World or capitalism,"

said Stephen. "What on earth have they got to do with me? I don't know what you're talking about."

"Don't you disapprove of capitalism?"

"No, why should I? Do you?"

"Of course I don't."

"Well then, why should I?"

There seemed to be a deadlock, and Hugh turned to Frances, and appealed to her to support his view that Freudian philosophy was both pernicious and out of date. "As a woman, for God's sake, Frances," he said, "surely you object?"

"Well, sort of," said Frances. The problem with Hugh was that he really was quite well informed in a muddled kind of way, he was probably quite well aware of the feminist arguments against Freudian faith, but he was too drunk to express himself. And she herself was also rather confused about Freud's views of women. While not quite able to accept the theory of penis envy, she was more and more convinced that what every woman wanted was a man, and that what every man wanted was a woman, or that if they didn't want that they ought to, and that the only possibility of happiness and harmlessness on earth were to be found where Freud would have us find them, and that there was no way out of this, and that there was no point in being reasonable, life wasn't reasonable, motives weren't very mixed, they were horribly pure, appallingly unmixed, life wasn't at all complex, it was truly of an unfair, terrifying, rigid, irreducible, wicked, amoral simplicity. One just couldn't accept the simplicity. It was almost improper to accept it. She could see Hugh's point. She smiled, ate a nut, smiled again, and said, "It's like religion. I object but I believe," she said. "Because that's how it is."

"You're a traitor to your kind," said Hugh.

"I don't see that," said Frances.

"You're supposed to be a free woman," he said. "You *can't* believe in Freud. And anyway, you can't deny that analysis is designed to stop people behaving in antisocial ways. And that therefore it's just another prop to society."

"That's just Laingian crap," said Stephen mildly. "And you're thinking of psychiatrists, not psychoanalysts, aren't you? Or perhaps you don't really know the difference?"

"Don't you be so fucking rude to me, son," said Hugh, and relapsed briefly into silence, from which he emerged a minute or two later with loud and snorting laughter. "Laingian crap, eh?" he said. "So Laing's out, is he? Who's in, then? Apart from Freud, of course?"

"Out, in," said Stephen, wearily. "You ought to be working for the *New Statesman* or the *Sunday Times*, not a bank. You could write those bits that tell people in their weekend cottages what they ought to be reading and what they ought to view on the telly and who's who in the *roman à clef*, and all that kind of thing. I've never known anyone so keen to keep up and so pleased to see other people on the way down."

"It's my age," said Hugh. "It's your fault. You've aged me prematurely. Fran, tell your daughter to take his daughter to bed, I can't stand all these children in the room. It makes me nervous."

"I quite like them about," said Frances, and it was true. She liked being in a room full of her own family, she felt safe with Natasha sitting there reading, with Daisy with the baby on her knee, with Hugh drunk and talkative, with Stephen limp and pleasant and intelligent. The light flickered from the fire, and glinted from the mirror on the wall, from the glasses, the gold rims of the coffee cups. It was so beautifully furnished, the cottage—everything was brown and red and black, yet nothing was too new, too shiny. The loose covers of the large chairs and settee were worn, the rugs which Natasha had made herself over the years were a little shabby, the curtains were jumble-sale curtains, an old lady's curtains, with a muted pattern of birds and acorns on a beige background. It was all just so, it had been put together with love and care and trouble and expense (but not too much expense). A large bunch of teasels and honesty stood in a jar on a little table: a brown jug of dried grasses stood on another. A bookcase held weekend books and games—cards, Scrabble, Monopoly. A heap of baby toys stood in a corner. Two sheep skulls and a badger skull stood on a wooden chest. A copper kettle stood in the hearth. A bunch of dried flowers dangled from the low ceiling. It felt safe, it felt like the country, undisturbed, with the black night and no lights in it outside the small windowpanes, timeless. It was an old cottage, it felt old and safe like a secure infancy. Why can't I make my home like this, thought Frances, why is it that I am so restlessly always going away, what on earth is it that makes Natasha able to do this, and me not?

She thought of the flight to Adra, of the hotel in the desert. She thought that perhaps nothing would ever seem exciting again. She wondered if she were growing old. Though it had seemed a good idea when she had said she would go. To get right away, to somewhere different, to do something absurd. But the spirit had gone out of her. Where had it gone to? Why had she never aimed for Natasha's virtues, Natasha's composure?

Natasha must have been very unhappy, with Hugh as a husband. How could she be as tolerant as she looked?

The younger children went to bed. Natasha made another pot of coffee. She ground the beans in a square wooden grinder on her knee, and boiled the kettle on a rod over the fire. She had a special attachment, for doing this, given by a Swedish friend. How could one have the patience to have a Swedish friend, to write letters, to stay in touch?

Hugh stumbled out to get some logs for the fire, and Stephen quietly remarked to Frances that he had been reading Freud's *Beyond the Pleasure Principle*, had she ever? and did she believe that the self longed more for life than for death? Frances replied that she had indeed read that work a long time ago, and had forgotten much of what it said, but was it not the work in which Freud admitted that there was a possibility that all instincts were struggling to restore an earlier state of things, and that an earlier state being inanimate, all living things strove for death? More than that, said Stephen, he says that it's possible that the extraordinarily violent instincts of sex arose by accident and are not particularly ancient.

Compared with the other yearnings of matter?

Precisely, said Stephen.

So to seek life was some silly new idea, the chance result of a Darwinian accident?

I suppose so.

And where does that leave us? asked Frances.

"More or less here," said Stephen. He looked sad and intent.

"Where does what leave us?" said Hugh, coming in with the logs.

"We were talking of the death wish," said Stephen. "And of things wanting to return to an earlier state."

"Schopenhauer?"

"No. Freud."

"Not Freud again." He poked a bit of log cautiously into the blazing middle of the fire. Frances watched him. She was thinking that any fancy that she could recall even a glimpse of her own childhood, of an ideal childhood, in this house, was an illusion, for it was not her past nor the cottage's past that surrounded her. The cottage had belonged to laborers, had been cold and dark. Her own past too had been quite otherwise. No wonder she could not re-create it. But what hopes should one have of any future? Should one merely regress to a field full of stones, one's own safe place? What about sex, what about salvation? The eels go back to the same beds, the swallows fly south in the summer. And she had gone back for a weekend to the flat Midlands. What had she found there? What held her like a stone around her neck, like a stone in her chest, heavy, solid, inert? A field of stones, a valley of bones.

"Freud says," said Stephen, smiling, "that the reason why things struggle so hard to stay alive against all the odds is that they want to die *in their own fashion.*"

"I wish my carp would struggle a little harder," said Natasha, pouring the smoky coffee. "More coffee, Frances? They keep floating up all bloated, poor darlings."

"Perhaps they *like* dying there," said Frances, joining with Natasha's wish to lighten the mood, afraid that she and Hugh, if this talk of death went on much longer, would start to brood on the death of their sister Alice, who had gassed herself for an unidentified reason. "They obviously feel it's their destiny, to die in your pond. They float up quite happily."

"And that little camellia that didn't take? I suppose that *liked* turning all brown and withered? I'm supposed to think it looks better like that, am I?"

"I thought it did look quite pretty," said Frances, who had been shown the withered shrub that morning.

"It's a new fashion, this admiration of death," said Hugh. Really, how he managed to talk at all, let alone talk reasonably well, with all that liquor inside him, was a mystery. "It's a post-Romantic fashion. People used to be frightened of it. Shrouds, skeletons, *memento mori*, all that. Now we stick the stuff around as decorations. Look at it. Dead flowers" (he waved dramatically at the teasels) "dead—dead *skulls*. Look at it."

"I remember finding that badger's skull," said Natasha. "I'd just gone for a pee behind a tree, and there it was."

"I thought death was supposed to be the modern taboo," said Frances. The subject was, after all, irresistible.

"Taboo? Taboo? Balls, it's the fashion. Well, not quite, it's more the fashion to say it's a taboo. But people talk about it all the time. It's all over the cinema, all over the telly. Haven't you noticed? Books on the subject every five minutes. It's morbid, that's what it is."

He poked the fire again, and escorted a panic-stricken wood-louse onto the floor. It scuttled off under a table. They all stared into the red-hot crater. The wood sighed and sang.

"I'd hate to be burned on a funeral pyre," said Natasha,

"like those people in the Sudan you gave me a book about, Fran."

"Even for me?" asked Hugh.

"Oh, for you I've been burned alive a million times," said Natasha.

"A brand from the burning. To Carthage then I came," said Stephen.

"Who said that?"

"T. S. Eliot. Or St. Augustine, as you prefer."

"To Carthage then I came. And to Adra I go," said Frances.

"Perhaps they *liked* being burned alive," said Frances. "But I can't really believe it. Can you?"

"No, not really. *You* ought to believe it, though. *You're* supposed to understand the minds of ancient races."

"I'll tell you a very sobering thing that somebody said to me the other day," said Frances. "You know that quotation, I forget who said it, about *'In death we join the great majority'*? Well, I've always thought that was very nice, and I said it to this fellow who was going on about how his mother was dying. And do you know what he said? He said it wasn't true any longer. He said there were more people alive now than ever have been alive in the whole history of mankind before, all put together. Do you think it can possibly be true? And if so, what a dreadful notion."

"It would make one feel doubly left out," said Hugh. "Dead, with all those teeming millions still having an endless rave-up. Horrible."

"It can't be true, can it, statistically?" said Natasha. "I must ask your mother. She's the population expert, she should know."

"She'd *say* it was true even if it wasn't," said Hugh. "You'd better not put the idea in her head. She *is* an irresponsible woman."

"In this exhibition at the Hayward Gallery," said Stephen, "there was this painting by Salvator Rosa of Empedocles

jumping into Etna. Did you see it, Frances? I think it was
you that told me to go.''

"Yes, I saw it. Did you like the exhibition?"

"I liked that one best."

"Did you really? I liked the philosopher reading under a
tree. He had bare feet."

"You *have* got a peaceful nature, Aunt Frances. I liked
Empedocles.''

"Whatever did he jump into Etna for?" asked Natasha.
"Was that the death wish getting too strong for him?"

"He jumped in to prove he was a god," said Frances.
"He'd been boasting."

"And was he a god?"

"No, of course not."

"How do you know?"

"Really, Natasha, what a question. You don't believe in
gods, do you?" Natasha laughed, shifting her position in her
chair, wriggling the toes of the foot she had been sitting on.

"*I* may not," she said, "but maybe *they* did. Anyway,
how do they know he wasn't one?"

"I can't remember. How do they know, Stephen?"

"They found his sandal," said Stephen. "Thrown up out
of the crater. A bronze sandal."

"And what did that prove?"

"It proved he'd been burned to a cinder, I suppose," said
Hugh.

"I don't see *why*," said Natasha. "Why ever does it prove
that?"

"I suppose the theory was that he'd leap up again out of
the molten lava like a phoenix. And as he didn't, he was
assumed dead."

"Reasonably enough," said Hugh.

"I don't see *why*," said Natasha. "If he really was a god,
he might have liked it in the depths of Etna, mightn't he? He
might have been tired of living amongst foolish mortals."

"He was some kind of philosopher, wasn't he?" said
Frances. "Perhaps he was an early Schopenhauer."

"What was his philosophy?" asked Natasha.

Nobody knew. Stephen remembered that the other philosophers portrayed in the exhibition, or at least the ones that Rosa seemed to like, were Stoics. But jumping into Etna did not seem a Stoic act.

"We could look him up," said Natasha. "Stephen, find something to look him up in."

Looking things up, grinding coffee beans, making rugs. Natasha had picked up her crochet: she was making a dress for her granddaughter. While Stephen looked through the shelf for information about Empedocles, Frances thought of the Rosa painting. Red and brown it had been, not unlike the colors of this comfortable interior, but not at all in any other ways comfortable: it had been on the contrary rocky and seething, an immense craterous romantic cavern, with Empedocles falling forward perilously from one foot into the red depths. The rock had had a bubbling viscous volcanic look about it: the whole painting suggested violent motion, and the philosopher himself, clothed as she recalled in sandals and brown robes, seemed made of the same stuff, to be longing to be absorbed into the same stuff.

Stephen had found a copy of Brewer's *Dictionary of Phrase & Fable*. He read the extract about Empedocles. It didn't say what kind of philosopher he was. Matthew Arnold had written a play about him. There was a quotation from Milton. Stephen read it out:

> He, who to be deemed
> A God, leapt fondly into Etna's flames,
> Empedocles.

"And thereby proved he wasn't," said Hugh.

"Or *was*," said Stephen. "Depending on one's view of godliness."

"How can one think it was a godly act, to jump into a volcano? He was just deluded."

"*He* can't have thought he was a god," said Natasha. "*He* can't have been deluded."

"Why not?" said Hugh. "People are always deluding themselves about that kind of thing. Part of the human spirit. There was a silly bugger on the television only last week, threw himself off a church tower somewhere in Lincolnshire, he thought he could fly. And look at all those stupid fools who keep boring holes in their heads and jumping out of top-floor windows."

"You're suggesting Empedocles was on a trip?" said Frances, rather provocatively. The subject of drugs was a dangerous one: Hugh himself had had a patch of smoking, which had thrilled him while it lasted, but the stuff had been too mild for him really, his constitution craved its daily pint of spirits, and he had luckily had too much sense to move on to anything harder. But he was ill placed to criticize his son, or any other of the rising hordes of the vast young majority, on the grounds of their possible addictions; this didn't prevent him from doing so, but it made him remarkably angry in the process of doing so. Once he had thrown a tea pot at Natasha, for suggesting that he mind his own business. She had to have stitches.

"Delusions of immortality," said Hugh. "Sounds like a trip, doesn't it?"

"I wouldn't know," said Frances. "I've never been on one. I only go on real trips, like to Adra. Anyway, I hate that kind of language. As bad as a 'dig,' a 'trip.' "

"Why didn't his sandals get burned as well?" asked Natasha.

They all paused, and thought about Empedocles' sandals.

"They were bronze, were they?" suggested Stephen. "Perhaps they were *real* bronze? Do you think? I'd always pictured them as being this kind of bronze vinyl stuff, but perhaps they were *real* bronze?"

"Horribly uncomfortable," said Hugh. "Metal shoes. Not at all the thing."

And they speculated for some time about the shoes of the

ancients, and whether or not bronze would melt in molten
lava, and how instant the death of Empedocles would have
been, and the nature of the Delphic oracle. It was all very
pleasant. Hugh was in a good mood, an exceptionally good
mood: he liked having his family around him, under his control, trapped there in the surrounding rural darkness. He was
rather proud of his sister. Frances's heart went out to him for
his pride. He could so easily have resented her, by a hair's
breadth he could have resented her, as dead Alice certainly
had done, and yet for some reason he didn't, he liked her,
he liked to have her around. He hadn't liked her so much
when she was with Karel, it was true, but then it hadn't
mattered, and his jealousy had been so obvious that it had
been quite harmless. He was a good man, Hugh, he let everything flow from the depths in him up to the surface, and
if he did it through increasing quantities of drink, who was
to blame him? She knew enough about him to feel that he,
like herself, suffered from periodic blacknesses, but instead
of sweating them out, he drank them out. He had accepted
himself as an incurable. What would Freud had said of his
self-help? At least he had kept himself in touch, at least he
did not stare like their father into empty space. An excess of
motion was certainly preferable to that deadly calm. One felt
reasonably alive, near Hugh, if only in the movement of
proximity. No wonder he had to force himself, to stoke himself, to galvanize himself. He was telling them now (the Delphic oracle forgotten) of the stock market, oil shares, interest
rates. They were all in a state of glorious flux, seething like
Etna. Hugh loved it when the news was bad. He loved money
with a crazy passion, he loved its fluctuations. Frances could
not follow a word he was saying, but she listened with pleasure, watching his dark animated face, his jabbing pointing
finger, his eyes flashing and dilating with pleasure at the
downfall of yet another secondary bank, the unexpected collapse of yet more shares. Hugh never made any money: he
was always making vast sums in theory, then losing them
again. In fact, he had a steady income, the rest was all fun

on the side. He dabbled, but he always knew when to get out. For years, Frances had pictures of him always on the verge of ruin, poised like Empedocles over a gulf of bankruptcy, for he did take risks, he borrowed and speculated, but for some reason things always calmed down, things remained much the same, the family continued undisrupted, Hugh kept the same position, Natasha continued to bake bread. He was telling Frances now that she ought to put all her money into something called Rosewood Investments, they were absolutely the thing, she ought to buy now.

"If I bought *now* everything you told me," said Frances, "I wouldn't have a penny to my name. You know you're always ringing me up and warning me not to do what you've said, and then thanking God when I say I haven't. And do you know why I never do what you say? It's not because I don't trust you, it's because I haven't any money."

They both laughed comfortably at the joke.

"I don't believe you haven't any money," said Hugh. "A successful woman like you. You must have a few thousands stacked away somewhere."

"Nonsense. What I earn, I spend. Life's very expensive for a single woman, you know. Four children, food bills, mortgage, housekeeper, cleaners, trains, airplanes, all that kind of thing. No, if you want somebody to invest something for you, you should get onto my husband."

"I tried Anthony. I always try Anthony."

"Did he listen?"

"Anthony once made ten thousand off a word of mine, you know."

"No, I didn't know. Did he really?"

She was mildly interested. If Anthony really had listened to Hugh, then Hugh couldn't be such a fool as he appeared, for Anthony, as far as money was concerned, was certainly very careful.

"What are these Rosewood Investments?" she said.

Hugh started to explain. She tried to listen, but failed. He drew her pictures of percentages on a piece of paper, but she couldn't follow. All she understood of money was what she earned in salary and odd checks for journalism or was given in grants, and what she paid out in cash, bills and income tax, and even that she had to have an accountant to explain. So she pretended to listen, and after a while she yawned and told him that his Rosewood Investments sounded immoral, and she couldn't possibly invest in something that was even connected with property companies.

"You don't know what a property company *is*," said Hugh, ready to begin all over again.

"No, and she doesn't want to," said Natasha, equably.

"There's *nothing* annoys me *more*," yelled Hugh, leaping to his feet and looking agitated, "than the average cultured person's stupidity about money. Why don't you make an effort to understand? You behave as though it were a mystery beyond the powers of human understanding. Why won't you *listen*, for God's sake?"

"It *is* a mystery beyond the powers of human understanding, that's why," said Frances. "Don't you agree, Stephen?"

But Stephen wasn't listening. He was leafing through Brewer, smiling to himself.

Anthony and Hugh, in the old days, had talked about money sometimes. But their styles had been so different that even though they talked about the same thing, they still seemed to be talking across a culture gap. For whereas Hugh was agitated and confidential in manner, Anthony had been conspiratorial and discreet. She didn't often think about Anthony these days. Remarkable, how completely he had dropped out of her memory, as though he had been a pure accident, a meaningless aberration. And yet he'd filled some seven years of her life, and together they had produced four children.

Natasha was remarking that it was time for bed, or at least time for her to go to bed. She yawned, and stretched, and put her feet down, feeling for her shoes, hooking them up elegantly with the ends of her stockinged toes. "Tidy the fire up a little, love," she said to Hugh. "I'm always afraid bits will roll out onto the hearthrug in the middle of the night and set it on fire. And have a look at the Aga for me, will you?

"Good night, Frances, good night, Stephen," she said, as she rose to her feet, picking up her picture book. But as she spoke, Stephen leaped to his feet, and started off up the stairs. "The baby," he muttered in explanation, as he went. And it was true, if one listened hard one could hear the very faintest cry, through three shut doors. He must have been tuned in, listening like a mother. Frances and Natasha smiled at one another, at the sight of his immediate fatherly concern, but Frances was disturbed by it, not amused. Natasha went upstairs, leaving Frances and Hugh alone together. Frances had thought she would have had a tête-à-tête with Stephen. Guiltily, she was glad to have been spared it. She did not feel up to dealing with his problems. Hugh's problems were so old, so seasoned, that they neither bored nor bothered her. She watched him tidying up the embers, as he had been instructed. Would he speak to her, would he not? He did not. But he sat down in silence when he had finished, and stared into the ash, and waited for her.

"I went to Eel Cottage this summer," she said, after a while.

He was silent, then he said, "Why ever did you do that?"

"I don't know. I just wanted to have a look. Have you ever been back?"

"No. Never. What was it like?"

"Not too different. It's been kind of—slightly—smartened up a bit. I can't explain."

He laughed. "It was a gloomy dump in some ways, wasn't it."

She thought. Her grandfather, her grandmother, the potted plants, the old books, the plates with faded pansies, the ditch, the yellow dog. Yes, it had been a gloomy dump. Compared with this warm, cozy, attractive interior, it had been both cramped and drafty, cluttered yet bare, ugly and tasteless, full of cheap mementoes and meaningless souvenirs. A Day at Hunstanton, a Day at Mablethorpe. A pottery crab from Cromer, a salt cellar shaped like a thatched cottage, peg rugs, tastelessly multicolor, not pleasantly monochrome like Natasha's. Plastic lampshades had replaced the paraffin lamps when electricity was brought to the village. Yes, it had been a gloomy dump. But it had been the real thing. Her grandmother had baked bread. It had been square, white, and heavy, it had stood in large yellow panchions, with a brown earthenware glaze, it had stood there to rise, and it had not risen much. Natasha's bread was infinitely better. Her grandmother had stewed mince without flavoring, wet, in an enamel dog dish, with half an unchopped onion. On her draining board (a wooden board, slimy with age) had stood at any point two dozen items, rusting, spotty, dull. Yet her kitchen had been the real thing. There was no escape.

"What do you think, Hugh," she said, "about escaping from the past? It's so nice here, I like it here so much."

"Oh yes, it's *nice* enough," he said, as though he knew what she meant.

"I've got this terrible stone in my chest," she said. "It's like some kind of gravity. I can't do anything about it."

"Perhaps you'll feel better in Adra."

"Perhaps. I just keep moving, to get away, but one never gets anywhere."

"You've had a hard time, Fran." He meant with Anthony, and Karel, and her operation.

"Not specially. I've had a good time, in many ways. Sometimes I feel fine. But I've had this long patch now, feeling not too good. It can't go on like this, can it? Is this middle age, do you think?"

"Nonsense. Of course not. You're young, still. You should get married again. Why didn't you marry Karel?"

"He was married to somebody else."

She was beginning to feel painfully sorry for herself: luxurious tears were forming in the wells of her eyes, they would easily spill over. Should she let them? Perhaps not.

"He could have left her. For you," said Hugh firmly. "I don't approve of all this messing about."

"You mess about yourself," said Frances, deciding not to cry after all. Crying would mean giving up hope, and she wouldn't, she refused, she couldn't.

"Oh well, to a certain extent we all do," said Hugh, complacently. "It's our age, after all."

"I don't," said Frances. "I haven't slept with anyone for years. Almost literally years. Well for months, anyway."

"Good heavens," said Hugh. "How interesting. What does it feel like?"

"Like a stone in my chest," she said, and laughed, feeling suddenly better.

"What a *terrible* thing," said Hugh, with exaggerated concern. "It can't be good for you, you must do something about it. You usen't to be like that, did you? It can't be for want of opportunities, can it?" he said gallantly.

"Not exactly," said Frances. "Though it's a funny thing, people really don't try very hard when they know they're not going to get anywhere, but how they know it, I don't know, if you know what I mean. The most stupid people are quick, you know. When Anthony left I was overwhelmed with offers. But when Karel left, they just left me alone." She paused. "Of course, it's partly that being with Karel meant that I didn't know anyone else. I was so happy with him."

"I never understood why you two split up."

"Perhaps I didn't like being happy? It stopped me working, being happy!"

"What's work?"

"You're right, what's work. Ambition is just another form of defect."

"As Freud doubtless said."

"As Freud did in fact say."

"Well, I'm sure Freud wouldn't like you to sit around like this. I'm sure he'd recommend you sleep with somebody. You can't sleep with me because I'm your brother, and I

believe it's not considered nice, but I could find you some
agreeable lovers when you get back from Adra."

"Bankers?"

"What about a nice financial journalist I know?"

"Why can't I have a banker?"

"Perhaps you'll find an archaeologist in Adra. Or an oil
man. Or what about the Minister of Culture? Isn't he a good
friend of yours?"

"He is, and you mustn't make jokes about him. He's a
very exceptional man."

"All the better."

"He's got a wife already."

"So has everybody of your age who's normal." He tossed
a pine cone into the fire. "It's time for the second round. In
your case, it's more than time."

"What about you, then?"

"Oh, I'm all right. Well, I have been all right. But only,
as you know, because there's something wrong with Natasha.
But now even Natasha is thinking of moving. She pulled
herself together one day and set off to go to a series of group
analysis sessions. To see why she put up with me for so
long."

"You're not serious."

"Perfectly serious."

"So that's why you're so anti-Freud."

"Partly. I mean, fuck it, if she can't work out what's wrong
with her herself she doesn't deserve to know, does she? Group
analysis. It's just an excuse for a party without drink."

"So you think she'll find out?"

"How the hell can she find out? None of those cunts is
going to have the wit to say to her, the reason why you've
stayed with your husband, Mrs. Ollerenshaw, is because in
the total scale of human beings, taking a wide view of the
spectrum, and forgetting his little personal failings, taking a
wide view, your husband is an exceptionally nice man."

"No, they're not. Do you really think you're exceptionally
nice, Hugh?"

"Well, I'm not bad, am I?"

"*I* like you. But I don't have to live with you."

"Eel Cottage. I remember Eel Cottage. We slept in the same bedroom and I used to explain to you the mysteries of sex. Do you think it's had a bad effect on us?"

"Could have. I remember finding it much more interesting than the mysteries of finance. But it must have been that that set you in your role of pedagogue."

"Did I used to demonstrate? I hope not."

"Not much." She gazed at him. The conversation was drawing them apart through its intimacy, finally, into their separate darknesses. She felt its pull.

"Perhaps my children are awake up there now, discussing the same subject. Do you think?"

"Imagine what it's like, when one of yours knows so much about it that you wake up and find yourself a grandfather. Or in your case, a grandmother."

"I've surely got a year or two to go."

"How old is Daisy? Fourteen? Not long, I'd say."

Hugh was thinking of Frances's nine-year-old body, its long round lines, its hard and skinny power. She had been tall and blond, long-legged round-bottomed, freckled, her skin white. She had been histrionic, an exhibitionist—she would dance naked around the room with a towel around her, she would pose in front of the peeling tilted mirror, making faces at herself, sticking her bum from side to side, stretching her neck, making her eyes roll seductively. Her pubic hair grew blond and early. Hugh's grew black and late. This had interested them both greatly. They had had their estrangements, but on the whole he had looked after her carefully. And now she sat there, hardened, thickened, with a stone in her chest, her skin not white but a curious colonial yellow, her hair thick and straight, long and untidy, her legs stretched out (still long) with cracked shoes on her narrow feet, her hands dangling limp and even, evenly spaced on the arms of the easy chair, and a large lump of diamond shining from one knuckle. She was off to Africa, to give a paper at a conference. Presumably that was what she wanted to do, or she wouldn't be doing it. Even as a child, she had seemed to have a reserve strength, a strength greater than his own: she had liked solitude, spending hours alone watching bugs and beetles (as their father before them), whereas he had liked solitude only out of defense, because nothing else was offered. Now, he could not spend an hour alone, and had organized his life so that he never was obliged to.

She was a career woman. He had always thought that she put her career first, in selfish ruthlessness, and that for it she had lost Anthony and Karel. But perhaps it wasn't so. She stared now into space, with a look like their father's on her face. He did not like it. But he couldn't think of anything to say to her. There was no need for her to be alone, she was a good-looking woman, much sought after. She sat inside a thorny palisade of her own making, cross and contemplative, not a captive but a queen. A queen of a small muddy village.

"Fran," he said, "do you know what you've grown up to look like? It's amazing. Do you remember that picture book at the Eel, *Historical Figures Through the Ages*? D'you remember the one of Boadicea? She looked *exactly* like you."

It came back to him so vividly, and he could see that she too remembered—Boadicea, Queen of the Iceni, sitting in her hut contemplating the overthrow of the Romans. She was staring into the peat fire, much as Frances was staring now, a goblet of wine at her elbow, a skin map spread on the floor at her feet. She was unhistorically clad in long flowing pre-Raphaelite robes of purple and red, with a low belt with studs around her hips, and her hair hung loose and matted around her hawklike features. On the next page, one saw her in action in her chariot, wheels flashing, knives flashing, hair flying, a spear in her hand.

Frances smiled. "Thank you," she said. "I always liked that picture. I've been modeling myself on Boadicea for years. Victorious in defeat. Wasn't that the caption?"

"Something like that." He stood up, stretched. "I must go to bed. It's late. I'll just go and see to the Aga."

She gathered up the coffee things, and followed him into the kitchen with them. He was riddling the ash from the bottom of the stove. She stacked the cups in the sink.

"If you open the back door," he said, "you might see the hedgehog. He comes at this time, sometimes, for his milk."

"Isn't he hibernating?" she said, but she opened the door and smelled the amazing damp sweetness of the English air, heavy with the smell of leaves and moss and graveyard. An owl hooted. The hedgehog's saucer stood empty, but as she picked it up she saw him approach, bundling blindly across the yard toward the light of the open door. He scuttled and bundled on small feet, hesitating when he found the saucer had gone. She filled it quickly, and put it down for him, and he approached again and drank. She and Hugh stood and watched him.

"He's nice, isn't he?" said Hugh. "But terribly stupid. I was trying to get the car in once, and he was there waiting. But he wouldn't get out of the way, he just rolled up into a ball and lay there. Natasha had to get out and pick him up to move him. She wrapped him in her headscarf, she didn't like to touch him. Then she had to burn the headscarf because of the fleas."

"What does he do when you're not here?"

"He must go somewhere else, I suppose, or drink something else. I can't think why they like milk anyway, can you?"

They shut the door on him.

"You go up first," said Hugh, "and have your turn in the bathroom. I'll just finish tidying up down here."

She wasn't halfway up the stairs before he had poured himself a large, final, oblivion-inducing drink: looking back (the stairs led straight from the room) she saw him holding it. He raised his glass to her, she sighed and mounted the stairs.

Before she got to bed, she had to go through the room with the children. There they all were, lying tossed and disheveled in their green and blue sleeping bags. Daisy, Joshua, Spike, and Pru. The glow of extreme health burned in their cheeks, their tousled hair glowed on the pillows, their lips were parted, and they heaved and sighed slightly, with respectful vibration, as she watched them. They smelled lovely, of hair and skin. They slept well, they were good children, they had worn themselves out. But Hugh was right, they were growing up. Even the baby was eight now. They had kept her so busy, worrying about them even when she wasn't with them had kept her so busy, guilt about them (not very profound, she had to admit) had occupied the surface reaches of her being with its endless little squalls and tempests, so that she had hardly had time to worry about herself. She had reeled from job to job, from country to country, from Karel to children, organizing meals and washing machines and schools and laundries, buying socks for Spike in Alexandria, rushing home from Glasgow to take Josh to the doctor about his balls, writing shopping lists even in the middle of lectures and seminars, consulting timetables, ringing stations, arranging fantastically elaborate schedules, shouting at domestic agencies, swearing at gasmen, bursting into tears one shaming day in front of her accountant because she'd left her bank statements in her lecture folder, never going to a hairdresser, wearing the same clothes till they fell to pieces, and listening to other people telling her how busy she must be till she believed it herself. And now it all seemed to be slowing down. They no longer needed her very much, the children. When she was at home, they would go off for hours on end, for whole days, swimming, fishing, to the cinema, playing football. They went on trains to visit friends in other parts of London, in other parts of the country. They were independent, they had learned independence early, the time would come when they would not need her at all. And what would she do then? Who would then be hers?

Stephen Ollerenshaw lay on his bed in his weird fake-raftered attic corner, and listened to the breathing of his daughter. Every sigh, every rustle went through him. He hadn't slept properly since she was born. It didn't seem right, to spend so much effort, simply to stay alive, to fear death so much, not only for oneself, but for others. Why weren't the human race like rabbits, or sheep? Why were they so hard to rear, yet so insistent on survival?

He thought of Frances, and his father Hugh. Hugh drank, and Frances traveled. He hadn't yet worked out what he would choose to do with his adult life. Their responses seemed to him to be luxuries, expensive evasions. (He didn't know much about other people: he would have been surprised to hear that alcoholism, like schizophrenia, flourished amongst the working classes. He thought that it was a city disease.) He was right, of course, about travel. Frances had struck it lucky, in that her cure and her evasion were of a singular purity, they had a fine creative therapeutic halo. But a halo for the rich and the clever and the lucky. He himself was neither lucky nor clever, though he supposed that by most standards he was rich.

He didn't resent the good luck of Frances. He wished her well. She had a splendid carelessness, he wished he could catch it. Her children didn't keep her awake at nights; they slept well, heavily, healthily. But she was no use as a model, she was a freak. Her talents were freakish, her perceptions were freakish. He had hoped, at one point, that by staying close to her (in her kitchen, in her Putney garden, by visiting her in hospital) he could catch her disease of survival, her mad tricks of recuperation. But no, it wasn't so. He was too normal, too dull. He hadn't got the stamina for living like that, at that pace, with that kind of energy. He saw himself as an ordinary person, as a member of the cooling human race. There seemed to him to be something nineteenth century about Frances's explorations and affairs, about Hugh's drinking. Grand, it was, but out of date and futile. There was even something sordid about so much will to live. He found himself speculating more and more about dead Alice. But nobody would tell him about Alice. It was as though she had passed out of life and out of memory. He rather suspected that Alice had not done it properly. By that, he meant that she had wished to be loved, had wished to be recovered, had wished for attention, as she knelt down by her unlit gas fire with her head in a towel. That, too, was sordid.

He himself did not wish for love. There was enough love. Hugh loved him, Natasha loved him, Frances loved him, both sets of grandparents (a complete four) loved him, Beata loved him, and his poor baby loved him far, far too much, far more than he deserved. His problems were not personal, his fears were not personal. Or did not seem to him to be so.

The baby whimpered in its sleep, and he reached out a hand and shook its cradle. The little creature inspired him with such pity and such terror, he could not bear it. What did it dream of? Birds dream in the egg, he had read recently in the paper. In her egg head, in her thin-boned beating skull, his baby dreamed. The membrane of her head still beat, softly, under her soft brown curls. He prayed, passionately, for the bones to close. Small things had always frightened him, small birds, bats, butterflies, mice—not for any dislike of them, but for pity and terror, terror and pity. Birds were always getting into the cottage, Natasha was frightened of them, and so was Hugh; it had always been his task to remove them, he had been so afraid of killing them, in his clumsiness, and once a fledgling had died of fright in his hands.

There was no escape from this fragility, this soft and bloody beating, these small bones, this perishable flesh. Since diagnosing Beata's illness (he had worked it out himself, from a book) he had read medical textbooks, constantly, with horror, shocked by the catalogue of all the illnesses that flesh is heir to. And the medical textbooks didn't mention road accidents, fires, lightning flashes, falling meteors, and all the other likely and unlikely causes of accidental death. Survival was a miracle.

He had had a brief period of respite, between the anxieties of puberty and the responsibilities of fatherhood. True to his age, he had found escape from the human condition not in drink or travel, but in drugs. While high, he had been for long periods of time unaware of mortality and its pressing implications. He had been able to forget about death, while concentrating hard on the pattern in the carpet. Lying in bed, now, rocking the cradle with a tired arm (the baby was restless, she was teething, and her cousins had overexcited her), he looked back to those happy days of grassy innocence, when the future had seemed so irrelevant. One would never get back there again. The Garden of Eden. He had hardly smoked at all since he had, one evening, caught his father at it: Hugh, giggling helplessly, talking inconsequentially, falling off his chair, had seemed such a parody of Hugh drunk, fierce, disputative, logical, irritable, that Stephen (although he excused his father's behavior on the grounds of inexperience) had decided to set a good example by abstaining. Drugs are out of fashion, he told his father. His father was very fashion conscious.

Various friends of his had met bad ends through drugs—not through grass, but through acid. They had thought themselves immortal, some of them: one had jumped out of a high window, another had tried to cross a motorway while hitchhiking to Leeds, apparently under the impression that he had the power to stop the traffic. Others had simply gone rather mad. Stephen's problem was that most of his delusions (he supposed they were delusions) came to him when he was quite sober and in his right mind. He had from an early age suffered from the more common suicidal impulses, and was surprised that more people did not fall out of high windows or off church steeples or cliff tops, or throw themselves under trains, or drive themselves into head-on collisions. Freud had said that we are all balanced between conflicting needs: the need to live, and the need to die. It was a miracle that the balance was so well struck in favor of living. In Beata, something had gone wrong, and in himself also, he sometimes thought. He was genuinely surprised that the average person was so well aware that a high jump would prove fatal. Perhaps he himself had a sense missing, a protective sense of danger, like those rare unfortunates who feel no bodily pain, and who have to learn, by intellectual processes, that they must not put their hands in the hot flame. (Or was the reverse true? Was he perhaps too much aware, as for this child of his? He did not know.)

He had never dared to take acid. For already, when looking out of a fourth-floor window, or gazing down a stairwell, he would think to himself: *the quickest way down is to jump.* And each time, it seemed like a truth, as well as a temptation.

The baby whimpered. He was worried about the baby. Something was wrong with her back, she didn't seem to sit up as well as she should at her age, and her head wobbled rather. The doctor said it was nothing, but he thought that even so he would get a second opinion. How appallingly badly constructed is the human body. Why aren't people made of plastic or wood, or some other more or less indestructible material, thought Stephen to himself, as he lay awake, and listened to an owl hoot in the well-stocked courtyard. God had organized man very badly. How sorry he must have felt, when he saw the sorrows and torments that Christ, his only son, had suffered. Why had he not in his great pity blotted out, on Good Friday, in the darkness, the entire creation? For the same reason, perhaps, that Stephen himself could not kill a dying rabbit, and was frightened of a frightened bird. God was weak and sorry, just like man, he turned away his face from pain.

Sometimes Stephen thought he might become a doctor. It would at least be a positive way of confronting his obsessions. It might even cure him of them. But he doubted if he had the intellectual energy. He hadn't got the right qualifications behind him, he'd have to start too many subjects all over again, and he'd lost too many brain cells already. And what use was one doctor, in view of the size of the problem?

He fell asleep, his white arm hooked into the cradle, so that when he woke up an hour later it was numb and rigid, and for some time he thought that he must have a terrible new creeping paralysis (multiple sclerosis, maybe?).

* * *

Karel Schmidt sat at his desk in the flat off the Fulham Road, and stared at a heap of bills. He had decided to sit down and pay some of them, but was not making much progress. Gas. Electricity. Telephone. Newsagent. They were all final notices. Karel always waited for final notices, assuming that everybody else did too. It never occurred to him to pay earlier, occasionally he discovered that others were more prompt, but he wrote them off as neurotics or eccentrics. He knew no better. He had been brought up in a household of final notices and unpaid bills. He even considered himself rather efficient. He had, for various reasons, little grasp of a norm.

He opened his checkbook, filled in the date, lit a cigarette, stared around the room, and listened to the roar of the traffic in the severe, straight, grim one-way road below. The flat was a first-floor flat, large and gloomy. He had never cared for it much, and didn't now. It was overfull of heavy old dark brown furniture, most of which his aunt and uncle had picked up cheap just before and during the war: it reflected their tastes and mood, for it had a continental, derelict, refugee look about it, and stood around the walls as though waiting to be rearranged. Joy hadn't much interest in furniture, though she had once in an unusual outburst of energy painted the walls of the living room a dark purple, which she had thought would conceal their irregularities. It had concealed the marks but not the bumps. Even Joy had agreed it wasn't a very cheerful color. It looked all right in other people's houses, but in theirs, it looked morbid.

The one good thing about the house was the view out the back. The living room filled the whole width of the building, and the front window looked out over the traffic, pouring relentlessly on its way north. Why this particular road had been selected as a throughway, nobody could remember. Perhaps because it was wide, dull, and inhabited by powerless people, many of them old ladies who watched the trucks from lofty bedsitters. But the back window looked out over a garden, over trees and bushes, as far as the eye could see.

The garden was inaccessible, for it was in fact a cemetery. But it was a garden, after all.

Karel finished paying his electricity bill, and stopped for a few minutes to think of Frances Wingate, off to her conference in Africa. The thought of her carrying on with normal life always upset him, indeed it annoyed him, and at times he felt like getting on an airplane and flying out there and getting hold of her and forcing her to come back. But he didn't suppose that would do much good, and anyway it would be terribly expensive, and he wasn't all that well off, though things had been looking up financially, he had been given a raise and a new appointment. It was just as well they were looking up in some direction, for in others they were appalling.

He missed Frances. He loved her, and that was that, and he had thought she loved him. No reason why she should, of course, but still, he had thought she did. They had had a good time together. What more had she wanted? What more could anyone possibly have wanted? Perhaps she really was a shallow person, as she had claimed from time to time, and had wanted a little more fun. They certainly hadn't managed to have much fun together. He thought of her in a hotel in Adra, alone in a hotel bedroom, accompanied in a hotel bedroom. They had only ever managed four days away together in the whole of their seven years. Had she been aggrieved, like a neglected wife? He had always thought her above such things, but maybe she wasn't. He had always suspected that she preferred to be on her own, autonomous, her own keeper. But maybe not, maybe he had disappointed her in some way. He didn't understand her, he didn't understand anyone.

Gas, fourteen pounds. Telephone, twenty-five. He must tell the children to lay off the telephone.

Since Frances had left, he had gone from bad to worse. At first he had been actively unhappy, and had spent his time contemplating strange forms of pursuit and revenge, but then he had settled down into a more passive misery. He had tried to be practical about it, he had taken on extra evening classes to fill in the time, he had struggled even less when boring people arrived to bore him. Let them have him if that was what they wanted. In a sense, Frances had shielded him from his own weaknesses, for in order to be with her, he had been obliged to organize himself a little, and at her house in Putney, in her bed in Putney, he was out of reach. In her bed, between her legs, was the only place where he felt safe and guiltless. Now, she had taken away that place, and left him. He was being pulled to pieces, as though by wild beasts. One could not of course compare Mrs. Mayfield or Ken Stuart or any of the other people who pursued him to wild beasts without sounding ridiculous, for they were all pathetic, sad, depressed and hopeless cases, without (one would have thought) a fang between them. But wild beasts they were, and they made Karel bleed. He dreaded them now, he dreaded all of them. Between them, they had made mincemeat of him. He couldn't face them any more. He didn't know what to do.

He had made the mistake, simply, of taking on too many. Whether he had done this through goodness, as Frances had come to believe, or through inertia, as he himself believed, or through masochism, as Joy believed, who can say? Certainly he had managed to defend himself at times by his theory that the human condition was so appalling that one should not even struggle to escape from it. He had seen his own behavior as chosen rather than helpless. In his heart, he knew he couldn't help but be how he was. He was a born victim, and, saved by a miracle from the holocaust of Europe, it was not in him to devise another fate. How could he say no, when the telephone rang, how could he hurry away from the mad and the lonely?

Once, he had undertaken his role with some goodwill. But now he found that everything was too much for him: he could not go on, and did not know how to stop. He had deceived himself into thinking himself of use, but now he knew that he was not. It had become physically impossible for him to respond to all the demands on his time and his patience.

There were simply too many people wanting a piece of him. He tried to combine his claimants, letting them come around together, but then they would quarrel and drink and smoke and fall over one another in the most appalling way, and then come back for yet another evening to complain about each other, making everything take twice as long. Each wanted him and him alone. However could he have been fool enough to let them think that they all could have him? He tried leaving the phone off the hook, to prevent people from ringing, but then they called around, and when they called, as some did, all the way from Croydon or Kentish Town, they had to stay even longer when they got there.

No doubt about it, he had got himself into a terrible mess, and it was all his own fault, or rather Frances's fault, for it was that last evening class, that extra evening class, that Frances-substitute, that had finally tipped the balance. He had himself imposed the last straw. There were two people in that class who seemed more tiresome and more demanding than any he had ever had before. One was, to make things worse, an extremely attractive girl: the other an elderly bachelor. The girl was Swedish: wide-eyed, beautiful, divorced. The bachelor was passionately interested in local history, and had joined Karel's class by mistake, but having joined it, would not let go. Between them, they pulled him apart. They would corner him at coffee breaks, lie in wait for him in the doorway, walk along the street with him, cadge lifts from him. In the end, of course, both of them ended up regularly in his flat. Both were very lonely people. They perturbed Karel, as such people always did, but what perturbed him most of all was his own growing hardness of heart. There was no mistaking it, he regarded them with rancor. He did not want to see them, never wanted to see them, was relieved when they fell ill and did not turn up. He found himself watching their maneuvers to gain his attention with malice rather than with compassion. (There was one occasion when, in an effort to get near him, one of them pushed the other right off the pavement into the gutter, as they walked to the pub for a drink.) Indeed, he found himself wondering whether or not they weren't actually encouraged to pursue him by the element of competition with the other.

Such observations about human behavior had, naturally, crossed his mind often before, but he had never before taken them so seriously. He had always believed that people could not help what they were like, and that any misery, however apparently self-imposed, deserves attention. This, in a sense, had been the basis of his being. And now he found himself changing into something quite different, he found himself blaming people, criticizing them, noticing their least attractive features instead of their redeeming ones. When people were unhappy, he found himself thinking, it was invariably their own selfish fault. They got what they deserved.

This was a revolution for him. He did not feel any the better for the fact that he realized he had been driven into his new position by his own folly—if he'd had any common sense, he would have restricted his attention to a chosen few, and then would have been able to go on thinking them badly done by, abused, tragic, deserving of compassion. The fact that he now saw them as coldly calculating selfish manipulators, actually capable of taking pleasure in tormenting him, hungry for his blood rather than his tears, was a result of his own policy. He should have been more sensible, have turned more away hungry from the door.

But what had goodness to do with common sense? He had tried to do the right thing by people, he had responded to their claims. That was all. He had played at being God, which of course he wasn't. It was an unpleasant awakening. He looked back on his own stupidity with alarm. Doctors know they cannot help all patients, psychiatrists discriminate amongst their cases, knowing some beyond help. Why couldn't he have done the same? And why ever had he imagined that he was indispensable?

His nastiest shock had come a few weeks ago, when he had actually lost his temper with one of them. Usually, he only lost his temper with people who could take it, like Joy, and one or two of his colleagues. But on this occasion he had lost it with Slater, an ex-student of his, who had called around while Karel was trying to write a lecture about agriculture and child labor in the late 1800s. He had called around to borrow a fiver, to complain about the way he was being treated at work, and to complain about his girlfriend. He was one of those self-denigrating men who think they are forever underappreciated by the rest of the world, and he would take his revenge by the most subtle and complicated form of bitching and malice. He had done this in class: though in fact reasonably competent, he had always taken the line that he was terribly stupid, a position from which he could safely sneer at the mistakes of those of his own level. Now almost thirty, he still continued in the same vein, and told Karel some lengthy story about his girlfriend's behavior, full of overt praise and covert hatred. The poor girl was clearly deep in, too far committed and too cleverly manipulated to escape: the behavior which Slater described was quite clearly simply her desperate thrashing to be free. She, like Karel, had been too kind to tell Slater to bugger off, as she should have done years earlier, and all the thanks she got was this endless devious abuse. No wonder the poor girl was late for appointments, tried to go out with others occasionally, talked to other men at parties. "Of course I don't blame her," said Slater, every now and then, drinking Karel's gin, "I don't *blame* her falling asleep over dinner, I mean she does get terribly tired at the hospital" (she was a nurse) "but you would think she'd have made a *bit* of an effort, wouldn't you? Of course I don't *blame* her."

Slater was an extremely unattractive and dreadful man. Karel had once been so worried by this that he had tried to see his good points, and had found some. Now he found himself wishing that his girlfriend would escape. Let her get away, while there was still time. For Slater was, simply, a dreadful man.

Having finished with his girl, Slater started on Karel himself. His approach with Karel was a mixture of flattery and malice, as doubtless it was with the girl. How was Karel? How was Joy? Joy was out at the moment, he saw. How was life at the Poly? Here followed some abuse of lecturers quite unknown to Slater. A man like you, with your intelligence, said Slater, you should have done better things. You can't want to waste your life at that place, can you? And more, much more, of the same, Karel, gazing desperately at his lecture notes (he had to deliver the lecture the next day, and the subject was one of his favorites, he had been hoping to produce something a little better than usual) listened for some time. He listened without patience. He was not at all interested in what Slater thought of his abilities, his own assessment of himself was grandiose beyond Slater's wildest dreams, though not perhaps in the terms Slater described. You ought to write a book, pursued Slater relentlessly. I don't *want* to write a book, said Karel, as pleasantly as possible. You're wasting yourself, all your students thought so, we all thought so much of you, said Slater.

And that was the point at which Karel lost his temper. There was no satisfaction in it, it was so long overdue. He told Slater that he might well have been able to do better for himself if he hadn't wasted so much time on people like Slater, who were so insensitive to other people's problems that they would call in without warning and stay for hours when their host was clearly trying to snatch an odd couple of hours to work. "I don't know about writing a book," he yelled, standing up and tugging at his hair rather desperately, "I can't even write a *lecture* because of bloody bores like you droping in and drinking my drink and borrowing my money and boring my *mind* out."

All right, all right, Slater said, rising to his feet, looking secretly satisfied by this response from his hero. It was that look of secret delight that finished Karel. Though he felt guilty enough—after all, how can one call a bore a bore and not feel guilty?—to respond when, two days later, Slater rang up, full of apologies, so sorry he had intruded, he hadn't realized Karel was so tired, he must have been overworking, and hadn't he been having personal troubles too? (How gossip about himself and Frances had reached the dingy mad suburbs of Slater's mind, Karel never knew—he had always assumed that she inhabited a world where people didn't gossip, that she was somehow of another order, exempt.) Why don't you come and have a drink with me, and let me give you back the fiver, said Slater.

Reluctantly, Karel agreed. He went to the agreed place at the agreed time, and Slater was not there. Karel waited a quarter of an hour, then left.

Slater rang again, the next day. So sorry he hadn't got there on time, he must have arrived just after Karel left. What about a meal? The nurse, who had always wanted to meet Karel, would cook it.

Groaning inwardly at the prospect, knowing he was being maneuvered into a position of extreme disadvantage, Karel accepted. And the night before Slater rang to say awfully sorry, he had flu, they'd have to put it off.

That was the end of Slater. He had had his revenge. Karel never heard another word from him, though he heard indirectly that he always spoke of him, when he spoke, with extreme venom. He transferred his allegiance to another ex-teacher, who was not very patient with him.

Karel had often wondered whether Slater had thought that Karel would actually be disappointed not to have dinner with him on that last occasion, or whether he had finely calculated the degree of relief, fury, and disgust that Karel had, at that moment of refusal, actually felt. Impossible to know what mad people think, how aware or unaware they are of their own devious games.

Karel was so relieved to have got rid of Slater that sometimes he toyed with the idea of getting rid of everybody, in one fell swoop, in one drastic reorganization. He would become a complete recluse. But this, of course, was impracticable. However would one find the nervous energy to annoy everybody, as he had managed to annoy Slater? The strain would kill him.

Another irony of the situation was that Joy, nowadays, seemed to be resolved on a course of getting rid of him. Why she couldn't have done this some time ago, when Frances was still available, he could all too well imagine. How extremely unpleasant people are, he reflected, and wrote out another check.

Joy had recently decided to become a lesbian. In her new view, she had always been one, but Karel couldn't really go along with that. It's true she'd never been very enthusiastic about sex with him, but that was for other reasons, surely. Anyway, it was now quite the fashion to be lesbian, and Joy was carrying on with the girl from the tobacconist's down the road. She claimed to have been carrying on for years, but this Karel doubted. Anyway, whatever the length of the affair, she had now brought it out into the open, and whenever anything at home annoyed her (which was often) she would flounce off to the tobacconist's. She used Vera (this was the other woman's name) as a counter in the complex game of bargaining that makes up any less than totally happy marriage. Sometimes she said she was going to move out completely, abandoning the children, who in her view were now old enough to look after themselves. Sometimes she said she would take the children with her and set up house somewhere else, in the country preferably. But she in fact did neither, preferring to move up and down the road at her own convenience, or rather at Karel's inconvenience. The whole affair was like some grotesque parody of his own affair with Frances, inflicted, he could not help thinking, as a conscious revenge. She was down the road now, while he wrote out checks, and the children were all out with friends.

He couldn't really blame her. He tried hard not to blame her. On the other hand, as ever, she wished to be blamed, and would taunt him so much that in the end, when her mockery went beyond the bounds of the tolerable, he would beat her up. With blackened eyes, a bleeding nose, bruises on face and arms, she would stagger off triumphantly to the tobacconist's, to bewail the violence of men. Then she would come back and begin again. He sometimes thought he would have minded less if her methods had been more sophisticated: she had in the old days had a fine style of invective, which he had found perversely attractive (indeed he could still remember a time when the savagery of her attack on life had impressed him, through its complete abandon, through its lack of the devious subterfuges of such as Mrs. Mayfield, Slater, and Stuart), but of late she had become less inventive, more crude. On the last occasion when he had attacked her, she had been sitting in the armchair late at night while he was marking some papers. After a while, bored, simply bored, she had started to pick a quarrel, about how he shouldn't have criticized one of the children for not finishing his supper. Karel, not caring much one way or the other, replied and went on with his work. She continued with the theme until he began to shout back, but he had just enough self-control left to confine himself to a little brief abuse. Then he went back to marking his papers. Joy, however, was not satisfied. She had started to throw things at him. Anything at hand—fag ends, paper clips, pencils. He wondered, not for the first time, whether she had gone mad. What should one do, with a madwoman? He remained indecisive while she finished off all the small objects in reach, and then picked up her coffee mug, a flowered pottery mug. She threw that at him, and missed, and began to look around for something else. It flashed across his mind, as he felt himself lose his temper, as he felt that dangerous spring unlock, that she was like a caged animal in a zoo, throwing bits of its dinner at its mate, and the comparison horrified him: it horrified him even while he took her by the hair and shook her up and down and banged her head on the floor.

As usual, when he had finished, she lay there with an air of smug triumph, then got up and went off to tell Vera.

Karel wondered how much more of it he would take, and how, if ever, the end would come. Perhaps he would murder her with the bread knife. Maybe that was what she was waiting for.

He hadn't felt murderous with Frances. He hadn't wanted to kill her, he had wanted to make love to her. Making love to her would have kept him happy forever, but she must have had more complicated views of life, or she wouldn't have left him. He had always hoped she would come back, but was now beginning to doubt it. He couldn't contemplate a replacement. She, for no good reason, had been exactly what he desired. He could never hope to find such a woman again, for he did not know what it was in her that he so desired. It was the whole thing, her whole self, the way she was. And it wasn't only loving her that was so satisfactory, it was as though loving her made everything else much better. He found it easier to be pleasant to Mrs. Mayfield when Frances was being pleasant to him. Maybe he shouldn't have found this surprising, but he did. And now that she was gone, he was becoming impatient with everybody, even with Mrs. Mayfield. He simply couldn't keep the whole thing up any more. He had failed. He had failed to be an egalitarian of love, so he would become an egalitarian of hate, and hate the lot of them. Why draw distinctions?

Karel hated distinctions. There was no justice in life, why seek for it or try to create it? What justice could ever have given to him and Frances such years of loving, and to others, no loving at all?

Karel's parents and brothers and sister had perished in the gas chambers. His mother had made distinctions: she had chosen Karel for salvation. Her favorite son, her baby. As the darkness closed in on them (they had been living in Cracow, his father a doctor, his mother a journalist), she had chosen Karel, aged three, and sent him off to England with her sister and her sister's husband. She had always meant to follow, but like so many, she left it too late. What consolation had it been, at the point of death, to know her baby was alive in Palmers Green? Karel could not bear to think of these matters. How could he not have felt himself rejected, denied the honor and the intimacy of death? The chosen, the elect, the rejected. His brothers and sister, dead. He thought at times he could remember them, but perhaps it was his aunt's memories he remembered—his aunt, weeping night after night by the hearth, her apron thrown over her head like a peasant, rocking herself backward and forward like a peasant, though she was a graduate of the University of Prague, while Karel, the favorite, cried for his cruel mother who had forgotten him and sent him to live in a dark single room.

Mrs. Mayfield lived alone, in a dark room.

He would give up the struggle. Why should he personally feel called upon to justify his survival by struggling singlehanded to redress the appalling imbalances of the natural scheme of things? Let others die, let them rot. He would disassociate himself. He would end up in a bedsitter like Mrs. Mayfield, with a milk bottle or two on the windowsill, boiling eggs in a kettle, a malevolent recluse. Adding by one unit to the world's immeasurable woe. Joining the legions of the great majority. Supporting, rather than defying, the myrmidons of solitude and death.

He contemplated this vision with a morbid satisfaction. It pleased him. He looked around, at the purple walls, the oak sideboard, the moquette chairs, the tatty Indian carpet, the littered desk, the overflowing bookshelves. Why set oneself up in this grand manner? It was unnatural. It was asking for trouble. He would sink into his proper place.

As he finished writing out the last check, the doorbell rang. He crossed furtively to the window and peered out from behind the brown curtain. Standing on the doorstep was an ex-colleague, no doubt in hope of a cup of tea or a free drink.

I'll start a new life today, thought Karel. I won't answer. And with an immense effort of the will, he managed to stand there, without going down to open the door. He went down at the second ring, of course. And as a reward for his oneminute effort, for his heroic attempt to adjust his worldpicture (or as a reward for his equally heroic failure to readjust, who can say?) the picture postcard which Frances Wingate had written to him at the beginning of the year was at that moment lifted from its resting place at the bottom of a mail bag a thousand miles away, and sent upon its way. Its journey from box to bag had taken nine months: the rest of its journey was to take a mere ten days. And to those who object to too much coincidence in fiction, perhaps one could point out that there is very little real coincidence in the post-card motif, though there are many other coincidences in this book. These days, the post being what it is, it would have been more of a miracle if the postcard had arrived on time, as Frances (unlike Tess of the D'Urbervilles) should have been sensible enough to realize, though (in this sense like Tess of the D'Urbervilles) her judgment too was clouded by emotion. Frances, in fact, had built her expectations of Karel on a perfectly accurate premise: that, if he received her card, he would respond. As, in ten days, he will do.

David Ollerenshaw, well on his way to Adra, with his foot down on the accelerator, watched the desert pass, and sang to himself, loudly and contentedly:

> *Jesus shall reign where'er the sun*
> *Doth his successive journeys run*
> *His kingdom stretch from shore to shore*
> *Till moons shall wax and wane no more. . . .*

he sang, thinking little of the content, but liking the tune, which he remembered well from his school days. He had, however, probably been prompted to choose this tune by the sight of the surrounding empty wastes, where neither Jesus nor Mohammed reigned, for there was nobody there at all. The following year, the whole area was to be struck by a terrible drought, but David was not to know that. And even if he did, he might have reflected that his valley of tin would probably come in handy somehow, even in a drought situation.

Meanwhile, he was well stocked with water, and with other forms of drink. Although capable of considerable abstinence, he would go in for bouts of heavy drinking, like a sailor on shore leave, and he did not see why he should not indulge in one of these at the end of his journey: he was preparing for the indulgence each night, after pitching his tent, by a nightcap of whiskey.

He changed tunes, and started on Greenland's icy mountains. He'd met a few missionaries on his travels in desolate outposts. Converting the heathen, the Turk and the Jew, the Eskimo, the Pacific islander, the African. Their task had always seemed to him mad: he was more likely to find gold in a tin mine, than they were to strike faith in the heathen human heart. But they went on prospecting. Likely places, unlikely places.

On the boat over, he had met a French couple; he had been unable to avoid meeting them, as they were all three placed together at the same first-class dining table for meals. At first he had thought them husband and wife, but after a while it became clear that they were brother and sister: middle-aged, olive-skinned, somberly dressed, they were on their way to visit their mother, who was dying in a nursing home in Algiers. He was a businessman: she an actress, it seemed. They were on poor terms, but united by their journey. In Paris, where both lived, they never met, they said. With the same features, the same gestures, the same ironic smile: we never meet, they said. Did David have brothers, sisters, a wife? No, none, nobody.

Black birds of passage. He had walked on the deck with them after their dinner, in the blue night, in the middle of the black Mediterranean. The woman, immobile as a figure-head in the slightly salty air, held a silk scarf around her throat with one gloved hand, as she looked south. Her brother, a man of fifty, covered her other gloved hand with his as it lay on the rail, "Death brings us together," the woman had said, not very dramatically, factually rather, and down in the bar he had heard some of their differences. She had signed a petition claiming to have had an abortion, out of female solidarity, she said: he was a Catholic, with a pub-

lic position, and six children. They told David these things
freely, as pop music from a coin machine filled the bar. They
sat, the three of them, around a plastic-topped steel-rimmed
round table, lit from beneath with lurid pink and green and
checkered lights, covered with brown melted smudges from
lighted cigarettes, and the other two discussed why it was
not possible, in these times, to live in the same city on
friendly terms with one's brother, one's sister. David listened
to these foreign conversations, volunteering nothing. He had
never inhabited a region where friendship had been possible,
of the sort these two had perhaps once enjoyed in infancy.
An only child.

People often told David things. He had heard some amazing stories, both in the prolonged and enforced intimacy of
communal effort (what else can one do, in the Falkland Islands, but tell stories?) and from passing strangers, such as
these. There must, he sometimes thought, be some rift in his
nature, unperceived by himself, down which people knew
they could let their confidences tumble out of sight. Other
people's garbage. He could understand the satisfaction. Once,
on an uninhabited island off the northwest coast of Scotland,
he had lost a gunmetal cigarette lighter down a crevice between two rocks. He liked to think that it was still there.

He rarely told people much in exchange. They didn't seem
to demand it. But he would make his own offerings. On this
occasion he showed them some of the objects that he carried
around in his khaki pockets: a dull topaz or two from his
valley, a little aspirin bottle of stream tin, a twig of straw
tin, a sign of previous habitation. (There was no one there
now: the water had dried up.) They looked at his relics with
interest.

The coin box played a popular song called "Souvenir."
The woman recited, somberly, more dramatically, "Souvenir, souvenir, que me veux-tu?" It was a poem by Verlaine,
she explained, that their father had recited frequently over
the dining table. They had been born and brought up in Algeria, she explained, and had not been back since the trou-

bles. They were returning to the land of their birth. "O temps,
suspends ton vol," she said, with feeling. She was an actress. Her solid cream neck rose from the throat of her dark-
green dress, a firm column. She looked so like her brother,
the same nose, the same eyes, the same gestures, and yet
they led in the same city lives so far removed, so mutually
hostile, that they never met.

"As pants the heart for cooling streams," sang David,
driving through the desert, prompted this time by the surrounding dryness. He thought of the Frenchwoman and her
brother, and of Frances Wingate, who was attending the conference, and whose lecture he had heard earlier that year. He
looked forward to meeting her. He was quite interested in
archaeology.

Frances Wingate sat on the airplane and stared down at the
desert. She was bored. Perhaps the stone in her chest was
boredom. Nothing seemed very interesting any more—
traveling was a drag, the conference was certain to be tedious, the desert below was extraordinarily tedious, and she
didn't even feel like the drink she'd ordered. She was terrified
of boredom, it was the worst threat, or so it seemed for the
moment. The absolute futility of all human effort struck her
in all its banal, heavyweight, unanswerable dullness. My
name is Ozymandias, King of Kings: Look on my works, ye
Mighty, and despair!

She tried, with an immense effort of the will, to make
herself think about something interesting: namely, Joe Ayida, Minister of Culture of Adra. He was, as she had told her
brother, quite an exceptional man. She had met him in London: he had come to talk to her about her trade route and her
trans-Saharan emporium. He had been extremely excited by
them, and also extremely well informed about the possibility
of similarly interesting discoveries on his own territory. She
had told him that it was more than likely that such discoveries
could and would be made. He had talked a great deal about
the history of Africa, and had been not at all annoying on

the subject: through him, she had glimpsed what it must be like to have lost one's past, and to stand on the verge of reclaiming it. The Greeks, the Romans, the Egyptians, he had said, they have blinded us for centuries. She agreed. She always agreed in theory, but Joe had made her feel that it mattered. They discussed the massive joke of Zimbabwe, the confusion created among Egyptologists by radio-carbon dating, the inability of the European mind to conceive that any good thing could come out of Africa. They have conceded us Homo habilis, but it is not enough, said Joe Ayida. We will rewrite the labels in the museums. Quite right, said Frances, carried along by his enthusiasm.

Joe Ayida wasn't an archaeologist, or even an anthropologist. He was an art historian. Of course, as they had frequently remarked to one another, the disciplines overlapped more and more these days. He was also a sculptor. To hear him talk of tradition and the individual talent was to enter into a world where old labels had meaning. Frances found it deeply exciting, and also beyond her. There was something in Joe Ayida that she could never catch. She was too old and came from the wrong culture. But she could recognize it, she had a feel of its quality. Hearing him speak, one heard words like *artist* and *nation* for the first time, with a kind of primal clarity.

Joe was ideally placed so to speak. His nation was a small one, his country large. It needed culture, it needed water, and minerals, and oil, it needed past, present, and future. It seemed that some of these commodities had now been discovered: perhaps Adra was about to become as rich as a Gulf State. She wondered what they would do with the money, if it were really there. Television stations, airports, roads, railways, hotels, washing machines? At the moment, most of the people of Adra were seminomadic: she had met plenty of them herself in her travels. They pitched their tents by small ancient trees, they wandered with their biblical cattle. The country would need a lot of money if it wanted to get any kind of modern living to its remoter inhabitants. And perhaps it didn't want to. Modernization wasn't so much taken for granted as a blessing, these days.

She wondered what Joe's intentions were. He was a dynamic man, and had certainly been a powerful force in organizing the conference, but he wasn't exactly prime minister yet, and there were other yet more powerful economic forces involved. It was going to cost Adra a lot of money to get at its newly discovered resources, and one of the many things Adra hadn't got was a lot of money. Loans, investments. The conference was doubtless intended to raise a few million pounds. It was a prestige project, to persuade the world of the seriousness of Adran intentions. A prestige project of the intellect, as the amazing hotel they were all going to stay in was a prestige project of a more earthly nature. She gazed at the brochure for it, which lay brightly colored on her table, provided by Air-Adra. It was really too amazing. The architect that designed it must have gone mad. It was an enormous building, the Hotel Sahara, and it was much wider at the top than it was at the bottom, like a kind of pyramid in reverse, each floor extending by one step out into the sky. A blue, dazzling, blistering Kodacolor sky. One wouldn't have thought such a construction possible. It looked quite illogical, as though it must surely fall over. It was as white as the sky was blue, and its base was surrounded with ornamental palm trees and fountains. A row of large Mercedes was drawn up in front of the vast entrance. Frances found herself hoping that she hadn't been given a room that hung out, as it were, into space. If a child had built such a building out of Lego bricks, she would have understood it. It was quite an amusing shape. But it wasn't for real.

The drink that she had ordered arrived, brought by a rather forbidding very black Adran girl. It was a Campari soda. Frances stared at it in horror. Whatever had happened to her, that she had started to order drinks she didn't like in order to have a change? At least it was an exciting color, as the hotel was an exciting shape. Such dull little pleasures would have to do her for the rest of her life, she thought glumly. For what

did the future hold? Nothing much. She'd be able to keep her
mind occupied while delivering her own paper, but that
wouldn't last long, and she knew she'd get horribly bored
listening to other people's. Interpreters were so dull, anyway.
She sipped the healthy pink drink. It wasn't too bad, but it
certainly wouldn't amuse one for eternity. Oh, God, she felt
bored. She wanted Karel. That short conversation with Hugh
about sex had upset her. She hadn't thought about sex for a
long time till then, but after all she wasn't as middle-aged as
she pretended to be. Why hadn't she tried anyone else, after
Karel? Was it the fear of annoying him, even in his everlast-
ing absence? Surely not. Perhaps it was the fear of being
bored by people, once she started having personal relation-
ships with them. She hadn't liked to admit it to herself when
she was younger, but now she didn't really mind: the fact
was that she found most other people frightfully dull. Most
other people *were* frightfully dull, and that was the end of it.
It wasn't really their fault, but one could guess what they
were going to say, and was tired with it before they'd said it.
And if one slept with a dull person, they would be sure to
hang around asking for more. Frances found herself in the
unfortunate position of knowing that people would hang
around asking for more whether they wanted it or not. She
seemed to have that kind of effect on people. And it was very
hard to get rid of them without being rude.

So there one was, alone. Here I am, she said to herself,
moving her lips over the words.

Karel had never bored her, not for an instant. She had
loved him so much that even when she couldn't understand
what he was saying, she had been happy to watch him say
it. How could he not reply to her postcard? How could she
love him so much, and other people not at all? Ah, she had
asked this question often, in their happy years. And had always found her own answer. It is because you are so lovely,
so amazing, she had cried, each time. For so he was.

The endless sand flowed under them. Work was all that
was left, with Karel gone and the children growing. But

somehow, when one knew one was good at it, it lost its charm. Why bother? What did it matter, one archaeologist more or less? One minister more or less?

Though that, of course, wasn't quite true. For Joe Ayida was in a position to influence his country's future.

Still, what was a country? My name is Ozymandias, King of Kings: Look on my works, ye Mighty, and despair! The lone and level sands stretch far away.

Oh, God, she did feel low. She knocked back the Campari and rang for another. The Adran girl came back and said they would be landing shortly and was Frances sure she wanted another drink. Yes, quite sure, said Frances, who was not at all sure. The drink never arrived.

But there were plenty of drinks at the hotel. So many, in fact, that Frances began to wonder whether it might not be more dignified to move on to heroin or cocaine and make an end of it.

She was met at the airport by a civil servant. It appeared that various other conference members had been traveling on the same flight: she had suspected that this might be so, and had deliberately avoided the eyes of people who might be trying to look at her. She was used to being looked at, and used to avoidance. They all shook hands politely on the tarmac. Frances began to feel slightly, but very slightly, better, as she stepped into the old routine. All one has to do, she told herself with a part of herself, is to *keep moving*, *keep talking*, and don't spend too much time alone. And you'll survive. What for? Don't ask, don't be naïve. While actually smiling, while actually speaking to a stranger (she said to herself, in the back of a diplomatic car, talking to a UNESCO man and a Polish woman engineer at the same time) one cannot possibly feel too terribly miserable.

The hotel was as surprising as its photograph, if not more so. They all exclaimed. The civil servant explained why it was like it was. He assured them it was very comfortable. And so it was. They stepped into a dense jungle of a foyer, beautifully air conditioned (for it was, even at this time of the year, unpleasantly hot outside), with mosaic paving, rippling fountains, heavenly Muzak. The manager met them, smiling happily, but without servility. What an honor, what a pleasure. The president of Zambia had visited him the week before. Before that, the English prince. And now so many distinguished guests. Their baggage would follow from the airport, would they like to see their rooms, would they like drinks in the lounge? Dinner would be served at eight. Tomorrow for work, this evening for society.

Frances liked this kind of thing, and she found herself responding like a Pavlovian dog. Thank Christ, she said to herself, for the large amount of silliness and vanity in one's makeup. Without it, one would indeed drop dead with boredom.

The conference members were eyeing one another uneasily. Should they have a drink, should they see their rooms? Frances said that she would see her room, and others followed suit.

She was, in fact, in an overhanging bit, just as she had predicted. It was clearly thought to be a particularly pleasant room, with views of nothing much in all directions. It was large and comfortable. She wandered around it for a while, opening closets, trying taps. They all worked, for which she awarded full marks. Out of the last window she looked through, she saw a large glinting swimming pool, lurid green-blue in the evening light. It was enormous, shaped like a kidney, with diving boards and chutes and floodlighting. Her spirits rose. She had brought her bathing suit. An after-dinner swim would be quite reviving.

Then she sat down on the bed, and burst into tears.

After a few minutes, her luggage arrived. It seemed to be an extremely efficient country. The man who brought it up didn't seem to expect a tip, either, for he dumped it and disappeared very abruptly.

She unpacked her clothes, her books, her papers, Karel's teeth. Then she had a bath. While she was in the bath, the phone rang: it was Joe Ayida, asking if she had arrived safely, asking how she felt. I'm fine, she said, what a glorious hotel. Do you think so, he said, ambiguously, and laughed. I'll see you at dinner, he said. Unless you come down first, for a drink.

I'll be down in half an hour, she said. And in half an hour, she went down to the bar, dressed rather smartly in a long black dress. The bar was large and opulent, marble floored, full of plants climbing up pillars and birds in white wire cages. Conference members stood about, drinking, and the television was on. The prime minister was speaking, as it seemed at some length. So there was television in Adra. She looked around for Joe, and wondered if the drinks were free, and if she ought to purchase some Adran currency. She spotted him, luckily, before she had to confront the problem. "Ah, my dear Frances," he cried with heart-warming certainty, disengaging himself from an aging Russian, "my dear, here you are. How delightful, how delightful."

He shook her hand, heartily. In Adra, emancipated women were honorary men, as he had explained to her, and could not be kissed.

"Joe," she said, "how nice to see you."

"How nice of you to come all this way," he said. And so they went on for some time. He provided her with a large drink, and introduced her to some of her prospective colleagues: she was well aware that she was very far from being the most important person there, and was pleased that he stayed with her. He stayed with her until they went in to dinner, and then abandoned her between a French economist and an Adran engineer. She tried hard with both, ate a vast amount of food, washed it down with as much wine as she could get into her glass, but was nevertheless glad, actually glad, when their chairman rose to his feet and made a welcoming speech. He spoke of the need for international co-operation, and to prove its need, his speech was duly translated into several languages. Luckily it was brief. It was followed by other speeches, also brief, one from a UNESCO man, one from Joe Ayida himself, one from some unexplained American. Then the chairman stood up again and announced the schedule, and explained how papers would be distributed and in which languages, and told them that an expedition had been arranged for the following week and he hoped they would all go, and that the rest of the evening was their own.

They drifted away from the table: Frances drifted rather rapidly, making for an Englishwoman who looked like a potential ally. The brief biographies they had been given said her name was Patsy Cornford and she was from the Department of the Environment, and so indeed she proved to be. She was quick to tell Frances that she was only there as an observer and wasn't supposed to have any views: however, she clearly had plenty. While she was expounding them, Joe Ayida came up and joined them. Frances asked if everybody had arrived. "There seem to be a lot of people," she said.

"Everybody is here," he said, "except a Russian who arrives late—she has problems with her visa, I think—and an Englishman, who drives himself."

"Wherever is he driving from?"

"Across the Sahara."

"Perhaps he got lost on the way. When was he supposed to get here?"

"Today, like yourselves. It is much safer on an airplane."

"What's his name?"

"His name is Ollerenshaw. A geologist, I believe."

"That's funny," said Frances. "My maiden name was Ollerenshaw."

"Isn't your father vice-chancellor of Wolverton University?" asked the woman from the Department of the Environment, and initiated a long conversation about new British universities, which excluded Joe Ayida completely and rather rudely. Frances struggled, and then gave in. It was going to be boring, after all.

Three hours later, at midnight, however, things had livened up a little. Some had retired to bed: others were sitting around drinking and playing cards. Frances had managed to bully the Department of the Environment woman (who was extremely pretty for one so neurotic) and one or two other stray possibles into a game of poker, though they hadn't got much beyond the stage of arguing about the rules they were playing by. Still, it was better than nothing. She was just thinking of proposing that they begin playing for real money instead of matchsticks when another member of the party, more daring (or, she suspected, a better and more dissatisfied card player), suggested that they drop the cards for a time and go for a swim. "Look," he said, waving, dramatically, at the kidney-shaped floodlit pool outside, "regarde, on ne peut pas resister."

Frances certainly couldn't resist. She rushed off to the elevator for her bathing things at once, persuading the Department woman to join her. Their rooms, they had discovered, were adjacent. The woman complained that she hadn't got her bathing things, Frances offered to lend her a spare set. Frances knew, from endless travel, that there is nothing more useful abroad than a bathing suit or two. Her own were extremely old: the bikini she had bought just after Daisy was born, and the one-piece garment which she offered to Patsy she had had since school. They changed, grabbed a heap of luxurious towels, and ran down to the pool, where a fat geologist and a bald engineer were already splashing and diving. The water was a perfect temperature: warm, soft, quivering blue, very mildly refreshing. She wondered if it was heated: it was probably cold in this part of the world at night, but the whole atmosphere was so artificial that one couldn't possibly tell. She lay on her back, her hair drifting like weed, her ears full of water, gazing upward at the white monument of the hotel, and the fairylights, orange and white and green, and a new crescent of a new moon, and stars competing ineffectively with the lights, and thought of other swims in other seas: the children on a beach in the south of France, howling with fear at the sight of the water (it had annoyed Anthony), an obscene swim at Venice on the dull and ugly Lido with a randy Italian, a desperate plunge into a hotel pool after hours of driving in Tunisia, as a child herself, on the vast intimidating sands of East Anglia, a swim in a river near her brother's cottage, in the icy Windrush, where one swam silently like an otter or a rat between the weedy flowering banks, on a level with secret holes and burrows. With Karel, there had never been much time for swimming. They had never had a holiday together, except that one with the frogs. She thought of the frogs, and smiled to herself as always. If one could smile about the frogs, one must be capable of recovery. She gazed up at the moon, and wished on it, like a child, as she always did when the moon was new, and on every first evening star: she wished for Karel to come back to her. Oh, God, she said, combining piety and superstition, let him come back, let me be his, let him be mine.

She wondered if Karel would have liked this hotel, this swimming pool. She paddled herself around a little, and watched the fat geologist dive in. She admired men, the way they didn't mind people seeing their bodies. Karel did mind. He was a modest man. His body was very private and beautiful. The Department woman was sitting very elegantly on a kind of bathmat, talking to an anthropologist. She looked very nice in Frances's school swimsuit; Frances suspected she wouldn't have worn it if she hadn't. What a weird scene. Joe Ayida wouldn't have liked it. Tolerant though he was, Western though he was, he wouldn't have liked it. He had gone home to his mysterious wife. She wouldn't know what kind of house they lived in. One would certainly never be invited to it. She had asked Joe's wife to dinner once, when she had been visiting London, and she had accepted, and turned up, and smiled politely, and eaten everything put in front of her (except the turnips, for which Frances could hardly blame her, for turnips were rather an acquired taste, though at that time one of her own favorite vegetables) and had said not a word. What did she think of London? She had smiled and nodded. What of Paris, what of Milan? She smiled happily. In the end, she said very nice. Yet she spoke good English, Joe asserted. Joe sculpted her, large and naked, but in company it was improper for her to speak, and it would certainly have been improper for her to disport herself in this lurid modern pool.

Frances noted rather enviously that the Department woman, who must be considerably younger than herself, hadn't got even a suggestion of fat. When Frances sat in certain positions, she noticed that there was a spare roll round her waist, and even an incipient double chin. On the other hand, she hadn't, she hoped, got the other woman's mad and manic laugh. How was it that one could tell so quickly that another person was slightly off course? The laugh floated over the pool. Frances swam over to the group—the fat geologist had joined them, and so had a nice-looking Bulgarian. The anthropologist who was talking to the Department woman was an Italian, a distinguished man, in his fifties, gray, but hardened and fit, grizzled as though by years of field work. His chest was covered with wiry dark-gray hair. His name was Emilio Spirelli, she had read a book of his once about kinship and family structures in nomadic peoples. He was watching her approach through the technicolor water, though maintaining a conversation at the same time, and when she arrived at the side he leaned over the pool edge, and offered her his arm to pull her up. His arm was amazingly strong, the hand had little hairs like wires all over it, he seemed to pull her out of the water without effort. The casual stylish gesture alarmed her slightly, as did her response to the touch of Spirelli's hand. He was like that, then, was he. She would have to be careful. The fact that she hadn't been touched by so nearly naked a man for a long time, together with Hugh's admonishments about celibacy, swam into her mind simultaneously, fish of the same color. She shook the water out of her hair and ears, to frighten them away. Oh, dear. Dripping, she sat there on the towel, squeezing out her hair.

"Dr. Wingate, I think," he said. She nodded, water falling from the tip of her nose. They all smiled. She remembered now, he was to present a paper on the effects of

development on a nomadic tribe in neighboring Chad, and
the projected consequences for a great many of the very few
Adrans who wandered around the northern territories of
Adra. It would be interesting; he was a very interesting man.
She also remembered that she had liked his book, because it
had argued a case for returning to Malinowski's simplistic
theories about family ties: he was opposed to the trend for
interpreting them in terms of property, arguing that property
was an extraordinarily recent development of civilization. He
was one of these avant-garde reactionaries that every profession throws up now and then—confusing, acute, unclassifi-
able.

"How nice to meet you," said Frances. "I do so look
forward to hearing your paper."

"And I you," said Spirelli. His English was not perfect:
nevertheless it was very much better than Frances's rather
unused Italian, and they managed to have quite an interesting
chat about families and kinship, a subject which naturally
attracted everyone. The geologist contributed the view that
in his experience the small modern family created strain and
neurosis and drove people into clinics, and did not Spirelli,
as an Italian, agree that large families were much better?
Spirelli did not necessarily agree, though he saw the point.
He himself, he said, came from a family completely dissipated (by which he meant dispersed, reasonably enough),
and that that was why he was so interested in kinship ties.
At this irony, he laughed, and asked them if they did not
think that it was common for people to choose a profession
that provided what they did not get in life. As compensation?
Like academics who grow old and gray writing pedantic
books about Blake and Lawrence, suggested Miss Cornford.
Or quiet novelists who write novels full of blood. That kind
of thing, he agreed, though Frances doubted whether he
picked up the literary allusions: he picked up the sense,
though, quickly enough. She liked him, but wished his name
didn't remind her of corsets, because that in turn kept re-
minding her of how fat she was or might be getting, and how

thin Miss Cornford was. They discussed the size of the modern family: Patsy Cornford had one sister, the geologist had one brother, Spirelli claimed two of each, all lost and dissipated, as it appeared, in all senses of the word. When Frances said she had four children, they all made clicking noises just as her mother would have done, which rather annoyed her. Still, she couldn't help feeling she had scored a point. "And your husband, what does he say? You leave him with babies?" asked the geologist.

"I haven't got a husband," said Frances, perhaps rashly, then tried to give a brief and forbidding account of her marital status, whereupon Spirelli asked her whether or not it was true that more and more women in England were bringing up their children alone, and whether or not the trend was pronounced enough to be counted a social phenomenon.

Frances tried to think about this, and said that it was hard to produce statistics. But she and Patsy Cornford between them could produce hardly any examples of first marriages with offspring lasting any length of time. "Perhaps getting married again is becoming a trend," said Frances. "Do you think, Patsy?" (First-name terms were inevitable: she was in for the woman's entire life story at some point during the conference.) Patsy did think so. But also it was quite common for mothers to bring the children up single-handed. More of the people Frances knew were doing this than weren't. She pondered the fact, it had never struck her so forcibly before. It wasn't that her acquaintance was a very large cross-section, but it was surely representative of something. And if so, of what? She asked Spirelli if it were so in Italy, and as he replied, half in Italian (it was not so, it seemed, but this was for economic reasons, educational reasons), she thought back to an incident the weekend before, which had, as it were, taken her by surprise. She'd been driving the children up to Hugh's and Natasha's, sitting in the kind of daze she always sat in while driving, and had stopped at a crossroads in one of the last villages they passed through: waiting for the light, she had seen a family on bicycles ap-

proach, two small children, and then their father. They were
laughing and shouting at one another, she smiled to herself
at the sight of them, it always touched her to see passing
strangers in momentary glimpses of amity. They weren't a
very special family—a little boy in a red woolly hat, a girl in
an anorak, the father a small workingman in a cap. And then,
their mother had followed, and quick as a flash, as she saw
the fourth member of the completed family, Frances had felt
her smile fade, her approval vanish, her own vicarious pleasure die, the image shattered, the transient harmony destroyed. It had frightened her, the way her spirits dropped so
instantly at the sight of the mother, bicycling behind. Why
not a mother? Why should she not join in too?

And she had driven on, thoughtfully, pondering this. The
truth was, she concluded, that she could no longer admit the
concept of a two-parent family. Such symmetry, such ideal
union utterly excluded her. She could not even smile at a
nuclear family's pleasure as it cycled along a road. She
wanted them split, broken, fragmented. She couldn't believe
they were really happy as a foursome: one of the parents
must be a drag, and if it wasn't the man, then it must be the
woman. Any other balance was impossible, unthinkable.

She had just been congratulating herself, as she drove
along, on the adaptability, the good nature, the charm of her
own children. She had been listening to their chat, idly, answering them from time to time, all the way from Putney.
She could manage. She could cope. No need for a man, must
have been her underlying thought. Or why be so shocked at
her own shock? She despised people who sacrificed themselves for their children and dragged their way through desolate, bitter marriages. Karel and Joy. For the sake of the
children. Her own children were fine, they had escaped her
fell hand. They were set free.

She could not conceive of family love. She was too selfish,
too uncooperative, too fond of her own way. That was it. It
was obvious. And she loved a man who was not the father
of her children, and he loved his family more than he loved

her. Moreover, she could not conceive of any life in which all the things she loved could come together, and therefore did not want to believe that anyone else could have such a perfect life. Ideological sour grapes. They dangled, blue and bitter. It was all bitter, whichever way one looked. However did it get to be like that? When were the anthropologists and sociologists going to explain that? Certainly, she said to herself, if those four people, that perfect family, at the village crossroads, had resembled for an instant a perfect family, they would not be able to keep up the illusion for long. Oh no. They would be quarreling by the next corner.

She thought of Hugh and Natasha, who had tried so hard. Hugh had tried to drown his nature in floods of alcohol, Natasha had slaved till exhaustion to produce the illusion of a home. And now she was attending group therapy sessions. They were the only couple Frances knew who were still married, even. Whatever had gone wrong? She did not often think in these simple terms. She looked down at her wet arm. The veins were prominent now, and knotty. Those on the inside on Karel's arm were huge and delicate, his skin was white and smoother than her own. She was aging, when she bent her arm there were wrinkles at her elbow. She should have had another baby, years ago, with Karel. Another family.

Spirelli had stopped talking about the education of women in Italy, and started on the difficulties of abortion in Portugal. She asked him about primitive cultures in which it was permitted for women to have children by different men. He described one or two. They didn't sound very nice. The geologist told them that he was too selfish ever to get married, that he liked to do things his own way and was very fussy about what he ate, liked to talk to himself, and was mean about money, too mean to support a wife. He found all this very amusing, and so did they. Then he asked Patsy Cornford if she was thinking of getting married. Frances obscurely feared an outburst at this question, especially as the girl had been rather quiet during the last ten minutes, but the outburst was clearly biding its time, for all that she said was that she was very selfish too and (darkly) it was time that certain people recognized the fact. Spirelli admitted to having had a wife at one point, but said that it hadn't worked out. "I have two adult sons," he said. It seemed they would not speak to him, they took their mother's part. "But an anthropologist like myself can have no family life," he said. The geologist agreed that those who went in for field work and conferences could have no family life. Then they turned on Frances, and asked her how or why she managed it, and she said she didn't know, it must be to prove that it could be done, and that she'd been lucky to have a rich if not a co-operative husband, and she went on to explain that naturally her work had suffered as a result of her family arrangements, how could it not have done? They told her she was making excuses, and the geologist said he must be going to bed, he was just going to plunge in again for a last swim, who would join him? In he went like a porpoise, puffing and blowing and cheerful, in his large flowered trunks. And Patsy Cornford, rather to their surprise, suddenly rose neatly and quietly to her feet, and walked over to the diving board, and dived in, perfectly, professionally, neatly. Spirelli and Frances sat and watched them, silently. It was late, everyone else had gone to bed, though there were still lavish lights glittering all over the ground floor of the hotel, and the upper stories were lit irregularly with small colored oblongs of brightness. They sat quietly, and listened to the slapping of the water, the breathing of the swimmers, the hum of the lights, the clattering of insects around the lights. It was a scene from nowhere, a modern Arabian Night.

And suddenly, they heard a noise. In the silence, it sounded important, ominous. It was only the sound of a car engine, as they realized after a while, but they found themselves listening to it with some attention. It seemed to be heading so directly for them, through the empty space. The hotel was built on the outskirts of the small town, near the very small and infrequently used airport. They wondered who could be arriving at this time of night. Frances had a sudden crazy inspiration that it was Karel, come at last to get her, as she had always known he would: how often had she not dreamed of him, stumbling over the hot sand, screeching to a halt outside her own front door, pulling her from her seat in the Institute, arriving (oh, God, how she had longed for him) at the side of her hospital bed. Oh, the reunions she had arranged in her mind. Why ever should he not, on an impulse, arrive in Adra? She summoned him, she willed him, she conjured him.

The apparition that finally materialized was not Karel, but it was almost as strange. Patsy and the geologist had climbed out of the pool to join their expectation: the car grew closer, grinding up the long drive. And here it was, in sight at last, a new green Peugeot. It pulled up smartly, by the side of the pool, an obvious place to approach for it was brightly lit (the manager had, finally, extinguished the splendid avenue that approached the splendid fountain-filled forecourt.) The four of them sat there, waiting to see who would emerge. And from the car came a man, an Englishman, a parody of an Englishman. There he stood, bespectacled, bare-kneed, desert-booted. He shaded his eyes like an explorer as he stared at them, presumably protecting his vision from the vulgar multicolored gaiety of the pool. (Closer inspection had revealed that the cluster of floodlights, in Adran colors, green, orange, and white, were arranged to throw patterns of hearts and diamonds on the colored tiles surrounding the pool. Frances meant to have words with Joe about those.) And then he staggered forward, rather dazed, uncertain, looking not at all well.

Spirelli, man of action, at once leaped to his feet and rushed forward. Frances, stumbling to hers, remembered how pleasantly strong his arm had felt, pulling her from the pool. Spirelli advanced with outstretched hand: the other man shook it hard. They exchanged some words. Frances joined them: "Ah," said Spirelli, "Dr. Wingate, you are just what is necessary, this is a countryman of yours, Dr. David Ollerenshaw, he has had a hard drive." More hands were shaken. The man looked on the verge of collapse. "Come and sit down," said Frances, helpfully, leading him to the wet bathmat.

They sat down. David Ollerenshaw said that he was perfectly all right, simply tired and hungry.

"Wherever have you come from?" they asked him.

"Oh, I drove down," he said.

"Wherever *from*?" they cried admiringly, picturing the map, the enormous Sahara, the empty space. "Oh, from the north," he said revived by their admiration, and proceeded to describe the final stages of his rather tiresome journey. (Spirelli disappeared discreetly, for some food.) It had been fine, but he had run into trouble nearly all the way. Something in the end had gone wrong with the car: he defended the car's honor warmly, insisting that it had been buggered about by children before he had embarked. He'd had to wait to fix that, then he'd decided to take a shortcut of a few hundred miles by a route that was marked on the map, or at least on one of his maps, but which, like all such routes, hadn't really existed. Luckily he'd had a compass and was used to that sort of terrain (Frances and the geologist, listening to him, had yearnings of envy, nostalgia, and horror mixed), but it had taken him a long time to get out, and he hadn't wanted to be late for the conference which he thought from his watch (which told him the date) was due to begin the next morning, so he'd just driven straight on, once he'd got back onto the right route. Anyway, there hadn't been anywhere to stop.

"When did you last eat?" said the fat geologist, wide-eyed.

"Yesterday morning," said David Ollerenshaw.

"Ah," said the geologist. "*I* would much rather have been late for the conference."

"Not," said David, "if you'd seen what I'd have been likely to acquire to eat en route.

"Anyway," he went on, "I'm not starving, you know, I'd

plenty of emergency rations in the car, I was just saving them up, for an emergency."

Nevertheless, when Spirelli returned with a plate of cold beans and chicken, he ate it with some satisfaction.

They all watched him, enjoying the harmless drama.

"Whyever did you *drive* here?" said Frances, finally, as he mopped up one of the last mouthfuls.

"Oh, I don't know," said David, "something I've always wanted to do, you know."

He finished off the beans.

"But right now," he said, "I think I'll have a swim."

They all fluttered and clicked and protested. Ought he, so tired, on a full stomach? That's the kind of remark my mother would make, he said, rising to his feet. Come on, you can dive in and fish me out, if I sink like a stone. You're already dressed for the job.

And he strode over to his car, and stripped off, returning in his respectable underpants.

"Here we go," he said, and dived in, not very gracefully, but with some force.

It was half an hour before they persuaded him to go to bed. The euphoria of fatigue and relief had taken him over, he was enjoying it. They were all enjoying it. There is nothing like an unexpected occurrence for producing a sense of intimacy among strangers, and Frances, in bed that night, was to reflect on the uncanny way in which the most disreputable members of the conference had, as it were, recognized one another at the outset, and sat up as though on purpose as a reception party. In England, in a more leisurely social clime, it might have taken them months to acknowledge one another's nature: she recalled one committee she had attended on which she had sat for six months without even speaking, socially, to the most likely-looking person on it, and then they had merely discussed the nature of the lunch and the mean quantity of drink which that particular committee provided. (One glass of sherry, followed by veal and ham and egg pie, it had invariably been, though he had said that was one better than one of his other committees, which simply offered Nescafé in mugs and Lyons fruit pies.) Here, there was clearly no time to let things take their natural dilatory course: with less than three weeks at their disposal, and an atmosphere so unreal surrounding them, they were precipitated into a kind of friendship, as on a ship on a holiday tour. David Ollerenshaw's appearance, looking so like a lost traveler from another age, had consolidated their burgeoning sense of clique: they accepted him, embraced him, he was theirs. Frances found herself thinking that this was how alliances in committees were formed—vaguely, by chance, over a bite to eat or a stray personal confidence. She hoped they would not disagree too much about any possible issues the conference might raise, if it was intended to raise any. Spirelli she liked, but could see that he would be a formidable adversary: however, surely an archaeologist and an anthropologist could agree? The fat geologist seemed to have the most amiable views on private life and manners, but who could tell what depths of obstinacy and imperialism might not lurk in his solid chest? David Ollerenshaw she was sure she could trust. He was too nice to be disagreeable. He was an eccentric, he was manic, he must be all right. And as for Patsy Cornford, she was only an observer, her views didn't count, and it appeared highly unlikely that she had strong views on anything but herself.

Eventually, they decided it was time to split up, to make their way to bed, Spirelli took charge of Ollerenshaw, promising to find him his room, to help him unload. They shook hands all around, bathing-suited, towel-draped. "I heard you lecture once," said David Ollerenshaw, to Frances Wingate, "I must tell you about it some time." "I look forward to that," said Frances.

And so they parted for the night, but Frances did not get rid of Patsy Cornford so easily. Patsy followed her into her room, naturally enough, to return the bathing suit, which she stripped off without any appearance of inhibition, and started to wander about naked, wrapped in a towel. Frances, herself uninhibited, immediately summed her up as an exhibitionist, justly but rather unkindly. Patsy had a white, full, heart-shaped face and lovely sloping shoulders and a long neck, and black very carefully cut hair falling in a sloping fringe around her face, and she had the kind of breasts that Frances had always envied to the point of anxiety—full, round, firm, separate, and as it were, upward-looking. Gazing at them now, Frances wondered how they had ever fitted into her school bathing suit. It was an odd thing about women, how small they seemed when clothed, how large when unclothed. Patsy had long legs and dark curly hair under her arms as well as lower down; Frances had noticed this before, and wondered whether not shaving was a new fashion that she hadn't got around to reading about in the color supplements. But she had, she noticed, shaved her legs. Clearly a highly deliberate young woman, Patsy Cornford. She was also highly intelligent, as she proceeded to tell Frances, while wandering around the room inspecting the furnishings and Frances's possessions. She had got a first in history at Cambridge, and had been persuaded to join the civil service, where she was sure she was wasting her talents.

Frances listened to this story, while she took off her bathing suit and put on her nightdress, and brushed her teeth vigorously, deploring yet again the pink spit that resulted, and resolving yet again to go to a dentist whenever she had half a moment. Since that rotten wisdom tooth her visits to the dentist had been nil. It had convinced her she was cracking up and going bad, and she didn't want to know about it. The bathroom fixtures were excellent, luxurious, gleaming, attractive. Unfortunately, hot water ran from both taps. She would have to speak to someone about that it in the morning. It didn't matter from the teeth-cleaning point of view, as when south she always (having learned the hard way) cleaned her teeth in bottled water, of which there was a large supply in the bathroom cabinet. It wasn't exactly Malvern water—in fact it had rather an unpleasant, slightly chalky, slightly effervescent taste—but it was doubtless healthy enough.

She missed a little of Patsy's story while rinsing out her mouth and washing up the bowl with both taps on, flowing hot and copious, but when she went back into the bedroom Patsy was still at it.

"So you see," she was saying, "it can only have been *envy*, can't it? I mean, why else did he get it, and not me? I'd have been much the most obvious choice, wouldn't I?"

"Yes, of course," said Frances, admiring the extremely pretty material of the curtains and covers—again in the Adran colors, white, orange, and green, but much more tastefully distributed, in a beautiful geometric pattern that looked as though it must have some respectable ancient lineage. She remembered Joe telling her that the Adran views on whether or not it was permissible to use natural forms in art were highly confused and emotional (owing to a mixed Muslim and African influence in the last thousand years), and that today some argued it was more ancient to use geometric designs, some that it was a recent Muslim innovation and must be abolished or at least discouraged. There were elements of tribal discord involved, as well. However it might be, here the geometrists had triumphed, and very beautifully. Joe himself was a naturalist, and sculpted largely from his wife, but, as he also claimed, he was no bigot.

She wondered whether Patsy would think her dull for having put on her nightdress.

"I'd say it was probably sexual jealousy, wouldn't you?" said Patsy. "I mean, I can't see why else he got the promotion and not me, can you?"

Frances could see all too clearly. She could also see all too clearly why Patsy had been sent out to Adra. Somebody in the office at home simply couldn't stand having her around any longer. In a kind of flash of light, like an extract from a film, she saw Patsy's furious, harassed superior, grinding his teeth, resolving to get rid of her, finding himself unable to do so, and discovering the loophole of Adra with a wave of intense relief. She saw them busily getting on in her absence with the work that never got done when she was there. She saw them dreading her return.

"What on earth are these," said Patsy, rather forwardly, picking up Karel's teeth, and staring at them.

Frances considered it an extremely indelicate question. What if they had been her own, as they might well have been?

"They're false teeth," said Frances, rather coldly.

"Good heavens," said Patsy, inspecting them closely. Frances wondered if she were going to say "Whose?" She did.

Frances paused, brushing her hair. Should she reply "None of your business" or should she say "They're my lover's"? Both replies entered her head simultaneously. She chose the latter.

"They're my lover's," she said, firmly.

"Good heavens," said Patsy, clearly awestruck. "Good heavens." She looked very intent. After all, she was only twenty-five, although so clever.

"And do you carry them around with you?"

"As you see."

"Why?"

"Why not?" Then, rather irritably, she added, "I do wish you'd put them down."

Patsy put them down, guiltily. What a tiresome person she must be to have in an office, always looking through one's personal possessions and asking tiresome questions.

"Do you carry them around as a *memento*?" she asked, after a moment, unable to let the subject drop.

"Not quite," said Frances. "They are the guardians of my virtue." And with that, she got into bed. Patsy was baffled, but not silenced. She started to relate another long office conspiracy, this time about a man she was sleeping with in another department, whose wife must have told Patsy's superior some quite false and unpleasant gossip about her. While she told this story, she was inspecting the dresses in Frances's wardrobe, and not failing to conceal her lack of enthusiasm. Frances crept further down into the flat tight-sheeted smooth foreign bed until her head was resting on the scroll of pillow. Patsy finished with the dresses and started on Frances's children, photos of whom she had stuck around her mirror. At the end of her story, she turned around on Frances, who jerked her eyes politely open, and said, "I think I'd have done better to stay on and become a professor, don't you? I can't think *why* I ever went into the civil service."

"It's not too late to change," said Frances. Such a combination of high intelligence (for the girl certainly was as clever as she claimed, her explanations of why people treated her badly were elaborate, and subtle in the extreme), paranoia, and stupidity had finally knocked her out, she had no more to say. She let her eyes impolitely shut again.

"I'd better go to bed, I suppose," said Patsy. She gazed at the spare bed in Frances's room. They had all been given twin-bedded rooms with baths. The hotel, like the one in Tockley, was too large in scale to provide single rooms, it seemed. "You wouldn't like me to sleep in here, would you?"

"No thanks," said Frances. She shut her eyes, and promptly fell asleep.

She dreamed that night that she was on an airplane. Suddenly there was a great deal of banging and thumping, and they were all told to get off it in a hurry. She tried to get off, but there were a lot of people eating meals in the aisles, and she had to climb over their tables, apologizing as she upset their heaped plates and wine glasses, then she had to climb over heaps and heaps of luggage, which turned into sandbags, which turned into dead bodies, and at the very threshold of the plane, with safety and the runway in front of her, she found herself about to put her foot on a dead man's face. She hesitated, the plane behind her went up in flames, and she woke.

The first day of the conference went well. Listening to the chairman's introductory speech, Frances promised herself

that she would stay awake all day, pay attention, and not let
her mind wander. The chairman spoke of internationalism
and nationalism. He spoke of cooperation between nations.
The rich and the poor. The need for sensible economic
planning. He said that his country should never become the
prey of the jackals. (Some stirred uneasily but with self-
satisfaction, recognizing themselves in the jackal role.) "We
have been a poor nation," he said, "a poor and unimportant
nation. Now we find we are in possession of a future and a
past beyond our imagination. We must discover our own rich
cultural heritage, stone by stone, and we must build a rich
future." And more of the same. The interesting thing was
that what he was saying was true. Frances recognized some
phrases evidently written by Joe Ayida: some of them were
even lifted straight out of his paper, *The Cultural Heritage
of Adra*. It was almost impossible for anyone from Europe
to realize how extraordinarily new, how unexploited the resources were here. Britain was so old, so crowded, so confused, so sated, so dug-up and reburied, so cross-threaded,
all its interests were so interdependent, so obscure. Here,
everything was new. Even the history was new.

The chairman had moved on to archaeology. "Our treasures may not be precisely of the magnitude of the Aswan
dam," he was saying, "but they will suffice to rewrite a
chapter in the history books of the world." She liked that
kind of thing. She knew what he was referring to: Joe had
hinted that there was an interesting new site in the hills a few
hundred miles north, ready for excavation. Someone was to
speak about it, later that week. The chairman moved on.
"We must learn our lessons from the mistakes of others,"
he was saying. "The Aswan dam had consequences which
are now well known, and which could have been foreseen.
Before we embark on large-scale alterations, which may af-
fect climatic conditions in widespread areas, areas even beyond our own territory, we must consult expert opinion in
many fields. . . ." And so on. There was one sentence that
stood out. He said, firmly, "We must beware of measuring

this country's wealth solely in terms of mineral resources. There are other less obvious resources which, if we do not destroy them now, will last forever. We must remember the false calculations of Aswan.'' What was he doing? she wondered. Appealing for international funds for the excavations, as seemed quite likely? They couldn't have struck oil in the middle of the site could they? There was no reason why not, of course. Stranger things had happened. She remembered the sad case of Perkins, who had discovered some very interesting indications in the middle of a modern cemetery in New Guinea, and who had politely decided not to dig further. And conflicts between sewers, gas pipes, and ancient relics were commonplace. The sewers always won, which was usually right. They must have found something pretty exciting, to start talking about the Aswan dam. Adran folie de grandeur, maybe. And maybe not. She had more reason than most to believe that the desert was full of the most interesting objects. That, doubtless, was why she was there.

The afternoon was devoted to papers on mineral resources. Frances listened dutifully to statistics about copper and wolfram, and stared at little colored maps that were presented to her from time to time. (Coyly, they were saving their tin discoveries for the next day.) It was all most interesting and very good for her, she was sure, and she had sensibly had nothing but chalky water to drink at lunch, and only a small meal: nevertheless, after about an hour and a half, her mind began to drift. She thought of all the other conferences she had attended, all the other committees. She had sat on some committees for years without even knowing what they were for. Once, when she had woken up to the subject matter, and the role she was supposed to be playing, she realized she was constitutionally ineligible to sit on it and had to resign. There was one which had infuriated her for six months or so with its ridiculous jargon: all the other members seemed to have been there for years, and they talked in initials and shortcuts, and she had noted with growing alarm that as she gradually acquired the jargon, so she gradually changed her views, and by the time she was thoroughly au fait with the committee's terms of reference and accounts, she had lost all desire to reform it, and had become as reactionary as all its other members.

She admired people who could do the thing well. Civil servants, who (unlike Patsy Cornford) could quietly get their minds around anything and produce order out of chaos and boredom. Chairmen who managed to be efficient and yet witty. Lawyers who could see inconsistencies in what seemed to her like logical statements. Mediators who could bridge impassable gulfs of opinion by the right formula of acceptable words, who could string a bridge of language between two craggy summits, avoiding the horrible plunge into the deadly chasm of a minority report.

Sometimes, however, people went berserk in public. There had been that conference at Uppsala, when old Hammerkind had started to read a quite dotty paper about the moral turpitude of radio-carbon dating and the great technological conspiracy. He had supported his theory, which otherwise might have got by, with quotations from the Scriptures and a plea for a return to a more reverent approach to prehistory, and had embellished it with some grotesque insults about careless Italian archaeologists and incompetent French ones, backing up his insults with some unfortunately not too grotesque illustrations. It had been quite a scene. She had herself, in deep excesses of boredom, wondered what would happen if she suddenly shouted out some rude words, or got up and danced on the table, or started to strip off all her clothes. Once a professor, whose gravity and calm she had always admired, confessed that he found it almost impossible to sit still for more than half an hour, and had to resort to the strangest devices to induce self-control. What was the average concentration span? she wondered—then woke up with a jerk, as her neighbor handed to her a pleasant little nodule of Adran manganese ore. The geologist was explaining how uneconomic it was to mine the stuff. She stared at it with respect and handed it on. Looking up, she caught David

Ollerenshaw's eye. He was sitting almost directly opposite. He winked at her, in an encouraging manner. He looked as lively and attentive as anything, after his ordeal in the desert. She envied his stamina, she liked his face. She would have a drink with him later, she had promised. Geology was his own subject, of course, that was why he was looking so wide awake.

She listened hard for the rest of the afternoon.

There was nothing much planned for the evening: they had two hours off until dinner, then dinner, then a film show about nomads. (How pleasant it was to have things organized. How agreeable her life was, really.) So she went upstairs to have a rest: belated air fatigue was telling on her, she was terribly tired. In the elevator, she was joined by Patsy Cornford, who was very excited because she had just had a telegram from her lover and another from a prospective lover. She showed them to Frances, proudly: they were bright green, an unusual color in telegrams, a kind of bright leaf green. One said I LOVE YOU DARLING PATSY, the other said HARLING COME HOME SOON. They speculated, in the elevator, as to why *Darling* should have been spelled once correctly, once incorrectly. Then Frances said she was going to have a short sleep and marched into her room and shut the door firmly: she wrote a letter to her children, allowing her gaze to wander over their four photographed faces, thinking of the mother octopus. The four faces stared back: Daisy, two years ago, blond and disdainful, a stern school photograph: Joshua, sitting on a bicycle grinning aimlessly in his good-natured fashion: Spike, savage and bored, leaning histrionically and waiflike, hands in his pockets, against the front door jamb: Pru, another smiling child, a very professional photo this one, a *Sunday Times* one, Pru sitting as a baby of six (she was now eight) in the garden, with a lot of leaves and flowers stuck in her hair. She wrote to them as well as she could, describing her flight, the hotel, the meals, the swimming pool. I'll be back soon, my darlings, she said at the end of the letter.

Then she lay down and fell asleep.

She woke in an hour, with her usual well-regulated internal timing: got up, had a bath, got dressed. The same black dress would have to do. She sorted out her conference papers: they had already got mixed up. She brushed her hair, polished up her shoes with a Kleenex, read a few pages of *The Charterhouse of Parma* (she'd been meaning to read it for years, and God could she see why), then read an article in the *Sunday Examiner* about old people dying alone and starving in the midst of plenty: she'd brought the *Sunday Examiner* all the way with her from Hugh's and Natasha's, it was reassuring to have an English paper around, even if it was out of date. The *Sunday Examiner* said that too many old ladies were dying alone and starving: the most recent had died in a pricey council block in a resort on the south coast, and somebody was in for trouble—the council, the social workers, the relatives. A witch hunt, she smelled a witch hunt. Probably somebody deserved it, but maybe not those who would get it. In the nomad film, they would doubtless be shown pictures of old folk left to die by the wayside when too old to plod on, and would be told by the commentary that this was a humane socially integrated way of dealing with old age. Sociologists and anthropologists were a strange lot. She looked forward to further discussions with Spirelli on the subject. Thinking of Spirelli, she drew her belly in sharply, and looked at herself in the mirror. Was the black dress too tight? She leafed through the *Sunday Examiner* again, and found a frivolous article about how one shouldn't be able to keep a pencil under one's breast. The idea to her, small-breasted, was laughable. A *pencil* under one's *breast*? She could as soon have hooked one under her lower eyelid. But maybe some people could. Maybe Patsy Cornford would be able to, in years to come.

She looked at her watch. It was time for a drink.

In the bar, she avoided a predatory-looking Spirelli who tried to intercept her, and made straight for David Ollerenshaw, who was talking to the Adran who had delivered the paper about minerals. They greeted her affably and bought her a drink. They were talking about geology. She tried too hard to prove that she had been paying attention all afternoon, by the occasionally intelligent question, and thought she didn't do too badly. Indeed, she got quite interested, and accompanied them into dinner where they continued to talk of the world copper market. She didn't mind that: it was what she was here for after all. She would have a chat with Ollerenshaw after the nomads.

The nomads were quaint but brief. They stood around aimlessly under a tree, tramped across the screen, fed their cattle and camels, made a few pots and baskets, and that was that. Maps followed showing their distribution. It was not a very glossy film, with a dull plot.

Afterward, some went to bed. Others decided to swim. Frances felt like a drink, and hesitated, wondering if it might not be thought too decadent to combine drinking and swimming. She was quite prepared to opt for the former, if there was going to be anyone to drink with. This, however, looked unlikely, so she went upstairs and put on her bikini, and found when she came down again that David Ollerenshaw was sitting by the edge of the pool with some glasses and a bottle of scotch. "Ah," he said, when he saw her. "Just the person I was waiting for."

"A man after my own heart," said Frances, somewhat to her own surprise, as David poured her a drink. She was not usually so forward, with strangers.

"Now you must tell me," she said, as she sat down by him, "what you were doing, at my lecture."

So he explained what he had been doing: that he had been in the same city, visiting his own institute, the Geological Institute, and that he was rather bored, because his rocks hadn't turned up. "I only saw that it was on by accident," he said. "There was a notice up, in the library. And I thought, why not?"

"Are you glad you went?"

"Of course I'm glad I went. You were in good form, I

thought. Not that I know what your form is usually. But you seemed in good spirits."

"Yes. I was, as far as I can remember. Or was I? No, come to think of it, I was feeling rather low, at the time. I had a terrible toothache. I had to have the tooth out, in Paris. Funny, how one forgets."

"Well, you didn't look as though you were suffering from a toothache, you'll be pleased to hear. Terrible, having a toothache away from an English dentist, isn't it? I remember once, in Nigeria . . ." and he poured himself another drink, and they embarked on a session of traveler's tales. Tooth extractions in wooden huts, typhoid in the back of Land-Rovers, suspected appendicitis half-way up a mountain: defective maps, gasoline problems, the lack of acceleration of Land-Rovers, snakes, sunsets. Field work in archaeology and geology seemed to be fraught with remarkably similar problems. "Horrible terrain, always," said David, enthusiastically, "and then one can't be quite sure if the stuff's there, or if it is, whether there's going to be enough of it, and if there is enough of it, whether it's going to be possible to get at it."

"Without spending a fortune."

"Yes, without spending a fortune."

"Your resources must be so much greater than ours, that kind of problem ought to be irrelevant."

"It never is, though."

And they discussed the excitement of the first indications—the aerial photographs, tracer plants that indicate the presence of a certain mineral, a piece of broken pot, a bone, a shape in the sand. The disappointments, the sense of rage at having wasted months of one's life in a hell hole, for nothing. "Though why I should care, I don't know," said David. "There's nothing in it for me, whether I find anything or not. I'm just doing a job. It's different for you, I suppose. What you find is all your own."

"Well, not exactly," said Frances, and explained briefly about the way in which even some of the most nonchalant countries had finally woken up to the fact that their treasures were being picked up idly from celebrated sites and carried home in tourists' pockets: they had introduced new regulations about exportation, and about time, too, she had to agree. It had taken months to clear some of her larger trunks from Tizouk.

Then they reverted, with one accord, to the subject of discomfort, and why it was that they were prepared to endure it—why, indeed, they could be suspected of actually enjoying it. Both agreed that heat was their worst thing, which was doubtless why both had ended up in Africa. "I tried the Falkland Islands," said David, "but it wasn't bad enough." They discussed the effects of heat on the British metabolism, and the horrible psychological shock of one's first experience of it: each seemed to have responded in the same way, which was not surprising, they said (comparing arms in the fairy-light), as they had the same complexions, fair skin, freckles. Frances described a night she had spent with her four children in Tunis, all of them melting and panting and furious and sleepless and desperate with that peculiar hot despair that seems so endless. "But what could I do?" said Frances. "A night in the Africa for the five of us would have cost something like *sixty pounds*, they told me. Sixty pounds, for air conditioning! I'm not mad yet. I will be, but I'm not yet." David described his first night in Tehran. Why do we do it? they asked one another. Are we simply masochists?

"Do you swim," she asked him, "in Arctic seas? That is a true test of a masochist."

"If you mean literally Arctic," he said, "it's more likely a death wish you're describing, than masochism. But I've tried some pretty chilly places, in my time." He thought of the Antarctic, and the happy penguins.

"I don't suppose I'll ever have to go and dig in the snow," said Frances. "There can't be much in the way of archaeology, under the North Pole."

He agreed. The swimming pool, however, he said, looked warm and inviting: why not try it?

They rolled in, lazily. They swam around.

"Hello," he said to her, in the middle of the pool, as her head rose from the dive, sleek like an otter's.

"Hello," she said, enchanted by the illusion of proximity, the illusion of belonging to the same species.

David was an energetic swimmer, and set a high standard: by the time they emerged, they were both a little breathless. Spirelli was waiting for them, as they pulled themselves out, with Patsy Cornford. He was about to offer his arm again, but she managed to evade the gesture. She was a little frightened of Spirelli. She did not want to touch him again. And yet, at the same time, a slight competitive spirit stirred in her, a spirit that had been quiet and subdued for a long time. She didn't like the look of Patsy getting on so well with Spirelli. Irresistibly, she set herself to charm. She felt David (a safer-seeming ally) watching her, with some amusement. But still, she couldn't stop. A bit of old mechanism had been put back into action, by a chance flick of a finger, and off it whirred, off it clicked, as efficiently as ever. Oh, dear, she thought to herself, oh, dear, oh, dear.

Spirelli seemed to appreciate her efforts: she had known he would, or she wouldn't have made them. He in turn told his own traveler's tales, tales as strange as those of Othello, of tribes whose heads grew beneath their shoulders, and Frances and Patsy listened, like two docile Desdemonas. Frances could see that Patsy was annoyed by her own arrival on the scene: she had been getting on well with Spirelli. The sight of her annoyance encouraged Frances to greater efforts of courtesy. She couldn't help it. Half-amused, half-horror-struck, she watched herself perform, and watched Patsy begin to sulk. Though if it were to come to it, she would have put the odds on Patsy. After all, she was younger, and better-looking. Perhaps she should form an alliance with her, not set up competition. It wasn't as though she wanted Spirelli, after all.

Virtuously, she returned her attention to David: they discussed the distribution of swimming pools among the undeveloped nations of the world. There were whole continents that Frances had never visited: she was beginning to feel ignorant. It was a good thing, to attend a conference every now and then, in order to be made to feel ignorant. Otherwise, as David agreed, one saw only one's own job. For months on end, said David, I hardly speak to anyone at all. That's why *I* like conferences, he said, pouring himself a large final drink. Suddenly, all this good company.

You adjust very well from one to the other, said Patsy.

Oh, I like extremes, said David. A lot of people or none at all.

In bed that night, staring through a dark window at a very large African moon, David wondered about these things. He was drunk, and, as usual when drunk, had a conviction that with a little introspection, all things would be made plain. If he thought about it enough, he would know why he continued, at his age, to plod off into deserts and suffer in strange places. He had to admit that there was a very high degree of straight masochism in his choices. He liked to suffer, and he liked to overcome suffering. He positively enjoyed it when things went wrong, when trucks dropped to pieces, and wells ran dry, and provisions got lost. Too easy a ride bored him. The easy explanation, that he was constantly trying to prove himself, seemed a likely one, and he thought there was something in it. It had been the explanation offered by a psychiatrist when David, at university, had had what he refused to refer to as a nervous breakdown. Closely questioned, he had admitted that, yes, his father had always made him work very hard, yes, his father had wanted him to study physics not geology, yes, he had always felt guilty and unhappy and inadequate as a child, yes, he had suffered terrible torments about masturbation and examinations and the guilt and sense of failure connected with both.

So, said the psychiatrist, you want to prove yourself a better man than your father, and you want to escape from him. How better to do it than by testing yourself in this way? (Two months' excessively solitary field work, as a post-graduate, had precipitated David's illness, and the doctor packed him off to bed for a month in a hospital.) David had agreed, and after a month had climbed out of bed, and had pursued his career as a geologist, continuing to test himself in extreme situations, although his father was now a feeble old shadow, a retired depressed teacher of general science in a Manchester comprehensive, and not worth proving anything to at all.

He thought of that first night in the Middle East, his first experience of extreme heat. Unbelievable, it had been. With his usual independence and faith in his own powers of endurance, he had refused to listen to advice about air conditioning, and had booked himself into a cheap small hotel. Why pay more? He could cope with bugs, he had no need for modern plumbing. But he had reckoned without the heat. He was in a daze from the moment when he stepped out of the airplane into the blinding light. He could hardly cross the tarmac to find a taxi. People talked at him and reeled away from him in a confused and meaningless way, dressed oddly, speaking odd languages, all inexplicably surviving and thriving in an atmosphere that ought not to have been able to support life, except possibly the life of large dry insects. He had somehow managed to get to his hotel, sign a register, allow himself to be pushed into an elevator and out of it, and had finally achieved his only aim, of falling upon the bed. And all night he lay there, sleepless, feeling the sweat pour from his body, feeling his joints melt and rot, mouth open, eyes open, limp, lifeless, aching, immovable. Sweat welled up in the sockets of his eyes and dripped over like great tears down his cheeks, until he felt that he would have wept, could he have found the fluid or the strength. He would have tried to read, to while away the long night, but he had not the strength to reach for his book. He would have rung the company, but there was of course no phone in the room. He saw himself condemned to an eternal hell of debilitation, immobile, lacking the energy even to cry for help, as in one of those nightmares where the sleeper struggles in vain to let

out the faintest of shrieks, or to move by half an inch an arm
or leg. He was trapped, like a fly in amber, in a new element,
and the element, solid like water, more solid than water, was
heat. Toward dawn, it had grown slightly cooler, and he had
managed to look at his watch, take a drink of water, and
doze off for an hour. But at sunrise the whole process began
again, with renewed intensity. He lay on the bed, and wept
tears, wasting precious liquor, not knowing how he would
ever feel well enough to let anyone know how ill he felt,
fearing he would lie there and die there and very quickly
deliquesce there.

In the morning, of course, a man from the company rang,
and then came around to collect him: with a superhuman
effort David pulled himself to his feet, put on some clothes
(he had lain there all night naked like a corpse, covered with
a wet towel) and managed to stagger across the exposed glare
of the pavement to a waiting car, from which he was delivered into the unimaginable relief of a cold air-conditioned
building. It had been quite an experience, and Frances was
right: it was the psychological shock that destroyed one so
completely. He had been through, since then, far worse conditions, but none had ever so alarmed him. It had been so
mysterious, the sense of total weakness, when all around
seemed normal, active, busy. But it only happens to one once
in a lifetime. One can train the body to accept all kinds of
trials. In the end, there weren't many trials left.

And it wasn't as though he could quite bring himself to
believe in the trial for the trial's sake. He believed in an end
product: he prided himself on the solidity of his end products. A valley of tin. Secretly, he thought archaeologists and
anthropologists were a frivolous lot: interesting, but frivolous, after the wrong thing, as were missionaries and moun-
taineers. Oil, zinc, tin, bauxite: they were real, they were
needed. I have harnessed my neuroses to a useful end,
thought David, staring out at the dark night, and the rather
theatrical stars. This was the way he had learned to consider
his own behavior. A psychiatrist might have agreed with him,

but he had long since given up consulting psychiatrists. He was a man who believed in self-help.

At least, thought David Ollerenshaw, I don't get in anybody else's way. (This was a thought that would arise in his mind in the most remote places: I'm not in anyone's way *here*, he would think, with satisfaction, alone in the Sahara, alone on a rocky shore.)

The conference quickly settled into its own pattern, a curious pattern in a curious limbo, of papers, discussions, meals, drinks, swimming. They inspected every aspect of the Adran economy, its resources and its prospects: they listened to long-range weather predictions over the Sahel, and the possibility of future droughts. They did not, of course, see the real Adra: they stayed marooned in the hotel, and watched film of the outside world. An expedition had been planned for the end of the conference: they were to be flown in a light aircraft to look at the tin mine and the new excavations in the north. It appeared that there had indeed been some exciting new archaeological discoveries, in a tin mine, as in Nigeria: Frances's wild conjectures, at her lecture, in response to David's question, had not been so wide of the mark. It wasn't exactly as though they were going to sink an oil well through an ancient site: there was no real reason why tin and figurines should not be harmoniously and jointly extracted—no real reason, that is, apart from the ancient reasons of the Sahara, lack of water, and lack of funds. The tin miners were already up there, extracting tin: there wasn't enough water left over for a team of archaeologists. An appeal would be made for funds. Frances would be asked to sign it, to agitate for it. (Her paper, which she delivered with aplomb, would be quoted, she realized, in this cause.) Indeed, she rather hoped she might be invited to play a more active role: one of the figurines that had been discovered was of a quite unexpected character, unlike anything that one might hope to find in Adra, and Frances, asked her opinion, and staring at its old enigmatic face, had felt such strong and sudden attraction,

THE REALMS OF GOLD 271

such a desire to stop messing about and return to some real
work, that the thought of a hot and waterless tin plateau had
begun to shimmer for her like an oasis.

Meanwhile, she swam in the pool, and ate too much, and
worried about her figure, and watched how other people behaved. The original group of late swimmers and late talkers
had, as Frances had predicted, solidified and become yet
more distinct, and, as she had also predicted without admit-
ting it to herself, Spirelli was proving rather a problem.
Randy, gray, and wiry, he seemed determined to avenge the
honor of his country, and the ghost of rejected Galletti. With
no Hunter to protect her, Frances turned, not wholly in self-
defense, to David, and forced upon them all many a late
foursome: for Patsy was as determined to forestall Spirelli's
advances to Frances as Frances was herself. Many strange
little games they played, by the poolside, in the bar, over a
game of cards: looks, smiles, nods, maneuvers. Frances liked
Spirelli: she couldn't help it. He was an interesting man, an
intelligent and original man, with a reliable air of confidence:
you'll be all right with me, he hourly implied, and she was
sure that in his sense it would be true. Luckily, she also liked
David, though in quite a different way.

She did not understand David. He talked a lot, which led
one to tell him a lot, but at the end of the day he had given
away nothing, the others all. She wondered about his solitary
life, and why he had chosen it: was he a homosexual perhaps? He told them once, in a way that told nothing, that he
had had a complete nervous collapse when ten years younger:
any of her friends she would have questioned more closely—
Was it sex? Was it family? she would happily have asked—
but it didn't seem quite right to interrogate him, for some
reason. And yet he wasn't withdrawn, far from it. He had an
amiable, sociable, communicative manner: he got excited
when talking about quite abstract matters (to hear him on
geology reminded her of her brother Hugh on the subject of
money). She liked his face and his freckles and his bare
English knees. She was pleased, childishly, to find a scientist

who would talk to her, a scientist that she found interesting. "I'm not a very *pure* scientist," David would say, when she expressed this view.

He was capable, at times, of the most extraordinary public behavior: a little dancing took place, one evening, to the music of a coin box, and David had leaped around in a most uninhibited fashion, all by himself. She liked that, though she was faintly embarrassed by it. And on one occasion, when they were all sitting by the pool, he had grabbed the Polish engineer (who was fully dressed) and slung her over his shoulder and wandered perilously with her to the end of the diving board, where he held her over the luminous water, threatening to drop her in. The Polish engineer, usually reserved and silent, had taken this in surprisingly good part, laughing and struggling as her black hair came loose from its bun, and finally tripping back along the diving board to dry land with a look of disheveled gaiety. Frances noted that the next night she came down for the first time in a severe dark-blue swimming suit, and swam powerfully and expertly around the pool with the rest of them.

Amusing though these diversions were, after ten days they began to pall slightly, and a feeling of claustrophobia set in. People began to talk of what they would do when they got home again, of jobs, of wives and children, of future conferences and expeditions. There was a feeling of not unpleasurable tedium, on the penultimate night of the conference, as Patsy, Frances, David, and Spirelli met for their customary drink before dinner: a mood not unlike the end of term, at a boarding school, where the prospect of release mingles with a faint sense of imminent loss of familiar companions and a desire for some final, reckless action. Patsy, demonstrating her response to the mood, was wearing a dress she had not produced before, a white dress which showed a great deal of brown and gleaming arm and bosom and thigh, and Spirelli rose to the occasion by ordering a large gin and French instead of his usual scotch. Frances herself had put on a necklace, she could not think why, following the same instinct that had prompted Patsy: it wasn't a very special necklace, it was a string of yellow glass beads she had had since childhood. David, in his khaki shirt, looked much the same as ever, but even David had a restless glint in his eyes. They talked a little, of the trip they were to make the next day to the tin mine, and of the dangers of light aircraft, and then Patsy yawned, and stretched, and said, "Oh, God, I *am* bored with this bar, I seem to have spent the last five *years* in this bar, if only there were somewhere else to go, just for a change." She looked around her, histrionically, at the tiled table tops and white wire bird cages and plants and flowers, and then turned to David and said, "I'll tell you what, David, why don't you take us all for a drive? There's no reason why we should stay shut up in this hotel, is there? Why don't you take us out for a spin in your nice new car?"

It seemed like a good idea, it was just what they wanted, they wondered why they hadn't thought of it before. There's nothing much to see, David told them, it's a very dull town, there's nothing to do and nothing to see: but they were not deterred. It will make a change, at least, said Patsy.

So after dinner, they met together again, and got into the car. To her annoyance Frances, who had determined to get in the front with David, found herself, through some strange last-minute maneuver that she was not quick enough to prevent, sitting in the back with Spirelli. Off they went, into the night, into the boring capital city of Adra. As David had predicted, there was not much to see: wide, well-lit streets (no shortage of space here), some large modern buildings, a mosque or two, a church, some Coca-Cola signs, some brightly colored fountains in the main square, ostentatiously wasting gallons of precious water. It was a flat, and arbitrary place. Not a bit like one's idea of Timbuktu, said Patsy, disappointed. Or does Timbuktu look like this, now?

There was one street that showed signs of animation: there were stalls, cafes, people sitting at little tables on the pavement, men selling nuts and ice cream. "This is the Champs-Élysées of Adra," said David, slowing down, as they drove past. "Or we could try the Old Quarter. But one can't take the car in. And one can't get a drink there. Or rather" —glancing sideways at Patsy, in her white dress—"you wouldn't be able to get a drink there."

"Is it picturesque?" asked Patsy.

"No, not really," said David, who had himself quite liked it, with its narrow poky streets and odd little corners and seedy hot shabby cafes, its sackfuls of beans and flour and inedible sweetmeats. There was no point in going there with two women. Frances one might have risked, possibly, but not Patsy Cornford.

So they settled for the Champs-Élysées. As they walked from the parked car to the least dull of the cafes, Spirelli put his arm around Frances's shoulders. So here we go, she thought. There was hardly enough spirit left in her to resist: his hand lay there, heavy and possessive and rather comfortable. The very slightest inclination on her own part would do the trick, she knew, and she knew that he would not miss it. She was annoyed with herself; she walked on, looking straight ahead. It was her own fault, it served her right. She thought of Karel, crossly. She had renounced him, but he wouldn't go, he hung around her, with all his treacheries like teeth on a string around his neck, bewitching her, preventing her from living. She would sleep with Spirelli, and be rid of Karel. What else was she supposed to do?

They sat at a little table, and ordered some soft drinks and some hard drinks, and ate some little dry nutty objects of a curious texture and an evidently local nature: the kind of thing one did not get in the Hotel Sahara. "This is the *real* Adra," said David, grinning at them over the plastic table-cloth. They watched the local life go by: Frances and Patsy were the only women in sight. And Frances allowed Spirelli to follow up the advantage he thought he had gained. Perhaps he had gained it after all. How strange it must be, she thought, to be a man, and to be so persistent. She watched Spirelli watching her, carefully, as they talked of this and that: he was waiting for a sign, like an auctioneer. She must be very careful not to nod or wink by accident, or she would find herself in possession. She must be very careful not to drink too much. (A horrible flash flicked through her mind, of a bad scene in a hotel at Luxor: drink, chat, quarrels, academic disputes of ridiculous ferocity, broken glasses and finally a ghastly hot night in bed with a red-haired Canadian cameraman and broken air conditioning.) Spirelli filled her glass.

When they had sat there for as long as seemed tolerable, Patsy, still restless, suggested a drive in the country. "There *isn't* any country," said David. "And anyway, it's dark."

"I want to see," said Patsy.

"Oh, all right," said David. "But it's not like the Cotswolds out there, I'm warning you."

"I don't care," said Patsy. "I want to see Africa."

When they got back to the car, Frances got into the back with Spirelli without protest. It was accepted that she would sit there with him.

The country was flat: the road ran through it straight as a ruler. Stunted trees grew on either side of it, for this was the fertile part of Adra. The road went on forever.

"You see," said David.

Frances sighed, heavily. Around them stretched the terrible space, and they looked out on it, as it passed. The earth was a kind of sandy red, stony and sandy at the same time. A little scrub grew near the road, fitfully cultivated, and beyond that, nothing. Frances felt that Spirelli was about to reach for her hand: oh well, so what, she thought, resigned, oh well, never mind. Idly, she tried one last spin of the wheel, one last conversational gambit, before the silence. What right had Karel to thrust her thus into the arms of strangers? One last desultory spin, and she would forget him.

"How flat it is here," she said. "It was so rocky, up at Tizouk. Flat places are rather frightening, don't you think?"

"I was born in a flat place," said David, from the front, responding gallantly, and it seemed, consciously, to her tired appeal. "I was born in Tockley, Lincs. Have you ever been to Tockley, Lincs? It's the flattest place in England."

"Tockley?" said Frances, sitting suddenly forward in her seat. "Really, Tockley? I thought you came from Sheffield."

"I do, but I was born in Tockley, my family come from there."

"But how extraordinary, so do mine."

"What a coincidence."

Spirelli sat back, Frances leaned forward. The game was over; indeed, Frances, engrossed in this new subject, had forgotten that it had existed. In the next five minutes, instead of finding herself involved in a contract with Spirelli, she found instead that she was related to David Ollerenshaw through a communal great-great-grandfather: her grandfather Ted had been his grandfather Enoch's first cousin. Astonished, delighted, amused, they traced connections: "But why had we never *heard* of each other?" said Frances, from time to time, and both agreed that it was typical of the Ollerenshaw family that they should not have heard of each other. Enoch the bad, Enoch the wicked, had been David's own grandfather, and had dandled him on his knee and played "This is the way the farmer rides" with him. What had they quarreled about, Enoch and Ted? Nobody could remember, nobody knew.

"My gran hated Enoch," said Frances.

"Enoch hated your grandma," said David.

"Perhaps that was what they quarreled over," said Frances, and they agreed that this might have been so, and agreed that both of them had vaguely heard of a sister of Ted, an Auntie Con, who had hated everybody, and had been as mad as a hatter.

"I don't know if one ought to be pleased to belong to such a family at all," said Frances. "A terrible lot, they are, really. Bad blood, I'd say."

"You look all right to me," said David.

"I look rather *like* you, in fact," said Frances, and as they drove back to the hotel and the others agreed that this was so: that there was a distinct family resemblance between the two of them, and how amazing it was that nobody had spotted it so far. And when they got back, they ordered a bottle of Adran champagne to celebrate, and sat up late over it, the four of them, discussing endogamy and exogamy, and the nuclear family, and genes and heredity, and incest. Spirelli, expert in family structures, drew them some diagrams of marriage patterns in Western Europe, and constructed for them a family tree, and proved to them that everybody was related to just about everybody, at remarkably few removes: but even he had to acknowledge that there was a certain degree of coincidence in the fact that David and Frances should have met so far from home, in the middle of Africa.

"Tell me," said Frances, finishing off her last glass, "did you have any sense of recognition, when you first saw me? Did you think, I recognize her?"

David shook his head. "No, I can't say I did. Did you?"

"I could easily persuade myself I did," she said. "But whether it would have been true or not, I don't know."

Spirelli, meanwhile, responding quickly to the change of play, was getting on with Patsy. Frances would have thought it beneath her dignity and his, but evidently this was not so. Frances felt reprieved, by sheer chance. How wise she had been to make a last conversational effort at that crucial moment, how kind of fate so elaborately to intervene. It was clearly much, much better for Patsy to sleep with Spirelli: both would enjoy it more. How astonishing people are, in the way they transfer their allegiances, she thought. And as she was thinking this, she caught Spirelli's eye, and he winked, he actually winked at her. She thought she was slightly offended. Carefully, she rose to her feet, to take her leave.

"I must go to bed," she said carefully, "if we have all those miles to fly tomorrow."

"I'll walk up with you," said David.

And they left Patsy and Spirelli sitting there, as thick as thieves, as they walked off toward the elevator.

"The sins of our fathers separated us," said David, as he pressed the button.

"One could say so," said Frances.

"I met this woman and her brother on the boat, coming over. They were going to see their mother, in a hospital in Algeria." He paused. "I wondered why they bothered."

"Families are incomprehensible," she said.

"I was an only child," he said.

They got into the elevator together, and ascended to the eighth floor. On the landing, they parted.

"Good night," he said.

"Good night," she said. "And thank you for the drive."

An undemonstrative lot, the Ollerenshaws.

When she got into her bedroom, Frances sat down on her bed and burst into tears. She was thinking that when the organizers of the conference had asked her to fill in her next of kin on her travel and insurance form, she hadn't known whose name to put.

She cried for quite a while, comfortably, tired. The stone in her chest was dissolving, after all: fate was on her side, after all. The tears poured down. In the morning, or the morning after, when she got back from the tin mine, she would write to Karel, she would write him a long letter, explaining how much she needed him, asking him to take her back. There was no point, no point at all, in being alone. How arrogant she had been, to think she could get him back with a postcard. It would take a letter, at least. If not two or three letters.

Resolved, comforted, she went into the bathroom and washed her face and cleaned her teeth. She was growing older, but Karel would not mind. Her skin was overexposed and veiny, she had wrinkles around her eyes, her hair was coarse and growing coarser, but Karel would not mind. Her teeth—no, she drew the line at looking at her teeth and wondering what Karel would think of them when he saw them again. His own weren't all that marvelous anyway, and she loved them, every one, even the false ones.

She got into bed. Next day, the tin mines. Piously, she

picked up and kissed each one of her children's photographs, and Karel's teeth. The tin mines, next day, and some rickety little light aircraft. She hoped it would not crash into a mountain, leaving her either dead (to be eaten by Spirelli) or alive (to eat Spirelli) as seemed to be the vogue these days. Before falling asleep, she looked at some photographs of the amazing figurine. Quite unlike anything, it was, with its naturalistic features (Negroid? Arab?—neither, really, in any recognizable way) and its stringy ropes of hair, all carved in terra cotta in a style no one had ever seen before. It had a witchy, androgynous, yet friendly look, almost a comic look, as one who appreciates the twists of fate. If she played her cards right, perhaps she could get Karel back, and get herself on the dig as well. She would have to see what she made of the site, the next day.

But the next day brought quite different prospects. It brought her, at seven o'clock in the morning, a pile of leaf-green telegrams, all demanding immediate action of one sort or another, and all, at first sight, equally incomprehensible.

She sat up in bed, gaping in horror at the pile on her breakfast tray, ripping open one after another, dreading to find news of the death or illness of children. Reading blindly, she could find no such news: none of them was from her ex-husband. So she had to calm down and begin again, under the agitated eye of the Adran girl, who did not dare to leave the room, so frightened was she by the ashy terror on Frances's countenance, and by the excess of telegrams.

After a while, Frances calmed down, and managed to read them and make some kind of sense from them. There were, in fact, only six: though there had seemed at first to be far more, and the envelopes, when opened, added to the impression of multiplicity. The most innocuous of them was from the *Sunday Examiner*, and said: PLEASE RING AT ONCE BILL MERRITON. She was used to that kind of thing, but it seemed more sinister in conjunction with the others. One of these said: SUNDAY EXAMINER CANDAL EXERT SELF COME

HOME MOTHER. Another read: MOTHER ILL COME HOME FA-
THER. Another read: HAVE YOU SEEN SUNDAY EXAMINER
MOTHER IN A STATE MAYBE BETTER HOME HOME H. Another
read: PLEASE COME HOME STEPHEN MISSING EVERYTHING
TERRIBLE WE NEED YOU YOUR CHILDREN ALL WELL NA-
TASHA. Finally, another one from the *Sunday Examiner* said:
PLEASE PHONE YOUR STORY EARLIEST EDITOR.

Frances stared at them. What on earth had happened?
What was this mysterious scandal (*candal* for *scandal*, she
assumed) that had hit her family in her absence? Was it her
mother's illness, had it caused her mother's illness? Her
mother had clearly been well enough to struggle to the telephone to send at least one of these telegrams. And what on
earth was the subplot about Stephen? (Briefly, she thanked
Natasha in her heart for those reassuring words about her
own children.) *Better home home*, said H, meaning *better
come home from Hugh*, she guessed. And what on earth was
the *Sunday Examiner* so very excited about, so suddenly?
Her relations with this paper had always been amiable, they
had published several articles by her, an adulatory interview
with her, and had covered her Tizouk expedition in glorious
color and for a large fee in their color magazine, but they
also had a reputation for hard-hitting exposés (not that an
exposé hits, it exposes) and ruthless investigations. Had they
been investigating her mother or her father and making them
ill? Were there scandals as yet undreamed of by her in the
Ollerenshaw family, skeletons stacked up in its closet, and
now about to rattle out and spill all their dusty bones over
the front pages of the Sunday papers? Surely not, surely she
would have heard about them, or sensed them. Was her
mother running an illegal abortion clinic, was her father a
spy or a bigamist? The possibilities, once probability was
discarded, were endless. She gaped at the sea of deadly crispy
green leaves, unsure what to do next.

The Adran girl hovered, quivered, approached, and poured
Frances a cup of coffee from the pot on her tray. What a
sensible, nice girl, thought Frances, and accepted the cup,

and drank. She was thinking hard. What should she do? How long would it take her to ring England? And whom should she ring, the possible hostile *Sunday Examiner*, or her probably hysterical family? And should she do what they all suggested, and catch the next flight home? The best thing would be to try to speak to Natasha. Her telegram, although containing as much menace as the others, had an air of reason about it, and anyway Natasha was always reasonable. She would try to ring Natasha, if only she could remember their number. And she would inquire, at once, about flights home.

"Please," she said to the Adran girl, who was still waiting. "I want to ring London. And to find out about airplanes to London."

The girl nodded helpfully, and smiled, and disappeared. A few minutes later, Frances had a call from Reception telling her that it would take at least two hours to put a call through to London, and that the only flight of the day left at ten that morning.

Clearly she needed official help. She began to pack, while wondering who could best help her, and finally rang the secretary of the conference, who seemed to get things going at a tremendous speed, booking her a seat on the plane, arranging transport, promising to get her call to London through in no time, and offering sympathy and calm efficiency all at the same time. "I'm sorry I shall miss the tin mine," she said, with some sincerity. "Another time, another time," was all he replied.

But he didn't manage to get her call through to Natasha, all the same. She waited around restlessly in the foyer, her luggage packed and waiting, only to be told that when the call got to London, Natasha's line was permanently engaged. This, if there had truly been a domestic crisis of the proportions indicated, was not surprising; she would have to wait till she got to London to find out what had happened. The tin mine expedition was due to set off before her flight for London so she was able to bid farewell, one by one, to the other members of the conference as they made their way through the foyer to the bus: she was touched when David Ollerenshaw offered to fly back to London with her. "After all," he said, "it's my family as well as yours, as we established yesterday. Why don't you let me come and help you sort it all out."

"Oh, it's probably nothing," said Frances. "Just some hysteria of my mother's. No, you stay and see your tin mine."

"I've seen it before," said David.

"All the more reason to see it again," said Frances.

"You could give me a ring, and tell me what has happened," said David.

"It's easier said than done, ringing Adra," she said: but they promised to communicate, and David went off on the bus, and Frances went off in her hired car to the airport, and caught the plane for London.

On the plane, the reason for at least some of the emergency became apparent to her, as she leafed through the sheaf of newspapers that had been thrust into her arms by the civil servant who saw her off. She wondered how she could have remained in happy ignorance for so long—through it wasn't really so long, today was only Wednesday, and the paper that had done the damage had been released to the world the preceding Sunday. In fact, as she considered it, it was more astonishing, far more astonishing, that the *Sunday Examiner* should have reached Adra so early than that it should have reached her so late. It was rather a tatty copy, perhaps some incoming passenger had left it lying around, and the airport newspaper man had sensibly reassembled and resold it.

The news, when she read it, combined the tragic and the grotesque and the crazily coincidental to such a degree that she did not know how to take it. The *Sunday Examiner*, as she recalled from her flight out, had been conducting an inquiry into the deaths of various old ladies from various causes in the preceding months, accompanied by a mildly political campaign against social workers, striking electricians, and various other offending bodies whom the paper chose to find neglectful of their duties. As luck would have it, there had been quite a few such deaths that autumn, and the preceding Sunday an old lady named Connie Olleren-shaw had been found dead in her cottage near Tockley. She had been dead for some months, which ruled out the striking electricians as the cause of death, and left neglectful relatives and social workers. The old lady had died, it appeared, of starvation: the paper implied that gruesome details could be given, were the paper not too delicate to print them. The paper also said that the old lady had several relatives living close by, and that she was the aunt of Sir Frank Ollerenshaw, vice-chancellor of Wolverton University.

Well, bugger me, thought Frances, gazing at a photograph of her parents, looking cruel and neglectful and affluent, on some public occasion.

The paper promised more details next week. Frances checked the dates: Connie Ollerenshaw's body had been found on Saturday, which meant the *Sunday Examiner* had had to do a rush job to get anything in the paper by Sunday, and that there would be more dirt next week. Including Frances's own story, as told to Bill Merriton, or as not told. Bill was a nice fellow, perhaps he had tried to contact her in a spirit of friendship rather than hostility, though one couldn't trust a journalist, ever. Obviously the paper hadn't, by Sunday, woken up to the fact that Connie Ollerenshaw, if she was Frank Ollerenshaw's aunt, must be Frances Wingate's great-aunt, or there would doubtless have been a picture of Frances as murderess adorning the inner page as well.

What bloody awful luck, she thought, that the *Sunday Examiner* should have been into the subject of old ladies dying of hypothermia and starvation and bad housing conditions. If they hadn't been, Connie Ollerenshaw might have been buried in peace, without creating a scandal. She could hardly blame her mother for feeling hysterical, if hysterical was all that she was feeling. She was beginning to feel rather hysterical herself, as the plane covered the endless spaces of the desert. Connie Ollerenshaw, her grandfather's sister, dying like that in a cottage with her stomach full of undigested cardboard and pages of newspaper. (The *Sunday Examiner* had not spared all details.) It was not nice to think of such a thing happening to anyone, let alone to a blood relation. She half wished she had let David fly with her, so that he could share this bizarre development in their family history. What on earth had happened to Connie? How had the welfare so completely overlooked her? She had heard of loops in the network, but surely not loops large enough to allow one whole old lady to starve to death, in the second half of the twentieth century, while relations sat in nearby Flaxam and Tockley eating bacon and eggs, and her parents dined on elaborately decorated large meals in Hall. She began, as the journey lengthened, and as she tried to eat a weird meal of chicken and mayonnaise, to sympathize with the investigatory zeal of the *Sunday Examiner*. Good luck to them, they were doing a good job, and how disgraceful, how wicked and shocking of her father, to let his very own aunt starve to death. What was the world coming to? One could carry disassociation to extremes, and he had done it. Had he felt no responsibility for her? Had he completely forgotten her existence, as he sometimes appeared to have forgotten the existence of the whole material world?

She couldn't remember that she had ever heard him make more than the vaguest allusions to Aunt Con. Her grandfather had never spoken of her either, but then he never spoke of anyone. And yet, from the sound of it, she had been living there all the time, only a few miles from Eel Cottage: she had been there, mad and alone, throughout Frances's childhood visits. Racking her memory, she thought she could dimly remember muttered remarks, overheard, not for the ears of children. What a sour and tiresome and quarrelsome lot the Ollerenshaws were, they had sucked in some poison with the very water of Tockley, it had poisoned their brains, that unnatural ditch water, she had always known it. Mentally unbalanced all of them, melancholics and suicides and witches, and now, in this newer generation, nomads, alcoholics, and archaeologists, with death running in their veins.

David Ollerenshaw had been born in Tockley, and those first few months of Tockley water, diluting the Cow and Gate powdered milk, had been enough to send him too, unlikely though it was, into the desert. She wondered how she would find them all, when she returned. Whom should she ring first? Her home? Natasha? And where in God's name had she left her car, she simply couldn't remember.

Families. Incomprehensible. What was it David had said to her the night before, about a couple who were going to visit their dying mother in Algeria? And here was she, bound on a similar errand. Ancient migrations. Perhaps David should have come with her; Constance was almost as much his great-aunt as hers, though neither had known of her existence, though David doubtless was still, even now, ignorant of her existence, or rather of her leaving of it. She thought about David, and of how surprised she had been to discover their relationship: the truth was (she might as well admit it) that she'd been astonished to learn that any member of the Ollerenshaw family apart from her father had ever made it to grammar school, let alone to university. Her mother had always taken the line that no good thing could come out of Tockley: the Ollerenshaws had been written off as peasants and shoemakers and shopkeepers, and Frances would never have thought of looking for a cousin among them, would never have dreamed of finding as acceptable a cousin as David. She had cousins on her mother's side, of course: there had always been plenty of Chadwicks to play with, discuss and dislike and compete with, and boast about. A surplus of them, in fact: a gifted, tiresome surplus. But her mother had always implied that her father's intellectual distinction had been a sheer fluke, a spontaneous generation, born out of mud of East Anglia unparented, like the ancient crocodile, and no more likely to have been repeated or paralleled than the virgin birth.

Frances, herself, had never been very keen on the Chadwicks. There were too many of them, and they were good at things that Frances could not do. Therefore she had not much

cared for the notion of family resemblances, of inherited
characteristics. She did not like people to say that she resembled her mother or her mother's sister (which she did not,
much, anyway). Nor did she like discussions about families,
which take up so much time in English social life. John
Sinclair-Davies had had one of the largest extended families
she had ever encountered, and although he managed to forget
about it while sitting in a tent in the desert, it seemed to rule
his life when back in England. She had always found it hard
to believe that John, so amusing, so charming, so delicate
and polite and attentive, so surprisingly adept with spade and
wrench and tow rope, was the same man as the effete bore
who would spend hours dropping names and tracing dull
network connections and being utterly uninteresting and un-
gracious whenever he happened to run into anyone of his
own extensive (but Frances-excluding) circle. How extraordinarily rude the well-bred can be, once they get onto the
subject of kinship. How bored she had been, on how many
occasions, listening to runic references to Sinclairs and Da-
vieses, to Chadwicks and Huxleys, to Haldanes and Stracheys.
She had allied herself with the ill-connected Ollerenshaws,
and the dull ditches of her father and his newts.

But now it seemed that even the insignificant Ollerenshaws
were going to prove a trouble. If one could discover a dead
Constance and a living David within the space of twenty-four
hours, what might not the future hold of contact and of com-
plication? England might be full of unknown second cousins,
running drug rings, murdering their mistresses, designing
nuclear reactors, entering monasteries, painting master-
pieces. Perhaps they would all gather together, in some terrible Midlands twilight. She had heard, from a friend, of a
gathering at Claridges, organized by an American millionaire, at which several hundred members of one family had
assembled, from all parts of the world: how had he felt, she
had asked him, to see so many of his kin, and did he recognize them as his kin? Oh yes, he said, you could tell us
easily. By the noses. She had found the idea alarming.

The plane continued, over the desert, on its way to Europe. She ate another mouthful of wilting lettuce. It tasted hygienic, as though it had been washed in disinfectant. Probably it had. Then she stared at the peculiar litter of plastic cutlery, cellophane, and polystyrene platters that occupied the table in front of her. What could it feel like, to be so hungry that one filled one's stomach with cardboard?

When Karel Schmidt's telegram arrived in Adra, it was read, solemnly, by the secretary of the conference, by various other official people, and finally by Patsy Cornford and David Ollerenshaw, who were thought to be most likely to know what to do about it. It was at first assumed that it was simply another telegram in the sequence which had arrived upon Frances Wingate's breakfast tray that morning, but Patsy and David, staring at it after a long and wearing day in the tin mines, were at last not so sure. It said: POSTCARD RECEIVED SEVERAL MONTHS LATE SORRY ABOUT SILENCE AM CATCHING NEXT PLANE TO ADRA SEE YOU SOON HARLING.

"Funny," said Patsy, "the way they always get *darling* wrong. It couldn't be from a man called Harling, could it?"

"No, it couldn't," said David.

"Well, then, who is it from? We ought to send him a telegram and tell him not to come all this way, he'll be terribly annoyed if he gets here and finds she's gone."

"Yes," said David, at this statement of the obvious.

"But we don't know who he is, do we?"

"No."

"Did she ever tell you about anyone? It couldn't be from her ex, could it?"

"Ex-husbands don't address one as darling, do they?"

"Oh, sometimes," said Patsy, vaguely, then went on: "Actually, I bet I know who it's from, it's from her lover with the false teeth."

"Did she have a lover with false teeth?"

"Yes, didn't you know?"

"What was he called?"

"I've no idea."

"I can't imagine what he wanted to fly out here for, when she'd have been going home on Friday anyway. Can you?"

"It doesn't look as though they've been very closely in touch lately," said David, staring at the telegram. And they were still staring at it, and speculating rather wildly about its intentions, when Karel Schmidt, looking distraught and harassed, as well he might, walked into the air-conditioned, fountain-bedewed, jungle-creepered, marble-tiled, fairylit lounge of the Hotel Sahara.

Janet Bird née Ollerenshaw was sitting in a television makeup chair staring at her own image with mingled fascination and alarm. She was ceasing to look like herself at all, as the makeup girl put on deep thick sticky pancake makeup, and applied mascara to her eyelashes, and back-combed her hair, and powdered her nose, and highlit her cheekbones. Janet was far too subdued to protest, but she couldn't help thinking that it wouldn't be wholly appropriate for her to appear on Midlands TV looking like a receptionist in a smart motel, when in fact she was supposed to be discussing the tragic and appalling death of Great-Aunt Con. The back-combing had the most dramatic effect. It made Janet's face, normally highly respectable, look pert and crazy and sexy. She wondered what words would come out of her mouth, if she spoke. There was a little part of her that rather enjoyed looking so improper.

Most of herself, however, was engaged in feeling guilty. She felt responsible for Great-Aunt Con's death. Not in any obvious way, such as a television interviewer or a social worker might suggest—she didn't feel the slightest guilt for not having visited the old girl, for it was well known in the neighborhood that Connie Ollerenshaw was a witch, and chased intruders from her overgrown premises with dogs and curses. But she did feel some obscure responsibility for having willed disaster. She had willed it, very strongly, the week before, and it had happened, pat, on the doormat, like a response straight from heaven. She'd been walking home with Hugh through the churchyard, thinking about supper and when to get the repairman to come and look at the washing machine, as Mark didn't seem to be able to fix it, when a wave of boredom so intense had swept through her that she had stopped in her tracks, and fixed her eyes on the evening star, which was winking away somewhere near the celebrated Perpendicular Steeple, and had said, as usual combining deities, Oh, God, Oh, God, Star light, star bright, First star I've seen tonight, Oh, God, please make *something* happen, anything, however awful, so long as it's *something*. (But not anything horrible to Hugh or me, she added as a proviso.) And then walked on. And when she got back, there it was, lying on the doormat, the evening paper, with its fearful headline. OLD WOMAN FOUND DEAD, it said, and smaller print announced that Miss Constance Ollerenshaw of Mays Cottage had been found dead in her bed, and seemed to have been dead for some time. She had been discovered by a neighbor, Mr. James Armstrong, of Mile End Farm, who had called to see how she was, as he hadn't seen her around for some time.

(Mr. James Armstrong, in fact, had said to his wife that morning, have you seen old Con around lately? His wife said no, pulling a face expressing distaste at the idea. I'll go down and have another go at getting her out, said James Armstrong, farmer. Perhaps she's dead, said Nancy Armstrong. If she's dead, she'll save me the trouble, said James. And dead she was.)

The evening paper had tried to hint that her death was the fault of the electricity workers who kept going on strike, but even Janet, not very good at reading between the lines of papers, knew that that was a lot of nonsense, for Mays Cottage had never been on the electric. And the paper had to change its line about that particular cause of death, as it was established the next day that she had been dead for months, even since the summer, and that hypothermia could not have played even a minor part in the tragedy. This interesting fact was blazed to the world the next day not by the *Tockley and Boothen Telegraph* but by the *Sunday Examiner*, a paper of high intellectual prestige, and undisputed integrity, and Janet, for once, found herself in the position of having a preview of the national news. For as she was giving Hugh his supper that evening, and wondering what Mark would say when he got back from the match (she had already got around to thinking that Mark might blame her for Great-Aunt Con's death, though not the wildest flight of fancy had yet suggested to her that anybody else would), she had been telephoned by the press.

They wanted to know all about Constance Ollerenshaw, her age, her habits, why she lived alone, was the cottage her own, when did Janet last see her, was there anyone else in the family who ever saw her. Janet replied, truthfully, that nobody saw her much, she didn't like people calling on her, and that she, Janet, had probably been the last person to visit her from the Ollerenshaw family. When was that? Oh, about six months ago, said Janet. In the spring.

The news had excited them greatly, and telephone call had succeeded telephone call, throughout the evening. The drama of events gave Janet the satisfaction of seeing Mark, for once, completely out of his depth, unable to work out any way to respond. (Should he blame her for having been to see Aunt Con so rarely? Should he blame her for having been to see her at all? Should he blame the whole Ollerenshaw family for its disgraceful connections? Should he allow himself to enjoy the slight tremor of importance that reached him from having his wife interrogated by the *Sunday Examiner*?) He could have to come down in favor of some, if not all, of these possibilities, but for some time he seemed genuinely confused. As Janet was also thoroughly confused, however, she couldn't really enjoy his confusion much.

It never occurred to her not to answer the press. Like most people unfamiliar with journalists, she accepted their interrogations with complete docility: it never crossed her mind not to respond. When they descended on her with cameras and tape recorders and notebooks, she gave them the freedom of her house, as though she were contracted to do so. And here she was now, in a television studio, about to take part in a local news program, and a discussion about care of the elderly and the collapse of family responsibility. It had, by this time, after some days of activity, become clear to her that there were some people who were out to make a fool of her, who were determined to cast her as the villain of the piece, but she was so sure that she wasn't that by now some faint stirrings of real opinion of her own had begun to coalesce in her mind, they were beginning to stick together and to thicken, like something stirred in a pan. She hadn't had the confidence to tell the Midlands TV people that she wasn't going to be on their program, but she was beginning to think that she might be able to say what she wanted to say rather than what they wanted her to say. Though she wasn't quite sure, yet. They were certainly clever at twisting one's remarks.

She felt almost safe, inside the thick greasy pancake make-up. It filled up the pores of her skin, it concealed blemishes it warmed her all over like a sunlamp, it hid her like impenetrable armor.

Mark had finally decided that she should never have been to see Aunt Con at all, and then she wouldn't have got herself mixed up in all this publicity and disgrace. He didn't seem to think this was a disgraceful attitude to hold, but he'd never been very good at self-criticism. And she'd had to admit to herself that her motives for going to see Aunt Con hadn't been very honorable. She had been asked so often to recall that insignificant-seeming visit that it had got a little blurred in her memory, but she thought she'd gone out of perversity, partly, to annoy her family, but in fact she hadn't annoyed them with it because it had been so awful that she'd never, until now, thought of telling anyone about it.

Great-Aunt Con wasn't at all popular with Janet's parents and grandparents, because she had belonged to the wrong side of the family. There had been some family feud, way

back in history, between her grandfather Enoch, and his first
cousin Ted Ollerenshaw, who had owned the nursery garden
at Eel Cottage. The row had been over something to do with
property—a will, a field, a paddock, something of that sort.
Janet suspected that even her elders had forgotten precisely
what the trouble had been about, but it had certainly lingered
on in the most remarkable way. Connie had been Ted's sister,
and report was that she was as mad as he was. The grand-
fathers were now dead, but Con had lingered on, living alone
in the rather large cottage that had come to her, from Bible-
crazed Albert Ollerenshaw. Eel Cottage no longer belonged
to Ollerenshaws, and when it had done, Janet had never visited it, so complete was the family rift, though she had known
that it existed, and indeed had always noticed it, with a kind
of thrill of appreciative horror, whenever she passed it on the
bus. Recently she had even been inside it, for it had been
bought up by friends of the Streets, health-food people who
went in for organic farming and gave occasional classes on
vegetarian cookery for the adult education program. Cynthia
Street had persuaded Janet to go around there with her for
tea one day, in one of her periodic energetic Janet-bullying
phases, and she had found it quite interesting. It was in Eel
Cottage that the thought of visiting Aunt Con had entered
her mind. Heather Stabler (who knew she was related to the
people who had owned the cottage before her) showed her
some books that had been there when they bought it, and she
had leafed through them, politely, as she sipped her watery
flowery tea, and ate her cress sandwiches. They were dark
spotted copies of Walter Scott and Shakespeare and Carlyle,
with wicked ogre Ted Ollerenshaw's firm signature in the
corner of each. She was ashamed to find herself surprised
that he could write so nicely. In the small-printed Shakespeare, oddly enough, somebody had written comments in
margins, in a handwriting more modern and more youthful
than Ted's. Perhaps they had been made by Frank, Ted's
clever son who had gone off to university and become a bi-
ologist, or something like that.

She was no more than politely interested, in these ghostly
memories (she didn't really want the books, and hoped
Heather wasn't going to offer them to her, as she was very
pregnant at the time and didn't want to have to lug worthless
old volumes all the way back to Tockley)—but livened up a
little when a few photographs and what looked like letters
fell out of Carlyle. The letters were in fact accounts—
accounts touching in their extreme modesty. On one day, Ted
Ollerenshaw had sold 3d of tomatoes, 4d of potatoes, 6d of
lettuces, 1d of beetroot, and 1½d of parsley, and had ex-
pended 6d on unspecified seed. Heather and Janet gazed at
these figures, and clucked and exclaimed and spoke of the
cost of living, and then Janet had looked at the photographs.
There was Ted, fat and Dutch, in his flat cap, his trousers
tucked into his socks, with a walking stick. He looked so
like Enoch, whatever could they have found to quarrel about?
History had made them interchangeable. And there was Mrs.
Ted, skinny and upright, an old witch, Enoch always called
her. And there was Ted's son as a little boy, in a sailor suit
in the photographic studio in Tockley: and again, on a rocking horse in what was recognizably the garden in front of Eel
Cottage. There was Ted's son, again as a grammar school
boy, in his uniform, and an out-of-focus one of him in what
seemed to be some graduation ceremony, wearing a cap and
gown. None of them were very good photographs—all re-
jects, no doubt, from a better batch which had ended up
elsewhere.

There was also a photograph of a young woman, heavily
braided and beaded and fringed, upright, unsmiling, stern,
beautiful. Her clear features gazed scornfully from the sepia
tint, across the decades. She looked savage and predatory,
grim and determined, and in her hand she held the handle of
a parasol, with threatening elegance. Who could this superior and arrogant person be? No Ollerenshaw, surely, for the
real Ollerenshaws (so it was said) ran to fat, and moreover
had never been well off enough to command such stylish
garments, such black-jet decorations. They had been peasant

people, 1d of beetroot people, and only a few of them, like Ted's son and her cousin David, had struggled out by their wits and climbed perilously up from the flat land, up the bean stalk of the grammar school, to the golden world above.

Have another cress sandwich, said Heather, and Janet took one, for although she wanted to sneer at the health food, she couldn't really, because it was so delicious, and Heather's home-ground brown bread was irresistible. So was the lovely peppery cress and the juicy tomatoes. She took a large bite (she'd been ravenously hungry ever since she started expecting the baby: would she perhaps end up a fat Ollerenshaw, despite her childhood skinniness?), and turned the photograph over.

My sister Connie, June 5, 1908, said the inscription, in Ted's script. So that was Connie. (Connie, dead like a dog in a ditch, with her stomach full of paper.)

Janet had asked Heather if she could have the photo, and had taken it home with her. It seemed a kind of talisman. It proved that Connie Ollerenshaw wasn't an old lunatic, a dirty old tramp, a vicious recluse, at all: she was a handsome young woman looking destiny coldly in the eye.

A week or two later, she'd taken it out and showed it to her mother and father, and her Uncle Alec, and her cousin Flo, and her Auntie Maureen, thinking they would say something at least of interest about it. And they did. They embarked on a long session of abuse about Ted, Ted's wife, Con, Ted's father, Eel Cottage, a wardrobe that had belonged to Ted's mother, Con's cottage, and various other ill-connected topics. Janet had listened, half-bored, half-fascinated. Then she asked them if any of them had ever seen Connie Ollerenshaw. Whereupon they all pursed their lips and shook their heads. (Maureen *was* a common woman, thought Janet, and Flo was just as bad, the way she let her baby suck a pacifier smeared with syrup was really the end, and so were her earrings, especially with that pink jumper)—and all denied Great-Aunt Con, with the exception of her father, Great-Aunt Con's cousin, who, fat and weak, recovering from his stroke, a privileged invalid, owned up to having known her quite well in the old days.

"But does she live quite alone, now?" she said. "Don't any of you ever go and see her?"

"Eh, there's no point," said her mother. "She's mad. Mad as a hatter. She sees no one."

"She'd chase you from the door," said Alec, and laughed with grim pleasure in the thought.

"What'll happen when she gets old?"

"What happens to anyone when they get old?" said her father. "They die, don't they?"

Janet was rather glad, subsequently, that social workers and investigating journalists had not overheard this interchange.

The next week, she set off herself to visit Great-Aunt Con. (She wasn't really her great-aunt at all of course—if she was anyone's great-aunt, she belonged to Ted's son's children, if he had any, but they probably didn't even know she existed, it was so long since Ted's son had left the district.) She thought to herself, it will make a nice walk, for myself and the baby. She walked long distances, in those days, having nothing better to do. She said to herself, perhaps she will like to see the baby. Some primitive edict of some long disrupted kinship network she was obeying, as she boarded the bus with her baby and folding pram, and asked for a ticket to Barton.

Con's cottage was two miles' walk from Barton. It was spring, it was fine and warm and the air, after the cold winter, met her cheeks mildly. The baby slept. The hedges were in bud and fluttering with birds, in the hedge bottoms there were celandines and coltsfoot and tiny white stars of chickweed. Loneliness possessed her sweetly, like a reassuring desolation. The grass was company, the birds were company. It was a pretty corner of country, less flat and dull than the rest of the county, with hedges and copses, and a little dell, where she had often come as a small child, the most famous place for bluebells in the neighborhood, and only a few miles from Tockley, in the least built up direction. If things were like this, she thought, I could perhaps live alone forever. Like Con.

The track was muddy, little used by vehicles, though there were wheel marks and hoof marks in the spring mud that bordered it. She wondered where Aunt Con bought her food. At the next village? From the farm next door? Did she grow her own? There was a little all-purpose shop a mile farther on, where the track met the next main road: it served a cluster of cottages, and perhaps also Great-Aunt Constance.

She had brought her a box of chocolates, she didn't quite know why. It lay on the end of the pram, on the blue pram rug. Black Magic.

A fat blackbird swooped in front of her, and into the hedge, like a familiar. And there was the cottage, behind the trees. She glimpsed its red roof.

As she approached the path, she began to falter. The cottage looked inaccessible. Surely nobody could have been down the path for years. Surely Con must be dead, thought Janet, three months before she died in fact.

The air of dereliction increased as one grew nearer. Nettles and other weeds struggled in the undergrowth, tall wild bushes, hawthorn and elder, tangled and struggled overhead. The path was deep in mud, wet and undrained, Janet's town shoes squelched and sunk into it, the light pram wheels left ruts. There were signs that the borders had once been cultivated—a few large stones stood around, as though by deliberation, gray and white, and one of them was strewn with the broken shells of snails, a thrush's anvil. From an overturned stone pot struggling clematis straggled dry and wild like an old woman's hair. A few purple flowers of honesty huddled and blossomed in the dark secret wetness. And strangest of all, a hawthorn tree which had fallen over, half-dead and rotten, soughing and waving in decline, athwart the path, still budded and blossomed, as though undeterred by death, the leaves still breaking from it in its grave.

It was hard to see the cottage, the path was so densely

overgrown. She had heard it was a large one, and so it was, she saw, as she fought her way through the tangles and over the bumps. It was large, and must once have been well cared for, for there were vestigial signs of flower beds, a garden seat, a shed, stone pots and urns. But all was overgrown, the shed was roofless and windowless, the pots were sinking into the green and yellow tendrils of the grass, the roses were like trees, fierce and thorny, brambles ramped wildly and savagely up to the front door. The one-time lawn was long and seeded, like a field. The windows of the cottage were boarded up, with planks and corrugated iron, except for one window on the ground floor. Plants stretched their creepers and suckers everywhere, creeping into crevices, picking at the stones.

Janet nearly gave up and went back, and a prophetic vision of Con's corpse flashed across her mind. But she was not a coward, she told herself, she had not come all this way for nothing. And there was something in her that loved the place. It was fierce and lonely, it was defiant. She liked it. And there, suddenly, stood her Great-Aunt Con, her face looming pale at the only window, the only cracked window.

She certainly looked like a witch. Her hair was white, her nose was hooked, and she shook her fist at Janet and the pram. She shook her fist threateningly. Janet could hear a dog barking. Janet advanced, across the lush, damp tangled lawn. She stopped, about two yards from the window. The old woman was shaking a stick now, and making it clear, by unmistakable gestures, that she would set the dog on Janet if Janet did not leave. "Great-Aunt Con," called Janet, "Great-Aunt Con. I'm Janet. Janet Ollerenshaw."

The old woman stopped shaking her fist and stick, and cupped her hand over her ear, then shook her head. She was deaf, she indicated.

The two of them stared at one another. A bird sang. And Janet picked up the box of chocolates, and advanced to the windowsill and put it down. The old woman watched intently, with seeming approval. Janet retreated, indeed ran back to the pram, suddenly overcome with terror, and was about to retreat, when she looked back and saw Great-Aunt Con beckoning and gesturing at her. She didn't want to go back, she didn't dare. She shook her head, and turned again, but this time Aunt Con rapped on the window pane with her stick. Janet faced her. Nothing would have induced her to go into the house. She knew it must smell, it must be in the last stages of decay, and she was fastidious. Nature could go wild, but not houses. She wanted to be back in her own polished tiled hygienic box. But the old woman, her blood relation, was still rapping and waving. What did she want with the baby? Did she want to see it? It would be ill luck, surely, to let her set eyes on the baby, she might wish it evil, she might cast a spell. Janet thought of those cracked gray shells in the snails' graveyard. Sacrifices, on a small altar. Witches in the old days sucked the blood of infants and pounded their bones in mortars, pounded them into paste. What could that old woman think about all day?

Janet turned to go, trying to keep calm. And as soon as she had turned away, it suddenly seemed to her that it was very silly, to be at all afraid. She wasn't a witch, the old woman, she was Connie Ollerenshaw, touched in the head, who liked to live alone. And Janet turned again, the last time, human, and saw the gray face mooning through the small dirty panes, and she picked up her baby so that Great-Aunt Con could see him. Con stopped rapping, and stared. Hugh slept on, wrapped up in his baby blanket. A curious family group. There seemed no point in doing anything more, once Con had seen the baby—the sight of him seemed to satisfy her—so Janet waved, with an appearance of bravery, and set off back down the path, to the track and the bus stop and her own tidy house. The old woman did not wave back. Her attention was now turned to the box of chocolates lying on the windowsill.

Janet felt rather pleased with herself, as she walked down the path. She had done her duty, she had visited her great-aunt, and she had got away free. Strange that she had wanted to see the baby, but now that Janet thought about it, hadn't

there been some talk once about Con herself and a baby?
Perhaps that was what had driven her mad—a dead baby, a
lost baby, a lost love. It was possible, but who now would
ever know? Secrets remain secret, they become even more
secret with the passage of time, with the shame of anxious
relatives, and the gossip of neighbors. Perhaps Con herself
couldn't remember what had thus cut her off from the dull
ditchlike flow of Ollerenshaw normality. The skeleton would
never rattle from its closet. And as for Janet, she had bought
herself off, she had offered a bribe of chocolates, and it had
been accepted. She had placated an ancient spirit, a spirit of
blood.

On the way down the drive, she noticed something that
she found at first frightening, then reassuring. Hanging from
the low branches of the bushes were other little offerings,
dangling from bits of string. They looked like sacrifices in
some pagan rite of propitiation, but on closer inspection they
proved to be bits of bacon fat, a piece of coconut, a piece of
cheese rind. Great-Aunt Con liked to feed the birds. And she
was well organized enough to get hold of cheese and nuts
and bacon, she didn't live on dandelions and nettles after all.

Feeling much better, Janet walked back to the bus stop. She
would never tell anyone about this visit, she resolved. She
would keep it to herself.

"Do you mean to say, Mrs. Bird," asked Ronnie Bennett,
interviewer, before a potential audience of some million people, "that you thought she would attack you and the baby if
you went any nearer? An old woman of eighty-eight?"

"She had a dog," said Janet, firmly, trying to avoid the
red inquisitorial eye of the camera.

"And you thought," said Ronnie Bennett, with manifest
disbelief, "that she would set the *dog* on you?"

"I felt she didn't want to see me," said Janet. "Or rather,
I felt she didn't mind *seeing* me, but she didn't want me to
get any nearer."

"And didn't you think to *tell* anybody about the conditions you found at Mays Cottage?"

"No, I didn't. Anyway, why should I have done? The Armstrongs must have known, they were always trying to get that cottage off her, or so I heard. And they lived much nearer than me."

"But didn't you think it was your duty, as a relation, to intervene?"

"No, I didn't," said Janet Bird. "I think people should mind their own business, that's what I think."

Although Janet Bird took the line that skeletons should stay in their closets, others, of course, did not, as we have seen. Constance's death really caused quite a lot of trouble. It made Janet Bird, her mother and father, James Armstrong and his wife, a social worker or two, and the local vicar, and Sir Frank Ollerenshaw appear in a most unfavorable public light. It drove Stella Ollerenshaw (no blood relation, as she hoped people would realize) into hospital in a state of collapse, and dragged her daughter Frances Wingate back early from Adra. It caused Karel Schmidt to miss Frances Wingate in Adra, and obliged David Ollerenshaw, a total stranger to Karel Schmidt, to accompany him back to London by air, leaving his beautiful green car in Africa. David Ollerenshaw had been willing to undertake the journey, for the press seemed to have been tormenting his cousin Janet, which he didn't approve, and he felt he should stand by his family, both its older and its more recently discovered members, in its time of trouble. Whether or not Constance Ollerenshaw was responsible for the disappearance of Stephen Ollerenshaw and his daughter still remained to be seen: it was quite possible that the two events were quite unconnected, and had simply happened to coincide in time.

Frances spent her first night in England with Natasha and Hugh, telling them not to worry about Stephen, who had disappeared from his flat in Brighton with his baby, leaving a worrying note: she also listened to a detailed account of her mother's alleged collapse. She also rang up her contacts at the *Sunday Examiner* and asked them what they thought they were playing at, couldn't old women be left to die in peace. You've got no sense of social responsibility, but we have, she was told by a flip friend, who was notorious even in the profession for hard drinking, large overdrafts, and wife-beating. Fuck social responsibility, said Frances, I want to speak to the editor.

The editor wasn't there, but Frances got hold of some subordinate who tried to turn the tables on her by hinting that it was people like herself, who despised the family unit, who lead to solitary deaths from neglect, and would she like to give him her view of the breakdown of marriage today? Frances rang off.

The next day she went up to Wolverton. She drove herself up, and as she drove she tried to come to terms with the fact that she did, after all, feel a sense of family guilt about the old woman's death. She shouldn't have been left to die, like that, of hunger. Somebody should have known, somebody should have called in. Her father, in short, ought to have known. He was her nearest living relative, and he had not given her a thought for years. It was grotesque of the papers to persecute him, grotesque of them to imply (as they seemed to be trying to do) that he had cut himself off (aided and encouraged by Stella) because the Ollerenshaws were so-cially embarrassing and better forgotten. It was grotesque, but there was some truth in it. Had she not herself been astonished to learn that David, her new-found cousin, had been able to rise from the same slough that had produced her father? And of what was that astonishment a measure?

Blood is thicker than water, she said to herself as she drove up in the M1.

She knew more details, now, about Connie's death. She had broken a leg, which had prevented her from getting over to the farm or down to the shop. She had dragged herself around for some time, eating what was in reach, and then had died. Neither the farmer nor the shopkeeper had registered her absence, which apparently wasn't as surprising as it seemed, for she was in the habit of quarreling with each for long periods, and each had assumed she was getting food from the other. Also, in the summer, she tended to look after herself more—she had vegetables in the garden, and fruit trees, and she would push an old pram around the lanes nearby, picking and scavenging. So nobody had missed her. Her dog was found dead on the bed.

The cottage was in a state of appalling neglect and had been shut up till it was discovered who now owned it. There was a will, a solicitor in Tockley had a copy, but he hadn't divulged its contents.

A horrible mess it all was, really. She hoped it wouldn't take too long to sort out. She wanted to get home again, to her children and her own affairs.

When she reached Wolverton, she found, as she had suspected, that her mother had taken refuge from unwelcome questioning and publicity in hysteria. She had not, however, foreseen that the hysteria would be so unmanageable. Her father, over lunch, tried to hint that things were bad, and he himself didn't look at all well. He kept shaking his head and sighing to himself, when he wasn't speaking. After lunch, he took her to the hospital, where her mother lay in a private room in a blue nightdress with a shawl around her shoulders, looking not so much aged as washed away. Her face, soft and youthful, looked as though a storm had passed over it, taking from it all memory, all expectation. The tension of waiting had gone, there was a blank drop in the tight skin around her wrinkled eyes, and the eyes themselves had that curious lusterless bland unseeing gaze that so often accompanies or succeeds acute mental distress. Her very hands were changed: they lay on the white-strapped smooth sheet, puffed and inert.

Frances half expected her not to recognize her, so changed was she, but she looked at Frances with a placid look, a terrible nod. "It's not my fault," she said, as though continuing a conversation, with a calm and interrogating inflection, as though Frances had been at her bedside for hours.

And she proceeded to recount the death of Alice, a story which Frances had successfully tried to avoid for years, and avoided now, by the expedient of shutting her ears and thinking hard about other things. She wondered what her father was thinking. He had crossed to the window, he was looking out, with his back to the room.

Lady Ollerenshaw didn't seem to be able to stop talking. Old sorrows, old grievances, were weighing on her mind, and she talked of them evenly, dully. Frances found herself putting her fingers in her ears and humming to herself slightly and very quietly, in order not to hear. After what seemed like hours and hours, a nurse came and tapped on the door and said that it was time for them to go, and they left. She and her father didn't say a word to one another, as they walked down the corridor, and down the stairs, and out into the courtyard, and into the car. They drove back to the lodge in silence.

"She'll get better," said Frances, over a cup of tea.

"Oh yes, I suppose so," said her father. She didn't know whether to speak to him, or not. She felt at a loss, useless.

Later in the evening, he asked her if she thought the *Sunday Examiner* would follow up its original attack, or whether it would forget the story. She said that she didn't know; she suspected, herself, that the heat was off. (She'd finally got hold, that morning, of her friend Bill Merriton on the *Examiner*, and he hadn't seemed particularly keen to pursue the story. He'd been much more interested in trying to find out whether she'd been doing anything worth reporting in Adra. I hear they've discovered uranium, he suggested: oh, I wouldn't say that exactly, said Frances. He could chase that one up for a while.) No, she said to her father, I wouldn't worry too much, if I were you. Something else is sure to happen before next weekend. There'll be some drug firm that needs exposing, or some race riot in a comprehensive school that needs investigating, don't you worry.

He said that her mother had only gone into hospital to get away from the journalists and the telephone, but that the longer she stayed there, the worse she seemed to get.

"She'll get better, perhaps, when the danger's over," said Frances, and he agreed. "Though she has been rather odd lately," he said. "Perhaps it's her age," Frances forbore to remark that her mother was well past the age where one might expect such a temporary oddness.

They talked, for a while, about the Ollerenshaw family, and Frances told him about her meeting with David. She had resolved to ask him if he knew the origins of the dispute between Ted and Enoch, but now she came face to face with the problem, she found that she dared not. He was too remote, and he had doubtless had good cause to remove himself; she did not wish to disturb him, she did not wish him to end up in a hospital bed. Let him deal with his life in his own manner, it was too late now to ask questions. So she contented herself with telling him about David, and Spirelli's views of kinship. Adra seemed a thousand miles away, as indeed it was, and she invoked it in her own defense, feeling as she had felt when a girl, invoking extra family activities by inexplicable runic references, as though to reassure herself that there was a world elsewhere. Her father was interested in Adra, he was usually interested in information. He had followed her career with admirable paternal attention.

Before they went to bed, he asked her if she would mind going to Tockley for him, to see the solicitor. "I'd better stay near your mother," he said. "I'd ask Hugh, but I think you're better at this kind of thing than he is.

"And there'll be a funeral to fix up, I suppose," he said.

Frances, rinsing out the coffee cups, saw herself as an adult, her parents declining feebly to the grave. The matriarch, arranging funerals. It was a role that she might have expected, but it seemed to have come to her rather suddenly.

"I'll have to get back to my children at some point," she said, as her father, in a placating movement, dried the cups, although the cleaning woman would be there as usual in the morning. "I've already been away a fortnight."

"Where are they at the moment?'"

"They're with Anthony and Sheila." Her husband, unlike herself, had married again, conveniently for Frances: Sheila liked to prove herself by being pleasant with the children. Frances thought of the children, back-talking, wisecracking, amusing, boiling themselves eggs and making cups of tea and studying physics and geometry and resolutely growing up, the rising generation.

"Do they like it there?"

"Oh yes. They like it anywhere, really."

"So you could spare a day or two more?"

"Yes. Of course." She thought, she hadn't sustained so long a personal conversation with her father for years. "You'll have to tell me, though," she said, "what to do about the funeral, and that kind of thing. And the will."

"The solicitors will help you with all that. They're a perfectly reliable firm. Brooks and Barnard. My father used to deal with them."

Frances wiped the clean white kitchen surfaces, and folded the dishcloth much more neatly than she would have done at home, and hung it over the edge of the sink.

"I suppose," said her father, rather helplessly, "I suppose I must be the next of kin."

Stella Ollerenshaw lay in her hospital bed and thought about the death of Constance Ollerenshaw. One had to die at some point, but surely not like that. She couldn't help thinking of her lying there all that time undiscovered. Not so long ago she'd read a very unpleasant item in the local paper, about an old woman in a council flat who had lived for four years in the same flat as her dead husband. When her husband's maggotty skeleton was found, he was just lying there in the bed, under a blanket. The old woman didn't seem to have noticed him at all. She was suffering from senile dementia.

When questioned closely, she said it was true that she hadn't seen her husband up and about lately.

David Ollerenshaw and Karel Schmidt caught the plane home from Adra together. They were getting on not too badly, despite the inconvenience of the situation. Karel had shown remarkable self-control when informed that he had missed Frances by a day, and wasted several hundred pounds in the effort. "Well, bugger that," he had said bleakly, and had sat down to recover. He had been unable to tell them anything at all about the crisis that had recalled Frances. He didn't read the *Sunday Examiner*, he only read the *Sunday Times*. "I don't even read the *Observer* any more," he said from time to time, as though that would contribute to the sum total of information about Frances's sudden disappearance.

The as yet undispersed conference members were delighted by his romantic arrival, which gave an unexpected thrill to their last evening. They fed him and bought him drinks and asked him about Frances and tried to prod him into the swimming pool, wondering what grand passion could have brought him so far; for Karel certainly had a quixotic look about him, a look of harassed desperation. He had a tatty, disheveled air, as of one whose clothes have been disintegrated by the constant fret of violent emotion, and they gazed at him with respect, a traveler from distant lands. Karel, conscious of his role, tried to live up to it, but he was feeling far too ill to leap dashingly into the swimming pool for their delight. He had had to have a cholera jab at the airport when leaving, and his arm was huge and swollen. He had been horribly sick on the flight, and the Adran food, delicious though it was, didn't seem to go down too well, so Karel, with his usual aggressive policy toward his own health, had firmly washed it down with a large quantity of Real Scotch Flora MacDonald Whisky, and swallowed a good many pills which kind geologists and engineers offered him. By the time he boarded the plane home the next morning, he was feeling extremely ill.

"It's my fault for lying," he told David, groaning into the paper bag provided. "I told the Poly I couldn't turn up because I was sick. And now I am."

David tried to cheer him up with the story of his first night in Tehran.

They had to change planes in Paris, and owing to a strike of airport workers were unable to find seats on the normal scheduled flights: they were nearly fitted onto a plane from Bombay, and would have been if Karel hadn't been feeling too ill to stand in a queue. This was just as well for them, as the plane blew up over the Channel, killing every one of the two hundred and seventeen passengers. Karel and David were lucky enough to spend the night in a hotel instead, and flew back to London the next morning, Friday morning, just as Frances Wingate was setting off to drive across the Midlands from Wolverton to Tockley, to bury her long-dead great-aunt.

Harold Barnard sat in his office and stared at Constance Ollerenshaw's will. He was wondering what his father could have been thinking of, to let her draw up such a tiresome document. It must have been quite obvious when she made it, twenty-five years earlier, that all its beneficiaries would be dead shortly, if they weren't then dead already. And now, of course, they were. The list of beneficiaries was short. Her dog—presumably any current dog. Her cat. (There might still be a cat roaming around there somewhere, of course— cats are good at survival.) The matron of Star Valley Nursing Home. (He had checked that one, and she had died in 1959.) And the cottage she had left, mysteriously, to the owner of a lodging house in Morecombe, who had died without issue the year after the will was made.

His father really ought to have kept her up to date on it, he thought. Though perhaps there wouldn't have been much point—she was dotty, had been for years, she might have tried to draw up something yet more inconvenient. The fact was that the firm of Brooks and Barnard had completely forgotten the existence of Constance Ollerenshaw. She had still been vaguely in their minds when Ted Ollerenshaw, her brother, was still alive, and somebody had mentioned her when Eel Cottage was sold, but that was a good many years ago now. Mays Cottage would probably go to the next of kin. If they wanted it. The Armstrongs at the farm had had their eye on it for years, but Constance had hated them so much that she had actually added a clause that the cottage shouldn't be sold to the Armstrongs. He wondered whether the clause would stand. The cottage, derelict though it was, might be quite valuable now. People were prepared to pay fancy prices for cottages, even in districts like this, and Mays Cottage was a period piece, completely unrestored, which in these days seemed to be an asset. Eel Cottage, which had changed hands several times since Ted died, had more than quadrupled in price, and would fetch an even better sum now.

He was waiting, now, for Ted's granddaughter, Dr. Frances Wingate. It did seem rather ironic that her father, who must have done very well for himself, seemed to be likely to inherit Connie's money (and there might be a bit more than the cottage, his father hadn't been very strict about cats and dogs in wills but he'd told her where to invest the odd hundred pounds or two, forty years earlier). There were plenty of other Ollerenshaws around on the spot, as it were, and several of them had been around to see him about the will: apart from the fact that they clearly weren't as well off as a vice-chancellor they now claimed that they had looked after Connie well in her old age, and were therefore more deserving of her money. In view of the circumstances of her death, he permitted himself to find this comic. But people have short memories. There was one of them who'd tried to go and see her, but only one: he'd seen her on the local TV news. She'd made quite a good impression. She'd given the old lady a box of Black Magic chocolates. When starving to death, Constance had eaten the box in which the chocolates came: relics of it had been found in her stomach. He hoped the young woman wouldn't get to hear that bit of information. It might upset her. And whoever's fault it was, it wasn't hers.

(She, of course, hadn't been around after the money.) Harold
Barnard inclined to take the line that it was nobody's fault.
If people chose to live alone, they chose to die alone. Though
they thereby sometimes created a good deal of work for their
solicitors. She had expressed a request, in her will, that she
should be buried in unconsecrated ground, and that the vicar
of St. Oswald's, Tockley, should attend. He wondered what
Frances Wingate would make of that. It wasn't all that easy
to bury people in unconsecrated ground, and the vicar of St.
Oswald's to whom she had been referred had been lying long
years in his highly respectable grave.

Frances Wingate parked her car in a side street, by the Church
of All Saints. How beautiful it was, the church. It wasn't the
famous church of Tockley; it was just another church. There
it stood, densely surrounded by building societies and Wimpy
Bars. How beautiful England was, how lovely a place is an
English town.

She was feeling a little light-headed, easily affected. She
hadn't quite got over the air travel shock, and all this rushing
around was making her feel rather emotional, and rather
tired. Perhaps she should stop rushing around the world and
settle down and live quietly in a nice place like Tockley.

She gathered together her bag, her gloves, her cigarettes,
and opened the car door. She sniffed. Her nostrils widened in
horror. For she was met by the most amazing smell. Whatever
could it be? Was it a spiritual smell, the smell of Great-Aunt
Con's decay, hanging like a miasma over Tockley? She had
heard of such delusions, they were well recognized. Nobody
else seemed to be stationary with horror, as she herself was.

But it was too distinctive to be a delusion. She locked the
car door, and walked along the pavement, sniffing experi-
mentally. Was it cows, was it pigs, was it manure? It was too
unpleasant to be any of these things, though it contained
elements that reminded her of them. Could it be something
burning? Perhaps what it reminded her of most was the smell
of burning chocolate, which she had smelled once before,

and most unpleasantly, on the flat green grass wastes of York race course, emanating from the local chocolate factory. But this was worse, worse even than that. Sweetish and piggy, it hung rotten in the air.

She would ask Mr. Barnard about it, and if he said there was no smell, she would go and see a psychiatrist as soon as she got home. Tockley hadn't smelled at all like this in the early summer. Perhaps it was the guilt of Con's death, after all.

Mr. Barnard was delighted to talk about the smell. He sat her down in his office, and gave her a cup of coffee and told her that Con's death was in no way her fault whatever the local and national press might suggest, and that it was certainly not polluting the atmosphere of Tockley: Con, he said, was neatly frozen (or as neatly as possible) in the morgue, awaiting burial. The smell, he explained, was the smell of cooking sugar beet, and it was a great local scandal, and how right she was to notice it. His firm, he said, represented those factions which were trying to prevent the smell of burning beet from filling the streets of Tockley, but there were other powerful interests who argued that it was a good smell, that there was no smell, or that even if there were an unpleasant smell, it was a smell upon which the prosperity of Tockley was founded, and as such must be accepted and made welcome. "We get used to it," he said, "but it certainly does strike a stranger."

"Yes, it certainly does," said Frances. She liked the look of Mr. Barnard, he was quite dashing in a quiet way, he wore side whiskers and a large wide striped collar and a colorful tie: she liked the way the hair receded from his high and intelligent brow. He was about her own age, she guessed: she had expected somebody much older, but as he shortly told her, he had some years ago taken over the position of his father, who had retired and was now dead.

Pleasant though Mr. Barnard was, however, he couldn't disguise the fact that Connie's will had left a few problems. He gave her some advice about undertakers, and the number of the police station, and she said she would have to think about whether or not she should disregard the will of the dead.

"A cremation would be simplest," said Mr. Barnard.

"I'll think about it over lunch," said Frances.

She then asked him if it would be all right if she went to have a look at Mays Cottage. She was thinking of going that afternoon. The police wouldn't mind, would they? she asked, and he said no, and looked in a little drawer of his desk and found her the keys. "Though I doubt if you'll need them," he said. "I think the door's off the hinges.

"I would come with you," he said, "but I've got some clients to see this afternoon. You won't be too shocked by what you find there, will you?"

"I've seen some nasty things in my time," said Frances, "though it's true that most of them have been a few thousand years old."

"You could bring me the keys back tomorrow," he said.

"I'll do that," she said. "And the dog, you said, was found dead? There's no need to look for the dog?"

"The dog was very very dead," said Harold Barnard gravely, and courteously escorted her out into the smell of beets.

She booked herself into the same hotel in which she had stayed earlier that year, and had some lunch there, thinking while she ate it of whether or not one ought to respect the wishes of a dead person to be buried eccentrically in unhallowed ground. She couldn't make her mind up. She of all people was aware that mankind had strong views about burials: burial rites were one of the oldest signs of culture, they were what distinguished man from beast. Impossible to dismiss such a significant passion as mere superstition, for if one dismissed that, how much else had to go? Perhaps she would have a better sense of her duty to Constance when she had been to visit her cottage. She would postpone judgment.

Harold Barnard had given her the vicar's phone number, in case she wanted to discuss the matter with the vicar. She rather fancied discussing burial rites with the vicar, perhaps she would give him a ring. (She was by now quite enjoying this disaster.) He had also given her the number of a distant relative of hers, called Janet Bird, who had been the last person to see Constance Ollerenshaw alive: she seems a reasonable person, he had said, you could get in touch with her. She's been having a tough time with the press, he said.

Frances had forgotten about the press: rightly, she suspected. The Constance story had been a nonstory, and they must have realized it by now. The British public was tired of dead old ladies and the gaps in the social services: its indignation was exhausted. Still, the family had had a bad time, however excessive her mother's reaction appeared. Perhaps she would ring Janet Bird, that evening. It would be interesting to meet yet another Ollerenshaw.

She felt rather tired after lunch, and went to lie down on one of the neat twin beds in her bedroom. (It wasn't the same room as the one she had stayed in earlier in the summer, it looked over a rubbish dump instead of over a parking lot, but it was in other respects identical.) When she woke up, it was after three, and the air was already turning slightly dark. Being a practical person, it occurred to her that it might well be quite dark by the time she had finished with the cottage, supposing that there was anything there of any interest, and that the cottage would probably not be connected up with electricity now, even if it had once been. Luckily, this was an autumn of power cuts, and the hotel had thoughtfully provided candles and matches; she slipped them into her bag, and set off.

Harold Barnard had drawn her a little map, but nevertheless at Barton she took the wrong turn, and got herself rather lost. The country, even though it was so near Eel Cottage, was quite different in character: slightly undulating, wooded, hedged. There was none of that sense of desolate rural openness and utility: it was secretive, alluring. The hedges were bright with red hips and berries: they glowed like little lanterns in the gathering dusk, and the dark clouds strained above them, white edged and flowing. These were the paths that Constance Ollerenshaw had walked with her old pram, gathering snails for supper.

She couldn't get the car up the path to the cottage, it was so overgrown. So she got out and walked. Unlike her cousin Janet, she was good at negotiating rough terrain, and careless of her shoes. (She could afford to be careless of her shoes.) She strode along, anxious to see the cottage before it was dusk, pushing her way through the bushes, which leaned toward her, ready to obscure the path altogether. It was like Sleeping Beauty's terrain, she said to herself, though it was no sleeping beauty that the Armstrongs had discovered there. An intense stillness, a trance, hung over everything. And there stood the cottage itself, ancient, decayed, dank, dark, beautiful. It stood alone, itself, gone wild, run wild.

She had been expecting the worst: later, she realized that it was partly in terms of her expectations that the place was so beautiful. But first impressions are all, and in the silent dusk she stood and stared. She had pictured decay, rusted corrugated iron, tin cans, broken bottles, rotten planks, dung heaps, the worst of the country, but instead there was a cottage, overgrown with thorns and brambles, crumbling and falling, but crumbling to nature only, not to man. Constance Ollerenshaw had lived simply and madly; there were no corrugated iron roofs covering her leaking rafters. A terrible purity marked the scene, and Frances approached it without fear. Even a corpse would not have alarmed her. She was used to corpses; human bones were her familiars. She walked up to the front door, through the long swaths of grass, her feet wet with mud and dew: Oh, so different, so beautifully different from the parched red mud of Adra, from the glaring altitudes of rocky, weathered Tizouk. England. A bird sang in a tree. Frances paused at the door, feeling in her pocket for the key. She bowed her head in respect to Constance Ollerenshaw, who had lived here alone for so long, whose death had been so solitary, so unremarked, who had let the creepers and brambles and roses grow in through her windows.

Harold Barnard was right: she did not need the key. The
door did not exactly swing open at her touch, but it was easy
enough to push open: the long-unpainted wood scraped over
the stone floor, for it drooped on its hinges, with a kind of
weary welcome. Though so densely overgrown and surrounded by trees, it was still light enough inside to see without the aid of candles, and Frances found herself in the main
room of the cottage: the main, front room. A door led off
the back to a kitchen: a staircase led up from one corner.

It was not nearly as desolate as she had supposed. There
was still furniture—a couch, chairs, a table with a fringed
velour cloth. There were even ornaments: a picture on the
wall, a lamp on the table, a vase on the mantelpiece. Embers
lay in the grate: knobby bits of wood. Perhaps Con had not
been mad after all: perhaps she had simply been a Natasha
of the country, without a town house. The Real Thing. A
desk stood in a corner, a solid wooden desk, ornate, carved,
woody, black. Apart from these objects, the room had a dignified emptiness: she wondered if it had always been like
this, or whether surface rubble had been swept up and removed by police or solicitors. The place was not exactly
clean: the stone floor was covered in leaves, the maroon
velour cloth was ragged and thick (she touched it tentatively,
with a nervous finger), thick and stiff with dust. There were
mouse droppings, bird droppings: maybe also rats? Frances
did not mind rats. She must remember to look out for a
possible cat.

A fraying plum-colored curtain, heavy with age and dirt,
hung between the main room and the kitchen: Frances pushed
it aside, and went through. The windows were small, and
branches leaned pressingly against them. They were small-
paned, made to let in the light with the smallest possible
escape of heat. How cold it must have been, in the past. She
was glad she had borrowed her father's jersey the night before. A row of pots stood on the windowsill: the plants were
dead and twiggy, dry and stiff, but they must once have grown
profusely, making the cottage green within, green without.

The floor, again, was stone, with a few peg rugs on it: Constance had cooked on a kitchen range, black and heavy, a Victorian range. It must once have been an expensive appliance. The sink was a deep stone sink, silted up now with leaves: Frances prodded at the leaves with a spoon, and beetles ran. There were spiders, too: an insects' paradise. On the stone slab by the sink stood some pans: curious, Frances peered in them, finding snail shells (she had heard that Constance ate snails, and why not?) a little mold, and in one lid-covered pan a sheep's head. Frances did not much care for the sheep's head: it had been picked too clean, and yet remained disgusting, the huge stupid eye sockets staring, the rather too healthy teeth still fixed in the jaw, and some of the bone pitted and worn and frilled into a tiny, holey pattern, an intricate membranous delicate web. It was a curious color too, green and red and blotchy, not white as bone should be. She did not care for it, she did not like to think of Constance eating the last scrap (or perhaps the cat had helped) and she put the lid on it again, and went upstairs, glad that Constance was not still lying there in wait, as she had been for the Armstrongs.

It was easy to see how Constance had broken her leg. The stairs, always a vulnerable part in any structure, were rickety and dangerous. There was no banister or hand rail, only a twisted dark red rope to hold on to, a faintly ecclesiastical rope; and that was broken. Several treads were broken right through. If I were to break my leg, thought Frances, how long would it take anyone to find me? She trod gingerly. There was nothing much to see up there, in fact: only a bedstead (the bedding and mattress had been, perhaps wisely, removed), a washstand, a bowl and a ewer (Frances cast her eye on them and decided that they would fetch a fancy price in an antique market, for they too were the real thing, pale green with a gilt rim, and many roses), and a wardrobe. She looked in the wardrobe: it was riddled and musty with worm and rot, and the clothes that hung in it were musty too, so she shut the door quickly. The other two rooms upstairs were

completely empty; apart from a few sticks of chopped-up
furniture: Constance must have demolished the other objects
in the house for firewood.

There was nothing more to see. She edged her way downstairs, and stood quietly in the middle of the now dark room.
It did not seem to her too bad, the way that Constance Ollerenshaw, her great-aunt, had lived and died. And the cottage felt all right. It even had a feeling of home. It was
contained, it was secret. It had none of the rural bleakness
of Eel Cottage, none of that open struggle. Nature had gently
enfolded it, had embraced it and taken it and thicketed it in,
with many thorns and briars; nature had wanted it, and had
not rejected it.

On the key ring, there was a key to the black desk. She lit
her candles and unlocked the desk, to see what was there.
She didn't know what she was expecting, Harold Barnard
had said there was nothing of value, but it was full of things,
every little drawer and pigeonhole was full. Bits of paper,
letters, photographs, medals, buttons, sewing eggs, bob-
bins, brooches, rings, old tickets, coins, pins, and bits and
pieces of a lifetime—of more than a lifetime, she realized,
as she started to go through them, for here were records going back into the dim reaches of the dusty Ollerenshaw past,
before dead Constance had been born. Ill-spelled letters in
spidery script announced a death in the family in Lincoln in
1870, a birth in Peterborough in 1875. Nearly as indecipher-
able as hieroglyphics, nearly as sparse in their information as
Phoenician shopping lists, they contained a past, a history.
There were a few Ollerenshaw birth certificates, some signed
with an X by illiterate parents: there was her own great-
grandparents' marriage certificate. Pitiful documentation, of
a family which had not set much store by the written word.
The objects were more eloquent: outdated coins (a little heap
of farthings, a silver threepenny bit); a tin Jubilee spoon, a
child's enamel Coronation badge. A worthless collection.
She thought of the prosperous relics of Tizouk, which had

brought her so much wealth: she thought of the elaborate leavings of the Chadwicks, the papers, the letters, the books, the heirlooms, the albums, the investments, the posthumous intrigues, the rings and houses that changed hands when even the most obscure member of the family died. The Ollerenshaws had lived quietly like mice, hoarding scraps, in their dark cottage. In one of the drawers she found a curious little pile of wooden pegs. She did not know what they were. She put one in her pocket. She would take it to the museum, perhaps, for identification.

And out of this darkness, her father had clambered, oddly gifted, oddly persevering, a freak escape. Or so she had always thought. But of course, there had been other Ollerenshaws who had climbed too. They had learned to write their names, they had managed to rise above the twelve shillings a week wage, the suppers of dry bread and onions. And as proof of their success, Joshua Ollerenshaw, shoemaker, had managed to buy the tied cottage from the estate, in 1880, for the sum of £64. In the heart of the agricultural depression (Frances knew a few dates, from Karel) the Ollerenshaws had managed to become independent. They had risen from the slavery of agricultural labor: they had become shoemakers, smallholders, small shopkeepers. Ambition had propelled them, as it propelled her and her father. They had worked long days amongst the beets and potatoes: they had worked long nights, men, women and children, at piecework, stitching shoes, ill-paid, persevering, thrifty, as she too had worked hard—she, the blessed and the lucky, the winner at cards, the finder of gold, unembarrassed by riches.

(The greatest stroke of luck in the family, though Frances was never to know it, lost as it was beyond the possibility of research, had been the marriage of an Ollerenshaw daughter to a shoemaker from Kettering in 1854: the shoe trade had prospered at that period, and the shoemaker had his own machine, and was able, from the fruit of his own labors, to buy another such machine for his in-laws. It had not made life easy, but it had made it possible. There was more hope for a working man in a stitching machine than in a spade or a needle.)

Constance, too, might have been one of the lucky ones. There were photographs of Constance, proving (as Janet Bird already knew) that she had been a handsome girl; even the poorest of women, carefully posed in their Sunday best for formal studio photographs at the end of the nineteenth century, managed a touch of style. And Constance had plenty of style. She had learned to read and write, at the village school: there were certificates to prove it. Later, she had admirers: there was a little bundle of love letters, tied with a blue ribbon. She had not used these to light the fire: she had not, in her final hunger, eaten these. And here, too, was the record of Constance's retreat: a birth certificate for a daughter born to Constance Ollerenshaw, June 15, 1914, in a nursing home in Lincoln: a death certificate for the same child, who had died eighteen months later. Bills for another nursing home (a mental home?). Postcards from her mother addressed to Aberdeen, where Constance had gone to work, in 1918. It was all there, the whole story.

There were even mementoes of the child's father, a little bundle tied with a black bootlace, and pushed into a large envelope with a black funereal border and a motif of green printed lilies. Frances looked at them, and wondered whether she should read them. It was growing cold; the candles flickered in the dark room. She wondered if the paraffin lamp still had any paraffin in it, but it was rusted and dry. She knelt by the hearth, and ignited the dry half-burned sticks in the grate: smoke poured up the long-disused chimney and billowed into the room. Doubtless the chimney was full of birds' nests, by now.

The child's father had been a married man, a seaman from the dwindling port of Boston. A limp cutting of the announcement of his death in the local paper was the first thing that fell from the sad packet. He had died young, aged thirty-five, crushed in a fall from his ship at anchor in the flat waters of the peaceful harbor of Boston. He had left a widow and two children. His singing would be much missed by the choir and congregation at St. Stephen's Church, the paper said, and there were two lines of appreciation from the vicar, George Wyatt Edmonton. He might have been a singer, but the scraps of his correspondence which had survived were not eloquent: on cheap, much-thumbed paper, in faded pencil, they declared: *Meet me at the Fortune of War, Skegness, Friday night: Can't make next weekend, try next: I miss you, my dearest dear.* Some were more revealing in tone—*Be brave, my dear, all will be well. When I return I will speak with the vicar. Be brave, my own Connie.* And so on, and so on. Poor man, seducer, con man, vacillator, lover, traitor, how could one tell? Connie's letters were not there, they might have told more. He thanked her for them, in the much folded scraps. And did not leave his wife, as he seemed at times between the laboriously looped lines to promise. He had died three years after his child's death, three years that Constance had spent in and out of mental homes, three years of which the packet held no record, no word.

Frances, by the blue fire, thought of Karel, as she read of Constance. She was sniffing hard, and wiping her nose with the back of her hand. Had Constance loved him, where had she met him, and had they been happy, how had she got to be so mad? Lost love, rejection, puerperal fever, guilt, interfering vicars, the death of a loved child, persecution by parents. (She had as yet found no record that the parents even knew of the child: Constance had left home and stayed from home, returning, it would seem, only after the baby died, up in Aberdeen.) Had it been slow, had it been sudden? Would it ever have been curable?

The last letter in the packet was from the vicar, George Wyatt Edmonton. It was addressed to Miss Constance Ollerenshaw, care of Mrs. Ollerenshaw, Mays Cottage, Hags Lane, Barton, Barton-by-Tockley. It was still in its original envelope. The date was a week after Constance's lover's death. It said:

The Vicarage
St. Oswald's
Tockley.

Dear Miss Ollerenshaw,

   I am hoping that this letter will reach you, and that
God may have restored you to a mind to read it. What
guilt I bear for his death, God knows, and I repent. I
wished you also to know that I repent of my hasty
words to you. I was a young man then, and myself
single. Forgive me, if you can, and my shortcomings
will lie more easily upon my conscience. Only the wise
know all ends.

Yours in Christ,

George Edmonton. (Burn this.)

Frances stared at this interesting missive with curiosity.
The rural plot was thickening, to include vindictive vicars—
possibly homosexual vicars, who can tell? John Lincoln, seaman and singer, must have been quite something to have
spread so much confusion around him. She wished there
were a photograph.

   The fire was going out: she crouched by it, feeding it with
leaves and twigs. She thought of feeding it with George Edmonton's letter, obeying its original instructions, but her archaeologist's training was too strong. He had requested a
burned offering, but had probably not deserved one. On the
other hand, Constance herself must have forgiven him, or
she would not have asked for the vicar of St. Oswald's to
reside over her funeral, now somewhat overdue. As Harold
Barnard had pointed out, the present vicar of St. Oswald's
was a sprightly young man called Fox, nothing at all to do
with his predecessor but one, Mr. Edmonton, who had died
in 1948, but Constance had clearly been in no mind, when
drawing up her will, to ponder on that kind of development.
She wondered if the elder Mr. Barnard had known anything
about the connection between Constance and Edmonton.

Even if he had, he too was now dead, and she could not imagine Harold knowing anything at all about such far-off events. He looked as though he would be more at home with property development and industrial estates. His business was clearly booming: he too had risen in the world, his clients would no longer include, except for old times' sake, such small fry as Ted Ollerenshaw and old Connie.

The fire had picked up again, but the room was full of smoke. It felt like midnight, though (looking at her watch) she saw it was only six o'clock. She felt curiously at home, and private, feeding twigs into her own hearth. Perhaps she herself would live here, taking over where Con had left off. Soon she would no longer need that large house in Putney. She would live here—tidy it up a little, perhaps, but not much—a bathroom, a telephone? no, no telephone—water, of course, there hadn't been a tap in the kitchen, there was probably a pump out the back somewhere. One would need water. She had had enough, in her desert days, of life without water.

The silence was intense. She sat and listened to it. There was nothing but the occasional rustle, as a bird moved in the boughs, as a draft moved the leaves on the floor. She thought of David Ollerenshaw, who lived alone, or as near alone as makes no difference. From choice, pure choice. She drew her knees up, hugging them, staring into the friendly little flames. She sat there for some time, thinking what a pity it was that she would have to go and have supper: otherwise she might have risked a little adventure, she might have risked sleeping the night there, where surely no ghost would disturb her—she was thinking of this, when she heard a rather large ghost, approaching. At first she thought it was an animal, the lost cat, beneficiary of a lifetime's milk, maybe (though any cat of Aunt Con's would surely be as good a forager as Aunt Con herself had been), but the noise was of something heavier. A cow, a badger? Karel, come from the South Western Poly and the Fulham Road to claim her? The Armstrongs with shotguns?

She sat there and waited, her heart beating with something

rather like fear. It was after all very dark, she was very much alone, nobody had any right to be there but herself, nobody knew she was there, and yet the footsteps were clearly human. Whoever it was, was making heavy weather of the approach: it was no silent tramp or footpad, she could hear breaking branches and muttering. And, after a moment, a flashlight shone in at the window, and a face peered at her. She and the face stared at one another with mutual alarm, frozen, until she worked out who it was. For it was, as it obviously would have been, only Harold Barnard.

"Come in," said Frances, not bothering to get up from her hearth, and he pushed his way in through the sagging door.

"You gave me a fright," he said, stamping and knocking the mud from his shoes. "You don't half look like the rest of your family. You could have been Constance herself, fifty years younger. In this light."

"You gave *me* rather a fright," said Frances, primly. "I wasn't expecting a visitor."

"Well, I go past the end of the road on my way home, and when I saw your car parked there, I thought I'd look in to see how you were getting on, see if I could lend you a torch. But I see you're well provided. You've made it look quite cozy in here."

"Was it much worse, when they found her? It wasn't nearly as bad as I'd expected."

"As a matter of fact, it wasn't bad at all. There wasn't much rubbish. Of course, she'd burned a lot. And she didn't seem to go in much for cans and newspapers and things like that. No bottles, either. We swept a bit out, but it wasn't that bad."

"She must have lived very—simply," said Frances.

"You can say that again," said Harold Barnard, thinking with pleasure of his stereo, his red setter, his trolley full of bottles and glasses, his hot plate covered with dinner, his shining Chippendale dining table, and his rather sexy wife, all waiting for him comfortably five miles down the road in their large double-glazed country residence.

"Did you find anything interesting, in the papers? There didn't look as though there was much there, but of course we haven't been through them thoroughly."

"Well, *I* think they're interesting," said Frances, "but then they're my family, aren't they?"

He smiled at her, pushing at a corner of the rotting mat with his toe.

"I wish I had a drink to offer you," said Frances. "But as you see, I haven't had time to settle in properly."

He laughed. "To tell you the truth," he said, confidingly, "as I drove past, and saw your car there, I had this silly picture—ridiculous, I know—I thought, perhaps she's fallen down those stairs, and broken her leg, and can't get out. I couldn't think what you were still doing here, in the dark, like this. I never thought of candles, or that you might have had a torch in the car. I drove right past, telling myself not to be so damn silly, and then I thought, that's what happened to old Connie, and I came back and had a look. When I saw the smoke from the chimney, I didn't know what to think."

"It was cold," said Frances, "so I lit a little fire."

"So I see. You're good at making yourself at home."

"I'm glad you called by. It was kind of you."

He paused, and stared at her. She had a curious look, crouched there in the firelight, her blond hair bleached but lit with red, her arms folded around her knees, shapeless in her large green jersey, her green masculine cable-stitch jersey.

"As you can't offer me a drink," he said, "why don't you come and have one with us? I'm sure my wife would be delighted to meet you."

He didn't like the idea of leaving her there on her own: that was one of the reasons why he asked her. Partly because it seemed wrong to leave her, partly because he was afraid she would set the place on fire, which would do him and his firm no good. And, in part, he wanted a little more: he liked her.

She sat there, considering. "I don't think I look fit to go

out for a drink," she said, insincerely, playing for time. "I'm a bit muddy."

"That wouldn't matter,"he said. He nearly added, we live very simply, but thought better of it, remembering the provenance of the phrase.

"I *was* thinking of ringing up that vicar this evening," she said.

"You'd still have time to do that. It's only"—he consulted his watch—"only five past six. And we live only five miles up the road. Do come."

"Oh, all right, thank you very much," said Frances, staggering to her numbed feet, abandoning the recluse's life rather promptly. "If you're sure it won't matter that I'm a bit cobwebby."

"It won't matter *at all*," said Harold Barnard, gallantly, pushing the door open for her to go through, when they had stamped out the remaining flames. He shone his flashlight for her on the tangled path, but she was better at making her way than he was. Still, he didn't complain. She liked a man that didn't complain. And she was seized with curiosity to know what his house was like, what his wife was like, what kind of life he led out here in the country.

"My wife *will* be pleased to meet you," said Harold, with a pleasing confidence, as he held her own car door open for her. "She's always taken an interest in archaeology. Belongs to the local archaeological society, and all that kind of thing. And she took me off to Greece last year for our holidays, to look at the ruins."

"How nice," said Frances, sincerely, wishing fleetingly that she were married to Harold Barnard and could take him off to Greece for his holidays, and belong to the local archaeological society.

"Just you follow me," he said, letting himself into his own new bright gray Citroën. "We'll be there in a couple of minutes."

She wondered whether he was the kind of driver who would drive ostentatiously slowly, in an elaborately careful way, or

whether he would take off in an abrupt, competitive and aggressive manner. He did the latter. She was flattered, concluded that he must know the small roads well, and put her
foot down on the accelerator. They were there, more or less
as he had predicted, in ten minutes, pulling up rather abruptly
on his well-graveled drive, in front of his large, low, highly
desirable residence. It dated, she supposed, from the twenties, that period of comfortable living, but had since been
much improved. A neat well-kept lawn spread around it:
discreetly planted trees screened it from the road. Light shone
from several windows, through several shades and thick-
nesses of curtain: an outside light shone, welcoming, from
the porch.

"How very nice," said Frances, climbing out of her car,
trying to dust the bits off her skirt. "What a lovely place to
live."

The front door opened, and the red setter ran out, wagging
his tail. Mrs. Barnard stood in the doorway, the light behind
her, her arms folded.

"I do hope she won't mind, my just arriving like this,"
murmured Frances, as they approached.

"She'll be delighted," said her husband for her happily:
and so indeed she seemed to be. "How lovely to meet you,"
said Mary Barnard, several times, as she showed Frances the
beautiful brown and gold deep-carpeted bathroom. "How
lovely to meet you," she said again, when Frances emerged,
looking a little tidier. "I thought you were just one of Harold's clients, how nice that it should be you."

This is what life ought to be like, thought Frances, as she
followed Mary Barnard down the stairs, past the prints of
boats at Boston, and Dutch landscapes at Lincoln. Nice people, pleased to see one, in a nice comfortable place. She
shivered on the edge of perfectly enjoying a perfectly ordinary experience, a perfectly ordinary encounter, an event so
rare, as she walked down the wide stairs. Everything was all
right, how could anything be wrong?

Mary Barnard was a very pretty woman: no wonder Harold Barnard had such an air of being pleased with himself, and all the world. No wonder he had been sure that Frances would meet with a fair reception. What resentments could ever be nourished in so attractive a bosom? Fortunate Harold, to lie on it each night. A county girl, brown-haired, well-bred, just marginally too well-spoken, well-dressed, she stood there quite unselfconsciously in front of a trolley full of drinks and glasses, asking Frances what she would have: it was satisfying even to behold so much satisfaction. Sex, of course, was what distinguished her: she looked as though she gave and got exactly what she wanted, and Frances found the suggestive way in which she handed her husband his drink quite enchanting. She was so pleased with the Barnards, and their delightful drawing room, that she felt herself on the verge of accepting their inevitable invitation to stay for dinner, and was rather relieved when an instant excuse sprang to her lips when the invitation arrived. "I'd *love* to stay," she said, looking at her watch, "but I really must leave in half an hour, I'm expecting a telephone call at the hotel."

"What a pity," said Mary, unruffled, sipping her sherry. "But still, how nice of you to come at all."

Frances wished she knew how long they had been married, and, if for long, whether they had had to work hard at continuing to feel so pleased with one another, but it didn't seem polite to ask. There didn't seem to be any traces of children around, but they could have been away at school. If there were no children, that would bear out her own theory that one could manage a man or some children, but not both at once: a conclusion markedly at odds, alas, with the arrangements both of nature and society. On balance she thought that the Barnards had just been lucky. However long they'd been at it, they'd been lucky with it, and they were still enjoying it. Such things don't happen often.

Being unable to discuss the happiness of the Barnards' marriage (though the subject would have interested all three), they spoke instead, briefly, of Constance's cottage and what it might fetch on the market, discussed property prices, and moved on to archaeology. Mary was, as her husband had claimed, an enthusiast: she had a row of rather large glossy books on the subject, two of them containing contributions by Frances, which Mary pointed out, proving thereby that she did not keep the books for decoration. Frances was rather ashamed of one of the contributions: she had been paid a vast amount of money for it and it had involved very little work, as is so often the case with that kind of enterprise: the more original labor, the less pay. Mary also had Sinclair-Davies's book about deserts, which Frances looked at with real pleasure, resolving not to be a recluse after all, but to try to get in touch with people like Sinclair-Davies again.

"I have a cousin who is an archaeologist," said Mary, as Frances sipped her drink, looked at Sinclair-Davies's elegant drawings, stroked the silky head of the friendly red dog, and sank yet deeper into her extraordinarily comfortable armchair, quite overcome with the possible and varied pleasant sensations of the material life. "I think you met him, once? He told me that he'd come across you somewhere. Hunter Wisbech, his name is."

"Good heavens, yes," said Frances, remembering the young man who had chatted her up so effectively that spring, the young man who had brought her tidings of Karel, and whose information had persuaded her to post the summoning postcard to Karel: and as she thought of Hunter, who had told her that Karel said he loved her, it became quite obvious to her that her postcard could not have been delivered. It was so extremely obvious that she wondered how she had ever doubted it. How very stupid she had been.

"So he's your cousin, is he?"

"Well, he's a sort of cousin," said Mary, and gave a very brief sketch of how Hunter fitted into the Wisbech-Hollander-Gibbon corner of county society: a sketch offered with judgment and propriety, and dropped when it became evident that Frances was not rising to a single one of the offered connections.

"And is he still abroad?"

"Yes, I think he has another year at the institute."

"I thought he was a very agreeable young man," said Frances, politely.

"Oh yes, *agreeable* enough," said Mary, with a droop of her eyes that made her look oddly like the absent Hunter: both, Frances thought, were sensual, one actively, one lazily so, but there was a marked resemblance.

"*Agreeable* enough," said Mary, "but terribly *idle*. Though he got himself married again, did you know? He married an Italian archaeologist. His first wife ran off with the doctor"—and she and Harold began to laugh, as at some private joke, but Frances, still inspecting them both eagerly for the secret of happy married sex, could not tell whether it was the laughter of happy criminals, or of happy innocents. Either way, they seemed more amused than censorious about Hunter's exploits, which they discussed at greater length over a second glass of sherry: then Frances rose, and said that she must go.

They saw her off, with detailed instructions of how to find her way back, and repeated invitations for more visits, while in the neighborhood: the weekend was upon them, she could see that it was likely she would have to stay till Monday, to get the funeral fixed. She had made her mind up about the cottage: if her father didn't want it (and it was inconceivable that he should), she would persuade him to let her buy it from him.

She drove back to the hotel, rang her father and reported on progress, rang her children and managed to avoid speaking to her ex-husband, and then put her feet up on the bed and wondered what to do. She half regretted leaving the Barnards, but hadn't really wanted to stay there till they bored her or she them. She had several telephone numbers in Tockley: the undertaker's, the vicar's, her cousin Janet Bird's. It seemed a little late to ring an undertaker, but she might well try the other two. Or maybe she would just go and have a meal and have an early night. But it seemed a little dull, as a prospect. The Barnards had engendered in her a social mood, which she needed to satisfy.

After a while, unable to make her mind up, she went down to the bar and had a drink and chatted to the barman and to a couple of businessmen and a barrister who claimed to be involved in the interesting case of the Tockley smell: then, fortified, she went back upstairs and rang the vicar. The vicar was eating his supper (she could hear noises of family meal-time in the background), but said she could go and see him in the morning. So she then rang Janet Bird.

Janet Bird was also eating her supper when Frances Wingate rang. The vicar had been eating shepherd's pie, cauliflower, and frozen peas. Janet Bird was eating shepherd's pie and frozen peas too, though she had no cauliflower. There is some limit to life's coincidences. Janet was alone, for her husband was out at a meeting, and she was waiting for something to happen, as usual. She was waiting with an increased expectation of restlessness, for so much that was unexpected had in fact happened of late: it no longer seemed unreasonable to expect more events.

So when the phone rang, she answered it almost hopefully. There was a woman on the other end, who said that she was called Frances Wingate, and that she was a great-niece of Constance Ollerenshaw, and had come up to fix the funeral, and that she was Janet's own second cousin or first cousin twice removed, or something like that, and she wondered if she could meet Janet. "I'm staying at the King's Head," she said, this confident unknown woman, "and I thought perhaps you might like to come round and have a drink with me. It would be interesting to hear more about Great-Aunt Con."

Janet panicked, slightly. What should she do? She couldn't go out, because of the baby. She wondered if this woman wanted to persecute her, like the press, for neglecting Constance.

"I can't come out," she said, "because of the baby."

"Oh, dear, what a shame." The other woman sounded
genuinely disappointed. There was a pause.

"But perhaps . . ." said Janet, reluctantly.

"Perhaps?" said Frances, encouragingly. Janet had not
been intending to issue an invitation, but she felt pushed into
saying, "Perhaps you could come round here. For a cup of
coffee."

That would be very nice, the other woman agreed. Frances
Wingate was her name, she repeated. They made arrangements: she would call round in an hour.

Janet returned to her cooling pie, rather alarmed by what
she had done. She had lost her appetite. It wasn't like her,
to invite anyone round like that. The other woman must have
forced her. She had forced her. Janet pushed a few peas
around the plate. It wasn't reasonable, she decided, to think
it might be an accusatory visit, for Frances Wingate was
Aunt Con's direct, own great-niece, therefore if there was
any guilt, any neglect, it was as much hers as Janet's.

Frances Wingate. She must be the granddaughter of Ted
Ollerenshaw, from Eel Cottage. The name was vaguely familiar: perhaps because Harold Barnard had mentioned it,
but she thought there was more to it than that.

She ate a cold mouthful, and carried her plate back into
the kitchen, and turned off the television, which had been
keeping her company with a program about a drought in
Africa. What had she offered? Coffee. It would have to be
Nescafé, she hoped Frances Wingate wouldn't mind. She got
out a tray, and two of the best wedding present cups. If she
put the coffee in a jug, perhaps she wouldn't notice. It all
tasted the same, really. She wished she had a piece of cake
to offer. But she never had a piece of cake. Thoughtfully, she
went back to the living room, and started to tidy up, thought
there was nothing to tidy. It was tidy already. And it was too
late to buy a new settee, a new chair, a new hearthrug, a new
house, to impress this visitor.

She was still aimlessly tidying magazines, like an actress
tidying an overneat stage set, when the doorbell rang, and as

it rang, as she saw the outline of Frances through the glazed
door, the connection she had been searching for came back
to her, recalled by the women's very silhouette. Of course,
she knew who Frances Wingate was. She had read a whole
article about her, a year or two ago, in the *Sunday Examiner*
color magazine. There had been a lot of photographs of her,
at home in her house in London, and in some kind of ruins
abroad, and there'd been a ridiculous interview, in which
Frances had said a lot of ridiculous things about being famous, and how she organized her home life, and whom she
had to dinner parties, and Janet had remembered it so well
because she had found it quite sickeningly offensive and irritating and silly, and here was this silly woman, standing on
her own doorstep, and ringing her own doorbell. Janet wished
she could remember what she had been famous for, but she
couldn't. Something ridiculous, no doubt. "I never use frozen vegetables," was one of the more infuriating things that
this woman had said, "because one of the things that I enjoy
most in life is queueing at the greengrocer's to see what
they've got, and I like peeling things too, I get a lot of pleasure out of peeling things." Too bad about the instant coffee,
thought Janet, as she opened the door.

The woman on the step was wearing a brown jacket, a
green man's sweater, and a black skirt unfashionably (or
fashionably) long, and her shoes were not at all clean. "Excuse me," were her first words, as she offered her hand to
be shaken, "I'm afraid I look rather a mess, I've had quite a
day, with one thing and another." Her hair could have done
with a brush, too.

"Oh, that's all right," said Janet, feebly. "There's only
me. My husband's still out, at this meeting." She was slightly
appeased by the fact that Frances wiped her shoes on the
mat: not very effectively, as the mud was dried on, but at
least it was a gesture.

"How lovely and cozy it is in here," said Frances, following Janet into the lounge, and taking it all in—the cheap
carpet, the cheap modern furniture, the pretentious orange

curtains, the pretentious Swedish candles, the desolate bleak
wilderness of boredom, the nest of coffee tables, the small,
not-quite-full bookshelf, the overfull magazine rack, the reproduction of a Dufy painting, the white Formica table, the
vase of dried leaves. "How nice," said Frances, insincerely,
as she allowed herself to be settled by the electric fire, in an
armchair. She warmed her hands in front of the fire. "How
nice to be able to get warm," she repeated. "I'm afraid I
came up without a proper coat, I've only just got back from
Africa, and I didn't have time to go and collect one."

It wasn't a good opening.

"From Africa?" said Janet, frostily, without interest. "I'll
get you a cup of coffee," said Janet.

Frances's heart sank, as she sat there for a moment on her
own. It was going to be ghastly. There was no point in having
come round at all; she'd have been better off ringing the
undertaker, or chatting up the barman in the hotel. She knew
this kind of house all too well: she knew all too many people
like Janet, tight-mouthed, slightly sour, overtidy (she looked
with alarm around the impeccable, polished, dull room),
critical, mean, not yet quite hardened into irremediable bitterness, but well on the way toward it. Frances shivered, and
reached out her hands to the red rings and the dangerous red
ache of the fire in the mushroom-tiled hearth (they were still
designing hearths from the thirties, up here), and watched
the big veins rise in the back of her hands. In so many houses
like this she had sipped glasses of sherry, drunk cups of
coffee, eaten small cakes (sometimes rather good cakes, for
people still bake, in some parts of the provinces), and listened to discussions about the education system, while waiting to catch her train home after a lecture, while waiting to
give a lecture. How many bitter little domestic disputes, how
many professional meannesses, how many ungenerous remarks she had witnessed in rooms like this, bred out of the
tiles and the white plaster walls. How many discussions about
television programs she had never seen, how many attempts
to pull the conversation away from television, how many

savage comments on heads of departments unfairly promoted, on the ignorance or stupidity of schoolchildren and students, on public figures arbitrarily disliked, on the distance from or closeness to London: how many insults she had received, in such rooms, from those whose only aim had seemed to be to score. Janet's husband must be a teacher: the room bore so familiar a stamp. The only endurable subject in such a place was children: the only subject which would bring flickers of grace, of humanity, of feeling.

"How old is your baby?" she asked, politely, when Janet brought in the tray with the coffee.

"Oh, he's nearly one," said Janet. She handed her a cup. "I'm sorry," she said, not meaning to, "that I haven't got any cake. Or even any cookies."

"Oh, I never eat cake," said Frances, untruthfully. "And what's he called, your baby?"

"Hugh."

"That's funny. My brother's called Hugh. Is it a family name, do you think?"

"Not that I know of. I called him Hugh because it wasn't a family name."

"Funny, that we should meet like this," said Frances, uneasily.

They got on badly. Janet was stiff, nervous, resentful: Frances simply wished she hadn't bothered, and wondered why she had inflicted on herself such a dull and disagreeable hour. She was wondering how soon she could safely leave. She hadn't in fact eaten anything since lunch, except a few olives and gherkins and peanuts, and was beginning to feel rather hungry: a piece of cake would have been quite welcome. She could tell that Janet didn't like her at all, but hadn't any idea how to set about interesting her, nor could she quite find the will to try. They talked, a little, about Constance, and her will, and the cottage and what would happen to it: Frances sympathized, formally, over Janet's troubles with the press and TV, thinking privately that either the girl was a fool to let herself in for the publicity, or that she had secretly enjoyed the thrill: she suspected the latter, for there is no limit to people's morbidity, and up here, any- thing must have been better than the normal tedium of life. They agreed that Constance's death was nobody's fault, and nobody need feel guilty. They uttered a good many plat- itudes, in the course of this discussion.

Janet's husband, it turned out, wasn't a teacher; he was a chemist, who worked on plastics. That figured, too. Janet inquired politely about Frances's visit to Africa: Frances re- plied briefly, well aware that a description of Adra would be unlikely to go down well. They talked, a little, about Eel Cottage, and Janet explained that the present owners were health-food people: Frances was quite pleased to hear this, it fitted in well with her conjectures on her visit in the sum- mer. All in all, it seemed a reasonable fate, that the Eel should have ended up like that.

The conversation slumped. Janet offered another cup of coffee, Frances declined. She looked at her watch, covertly. It was nine o'clock: too late for a meal in the hotel, but she'd noticed a Chinese restaurant and an Indian one, either of which would do.

"Would you want to come to the funeral?" she asked, for want of anything better to say. "When I get it organized?"

"I don't see the point, really," said Janet. She paused. "I've never been to a funeral," she added.

"There has to be a first time for everything," said Fran- ces, fatuously. She felt sorry for Janet Bird, cooped up here with her little baby, but it wasn't her fault, what could she do?

"Well, perhaps I will," said Janet. And she looked at Frances, and said, "After all, there's not much else to do around here, is there?"

Frances laughed. "That's one way of putting it," she said. She reached for her bag. She would have one cigarette, and then she would go. "Do you mind if I smoke? Would you like one?"

Frances hardly ever smoked: she smoked intermittently,

always less than a packet a week. Sometimes a packet would stay in her bag till it fell apart. Janet accepted one, to her surprise. Things seemed slightly, just marginally better, as Frances leaned forward with a lighted match.

"I read an article about you," said Janet, as she neatly knocked ash into a Zodiac-patterned ashtray. "In the *Sunday Examiner*."

"Oh, God," said Frances, "how ghastly. Did you really? I always hope people won't really read that kind of rubbish. I never do. But I suppose somebody must. It was horrible, didn't you think?"

"Your house looked very nice," said Janet, primly.

"It is very nice. I quite liked those photos, but I've never been able to make them send me copies. And the African ones were really very good."

"Where were they taken?"

"In Carthage. They flew out, specially. I kept saying, what a waste of money, why don't you fake it, you could easily make my back garden look like Carthage, but they wouldn't. They're purists, photographers."

Janet looked resentful still, as well she might: but she also looked faintly interested. Frances began to feel that a little perseverance might well effect some kind of a thaw, and was thinking what a pity it was that they hadn't got a drink (she could really have done with a drink) when the phone went. Janet answered it with the air of one who has not too much expected a call. Frances watched her as she spoke. It was clearly her husband on the line: Frances saw her whole body stiffen. Poor woman, she thought, poor woman. She knew that look. So that was how it was. She might have known.

The husband was saying he would be back soon, and was bringing a friend, and would she put the kettle on, or something along those lines, because Janet answered, "But I've got somebody here, myself."

This did not go down well, for Janet continued to defend herself: no, it hadn't been pre-arranged, no, she couldn't have told him about it earlier, yes, she supposed there might be enough shepherd's pie left for two. By the time she put the phone down, she was looking faintly desperate, and anxious, as though she knew too well that she had revealed too much.

"Is that your husband on his way home?" said Frances, trying to be helpful. "Perhaps I'd better push off, he's probably had quite enough of the Ollerenshaw family lately."

"No, don't go," said Janet. "He won't mind."

He so obviously would and did mind that Frances, watching that shadow of terror on Janet's face, felt quite overcome with sympathy. How could she leave her here, to await such a homecoming? Yet how could she stay, so unwelcome?

"I'll tell you what," said Frances. "I've had an idea. When your husband and his friend get back, why don't you come out with me for an hour? We could have a drink at the hotel, or something. That would be more of a pleasant change than a funeral."

"Oh, I don't see how I could," said Janet.

"Of course you could," said Frances, in a healthy, bullying tone. "It's good for one, to get out every now and then. I know what it's like, with small babies. They're a terrible tie."

"*You* don't seem to have found them very tying," said Janet, with spiriting asperity.

"Oh, I don't know," said Frances. "Even I've stayed at home once in a while."

She could see that Janet was going to agree: it seemed a good plan, and once agreed, they began to get on better.

"You ought to make your husband baby-sit every now and then," said Frances. "On principle."

"Oh, he does offer, sometimes," said Janet. "But he usually offers when he knows I don't want to go."

"Well, there's not much he can do about it this time. We'll present him with a fait accompli. We'll say we've got to go and discuss your great-aunt's will. He can't do anything about that, can he?"

"I don't suppose so," said Janet. And then added, surprisingly, "I don't suppose he could do much about anything I really decided to do. It's just that I can't decide myself."

"Well, there's not much scope for action, with a baby around. You'll have to wait a bit."

"Yes, I will."

"You know," said Frances, who was beginning to think that the curtains weren't so pretentious after all, they were really quite an attractive shade of orange, and she rather liked the red piano, "you know, you're the second new relation I've found recently. It's just occurred to me, you must know David Ollerenshaw, he must be your first cousin, unless I've got everything hopelessly mixed up."

Janet did, of course, know David: they discussed David, happily. How much easier conversation becomes, with a person in common: Frances felt that the Ollerenshaw network might well one day approach the density of the Sinclair-Davieses. Janet had known David since childhood, of course, though he had been some years older than she: he had always been regarded as the clever one of the family, rather more attractively clever than his father, whom nobody had ever liked. He had "turned his nose up," Janet said, implying that she too thought the phrase funny: and as for his mother, as for Auntie Evie—well, she had been a very unpopular character, critical, carping, nothing good enough for her, and religious, too. There was one good thing you could say for the Ollerenshaws, at least they had never been religious. They hadn't gone round nosing into other people's affairs, telling other people what to do. Poor David, said Frances, he must have had a tough childhood. Yes, said Janet, but he was always so nice, he was always so nice to me, he was good natured. I was nothing, I was just another little cousin, but he was always nice to me. Why shouldn't he have been, said Frances, and Janet said, oh, I don't know, when I was a child I never expected anyone to be nice to me. I haven't seen him for years, she said.

"He's never shown any signs of getting married, has he?" said Frances, vulgarly curious, as usual, about other people's

sex lives, and wondering whether her original hazard of repressed or unacknowledged homosexuality might be correct.

"Not that I know of," said Janet. "But then, I really haven't
heard much of him for years. Not since he started all these
travels. I think the last time I saw him was the day he got his
degree. I must have been about fourteen. His parents gave
this horrible party and we all went of to Manchester to see
David shown off—poor old David, he *did* look miserable. I
was miserable too, I was wearing a dreadful green dress that
didn't fit. My party dress." She laughed. "I think I was so
upset by how awful I looked that I hardly spoke to him. And
his father made this terrible speech, about how he had encouraged David, and bought him books, and made him work,
and all that—you'd have thought he'd got the degree himself
the way he carried on, and David looked so embarrassed,
though I suppose in a way it was true, do you think? It's a
terrible thing, what parents do to their children. Don't you
think?"

Frances did think so, and they talked for a while of their
non-Ollerenshaw mothers and their Ollerenshaw fathers, and
what they felt about them: they agreed that their fathers, who
seemed to share a capacity for staring into space, had, unlike
David's father, been noninterventionists of the first order,
and had erred, if at all, in the direction of neglect and indif-
ference. "I suppose one's never satisfied," said Frances.

"Sometimes I wonder about what will happen to my
baby," said Janet. "It's such a responsibility, trying to bring
up a baby. Sometimes I feel like giving up. But of course,
that's the only thing one can't do."

"It doesn't seem so bad, as they begin to grow up," said
Frances. "They begin to seem so obviously themselves. One
doesn't feel so directly responsible, when they grow older.
My eldest will be old enough to get married, next year."

"That's comforting," said Janet, without a flicker of surprise: usually, when Frances made such a remark, people
hastened to tell her that she looked far too young to have so
old a child. Either those days were over, and she looked her

considerable age, or Janet was herself so young that she regarded Frances as a member of a different generation. Either
way, Frances found she did not mind. It was of course true
that Daisy was old enough to marry, legally, next year, though
probably she would not: the problems of Stephen and his
young wife might one day be hers. (Where was Stephen? She
must ring Natasha, in the morning, for more news.)

There was a silence. Both women stared at the bar of the
fire, contemplative. "I know what you mean," said Janet,
"about being obviously themselves. They are, of course. But
I just don't see how it happens. I mean . . ." she hesitated,
unused to such concepts, such conversations, "I mean, I feel
I am myself, and that I've got to look after it. But I don't
know what it is. I know it's there, that's all. That's why I
don't think it was at all awful about Aunt Con, she was being
herself, if you know what I mean, everyone could see what
she was being." She paused, gathered courage, went on.
"And as for you, it's easy for you to know who you are. Even
the *Examiner* color supplement tells you who you are. Anyway" (still slightly reproachful) "I can tell from looking at
you, who you are."

"How do you mean?" asked Frances. Janet Bird was not
a fool, not a fool at all. She was so pleased, so grateful, that
she had thought of ringing her.

"Well, you know what I mean," said Janet Bird, gesturing, in a slightly camp, a surprisingly confident manner, at
Frances's jersey, and her muddy shoes. "I mean to say, look
at your clothes. When would I ever dress up like that?"

"I'm not *dressed* up," wailed Frances, "this is what I
wear, I can't help it. And you mustn't," she continued, well
aware of the issues, "you mustn't get cross about a silly
article in a paper, I never know what to say, but one has to
say *something*, after all. . . ."

"It said you liked peeling vegetables," said Janet. "That
must have been a lie. Surely that must have been a lie."

Frances considered for an instant. It had in fact been the
truth, that remark, though a truth, she agreed, fit only for

Pseud's Corner: she did like peeling potatoes, mushrooms, carrots, leeks, even the crazy Jerusalem artichoke. Truth, however, is relative. "Yes," she agreed, "of course it was a lie."

On the basis of such a mutual deception (for Janet too, as we have seen, liked peeling vegetables), they felt quite friendly.

"You know," said Janet, "when all this row came up, I was interviewed on the television. The local news. They made me up to look like somebody quite different. And I thought, why isn't that person me? And why could I never do that for myself? Interesting, isn't it?"

Frances was just about to reply that it was indeed extremely interesting, and that it was the kind of question that had often perplexed her, when they heard a car pull up outside, and the sound of footsteps. Both fell silent, in a moment of conspiracy. Frances herself was used to such homecomings; she felt considerable womanly solidarity with her new cousin. "Don't forget," she said (whispering, despite herself just very slightly nervous at the thought of the advent of a cross man, even though it was the advent of a cross twenty-nine-year-old man who was in no way her own problem), "don't forget, you've got to come out with me. We've got to talk about a funeral."

"All right," whispered Janet.

And in walked her husband Mark, and his colleague Bill David. Frances rose to her feet to greet them, prepared (indeed intending) to be charming, but she could see at once that there was going to be little opportunity to charm Mark Bird: he was one of those men on whom effort is wasted, one of those men on whom she never managed to have any effect at all. Neatly dressed, well-shaven, angry with some permanent grievance, he stood there on his own hearth, rocking backward and forward slightly, while Janet made introductions, explained (rather bravely, Frances thought) her own immediate plans, and disappeared into the kitchen to warm up the portion of shepherd's pie. "You've just been out to a meeting, Janet tells me," said Frances, unable to prevent herself from social niceties, "about a new pedestrian precinct, is that right?" Mark nodded. "You take an interest in local politics?"

"Well, somebody has to," said Mark. "If we don't speak up, there are others who will." He implied dark moneyed storms of malice, of corruption.

Frances tried to guess which side he would be on—for or against the precinct—and found that she had no idea: Janet hadn't been interested enough to tell her. "Tell me," she asked, smiling brightly at Mark and Bill, "which side did you go to support, the anti-precinct, or the pro-precinct?"

Mark Bird stared at her in feigned, in overdone horror. " 'Which side,' did you say?" he said, rudely, as though the question had betrayed imbecility.

"Yes, that's what I said," said Frances snappily. What a horrid little bully, she thought to herself.

"Do you mean to say," said Mark, "that there are still people in the British Isles who don't realize that the pedestrian precinct was the most"—and Frances still, even at this point, couldn't tell if he was going to say "brilliant" or "disastrous"—"one of the most"—and the word, when it came, was spat out with a most unpleasant vehemence—"*outmoded* concepts in town planning?"

"Come, come now, Mark," said Bill, uneasily, embarrassed, marginally more susceptible to the presence of a woman and a stranger: "Come along, you know that's not quite true, there are still areas where a precinct might be a perfectly appropriate way of dealing with shopping problems—"

"But we're talking about *Tockley*," said Mark, with all the violence of illogic. "We're not talking about all those other areas, we're talking about Tockley, or *I* am, anyway."

"Yes, yes," said Frances, soothingly. "Do explain to me why it is that a pedestrian precinct would be so unsuitable in Tockley."

They explained, Bill fairly politely, Mark with such

weighted innuendoes about her ignorance and folly that she
hoped, for Janet's sake, that Janet couldn't hear through
the hatch. How extraordinary people are, she thought, as she
listened to Mark and Bill describe town planning acts, and
condemn the views of distinguished architects, and rail
against the Council and the Ministry of Transport and the
Department of the Environment and a local solicitor: how
amazing, to tell me all this, when all I asked was a polite
question, and when, according to their evident assessment of
my intellect, I am quite incapable of following a single word
that they are saying.

They were in the process of informing her about car parking statistics in towns of comparable size, sparing her none
of the figures, and gazing at her accusingly as though she
would, if given a chance, reveal some other dangerous her-
esy, when Janet came back, with her coat already on.

"I won't be late back," she said to Mark. "Hugh won't
wake, he's been sleeping much better lately, but if he does,
we'll be at—at the King's Head, won't we—er, won't we,
Frances?"

The use of the Christian name was an act of marital defi-
ance: Mark registered it, but at the same time registered the
name of the hotel where Frances was staying. There was
nothing wrong with the King's Head: it was the best hotel in
town, a hotel where he certainly could not afford to eat whenever he fancied, a hotel where bar and restaurant had witnessed many a transaction of civic importance. Quickly,
Mark changed his tack, and looked at Frances with something remarkably like an old-fashioned leer.

"Well, don't have too much to drink, you girls, will you?"
he said. "Janet's got a very weak head, I'm afraid. Half a
glass of sherry and she's half seas over."

What an extraordinary remark, thought Frances, but all
she said was, "Oh, you needn't worry, I'll look after her and
get her back all right."

"Is that your car outside?" said Mark, adding more to his
mental calculations about Frances's status. A horrid man,

whatever could have gone wrong with him? He was stiff and unnatural, and his head didn't properly fit on his neck.

"Yes, that's mine," she agreed. She moved toward the door. "We'd better get off," she said, "or we'll never get back again, will we?"

He laughed at this nonpleasantry, a hard, unnatural, amused laugh, and followed them to the door to see them out. There stood her car, parked at the end of the cement path. She looked at it with longing. She wanted to get moving, claustrophobia was sweeping rapidly over her, she would have felt frantic if she had had to hang around a moment longer, waiting for a taxi.

Safely in the car, she turned to Janet, as she started the engine, and asked, "Do you drive?" She already knew the answer. Janet shook her head. "Mark tried to teach me once, but I don't think I'd ever be able to. And then there wouldn't be much point, because Mark always takes the car to get to work. . . ."

Her voice trailed away: Frances could see it all, the caged days, the walks with the pram, and not even a car at the end of the garden path. No way out. She would buy Janet a large drink, at the King's Head.

The town looked good, in the night. They drove down the dark High Street. The Indian restaurant was still open: so was the Great Wall of China. Everything else was shut. The church spire, the famous church spire, was floodlit. Tedium and beauty lay like a quiet pall. How can one have content, without content?

The hotel was brightly lit, welcoming, its large front doors open. Cars were leaving the parking lot: there was activity, movement, the sound of voices and laughter. Friday night, the liveliest night of the week. Frances parked the car, and she and Janet got out, and walked up the steps of the hotel and through its large revolving doors. The porter smiled, nodded, came up to Frances. "Dr. Wingate?" he said, politely. "Two gentlemen were looking for you, madam. I told them I didn't know when you'd be back, but they said they'd wait. They're in the bar, madam." He looked at the ornate gilt clock in the high hall. "Been there some time, now," he said.

"Oh, dear," said Frances, to Janet, as they crossed to the entrance of the bar. "I wonder who that could be?" A solicitor, an undertaker, a vicar, her brother: one or two of these, she thought it might be. But it wasn't. There, in the bar at the King's Head, looking, as the porter had said, as though they had been there for some time, sat David Ollerenshaw and Karel Schmidt.

For the second time in his life, Karel Schmidt had the satisfaction of seeing Frances Wingate's face turn gray with shock. She stood there in the door of the bar, gaping, her eyes fixed; her mouth dropped open and all the blood poured out of her, leaving her that peculiar tint of yellow-gray that had at first so enraptured him. Her recovery was terrific. She took a deep breath—he could see her, right across the room, take a deep breath, as though gasping for air—and as he rose to his feet, she ploughed toward him, the color coming back, life coming back, everything returning to its proper place, her hair settling back on the nape of her neck, for there he was, there was Karel, looking exactly, but exactly like Karel himself.

She reached their table, stopped, stared again, smiled. "What on earth, but what on earth, are you two doing here?" she asked.

"Looking for you, of course," said Karel.

"Whatever for?" said Frances, already on the attack: she was not one to succumb too easily to surprise tactics.

"I got your postcard, that's why," said Karel. "I got it a day or two ago. I've been looking for you ever since. All over the place."

"You got my postcard?" she repeated, stupidly. And then began to laugh. "But of course you got my postcard," she said. "Of course that would be it. I must have known you couldn't have had it any earlier. Can I sit down?"

She pulled herself a chair, pulled one out for Janet. She sat down by Karel, she put her hand on his sleeve. "I need a drink," she said. "Shall we have a drink?" She peered more closely at Karel. "My goodness me, Karel," she said in a reproving, maternal, amazed tone. "My goodness me, you do look ill. Whatever have you been doing to yourself?"

Over a drink and some small onions (I still haven't eaten, thought Frances to herself, through the confusion), he explained what he had been doing to himself, and she explained what she had been doing to herself, and Janet and David explained what they were up to also. The explanations took some time, and by the end of them everybody was in an elated mood, even the sickly Karel, whose arm was by now redder and more swollen than ever. "Well, well, well," said Frances happily, "this is quite an evening, don't you think? More fun than a funeral, Janet, don't you think?" And both women laughed, at their own joke.

After a while it emerged that neither Karel nor David had eaten either, and the bar had run out of onions and crisps. "You should have eaten earlier," said Frances, "especially when you're so ill."

"I didn't want to miss you," said Karel.

"Well, you've been missing me for months and months now, I can't see what difference an hour or two would have made. You might have warned me, you know. When I saw you, I nearly died of shock."

"So I saw," he said.

They looked at each other: there they both were, again, after all. No wonder they were pleased with themselves.

David was quite pleased with himself, too. He had organized Karel, a hopeless traveler, with exemplary efficiency: he had tracked Frances down like a detective, and here, as a reward for his efforts, was his own little cousin Jan, looking quite pink and cheerful, and giggling rather a lot with excitement and gin and tonic. It was all very satisfactory.

One could always rely on Frances, thought Karel, to rise

to an occasion. They would have to have something to eat, but she would know what to do. He sat back, admiringly, and watched her.

"Well, this is quite a party," said Frances, as though she had arranged it all herself. "I'll tell you what I'm going to do. I'm going to go and get one last round of drinks, then I'm going to find us somewhere for a meal. You'll come too, won't you, Janet? Janet only had shepherd's pie," she told the others, "she can surely manage another meal."

Janet felt that she could quite easily eat another meal. Excitement makes one hungry.

They watched Frances depart to the bar, then disappear to the telephone: the drinks arrived on a tray, and as they were drinking them, she returned triumphant.

"There," she said, "I've fixed it all up. There's a restaurant in a village five miles out which does late meals, and they'll be delighted to see us in half an hour. We'll get a cab off the station rank, I think we're in no state for driving. There," she said, sinking down, picking up her glass, "There, what about that for efficiency?"

"Full marks, I think," said David. "And now, tell me some more about Constance."

"No, no, we've talked enough about Constance, I wanted to hear about Karel in Africa. Was he terribly cross to find I'd already left?"

"I think he was past being cross, by that stage," said David, and obediently, as they finished their drinks and went out again into the night and the smell of the beet, and picked a cab up from the rank just outside the door, he described Karel's arrival, and told Frances what Patsy had said, what Spirelli had said, what the hotel manager had said, and how Karel had refused to leap into the swimming pool. The dark night passed by, and the air grew clearer and Frances listened, and held Karel's hand. It was all right, of course it was all right. The restaurant (recommended through a quick phone call to Harold Barnard) was all right too: it was a country inn, a cheery mixture of ancient and modern, with slot machines in the bar, and little pink lampshades in the dining room. The food, as Harold Barnard had promised, was excellent, and the clients (businessmen, professional men) looked prosperous and happy and fat, as they munched their way through smoked salmon and fried whitebait and homemade pâté glistening with little green peppers and brochettes of scallop and nice red tournedos and green salads and spinach and a delicious raspberry flan. Janet, who had often heard tell of this place (it was the only local Good Food place, and Mark tended to sneer at it and its clientele because it was so expensive), looked around her with satisfaction: no doubt most of what Mark said about it was true, but it wasn't true (as he asserted) that the food wasn't good, and she was rather glad that Frances's telephone call had interrupted her shepherd's pie, because this was much, much more agreeable.

The only person who didn't seem to be doing too well with his dinner was Karel. He managed his soup, but began to slow down rather noticeably on the steak.

But in the hall, on the way out, waiting for the women to emerge from the cloakroom, he inserted an idle coin into the slot machine, and won the jackpot. It seemed appropriate. He filled his pockets with silver shillings. Frances, flashing credit cards, had paid the enormous bill for dinner: he would make it up to her, later.

The air outside, as they stood and waited for the cab to arrive to pick them up again, was cool and dank. A light rain was falling. They waited in the stable yard, where loose boxes now housed Jaguars and Mercedes, and smelled the cold smell of grass and stone, a vestigial scent of straw and apples, a smell of raw-turned earth. "England," said David, breathing it in. "How lovely to be in England. I don't know why one ever goes away."

By the time Frances got Karel to bed, he was really rather ill. She put him in the twin bed, where she had so often imagined him, and examined his bare arm. It was swollen.

She stroked it, anxiously, then went to look for her thermometer. He sat and watched her, as she looked through her bag.

"I think I'm delirious," he said, as she turned back to him. She advanced upon him, put the thermometer in his mouth, and sat there by him, holding his hand, like a nurse.

"You're silly," she said. "You don't look after yourself properly. Fancy rushing off there like that, when I was coming home in a couple of days anyway. Whatever did you go and do that for? Apart from anything else, what a terrible waste of money."

Karel took the thermometer out. "I wanted to impress you," he said. He put it back in again, then took it out to add. "It was a gesture, that's all."

"It certainly was," agreed Frances, kicking off her shoes, and starting to peel off her stockings. Her feet ached. It had been a very long day. "If you ask me," she said, wondering how her feet had managed to get so dirty, through shoes and stockings, "it was a very *childish* gesture. You're not twenty-one now, you know."

"No, I know. It was my last fling."

She looked at the thermometer. His temperature was up, by a degree and a half.

"Do you think you've got cholera?" she asked him. "Is it one of those things where they give you a mild dose?"

"I haven't got any other cholera symptoms, have I?"

"No, I don't suppose you can have got cholera. You're probably just suffering from exhaustion."

"Your cousin David's got stamina, hasn't he? I've been dragging him all over the place, and he never turned a hair."

"He's used to it."

She sat down on his bed. She regarded him. "You'd better drink a lot of water," she said, finally, thoughtfully. "I'll go and get you a glass or two."

She organized him, as best she could: three glasses of water, some soluble aspirin.

"I should have made you go to bed much earlier," she said. "It was my fault, dragging you off for a fancy meal."

"One has to eat."

She took off her large green sweater, and threw it onto a chair. She was wearing a familiar black garment underneath it. She had had it for years. She didn't look any different, at all.

"Come to bed," he said.

She considered it. "I don't know if I should, really," she said. "I don't think it would do you any good."

"We could try."

"We could just hold each other," she said, judiciously. "I think that would be all right. Though it's a very small bed. They don't seem to make proper beds these days."

She undressed, went into the bathroom, brushed her teeth, returned. "I love you, Karel," she said, staring down at him. "I always did, you know."

And she got into the small bed.

An hour later, she had to get out again, and go back to her own bed. It was intolerable, in bed with Karel: he was burning hot to the touch, and the bed was too narrow to escape. The discomfort was appalling: treacherously, she abandoned him, yet again. He tossed and moaned. "Oh, fucking hell," she heard him muttering to himself in familiar style. Uneasily, amused, she fell asleep. There he was again, after all, and after all, there was plenty of time.

Frances found herself busy in the morning. She had to get a doctor for Karel, an undertaker and a vicar for Aunt Constance: she had to ring her children, to see if Anthony and Sheila could hang on to them for a day or two more; to ring Natasha, to see if there was any news of Stephen, and her father, for news of her mother. All these calls went off reasonably well, apart from the one to Natasha: there was no news of Stephen, or his baby. Both had disappeared completely. Frances stored this information: she would get it out, to worry about later.

The doctor said Karel ought to stay in bed. So he stayed there, getting hotter and hotter. I'd been so looking forward to having a good feel of you, said Frances, but it's as though there's some spell on you, to make me wait. She laid her hand on the smooth skin of his shoulder. "I love your shoulder *particularly*," she said, "but it really is too hot." She lent him a copy of *The Charterhouse of Parma* to read while she went off to look for David and an undertaker.

She was rather glad of David's moral support with the undertaker: not that he wasn't a nice man, he was very pleasant and made the negotiations as simple as possible, but it was a relief to have somebody else there. It seemed so respectable, to be talking to an undertaker with one's own cousin. They ordered a plain oak coffin: not a very large one. As they all realized, though not quite sure how to express it, there hadn't been much left of Constance.

"A funny business, funeral rites," said Frances, as she drove David along a leafy suburban road to see the vicar, Mr. Fox. "What are you going to have done with yours?"

"I haven't really thought about it much," said David. "Leave it to medical research, do you think?"

"You'd have thought they'd get far too many corpses left to them," said Frances. "An embarrassment of corpses."

"I wonder why she wanted to be buried in unhallowed ground. Seems a bit odd, doesn't it?"

"A sense of guilt, do you suppose? Thought she wasn't worthy. Or perhaps she just hated the church. There was some mixup, with a vicar."

"Really? I can't imagine anyone caring tuppence about hallowed or unhallowed ground. But people do. Murderers' fathers, and people like that. People are odd."

"All superstition, you think?" said Frances, as she turned up the vicar's pebbled drive. Two small children were playing in the drive: they stared up resentfully as the car passed them. Another child was yelling in a shrubbery, and Mrs. Fox, who opened the door to them, was covered in wet paint, and had her hair done up in a towel. "I'm just doing a bit of decorating," she said, "excuse me," and disappeared with her paint brush into the back regions of the large Victorian house.

It needed a bit of decorating, Frances thought. She had rarely seen a home so subdued to the demands of children. Toys, bicycles, strollers, lay about: the walls were covered in drawings and graffiti. It was going to be a long day's work for Mrs. Fox.

Mr. Fox, who received them in his study, was very pleased with himself. He had solved the problem of unhallowed ground to his own great satisfaction. "It's simple," he said, "we'll bury her in the new plot that's just been annexed on to St. Martin's at Barton. She didn't specify St. Oswald's, did she? It's very overcrowded at St. Oswald's. No, we'll slip her into the new extension at St. Martin's. It's being consecrated at the end of next week. So we're just in time." Frances wondered whether Constance might not have objected to being consecrated after interment, but the vicar, a casuist, waved aside this objection. "No, no," he said, "how could she object? One can't be *too* particular, can one? Think how much simpler it will be, in a properly organized cemetery. It's a very pleasant church, St. Martin's. She must have known it well. After all, one can't go burying old ladies at the bottom of the garden, can one? Have a glass of sherry."

It was too early for sherry, by any standards: certainly, Frances would have thought, by a vicar's standards. Perhaps he was absentminded. "You will say a few words, though, won't you?" she asked him. "As Constance requested?"

"Well, it wasn't me particularly she requested, as you know," said Mr. Fox, "and I can't say I ever met the old lady. But I'll do my best. I'll do my best. Life's rich pattern made richer by its eccentrics, something along those lines? We all rest in peace with God, however lonely our chosen paths?"

He laughed, in a disconcerting way, and proceeded to tell them about the interesting ceremony of consecration: a time-hallowed ritual, he said, and really rather affecting. The priest walks around the plot, reading these words—He started to look the service up, but couldn't find the right reference book, which wasn't surprising, as his study was as confused as the

rest of the house, a sea of papers and books and bits of
woodwork and small models of airplanes. Too many small
children had driven him mad, thought Frances compassion-
ately, as she watched him scrabble unsuccessfully through
his piles of books. They arranged that the funeral should take
place on Monday. Despite the air of confusion, he had been,
she realized, remarkably efficient on their behalf. She thanked
him.

Back they went to Karel, who was getting very bored with
The Charterhouse of Parma. "I'm not up to this serious
stuff," he pleaded. "Do get me something with a bit less
action in it. Please."

They promised to find him something, and went off to call
on Harold Barnard to report on progress. On the way back
they bought Karel a copy of the latest Kingsley Amis from
W. H. Smith's. "That's more like it," he said.

David and Frances had lunch downstairs in the hotel, but
Karel had to have his in bed. He lay there, drinking cream
of vegetable soup, and thinking of all the things he would do
to Frances when he was well enough to do them. He had to
stay in bed the next day too, but on Monday, he was well
enough to get up for the funeral: on Tuesday, he would return
to work.

The funeral was a very odd affair. It was attended by Frances and Karel, David and Janet, Sir Frank Ollerenshaw, and
Frances's brother Hugh: also by Mr. Fox, Harold Barnard,
and a photographer or two from the local press. (The national
press, as Frances had hoped, had completely forgotten the
life and death of Constance, and were busily engaged upon
exposing corruption in the police force, an enterprise much
more worthy of their talents.) The ceremony took place at
three o'clock in the afternoon: before it, the relatives (including Karel, as an honorary relative) lunched together at
the King's Head. Frances had been afraid the occasion might
prove rather trying, but to her surprise and relief her father
assumed his charming public role, and set out to be charming
to David and Janet, whose very existence he had hitherto

ignored: he was also quite excessively charming to Karel.
Indeed, his deference to Karel could only be regarded with
suspicion, both she and Karel independently decided, but
neither chose to reject it, and both pursued, politely, and
with the most profound inner satisfaction, their feet hooked
together beneath the table, a conversation about the future
expansion of the functions of the polytechnics, and whether
they should draw closer or not to the university system. Hugh,
more inclined than his father to show a primitive jealousy of
Karel, tried at first to resist the spectacle of what seemed to
be a fait accompli, but after a while he thawed out, made a
few louche innuendoes, and turned the conversation to the
old days at the Eel.

Frances had never expected to hear her father speak of his
childhood, nor was she satisfied now. But he did say, after a
while, as they reached the crystallized Stilton, "I wouldn't
mind a drive, to look at the old places, after we've buried
Aunt Con."

They buried Aunt Con, as Mr. Fox had suggested, in the
new extension of St. Martin's churchyard. The church was
built of a golden stone, peculiar to a small locality of the
county: it crumbled and deepened in the dark afternoon air,
yellow gold, soft, old. The dark yews and cypresses grew
sadly and suitably, and little rose bushes stood amongst
the graves, with the perpetual rose blossoming, that ever-
flowering bloom, crinkled and classic. On the graves lay
green chips, and in the vases rotted chrysanthemums. The
churchyard extension lay over the yellow lichen-covered
dense decaying churchyard wall: it looked like a field: it was
a field. Constance Ollerenshaw's grave was of yellow clay,
for the earth here was yellow. Beyond the field was the river,
that flowed in the end, wide and flat, into the North Sea, and
beside it stood cows, black and white, as on a pastoral vase,
a Doulton vase. (In the calm estuary of this river John Lincoln, lover of Constance Ollerenshaw, had drowned, not quite
by accident, more than half a century ago. He had been
drinking, or so it was said at the time.)

Karel, raising his eyes from the too open earth, and staring at the middle distance where the cows browsed, peacefully, as though in another age, reflected on his own passion for the rural England he saw so rarely, his haven, his place of exile, his unknown land, his subject, his livelihood: and on Frances, who came from this land. The eighteenth-century cows munched on, undisturbed, in their golden age, by the still waters, by the bending willows, in the autumn light. His own, and not his own. He was feeling better, out in the open air.

Janet was gazing at some interesting withered plants grow-ing at the foot of the wall. They were tall and gray and in-teresting with mildew of some sort: a silvery poisonous gray. She was thinking about the new houses that had been built just outside the church, on what had been a village green. They were all still for sale, though they had been finished for some time. No doubt a fancy price was being asked. She was not surprised that nobody wanted to buy them, for though the situation was pretty, the houses themselves were a most extraordinary shape: they had sliced and leaning roofs, like the blocks of cheese her father used to cut in the old shop in the old days, a shape perfectly appropriate for cheese, but not at all for houses. They had quite ruined the approach to the church. Barton had once been a pretty village. Why hadn't Mark and his mates attached themselves in the preservation of Church Lane, Barton, instead of to the gravel pits and the shopping precincts?

David Ollerenshaw was looking up at the weathercock, as the coffin was lowered: he noted that it was bright green. Whereas the four arrows on the church tower in the last vil-lage they had passed had been cleaned, and shone gold like shafts of sunlight. He thought about his gunmetal cigarette lighter, lying in a crevice on Handa Island, and wondered what color it had turned by now. He also wondered what color Aunt Constance had turned by now. How much pleas-anter the inorganic is, than the organic. He thought Sir Frank Ollerenshaw a brave man, to have mastered the dissection of newts, and to have solved the obscure and living mysteries of their biochemistry. He had never liked to admit it, even to himself, but he had never cared for zoology at school: squeamish, like a girl, he had flinched from the eyes of cows and the muscles of frogs. The inorganic was pure. He closed his hand in his pocket, on his stream topaz. Frances, he thought, was in a way her father's daughter, for in her pocket she kept (she had showed him) some ancient knuckle bones and two teeth, as well as a more acceptable coin or two. Lucky charms she had said.

Hugh Ollerenshaw was staring at the earth at his feet, in which was embedded half a cigarette card (or was it a bubble gum card? they probably didn't make cigarette cards these days, they must be period pieces by now, antique shop pieces, those toys of his childhood, fetching a fiver each on the Portobello Road). The card portrayed a rugby player, in red and white gear. Arsenal. He peered more closely, but couldn't quite make out the muddy features. Peter Simpson? Peter Storey? He wondered which team was supported by the small vandals of the village of Barton.

Frances Wingate, watching the coffin sink, hearing the rather well-chosen words of Mr. Fox (a man who filled her with increasing admiration), was thinking, somewhat pedantically and quite happily, of the funeral customs of the Romans and the Phoenicians, the purpose of mourning, and the need for ritual. She felt quite content to see Constance sink so gracefully to rest. Death, in this style, held no horrors. Death had produced a great deal of beauty. The Appian Way had struck her many years ago as the most beautiful road in the world, despite the agony that had been suffered there, and she had always liked churchyards and cemeteries. Highgate. Mycenae. Père Lachaise. The Protestant Cemetery in Rome. Gray's churchyard of the "Elegy." She had pottered around them all, taking an interest. Piacular rites. This country churchyard had an impressive, sequestered, harmonious, weathered beauty; one could not lie here restless, even though one no longer, so lying, joined the great majority. She spared a thought for John Lincoln, who could never have foreseen such an ending, and gazed at Karel, gazing at the cows. He had escaped the worst crime of history. He would escape Boston harbor, too. She thought of death and Durkheim, thanked God for Karel's salvation, and speculated about the origins of the religious sentiment. Ritual does not solve, but, like tears, it assuages, she thought.

As for Sir Frank Ollerenshaw and Harold Barnard, who knows what they were thinking? Omniscience has its limits. The speculations of Sir Frank are beyond speculation, but Harold Barnard may well have been thinking about the Tockley smell, the price of sugar, the Common Market, the property market, the possible price of Mays Cottage, the income of a vice-chancellor, or the identity of the unexplained Karel Schmidt. He was probably thinking about all these things at once.

The Reverend Miles Fox was wondering whether it would be improper to put his beret on when the so-called service was over. His ears were cold. The Reverend Miles Fox was a true believer, and simultaneously he prayed for the attention of God the Father, his Son Jesus Christ, and the Holy Spirit. All of these three seemed to him equally significant. The Reverend Miles Fox was one of those who have an understanding of the Trinity. It had made his life simple in ecclesiastical terms, this understanding: but it was hard to get it across to his wife, his children, or to people like Dr. Frances Wingate. He constantly felt that he was cheating, even within the church: he had had it too easy, theologically. Why did he have no crises of faith, like other vicars? Why was it for him so plain and easy? Father, Son, and Holy Ghost. Sometimes he thought that his wife was not even a Christian: she was simply a fellow traveler, with (poor woman) a miserably cheap ticket. He prayed for Constance Ollerenshaw, who had gone astray, but who had done no harm to anyone. Oh, God, he prayed, lay her to rest, gather her to rest. Oh, God, he commented, familiarly, they will surely not mind if I put on my beret. He found no obstacle, in his intercourse with God.

It was tea time, when they called at Eel Cottage. Janet, who knew the people who lived there, had rung Heather Stabler to ask if they could look in: she knew perfectly well that Heather would not mind, for it is not every day that a vice-chancellor with a title who has been accused of culpable neglect of elderly relatives arrives upon one's doorstep in the East Midlands. She could well imagine the flurry of sandwich-making that Heather Stabler would be thrown into by the visit, but I am afraid the thought quite amused her—an amusement not very malicious, for she knew that Heather would acquit herself well with the sandwiches and home-made bread, despite entreaties not to bother, and that in retrospect she would be glad of the opportunity. Janet thought she ought to go home to Hugh and her mother, who was minding the baby, but it was put to her that it would be much easier if she went at least as far as the Eel, to effect introductions. She saw the force of that, for she herself would not at all have liked to arrive upon a strange doorstep more or less unexpected, even if the doorstep had once been her own, and she could see that these other Ollerenshaws, however confident they might appear, might also have their hesitations. Indeed, she could see that Frances, upon closer observation, had many hesitations: her behavior toward her father was quite subdued, and her behavior toward Karel was carefully watchful.

In the Eel, they drank jasmine tea, and ate cress sandwiches, and Sir Frank admired the new red Aga, and reminisced a little about the inconveniences of the old black range. He was clearly affected by the visit, and shook his head from time to time, and sighed. Hugh and Frances were allowed to go upstairs to see the bedroom where they used to sleep and discuss sex and the atom bomb: it was still a child's bedroom, with a picture of Babar on the wall, a small bed, and a cot. "What are you going to do about Karel?" said Hugh, as they

stood there alone together in the little room. "I don't quite
know," said Frances, with unusual diffidence. "I'll have to
wait to see what he says, won't I?"

While the others talked of nursery gardening and its profits
(Peter Stabler had just got in from work, with a new scheme
for growing artichokes), Frances took Karel down to see the
ditch. You must come, she said, it is the most important
place of my childhood, all my behavior will be made plain
when you see it.

They walked through the cabbage field. It was almost dark.
Karel was feeling much better: he had recovered from Africa
and cholera, and was beginning to feel pleased with his own
gesture. It would pay off, shortly, he could see.

The ditch was as disgusting as it had been earlier that
summer, on Frances's last visit. Gazing at its scummy surface he said to her, "Do you remember those frogs, darling?
I often think of those frogs."

"It was partly those frogs that made me send you that
postcard," she said. "I loved them, didn't you? I love you
too," she added.

"So this is where you spent your childhood," he said,
standing on the top of the muddy bank.

"It used to be lovely, once," she said, and started to
scramble down the steep bank to the water's edge, to look
more closely at the nasty mixture of garbage: it was dark,
she slipped and fell. Ow, help, yelled Frances, as Karel,
trying to catch her, slipped and fell after her, on top of her.
Luckily, they missed the water. Karel held her, inside her
jacket, outside her father's green jersey. Help, help, said
Frances, as they lay there rather awkwardly in the mud. What
horrible places we always seem to end up in, said Karel.

When they got back to the cottage, covered in dirt, Peter
Stabler was agreeing with Hugh that despite the country's
grave economic crisis, there were still plenty of people in the
Midlands who would be delighted to buy artichokes, and that
he would have a go. "What on earth have you two been up

to?'' asked Hugh, as Karel and Frances appeared. ''We fell over,'' said Frances.

''We very nearly,'' said Karel, ''fell right into the ditch.''

They took in Mays Cottage on the way back to Tockley: it was too dark to see anything much, which pleased Frances, as she felt possessive about the place. Then they went back to the hotel, and had some drinks: Janet went home, and Sir Frank drove himself off, back to Wolverton, leaving the others to hold a small wake in Frances and Karel's bedroom. Hugh, who had not touched a drop at lunchtime, seemed less willing on this occasion to abstain, and David also was in a drinking mood. David, alone of all of them, had been somewhat depressed by the serious aspects of the day and also by a brief encounter with the mother of Janet Bird, whom he recalled from his childhood. He felt sorry for Janet. He did not think life would offer her very much. On the other hand, he alone of all of them was likely to die, like Constance, quite alone, and quite unmissed, and the prospect had very slightly alarmed him. It was all very well, to take the long view. He had a large drink. There would be some bad moments, before the long view paid off.

Hugh had intended to drive back to London that night, but drink overtook him. He rang Natasha, and said he would stay. Nobody was feeling very hungry, after the sandwiches at tea time, so they ordered some more sandwiches, and ate them in the lounge (which was quiet, on a Monday), washed down with a bottle or two of wine. It took a long time to persuade Hugh that it was time to go to bed: a yawning waiter and the emptiness of the last bottle finally dislodged him. Karel and Frances went upstairs to bed. In bed, Frances turned on her elbow to Karel, and said, forestalling. ''You know that postcard I sent you? It was partly the frogs, but it was partly a boy called Hunter Wisbech. Whatever did you say to Hunter Wisbech, about me?''

Karel looked puzzled. ''Whoever was Hunter Wisbech?'' he asked.

''Oh, you must remember,'' said Frances. ''He came to

give a talk at your Poly. Just like me. Surely you remember him? I met him in February. On my lecture tour."

"Was he that young chap with the long curly hair who kept going on about how his wife had run off with the doctor?"

"Yes, that was him."

"He wasn't at all like you, love. He was a quite different kind of person. And I don't remember saying anything much to him. He did all the talking, I think. Why, what did he say I said about you? I can't have said anything awful about you, I never have done, in my life. I always defend you, you know."

Frances didn't quite care for the notion that she was so constantly attacked, in her absence: nevertheless, she pursued the subject.

"You must have got on very intimate terms with Hunter Wisbech, whose name you have so completely forgotten," she said, accusingly. "Because he said to me that you said to him that you loved me. He said it over lunch, too."

"Did he? Well, perhaps I did. What's so surprising about that? I did love you, I still do. Why shouldn't I?"

"But it's not the kind of thing that one says to a total stranger."

"No, perhaps not." Karel thought hard, trying to remember: he was feeling much better, and was looking forward to getting this conversation over with, though at the same time it was a luxury, to delay the only possible conclusion by talk. "No," he said, "now I think about it, we did talk about you. It was he that brought the subject up, I think. We went off to the pub, after the lecture, and had a few drinks, and he said he knew Derek Palmer, who also knew you, and that's how we got onto it. I didn't say anything bad about you, you know. I never would. You mustn't be paranoid, my darling."

"I'm not. I was just interested. You must have been drunk, both of you," she said, speculatively, imagining the scene.

"Yes, I suppose we were." He reflected. "And anyway," he said, "how did you and Hunter get onto intimate terms about the subject of me, come to that? That's not the kind of thing one discusses with a total stranger, either, is it?''

As he spoke, an image of Hunter lying asleep on her bed in the hotel flashed across her mind: it seemed to have flashed simultaneously across Karel's mind, too, because before she had time to answer his question, he followed it up with, ''And I hope to God you didn't get *too* intimate with him, did you?''

''Of course not,'' she said indignantly as other images, of Galletti and Spirelli, of the Canadian cameraman in Luxor, flashed rapidly across the screen of her brain: she hoped that Karel wasn't receiving them too, but she knew he was: on the other hand, if he was receiving them at all he must surely be receiving everything else as well?

''Oh, God, Karel,'' she said, sinking down off her elbow into the narrow bed, ''I missed you, I really missed you so much.''

''Yes,'' he said. He was feeling quite himself again. He told her so. Yes, she said, burying herself against him under the white sheets, she could see that this was so.

All in all, it had been quite an enjoyable day.

The same could not be said for Stephen's funeral. Stephen's funeral was a nightmare. Heroically, Frances organized that one too, for Natasha was too ill, and Hugh too distraught. It was something to do, at least, and by chance she now knew how to do it.

Stephen had died early one morning, in a wood, in Sussex. He had killed himself and the baby. Stephen's doctor believed that he had done it because of a misapprehension about the baby's health. He gave evidence at the inquest, saying that Stephen had visited him frequently with small complaints, and had perhaps remained unconvinced that his daughter was a perfectly healthy slow developer. He also testified that Stephen had been overburdened with his studies and the care of the child, and had become depressed. Are you suggesting, asked the coroner, that he took the child's life because he feared for her future? The doctor agreed that this might have been the case. It was a merciful explanation, and the coroner accepted it.

Stephen's flat had been found littered with medical textbooks. A pediatric encyclopedia had been found, with the passages on metabolic and degenerative diseases of the muscles heavily marked. Perhaps he had thought the child was suffering from Oppenheim's disease, from Thomson's disease, from the first stages of muscular dystrophy.

The coroner concluded that the balance of his mind had been disturbed. He expressed the deepest sympathy with the bereaved family.

Stephen's wife was still in hospital, and paid no attention to this tragedy. Frances, in irrational moments, found herself bitterly resenting the wife. One has to blame somebody, sometimes.

Stephen himself had been well aware that they would conclude that the balance of his mind had been disturbed, and he conceded that in worldy terms, perhaps it was: nevertheless, he had wished to set the record straight, to explain his own logic, and to this end he had written a long letter, describing his state of mind.

He had not, as the doctor had helpfully suggested, believed his daughter to be fatally ill. The textbooks, alarming though they were, had offered little support for such a belief. He had accepted the doctor's diagnosis, that she was a slow (and not even a very slow) developer. *All* babies' heads wobble, the doctor had said, and Stephen had believed him. Nevertheless, he had continued to read the textbooks, and had discovered that although his child might so far have been lucky, there were plenty of problems lying in store. And even if she escaped them all, what of those that didn't? Horrified by the photographic illustrations, he stared at the limp bodies of small doomed long-dead babies, at the distorted bodies of children: their faces, like the faces of convicts in newspapers, had been blacked out, through some respect for their privacy, for their dreadful isolation. As Janet Bird, an Anglo-Saxon post-war woman, brooded over the fate of the Jews, he, a healthy father of a healthy child, brooded over illness and death.

Thinking about these things, Stephen made himself ill. Depression and inertia overcame him. It was as much as he could do to get himself out of bed in the mornings to get the child her breakfast, and he found himself forgetting to feed himself. Beata's way.

He would relapse into bed again, feebly, while the baby crawled around the room, pleased with little. Occasionally, he would get himself up, and go to visit a friend of his who was suffering from the aftereffects of LSD: useless duty visits, for the friend, who lived with an aunt, had become more or less speechless, and did not seem to recognize Stephen, or anyone else either. The aunt feared permanent brain damage. The doctors were marginally more optimistic. Stephen did not know what he thought about the case. He would sit there, drink a cup of tea, chat to the aunt, and every now and then make an attempt to speak to Sebastian. Sebastian would answer, occasionally, extremely politely, dully, briefly. Sebastian had once been witty, energetic, eccentric, and a great talker.

Stephen did not know what he thought about Sebastian, or why he kept on going to see him; to please the aunt, maybe. He liked aunts. This aunt claimed that Sebastian had lost all sense of time, and would get up for breakfast in the middle of the night, also that he would sometimes become extremely vocal, and talk a great deal, but that she could never understand a word of what he was saying in such spasms. Stephen wondered if there was anything interesting going on in his head, or whether whatever was in there had simply been ruined. How could one tell? His experiences with Beata had long since put him off the belief that madness is sanity, and sanity madness. But what, after all, was sanity?

It was while he was in this frame of mind that the news of Constance Ollerenshaw's bizarre end hit the Sunday papers.

He spent all Sunday thinking about it. In the evening, he rang Hugh and Natasha, to find out if they had anything to say about it, but they hadn't, much: they were annoyed, indignant, but by no means overwhelmed. Indeed, Hugh had even been quite witty about the subject. A well-balanced man, Hugh. So Stephen had given the baby its supper, put it to bed, and sat down by his gas fire to brood. Like a medieval contemplative, he dedicated himself to mortality, decay, the corruption of the flesh, disease. The end of all things.

Frances, in her worst moments, wept, like a woman. Karel also had a gift for weeping. Stephen lacked this gift, so he sat there and thought, instead. He felt himself on the verge of some revelation. It was sure to come: it needed no artificial invocation.

The revelation was one of extreme simplicity. It came to him like a light from heaven. It was better to be dead than alive: this was the knowledge that came to him. It seemed to descend upon him personally. Being alive was sordid, degrading, sickly, unimaginable: to struggle on through another fifty years, tormented by fear and guilt and sorrow, was a fate nobody should ever embrace. That others did was not his affair. Man had been created sick and dying: for seventy years he feebly struggled to avoid his proper end. There was something overwhelmingly disgusting about man's efforts, against all the odds, to stay alive. One spent one's life in inoculating oneself, swallowing medicaments, trying to destroy disease, and all to no end, for the end was death. How sickly, how pitiable, how contemptible. Eating corpses in extremis, like those cannibals in the Andes. Condemned to a life of soul-destroying fear, one died in the end anyway, the soul destroyed and rotted by terror. Whereas if one left now, if one leapt now, unsubdued, into the flames, one would be freed, one would have conquered flesh and death, one would have departed whole, intact, undestroyed.

The certainty played around him like fire. This was it, then. He must leave himself no time to forget, no time to lose his knowledge, no time to die and rot like Sebastian and

Constance, no time to wither, lingeringly, like Beata, whose feeble balance between life and death was the worst defeat, the most miserable compromise of all. If it was to be done, let it be done properly. The flames were light and bright, painless, without heat. The refining fire.

He started to pack up his things. It was midnight. It crossed his mind to leave the baby behind, but of course it was out of the question to leave her, whom he so loved, to a life that he had rejected. He thought of his parents, his family: they would suffer, of course, but then they had so many other things to suffer for that one more, in his view, wouldn't make much difference. Should he write them a note? He hesitated. He ought to write something to somebody, to explain what had lead to his resolution: otherwise, they might think he was doing it out of some kind of misery, which was not quite the case. He couldn't quite face writing to his parents, direct. So he wrote them a brief note of farewell, then a longer letter, to Frances, in which he enclosed the note for Hugh and Natasha. His letter to Frances was, he thought, quite clear: he explained that living was disagreeable, and worse than disagreeable, humiliating and destructive, and that he had decided that it would be much better to depart while the way was open before him. *Don't think I haven't loved you, Aunt Frances*, he concluded (he enjoyed calling her "Aunt": it had a pleasant element of the ridiculous), *don't think I haven't been impressed by your approach. I have. But it's not for me. Good luck to you, Frances, and goodbye.*

He addressed this to her home in Putney: she was, he thought, still in Africa, but she would be home soon, and there was no hurry. He left a note on his mantelpiece, saying, *Have gone, and won't be back* for his landlady. Then he picked up his baby, wrapped her up, put her in a knapsack with the sleeping bag and the sleeping pills, and set off through the dark town (it was after midnight), posting the letter on his way to his destination.

He walked till nearly morning. He knew the right place. They wouldn't find him till next weekend, probably: it was a very secret place, but people sometimes walked there at weekends. He made himself and the baby comfortable, gave both an overdose, and fell asleep as the dawn broke.

They weren't found the next weekend: they were found ten days later, two days after Constance's funeral. The police had been out to look, prompted by Frances, who found Stephen's letter only on her return to Putney from Tockley.

They were lying in a hollow in a wood, under tree roots, wrapped up in the sleeping bag together.

Frances wept herself into a stupor. Sodden with tears, she stumbled from police to undertaker, yet again. For days she wept almost without ceasing. If only he had left the baby, she would moan, rocking herself backward and forward, swollen and blotched. I would have had her, I would have had her, what's a baby more or less to me?

He didn't want to leave her behind, said Karel, who understood such things.

If Karel hadn't been there, she didn't know what she would have done. He moved in with her, of course, and they took up life together as though there had been no break. He looked after her, held her while she cried, comforted her, distracted the children, and coped with the incessant flow of telephone calls from family and sympathizers.

Stephen was cremated, in a London crematorium: it was pouring with rain as Karel drove slowly past the gravestones, up the interminable drive, to the chapel. Frances did not notice the chapel or the gravestones. Natasha did not attend, but her parents and Hugh got themselves there. Standing in the chapel listening to the piped music, Frances remembered the country churchyard, and Mr. Fox in his beret, and the rose bushes and the cows and the yellow stone, and she thought to herself truly and bitterly that they had been an utter, utter irrelevance. This was the place: this was death. How can one make a friend of death, how can one accept graciously the wicked deal? It was better not to pretend. All ritual is a hollow mockery. The tears poured down her face, and Hugh squeezed her elbow. "Men do not weep for the dead because they fear them; they fear them because they weep for them," Durkheim had said, in an attempt to explain mourning. But there was no explanation. An affirmation of life, of culture: a demonstration of the poverty of life and culture: what did it matter what that churchyard or this black conveyor belt represented? Nobody had felt the slightest desire to make matters better by burying Stephen in the Cotswolds churchyard, or even by alleviating this grim ceremony with some well-chosen words. Nobody cared, because they cared. Stephen was dead, and that was that. It was the thing, these days, to speak of making death less frightful, more dignified, more familiar. Perhaps there was something to be said for it. But for her part, she had drawn too far away from any human continuity to wish to know. Death and love. How dreadfully they contradict all culture, all process, all human effort. Stephen had been right. The silly curtains swished together, and Stephen and his child disappeared together into the red crater, made one with nature, transformed to black ash.

Drearily, they all trudged off back through the rain to culture, process, and effort. They were wedded to them, after all.

Through the following days and weeks, Frances read Stephen's letter again and again, searching for clues. What could have been done, who could have helped? They should have known, that last weekend in the Cotswolds, that there was something wrong with Stephen: she had known it, but she had done nothing. She had flown off frivolously to Adra, to sit around a swimming pool drinking and gossiping. She reproached herself. What had any of them said, in the evening, when they had talked of Freud and the death wish and Empedocles, that had tipped the balance?

Karel reassured her. It was not their fault; it was nobody's fault. Nothing could have been done to prevent it. He had made up his mind, and he had done it, and that was that.

Gradually, she calmed down. It was true that it was not

her fault: she had always been good to Stephen, and had always had plenty of time for him. Indeed, as Karel pointed out to her, she had clearly represented for him one of the only possible patterns of living. He had loved and admired her: he said so in his last letter to her. If anybody cheered him up, it was you, said Karel: look, he more or less says so. But poor thing, poor thing, Frances would weep, what can it have been like, to feel so desperate? She could not imagine his state of mind: she did not know how he could have brought himself to it.

Her own parents were quite subdued by the event. Lady Ollerenshaw pulled herself together and emerged from hospital and started living again, with a rather impressive humility. Sir Frank stared a little more blankly still, as though fate had conformed his worst suspicions about life, and said nothing. Hugh drank and wept: Natasha took to her bed tranquilized for days and in the end rose like a ghost, and picked up the threads of living. She stopped dyeing her hair, and withdrew her other younger children from boarding school: both courses of action seemed like mistakes, but nobody felt like arguing with her.

In the end, Frances got over it. One gets used to anything. She even began to see it in a better light, once the shock was over. After all, Stephen had been in some curious way true to himself: one could even see that his act had a kind of integrity and finality that exonerated all bystanders from guilt. He had blamed no one. He had not even, as far as one could gather, endured any very striking suffering before his death. One could regard it perhaps as a tragic accident.

Or perhaps it was not even as bad as a tragic accident. An accident cuts people off, unwilling, surprised: illness rips people panting and reluctant from life. Stephen had chosen to leave. Reperusing his last words, in a tearless calm, months later, it occurred to Frances that perhaps it was not so bad. Perhaps, in some way, it was all right. With a certain admirable determination, he had faced his own nature, and the terms of life and death, and seen what to do. He had had the

revelation she had always been denied, which she had
glimpsed so often in the distance. It was a revelation that she
did not want at all. She would continue to live, herself. He
had spared her, and taken it all upon himself.

She taught herself, over the years, to see his death as a
healing of some kind, the end of a long illness, a sacrifice.
Taken from them for their better health. Her own children,
certainly, mercifully, showed no inheritance of the more unwelcome Ollerenshaw traits. Stephen had taken it all away
with him. She thought of Stephen, years later, in Prague. She
and Karel never got to Pilsen, but they got to Prague, where
Karel's mother's family had lived, and while she was there it
was as much Stephen as Karel that came into her thoughts:
walking around the Jewish cemetery with the slanting apoc-
alyptic tombstones, staring at dangerous scaffolding and great
blackened stone eagles on doorways, she thought that perhaps it was the reinforcement, the double heritage that had
killed Stephen. For here was Karel, still alive, despite all still
alive, a man with no hatred in him, the only man in Europe.
Karel wept, in bed that night in Prague, because they had
been to visit his aunt, and she was now an old woman, living
not too well. The light had gone out in the middle of the meal
she had cooked them, and she had been distressed by the
forced failure of her hospitality, but for all that she refused
to return to London, for she felt more at home in Prague.
And Karel in bed had turned to Frances and wept, as she had
wept for Stephen, and it all seemed a part of the same fate.
A fate which had spared them, and left them with so much,
with each other. What could one do, what sense could one
make of it? One could only give thanks.

Karel lost a tooth, in Prague, as she had lost one in Paris:
it's the anxiety of travel that makes one's teeth go bad abroad,
they concluded, as they stared at the incisor that Karel could
ill afford to lose, extracted by a Czech dentist who was a
friend of the aunt, and who had once, when a young man in
another world, met Karel's mother. Europe and death. Karel
wept into the broad shoulder of Frances, and she stared at

the hotel ceiling (the aunt could not accommodate them, for she lived, as she had lived in Palmers Green, in a single room) and she thanked God for his survival, for there was no one else to thank. Karel, she said, don't cry, Karel, don't, please don't—though she did not mind, for to have him there was more than she, ambitious as she was, had ever hoped, and his tears, and the sight of his teeth hanging on the doorknob of the wardrobe, and the thought of his lonely aunt, and his dead mother and brothers and sister and father and dead Stephen's dust and ashes rising from a crematorium chimney, were all part of a salvation so unexpected, that she lay there with him, perishing and fading, it was true, but who cared, who cared, if one can salvage one moment from the sentence of death let us do so, let us catch at it, for we owe it to the dead, to the others, and it is all the living and the lucky can do for the dead, all they can do, given the chance, is to rejoice: overcome with joy she lay there, as he wept himself to sleep on her shoulder, overcome with joy she lay awake and thought of the gold baroque of Prague, and Kafka the mad Jew, and of those perilous gravestones, gravestones, her profession, her trade, her living, on account of which (account, account) she lay here with Karel in this double bed.

More years later, she stood with Karel in another graveyard, in the Precinct of Tanit in Carthage, and talked to an archaeologist of child sacrifice. She had never really understood her Phoenicians: nor had she been able to understand how Stephen could take the child's life as well as his own. His own, yes; that she had accepted. She stood there, grayhaired now in the bright North African light. There stood the little urns. Bones of children, bones of mice, bones of saints, relics. Lucky Mr. Fox, to believe in the resurrection. Whatever had the Phoenicians believed? She did not want to know, she did not want to understand, she turned away. She could not believe in the resurrection, or in the revelation, and anything more sinister she did not wish to comprehend. She was a modern woman. Her children were grown up now. (Daisy had become a physicist: her mother's pride in this was immense. She had also married Bob Schmidt, after a highly incestuous courtship, and was about to produce the child that Karel and Frances, in belated deference to the population problem, had refrained from producing. But further forward one cannot look. Or not yet.)

From these projections, it may be concluded that Frances's reunion with Karel, though achieved in ill health, and cemented by death and tears, proved permanent. Their separation had been an aberration: both remembered it with amusement, as a happily married couple might remember a harmless affair; both agreed that, postcard or no postcard, they would have got together in the end. Karel's wife went off to the country, as she had often threatened to do, to live in a lesbian commune: she left the children with Karel and Frances. Frances ran her large household with great satisfaction, feeling that her energies, which she had feared were going to waste, were properly taxed at last. The children bickered and quarreled a little at first, but after a few months settled down well.

Joy, contrary to Karel's expectations, and contrary to those of Frances (who had not dared to hope for so unlikely and so happy a resolution), turned out to have been truly lesbian after all. It was no wonder that she had been so cross with Karel for so much of the time. As the months passed, she became almost pleasant. Frances, through the inevitable social contacts brought about by the children, found herself becoming interested, against her will, in the homosexual movements of the seventies: she even went to a meeting or two, and was much impressed by them. Despite these liberal gestures, Joy continued to dislike and distrust Frances, and could never bring herself to be very civil to her. Frances didn't much mind: she had done little to deserve Joy's civility. She had ruthlessly and fairly persistently pursued her husband, and had got him, finally. She was quite content with the resolution, and could well afford to be pleased to see that Joy herself was less discontented. In fact, she was rather pleased that Joy did not wish to become too friendly, as in fact she didn't like Joy much, either. So there you are. Invent a more suitable ending if you can.

Frances bought Mays Cottage from her father. He certainly didn't want it and Frances did. To her astonishment, he allowed her to pay very nearly the market price for it (a sum rather more than a hundred times what her predecessor had paid for it in 1880). This interesting fact was to intrigue and perplex her for the rest of her life, and she invented various explanations for his surprising conduct, none of them wholly satisfactory. However one looked at the transaction, it involved blood money, of one sort or another, and it was money that she could well afford. Perhaps her father guessed the pride she felt in her own power of purchase, and wished to allow her to enjoy it? But she felt there was more to it than that.

She tidied the cottage up, gradually: on the first few visits, she managed to get there alone with Karel, and they slept together among the cobwebs, making good lost months and years, in a terrifying, a safe, a giddy, a precarious, a secure and all-excluding secluded conclusion, as final in its own way as Stephen's had been: as final, as ruthless, and, it seemed, as natural. Resent it, if you like. She will not care: she is not listening. A happy ending, you may say. After a few months, the cottage was fit for their large family, and they would all (or most, for the children had reached the drifting stage) go up for weekends and holidays. When asked where her country cottage was, Frances would say, "Near Tockley," and people would look at her as though she were mad, and she would laugh, and say, it may not be paradise, but it suits me. It never looked as nice as Hugh and Natasha's cottage, but she liked it. It combined elements. It was not quite as spectacular a rediscovery and reclamation as Tizouk, but it offered many private satisfactions. It even proved, in its own way, to be of historical, if not of archaeological interest, for one day when Karel was doing some repairs he found walled up in a closet three shoes—a man's, a woman's, and a child's—with a small porridge bowl. Ollerenshaw shoes, dating from the mid-nineteenth century. He took them to the museum, and found that the practice of shoe burial, if not exactly of shoe sacrifice, was not uncommon, and that such discoveries were occasionally found associated with other offerings—knives, coins, on one occasion a couple of slaughtered chickens. An interesting footnote to the history of the agricultural laborer, he said. Frances, staring at the strange little family of shoes, said, well, they were always an odd lot, Aunt Con clearly wasn't the first, was she?

Having the cottage meant that she could keep in touch with Janet, which pleased them both. She would pick Janet and little Hugh up from Tockley in the car, and drive them out for a meal, and her children and Karel's would play with the baby, while the adults talked. Mark usually refused to come, to Frances's relief. She tried a little subversion on Janet, but wasn't very successful. Janet remained self-contained, dry, only intermittently communicative: she wasn't prepared to discuss her marriage with anybody, after that initial disoriented evening. But she liked to see Frances. It made a change, to see Frances. Gradually, Janet came to believe that instead of confronting a life of boredom, she was merely biding her time. There was Frances at forty, as lively as anything, digging her garden, painting walls, writing articles, riding (she had taken up riding, to stop getting fat), so how could her own life be over, when she wasn't even thirty? Even if the gas mains didn't blow up under Aragon Court, something else might happen, after all.

Frances and Karel tried to keep in touch with David Ollerenshaw as well, but it wasn't very easy. He was rarely in England. He sent them postcards from foreign parts: he spent another six months in Africa, then moved on to the Middle East. (Frances had missed the dig in Adra, through her domestic complications: it proved to be an enigmatic but fascinating affair and she was annoyed she hadn't been there. But one can't have everything.) David sent them, for a wedding present, a lump of pale-yellow silica glass that he had picked up himself in the desert: scooped, pitted, smoothly irregular, carved and weathered by the desert wind, apparently translucent but finally opaque, it had seemed an appropriate gift.

They did manage to meet, occasionally, when he was in London: he came to dinner in Putney several times, and talked of the old days. He and Karel got on well. Frances found herself slightly piqued by their friendship, for she regarded each as her own discovery: she would grow quietly sulky while listening to them discuss world resources and recessions and the new science of cliometrics. A luxury, in these good years.

Once, David invited them around to his London pied-à-terre for a drink, and took them out for a meal. It was one of the biggest surprises of Frances's life. She had been certain that David would live in some shabby neglected hovel or bedsitter, like Mrs. Mayfield, and his address (in Earls Court) promised no better. But his tiny flat, in size alone resembling a bedsitter, was quite unexpected. It was carefully furnished, spotless, even elegant. A stereo record player, a large collection of records, shelves of books, a fine series of orchid prints, and (most inexplicable of all) some interesting pieces of porcelain bore witness to interests of which she could never have dreamed. On the mantelpiece stood some geological objects: satin spar from the Midlands, a polished block of pudding-stone, some green olivine from the Red Sea, desert roses, a lump of pink crystalline corundum, and a very large block of smoky quartz. She gazed into the block of quartz: it was dense and translucent within, streaked by refraction, like a petrified forest. Human nature is truly impenetrable, she said to herself.

On the way home, she said to Karel, what a surprising place. But Karel didn't know what she was talking about. David's place hadn't surprised him at all.

ABOUT THE AUTHOR

MARGARET DRABBLE is the author of nine previous novels and a biography of Arnold Bennett. She lives in London.